Se

ANNE WEALE

Heartline
Books

Published by Heartline Books Limited in 2002

Copyright © Anne Weale 2002

Anne Weale has asserted her rights under the Copyright, Designs and Patents Act, 1988 to be identified as the author of this work.

This is a work of fiction. Names and characters are the product of the author's imagination and any resemblance to any actual persons, living or dead, is purely coincidental.

All rights reserved. No part of this publication may be reproduced, stored in or introduced into a retrieval system or transmitted by any form, or by any means (electronic, mechanical, photocopying, recording or otherwise) without the prior written permission of the publisher. Any person who takes any unauthorised action in relation to this publication may be liable to criminal prosecution and civil claims for damages.

Heartline Books Limited and Heartline Books logo are trademarks of the publisher.

First published in the United Kingdom in 2002 by Heartline Books Limited.

Heartline Books Limited
PO Box 22598, London W8 7GB

Heartline Books Ltd. Reg No: 03986653

ISBN 1-903867-40-1

Styled by Oxford Designers & Illustrators

Printed and bound in Great Britain by
Cox & Wyman, Reading, Berkshire

ANNE WEALE

Anne's first romance was published when she was a 25-year-old newspaper reporter. At thirty she gave up staff journalism to start a family and concentrate on writing books.

Her backlist of more than 80 titles includes five long novels and over 60 romances for Mills & Boon, which adds up to five million words of popular fiction. Considering that Anne has moved house 17 times since marriage took her to the backwoods of South East Asia, this is not a bad output.

Currently her life is divided between a small village in Spain and a summer pad in the Channel Islands.

A lot of her free time is spent on the Internet. She writes a column about her favourite websites and can be reached by email at anne@anneweale.com

Heartline are delighted to welcome Anne on board with her first Heartline novel SEA CHANGE.

PUBLISHER'S NOTE: Heartline Books regret that they can accept no responsibility for the accuracy, reliability, security or suitability of any of the website addresses included within the pages of SEA CHANGE by Anne Weale.

Heartline Books – Romance at its best

Call the Heartline Hotline on 0845 6000 504 and order any book you may have missed – you can now pay over the phone by credit or debit card.

Have you visited the Heartline website yet?

If you haven't – and even for those of you who have – it's well worth a trip as we are constantly updating our site.

So log on to www.heartlinebooks.com where you can…

- ♥ Order one or more books – including titles you may have missed – and pay by credit or debit card
- ♥ Check out special offers and events, such as celebrity interviews
- ♥ Find details of our writing classes for aspiring authors
- ♥ Read more about Heartline authors
- ♥ Enter competitions
- ♥ Browse through our catalogue

And much, much more…

Dear Reader

I have always loved the sea, or the ocean as you may call it, depending on where you live. Islands, rivers and oceans have been a recurring theme in my life and my stories; and men who brave the sea in its wildest moods have always been high on my list of heroes.

Since I began exploring the World Wide Web, one of my greatest pleasures has been following, online, the many round-the-world yacht races, including the dramatic rescue by the Italian yachtsman, Giovanni Soldini, of the French yachtswoman, Isabelle Austissier, after her boat capsized in the Southern Ocean.

Within hours of that heroic rescue being reported, I found myself thinking, 'What if the situation had been reversed…if a woman had rescued a man…a man she had every reason to dislike?' Once a writer's imagination has started working, there is no stopping it until she has brought her story to its conclusion.

I am always sorry to part from the people in my stories. But, despite all the challenges and difficulties I have shared with them, I know they have a happy future ahead, and I say goodbye to them with the hope that they will find readers who, by the last page, will share my affection for them.

Happy reading – Anne

chapter one

The first time she saw Scott Randall in the flesh was at the eve-of-race party for two hundred people in an upstairs room at the Charleston Maritime Centre.

The room, decorated with signal flags to give it a nautical air, had a panoramic view of the Cooper River, one of the two great rivers that embraced downtown Charleston and fed a huge almost land-locked bay before flowing into the Atlantic.

Maddie had known beforehand that Scott Randall was going to be there. But she didn't expect to have any direct contact with him. In a large room, crowded with people, many of them outgoing Americans who had no problem getting along with strangers, she was the last person he was likely to notice.

She noticed Scott Randall the moment he arrived. He was tall even by American standards. To Maddie, here for the first time, the US seemed a land of giants. In Guernsey, a small island not far from the north coast of France, where she had grown up, most of the elderly local people were on the short side like her grandfather. The young islanders were taller and Maddie had been the tallest in her class at school. Tall and ungainly was how she saw herself.

Watching Scott Randall from a distance – his dark head clearly visible as he circulated in the throng of friends, relations, helpers, sponsors and media people – Maddie remembered a phrase in a press story about him. 'He's a guy who runs on pure adrenaline,' an interviewer had written.

Not sure what it meant, she had looked up adrenaline in

her dictionary. 'A hormone secreted in response to stress that increases heart rate, pulse rate, and blood pressure,' she had read. In most people's lives, stress was something to be endured or avoided. Scott Randall appeared to court it and to thrive on it. His vitality and energy were palpable from the far side of the room.

There were other men present who were equally fit, equally intrepid. But they lacked his imposing physique and distinguished looks. He could not be described as handsome. Most people had one feature which dominated their face. It was hard to pick out his. His profile was angular and, at first glance, hard. But his mouth was not lizard-lipped and taut with repressed impatience like her grandfather's.

Scott's mouth had an amused tilt, even when he wasn't smiling. Seen head on, when he turned in her direction, the end of his beaky nose looked slightly out of alignment with the bridge. As if it had suffered an impact when he was younger and never quite returned to its intended shape. Not that anyone close to him would notice that detail while they were caught in the focus of those astonishingly brilliant blue eyes, which from time to time flashed round the room like the beam from a lighthouse.

Maddie didn't expect to find that blue gaze focused on her. Or indeed for anyone else to pay attention to her. Although she was the only woman involved in tomorrow's event, she was not sufficiently feminine to be targeted by the press.

Also she was not good at interviews; journalists asking questions made her uneasy. She was a deeply private person, most at ease with children and the elderly. Her innermost thoughts were shared only with Bertie, the now shabby and one-eyed old teddy bear which had belonged to her father before her. Her mother had vanished before Maddie was old enough to remember her.

The party had been in progress for about an hour, and

Maddie was thinking about leaving, when a voice said, 'May I fetch you another drink?'

The accent was American but the man addressing her was Japanese; the only person at the party with whom she was already on friendly terms.

He was about the same age as her grandfather but, in character, totally different from the dour man who had raised her. Shigeru was a popular figure, held in respect and affection by everyone who knew him.

When he had taken her empty glass to the bar and brought her another soft drink, he stayed with her, chatting in the amiable way which made her relax and respond. He was the first Japanese person she had met, but he didn't have the formal manners she associated with people of his nationality.

They were talking about tomorrow when a voice said warmly, 'Shigeru...how are you?' and she looked up to find Scott Randall only a stride away.

Shigeru broke off what he was saying, his deeply lined face lighting up with pleasure at the sight of the younger man. Then he held out his arms and, to Maddie's surprise, they embraced each other as fondly as if they were father and son.

'It's great to see you again. How've you been?' asked Scott, as they drew apart and beamed at each other.

To Maddie, unused to such demonstrations, there was something both startling and moving about their uninhibited display of mutual affection. In that moment she warmed towards Scott and was ready to like him despite the off-putting aspects of his reputation.

After Shigeru had said he was fine and asked how Scott was, the older man turned to her. 'Have you met Scott, Madeleine?'

Normally he called her Maddie, but perhaps he thought her full name was more appropriate for an introduction.

'No, I haven't.' Knowing she was blushing, she stuck

out her hand and said a stiff, 'How d'you do?' instead of 'Hello' or 'Hi', the usual casual greeting at a party of this sort.

As the unlikely happened and Scott noticed her, the expression of delight and affection he had shown on greeting Shigeru changed to polite indifference.

His 'Hi' sounded curiously formal. His brown fingers closed firmly over hers, but only for a few seconds. He did not retain her hand, or say, 'Madeleine...glad to know you,' repeating her name to fix it in his memory the way most Americans did, she had noticed.

It was obvious that, as far as he was concerned, she was the least interesting-looking female whose existence he had ever been obliged to acknowledge, and he didn't want to waste a second longer than he must on her.

This was made even clearer when he turned his attention back to Shigeru, saying, 'I have to run...things to do. Why not stop by later, if you feel like it. You know where to find me?'

The other man nodded. 'I'll do that.'

Scott turned to Maddie. 'Good luck.'

'Thank you...the same to you.'

As they watched him heading for the exit, steering a path through the chattering groups of people, Shigeru said, 'How I should like to change places with him...to be a young man in my prime instead of an old one.' He sighed, and then laughed and shrugged. 'Have you had enough of this, Maddie? Shall I walk you home?'

'Thank you.' There was not much point in her staying at the party without him. No one else was likely to talk to her and she hadn't yet mastered the art of making friendly approaches to people she didn't know – at least not the sort of people here. She had no problem chatting up small children or senior citizens. It was the people in between those groups who daunted her.

If he hadn't already arranged to join Scott Randall later,

she might have suggested to her Japanese friend that they go into town together. Maddie's first encounter with Charleston had been in the pages of one of the world's classic love stories, *Gone With The Wind*. It was to Charleston that Rhett Butler had returned after the American Civil War and the failure of his marriage to the captivating Scarlett O'Hara. Having read the book twice in her teens, but never having seen the movie, Maddie did not associate Rhett and Scarlett with the actors who had portrayed them on the screen; she had her own ideas of how they had looked. In her mind's eye, Rhett bore a strong resemblance to Scott Randall.

Charleston, she had been told, still retained much of the grace it had had in Rhett Butler's time. She longed to explore its cobblestone streets, admire the stately mansions built by rice and indigo planters and taste she-crab soup and, perhaps, even the Planters' Punch cocktail which had been invented here. But to her frustration, the last minute preparations had left no time for sight-seeing.

Perhaps there would be time to look round when she got back here…if she got back.

'Are you nervous about tomorrow?' Shigeru asked.

She shook her head. 'Maybe I should be, but I'm not. I'll be glad to get started.'

Shigeru nodded. 'Me too. I don't like cities…though Charleston is better than most.'

He walked her to where her boat *Sea Spray* was berthed. 'See you in Cape Town. Take care.' With a pat on her shoulder and then a half-formal bow, he turned in the direction of his own berth.

Maddie went below. The between decks accommodation on *Sea Spray* was considerably more spacious than on the fast boats custom-built for professional yachtsmen such as Scott Randall. Her cabin was about the size of a small caravan.

'Hi Bertie,' she said to the bear, sitting with his back to

the bulkhead behind her bunk. 'You didn't miss much. If Shigeru hadn't been there, I'd have come back sooner.'

The habit of talking to the bear when no one else was in earshot had been formed long ago in her childhood. In those days they had carried on long conversations, Bertie's features as immobile as a ventriloquist's but his friendly growly voice clearly audible to her.

Although it had been her intention to have an early night, now she was back on board she knew she wasn't going to be able to sleep for hours yet. The Market area of Charleston, with its restaurants and pavement cafés, was only a short walk away. She decided to go in search of a bowl of the she-crab soup she had heard about. This might not have been a good idea had she been a small, pretty, feminine female. But no one was going to molest someone who looked as if they could stand up for themselves. In fact, with her short spiky haircut and unisex sailing clothes, it was more than likely that at first glance she'd be mistaken for a youth. After all, it had happened before, when she'd been working in her grandfather's boatyard.

Half an hour later, sitting alone at a table for two by the window of a small restaurant, she saw Shigeru and Scott Randall walking past. Quickly sinking down in her chair, Maddie gave a deep sigh of relief as she realised that they hadn't seen her.

Ever since her teens, Maddie had heard of Scott and admired his achievements. Far removed from her modest orbit, he'd already been making a considerable mark in the world of ocean racing while she was still at school.

Some of her classmates had seen him on TV. But Maddie's grandfather thought that television was the invention of the devil and refused to have a set in the house.

Left in her grandfather's care after the disappearance of her mother and the death of her father, who'd been the despotic old man's only son, Maddie had been forced to endure a strange, narrow upbringing. In Pierre Sardrette's youth, the little island where he and his granddaughter were born had been a quiet and peaceful place. Many people spoke a Norman-French patois; there was much intermarriage and seaweed, called *vraic,* was harvested from the beaches.

Today, the island's economy depended on offshore banking rather than agriculture and fishing, the narrow roads were busy with cars, and large cruise ships dropped anchor in the deep water channel outside the main harbour, so that their passengers could take advantage of the island's tax-free shopping.

In a futile attempt to stop his world changing, Maddie's grandfather had made his household a bastion of the old ways, imposing his will on his housekeeper and the girl who was a poor substitute for the grandson he had wanted.

Even now, at twenty-one, Maddie knew that there was so much missing from her life, which appeared to be totally unlike that lived by other girls of her age. She had never spent Saturday afternoons shopping and gossiping with friends in the crowded High Street and the Pollet, or spent Saturday nights having fun in the island's discos. Her social life had always been virtually non-existent. Not only because her grandfather disapproved of her mixing with her contemporaries, but because she didn't fit in with them.

Most of the girls at school had thought her a boring swot; boys had always ignored her. There was nothing about her to interest the opposite sex. She wasn't pretty. She was overweight. She didn't wear make-up or sexy clothes, and she didn't know how to flirt.

In the privacy of her bedroom, she copied the way the popular girls behaved, but she instinctively knew that their mannerisms didn't suit her, and there would be absolutely no point in her trying to act like that in public.

Her thoughts were interrupted by the waitress asking,

'Would you like to check out our desserts?' and handing her a laminated card printed with a long list of wickedly indulgent, heavily cream-laden puddings.

Needing time to make a choice from this abundance of tempting deserts, Maddie said, 'Could I think about it for a minute?'

'Sure...take your time. They're *all* delicious,' said the waitress, moving away.

Maddie read the list which was illustrated with photographs calculated to make any sweet-toothed diner salivate. At the same time she saw in her mind's eye the tall, lean figure of the man whom she seen in reality a few minutes earlier. It was impossible to imagine Scott Randall eating one of these gooey confections. She knew instinctively that he would regard them as junk food eaten by people with no self-control.

Or if, on rare occasions, he *did* eat a rich dessert, his super-active metabolism would probably zap the calories before they had a chance to be converted into unsightly flab.

For a moment her will-power stiffened, then weakened again at the thought that, if anything were to go wrong between now and her next time ashore, this might be her last chance – ever! – to taste the delicious smoothness of cream and chocolate on her tongue.

Why not have a final splurge, the voice of her weaker self murmured seductively. One helping of cheesecake with frosting isn't going to make any difference.

The waitress came back. 'Are you ready to order?'

She had blue eyes. Not as deeply blue as the eyes that had looked at Maddie with total indifference a few hours earlier, but blue enough to remind her of them.

Slightly to her own surprise, she heard herself saying, 'I didn't realise how late it was. I have to leave. May I have the check, please?'

A few minutes later she was on her way back to *Sea*

Spray, feeling a mixture of deprivation and virtue. But she knew it would take a huge amount of self-denial to transform herself into the kind of person who would have activated Scott Randall's interest at the party. And as, apart from being fellow competitors, they had nothing else in common, what was the point anyway?

An hour later, after saying goodnight to Shigeru, Scott took advantage of the marina's excellent facilities to have a final luxurious power shower. It was the last time he would enjoy the sensation of hot water beating down on his body for many months.

Perhaps the last time ever.

Like the faraway glimmer of lightning from a distant storm, this thought passed through his brain for no more than a nanosecond. Risk was something he had lived with for a long time. He enjoyed life too much to waste time thinking about worst-case scenarios. He took all possible precautions against things going wrong and then hoped that luck was with him – as it had been so far.

For the final minutes in the shower he switched the water from hot to cold, then turned off the spray and stepped out of the glass-walled cabinet to roughly towel his thick black hair – a legacy from generations of Italian counts. From the evidence of their portraits, still in his family's possession, they'd all had dark eyes and swarthy complexions. He had the same olive skin, but the colour of his eyes came from the genes handed down by his American forbears.

Unlike his contemporaries at Harvard, most of them now climbing the ladder to chief executive status – and trying to keep fit on machines in expensive gymnasiums – Scott's physique showed none of the signs of a life lived behind a desk or the wheel of a car; or of evenings spent in bars and restaurants. His muscular body carried no surplus flesh because, except when ashore, his life was one of continuous exertion. He was fit in the way that wild animals are fit, or males whose cultures are closer to primitive man than to over-civilised, twenty-first century man.

When he had finished drying and finger-combing his damp hair, with the casualness of a man who gives little thought to his appearance beyond keeping clean and neat, he slung his towel over his shoulder and left the washroom reserved for the use of participants in tomorrow's race.

Back on board his boat, *Aquamarine*, he would have liked to play a music tape. But when in harbour he observed the rules, laid down long ago by the person who'd originally taught him to sail. One of which was: 'Do not disturb your neighbours.'

To that end, his mother had also taught him how to tie back the halyards so that they didn't make the sort of noise which he was hearing now from boats berthed nearby whose owners had not had as strict a mentor.

Thinking about his mother reminded him of the girl whom Shigeru had introduced at the party. Scott didn't approve of women taking part in single-handed races. Even when they were middle-aged and had been sailing all their lives, he wasn't comfortable with them tackling the high-risk stuff.

In his opinion it was madness to let someone as young as Madeleine Sardrette – he recalled her surname from the race office lists – compete in the world's toughest sailing race. As far as he was concerned, women were designed by nature to withstand completely different kinds of stresses from those she was taking on.

Remembering her hostile expression as they shook hands, he wondered why she had reddened during that brief contact. Perhaps she was at ease with old men like Shigeru but felt threatened in some way by younger men? Not sexually threatened, that was for sure. No one was likely to make a pass at a girl with such an unflattering, hedgehog-type of haircut, who went to parties dressed in such drab, shapeless clothes, and clearly didn't believe in wearing earrings, or rings, or even minimal make-up.

Accustomed to women who enjoyed their femininity, he'd found Madeleine Sardrette almost impossible to fathom. He wondered what her parents made of her? Having chosen to call her Madeleine, presumably they'd been expecting her to grow up to be as sweet and tempting as those little sponge cakes named after a French pastry-cook. Unfortunately, he could see nothing sweet and tempting about Madeleine.

Although he had felt obliged to wish her luck, Scott thought it more than likely that she would be one of the race's first drop-outs.

As he lay down in his bunk, his thoughts switched from Madeleine Sardrette to a more important matter: the decision confronting him at the end of the race.

It was a dilemma he had wrestled with all his adult life. And it was still as difficult to resolve as it had ever been.

Author's note: For readers who share my enthusiasm for the World Wide Web, I have selected websites which will, I hope, enhance your enjoyment of this story. All the URLs (web addresses) at the end of each chapter have been checked, but of course I can't guarantee that they will always be accessible. However I have tried to choose sites that are likely to have a long life.

Charleston
www.charlestonphotographs.com

Teddy bears
www.teddybears.com

Gone With The Wind
www.dreamweb.org/GoneWithTheWindRing/

Rhett Butler
http://www.franklymydear.com/history/cast-clark.html

American Civil War
www.civilwarhome.com

Vraic
http://www.allinsongallery.com/blampied/stmalo.html

Madeleines
http://www.travellady.com/articles/article-chocolatefantasies.html

chapter two

From Charleston, the twenty competitors from twelve countries taking part in the Slocum Race, one of the world's most gruelling sporting challenges, set sail for their first port of call, Cape Town, at the southern tip of Africa.

It was now late September. Those who completed the course and returned to Charleston next spring would have sailed 27,000 miles. The first leg, through the North and South Atlantic, was not the most hazardous of the race's four stages; but they would encounter heavy currents from the Gulf Stream, tropical depressions, the windless calms known as doldrums, and a lot of commercial shipping.

The leg would demand tactical skills which Maddie was not sure she possessed, even though she had some experience of sailing in the English Channel, one of the world's most crowded shipping lanes, and had learned to sail in the Channel Islands where, over the centuries, hundreds of vessels had foundered on the surrounding rocks and reefs.

However, to her relief, early in December she opened the hatch to the cockpit one morning and saw, in the distance, the towering outline of the famous Table Mountain. She had not made good time, but at least she had made it. Soon she would be ashore again.

When all the competitors, except those who had already withdrawn, had arrived at their destination, the Royal Cape Yacht Club held a champagne reception and buffet supper for them.

Looking across the room at Sardrette, as he thought of her, Scott was suddenly reminded of a book his mother had given him. Its author, the legendary yachtsman Sir Francis Chichester, had been her hero.

On the title page Sofia Randall had written, 'For Scott, in the hope that he will develop the same qualities of tenacity, courage and dedication to his dreams as the author of this inspiring story'.

He had the book on board *Aquamarine*; it was a kind of talisman. Not that he believed in the magical power of objects, but he liked to have it with him. He had read it so many times he knew it almost by heart.

Long ago, at a children's birthday party, his mother had moved away from the group of gossiping mothers and beckoned him to her. 'Do go and be nice to that child in the red shirt, Scotty,' she had murmured in his ear. 'She doesn't seem to know anyone.'

Not too willingly, he had done as he was told and, later, at bedtime, been rewarded by his mother saying warmly, 'If it hadn't been for you, that little girl would have had a miserable time at the party. I was proud of the way you looked after her. Looking out for lonely people is always a good thing to do. There are a lot of them about.'

On impulse he crossed to where Sardrette was standing with her back to the room, pretending to be deeply interested in a painting.

When he looked at it over her shoulder he was surprised to recognise it as a copy of a picture he knew well; an oil painting of Chichester's ketch, *Gypsy Moth IV,* in the mountainous seas of the Southern Ocean.

'Do you like it?' he asked, from behind her.

The question made Maddie jump. She turned. When she saw who had spoken to her, she was even more startled but did her best not to show it. 'Yes, I do,' she said politely. 'Do you?'

'It's one of my favourite modern marine paintings. You

can really feel the power of that huge wave. What do you think of Cape Town? Have you been here before?'

She shook her head. 'I expect you have.'

'A couple of times, yes. It's a nice place with very hospitable people. When there's more time to look around, there's a lot to see.'

'I'm sure there is.' She wished she could think of more to say. She sensed that he had a low threshold of boredom and would not stay long if she failed to come up with something more interesting than her contributions to the conversation so far. But party small talk was like a foreign language to her. She had never had a chance to practise it.

'Are you looking forward to the next leg?' he asked.

'I wouldn't say "looking forward",' she answered cautiously. 'But hopefully –' Before she could add, '– it won't be as tricky as the stretch from New Zealand to Cape Horn,' they were joined by two middle-aged ladies, probably yacht club officials' wives, who obviously wanted to meet him but were less interested in her.

Scott Randall was charming to them for about three minutes before deftly excusing himself. The two matrons then wished Maddie good luck and drifted away, leaving her on her own again. She decided it was time to leave. Nobody would notice her departure and parties were not an environment she felt comfortable in.

Watching her sidle from the room, Scott was aware that he hadn't done as good a job with her as with the little girl at the children's party. But people who were as painfully gauche as Sardrette should really keep away from parties.

She was wearing the loose cotton top worn by fishermen and known as a slop. Hers was the colour favoured by Breton fishermen; the same colour as his cotton pants, known as Nantucket reds, had been when he bought them. Since then sun and spray had faded them down to pale ice-cream pink.

Any girl whose party outfit was a slop and baggy navy trousers had to be lacking the gene that made normal women want to dress up and look their best. Though, before she disappeared from view, he noticed that she did appear to have lost a little of her flab since the last time he saw her. But then most people lost weight while long-haul racing. It used up a lot of energy. Prolonged foul weather demanding round-the-clock exertion, often for days on end, could result in the loss of six or seven pounds. Most competitors couldn't afford such losses and had to be careful not to miss meals or to become dehydrated.

It could be that Sardrette, if she made it back to Charleston, would end the race looking a lot more presentable, weight-wise. Unless, of course, she had slipped away early to indulge in a food-binge before the race resumed. Or it could be she had run out of chocolate on the first leg and was going to make sure that didn't happen en route to their next stop-over in New Zealand.

By the time Maddie had crossed the Indian Ocean to berth at Auckland, on the North Island of New Zealand, it was February.

By now seven of the contenders in the 27,000-mile race were out of the running. They had either capsized, been dismasted or run aground. One of the unlucky boats had been Shigeru's. To her relief he was safe but unable to continue, so she did not have his company to look forward to.

When Maddie arrived, the first thing she wanted was to wash her salt-sticky hair in fresh water; a luxury she had to forego while at sea. By this time her hair was longer than it had been for years and she wondered whether to let it grow long enough to tie back.

She was on deck, towelling it dry, when she heard someone say her name, and looked round to see a man who introduced himself as a reporter from the *New Zealand Herald*.

The first question he asked her was, 'How do you feel about Scott Randall's statement on radio that women shouldn't be allowed to enter this race, Ms Sardrette?'

'I didn't know he had said that. Are you sure you've got it right?'

'Hear it for yourself.'

He unslung a small pack from his shoulder and took out a pocket-sized tape recorder. Moments later she heard an unknown voice with a Kiwi accent asking, 'How do you feel about women competing in long, dangerous ocean races?'

There was a pause before Scott's voice, instantly recognisable to anyone who had heard it before, said, 'Although it may enrage the extreme feminists, I don't think many men are happy about women being exposed to physical dangers. It's instinctive, or should be, for us to want to protect them from the worst kind of risks: avalanches, high altitude sickness, storms at sea, et cetera. That said, there are some brilliant women sailors. But why they want to undergo the kind of hardships ocean racing involves is something I've never understood.'

'Maybe to prove themselves equal to men?' the interviewer suggested.

'That's something else that's hard to understand,' was Scott's answer. 'Men and women are different in almost every way. Women are capable of amazing endurance and fortitude, for example in giving birth and in protecting their children from harm or hardship. But they weren't designed by nature to climb to the top of a mast in the teeth of a gale or to be flung around the way sailors are in storm conditions.'

'So you aren't too happy about having someone as young and inexperienced as Madeleine Sardrette competing in the Slocum,' said the interviewer, his tone making it a statement rather than a question.

'Absolutely not!' Scott's reply could not have been more adamant. 'I don't think she has a clue what the next lap of the race, through the Southern Ocean, will be like. Nor do I think the race organisers should have accepted her application.'

'But she did have the required qualifications,' the interviewer reminded him.

By this time Maddie could hardly contain her indignation. She had read somewhere that the best way to control an upsurge of rage was to hold your breath and count to ten. She did it now, while listening to Scott saying, 'Maybe so, but there is no experience that compares with, or prepares sailors for, the hazards between here and Cape Horn. It's the world's wildest, most treacherous ocean.'

The interview continued for several more minutes. Somehow Maddie managed not to explode. When it was over, she said, 'That's Mr Randall's opinion. The race organisers think differently.'

'But what do *you* think?' the reporter asked her.

'Sorry...no comment. You'll have to excuse me. I have a lot to do.' She went below, closing the hatch behind her.

When, later, she ventured out, the reporter seemed to have vanished, though she kept a sharp eye out for him on her way round to *Aquamarine*'s mooring.

She found Scott sitting in the cockpit, studying some papers attached to a clipboard.

'I'd like to speak to you,' she said brusquely.

He looked up and saw her glowering at him. Instead of inviting her to join him, he put the clipboard aside and – light-footed for so tall a man – stepped out of the cockpit and from the deck to the walkway where she was standing.

'What can I do for you, Madeleine?'

'For a start you could keep your opinions about women sailors to yourself. I've just had a local journalist asking me to comment on a radio interview you gave. I refused...because what I'd have liked to say would not have been complimentary, to put it mildly. You may be one of the stars of the ocean racing fraternity, but that doesn't give you the right to denigrate the also-rans.'

Scott folded his arms across his chest. Even though she was fizzing with animosity, a part of her was aware of the breadth and power of his shoulders under a close-fitting navy T-shirt and the sinewy strength of his sun-tanned forearms.

'I don't recall denigrating anyone.' His tone was as calm as hers was heated.

'You said I shouldn't be allowed to compete...that I didn't know what I was doing. How else would you describe those comments except as disparaging to me and to women sailors in general?'

'If you were running the race, would you allow sixteen-year-olds to compete?' he asked.

'No, of course not...but what has that to do with it? I'm not a teenager.'

'But you wouldn't argue that teenagers, even if they've been sailing since childhood, are not up to this kind of race?'

'No, but – '

'Why not?'

'Because they're just not old enough. They may have the technical skills but they don't have the –' She was momentarily stumped for a word to describe what it was they lacked.

'I don't consider you're old enough. I doubt if anyone under twenty-five has the mettle to deal with the hazards of the next lap. If you're wise you'll pull out,' he said quietly. 'No one will think less of you. You've already proved your abilities by getting as far as this. The Southern Ocean will still be there when you're five years older and tougher than you are now.'

'That's an outrageous thing to say,' Maddie blazed at him fiercely. 'I've a bloody good mind to report you to the race office. It has to be against the rules to try to talk someone out of competing. Not that I'm any competition as far as you're concerned; I know that. Which makes it all the more contemptible –'

'You're losing your cool,' he cut in. 'If you want to report me, that's your privilege. But before you do, calm down and ask yourself what reason I could have for wanting you out of the race apart from a disinterested concern for your safety and survival.'

That silenced her for some moments. Then, making an effort to speak in a more even tone, she said, 'You could be a closet misogynist. The fact that you play the field doesn't mean that you really like women.' As soon as the words were out, she knew that they were ill-judged.

Scott's blue eyes narrowed slightly, making the colour of his irises seem even bluer.

'What makes you think I play the field?'

Already regretting that impetuous comment, she said, 'You have that reputation. Anyway lots of men still make women feel unwelcome in areas they regard as strictly masculine preserves.'

'In case you hadn't noticed, there are quite a few women who would like to make men feel totally superfluous in all spheres,' he said dryly. 'I don't think it serves any purpose to get into a sex-war. For the record, my ideas about women were formed by my two sisters...of whom I'm extremely fond. Do you have brothers?'

Maddie shook her head.

'It makes a difference,' said Scott. 'If you'd grown up with brothers, you'd feel more comfortable with men.'

Maddie's chin came up. 'I don't feel *un*comfortable with men...unless they take patronising attitudes, as you did in that broadcast.'

'I have the impression that you've been on your guard with me since Shigeru introduced us,' he remarked. 'You seemed quite edgy at Cape Town.'

'Perhaps instinct told me you didn't approve of me,' she retorted coldly.

'There's nothing personal about it. I'm concerned for your safety.'

'And perhaps it has crossed your mind that, if a female of my age can do it, the whole thing will seem less heroic than when it was an exclusively male achievement,' she retorted frostily, aware, as she spoke, that she sounded like the most aggressive type of feminist.

Knowing she had made a botch of the whole encounter, she turned on her heel and marched back the way she had come. She could guess what he would be thinking: 'Let the silly bitch sink and to hell with her if that's her attitude.'

In fact Scott was in two minds about catching her up and trying to make her see reason. But he knew that what he should have done, instead of voicing his concern in the recent radio interview, was to tackle the organising committee before the race began.

There were others who thought as he did that Maddie, as Shigeru had called her, was too young to be exposed to the kind of hazards ahead of them. If he had acted immediately on his first reaction to learning that such a young girl had entered the race, it might have been possible to get the rules amended. Now it was too late. All he had succeeded in doing was making an enemy of her.

Which wouldn't have bothered him too much except for an intuitive feeling that, behind her prickly façade, Maddie Sardrette was more vulnerable than she wanted anyone to know.

As she disappeared out of sight and Scott returned to the cockpit to resume what he had been doing before she disturbed him, he was inclined to dismiss the feeling as groundless. Intuition was a feminine faculty. The women in his family based most of their judgements on it, while he and his father drew their conclusions from factual evidence.

Judged by her appearance and behaviour, the girl from Guernsey was capable of holding her own in most circumstances. She hadn't hesitated to come storming round to castigate him about his radio comments.

He checked his watch. In an hour he was being picked up by friends who lived outside Auckland. Meantime he had things to do which were more important than worrying about Sardrette.

During the next lap of the race, they would all be taking chances with their futures...

Back on board her own boat, Maddie was regretting the impulse to confront Scott. Telling him what she thought of him had done more harm than good. Now she had made an enemy of the man. A stupid thing to do considering that he was the favourite to win and popular with the media. In any public confrontation between them, he would always be given the last word and might make people believe that his views about women of her age being debarred from the toughest sailing races were valid.

The third leg of the race was across the notorious Southern Ocean to Cape Horn, the southernmost point of South America.

Maddie was afraid of the Southern Ocean. Terrible things had happened there. Icebergs and rogue waves the size of apartment blocks were among the dangers. Many times in the next ten days, as wind and sea raged and she and her boat were battered and bruised, she felt she had been mad to come.

At last the ferocious weather eased and Maddie knew that she had to have a long sleep, or she would be in danger of making the careless errors which happened when single-handed sailors were fatigued to the point of exhaustion.

She collapsed into her bunk about seven o'clock in the evening, and when she woke up it was almost five in the morning. Luckily, during her ten hours' oblivion nothing disastrous had happened – at least not to her.

When she checked the messages from the race operations centre she was dismayed to find that, three hours earlier, the centre had alerted all the remaining competitors to a capsize. To her amazement, the most likely winner of the race, and the least likely person for a disaster to happen to, was now in desperate peril of losing his life. While she was dead to the world, an emergency position-indicating radio beacon registered to Scott Randall had been activated. Exactly what had happened was not known, but the weather in his area was already bad and getting worse. His chances of survival were not good.

Maddie immediately made contact with the operations centre and was soon receiving the latest update on the situation. This was even more alarming. The boats closest to Scott, and the skippers best-qualified to handle the situation, were, for various reasons, unable to respond to the emergency. There was only one person who might be able to reach him – herself.

Royal Cape Yacht Club
www.rcyc.co.za/guide.htm

Table Mountain
www.cape-town.org

Sir Francis Chichester
www.gileschichestermep.org.uk/francis-chichester.htm
and
www.mmbc.bc.ca/source/schoolnet/adventure/chichester.html
and
www.webcom.com/~trw/London/52235716.html

Nantucket reds
www.nantucketreds.com

Auckland
www.aucklandnz.com/gallery.index.asp
and
http:/nz.com/NZ/NZTour/Auckland/CityOfSails.html

chapter three

The next eighteen hours were a nightmare. Conscious that a man's life – if it were not lost already – depended on her, Maddie battled with hurricane winds and huge waves to reach the position where Scott's boat had turned turtle.

His satellite phone was dead, but the two emergency beacons were continuing to transmit his position. Whether he had been swept away in the catastrophe, or was still on board the wrecked vessel, there was no means of telling. All she could do was get there as fast as possible. There was no hope of any national rescue service coming to his aid. His only chance of survival was if she and *Sea Spray* reached him in time.

By the time she reached the area where he should be, the atrocious weather had abated to what seemed, by comparison, fairly moderate conditions.

On finding the upturned yacht, Maddie made two close passes, yelling as loud as she could to alert Scott to her arrival. The lack of response made her sick with dread that either he wasn't inside, or wasn't alive.

Then, as she began the third pass, she saw him emerging from the escape hatch that all the specially designed boats had in their transoms.

Maddie felt weak with relief. All her previous feelings about him – dislike, resentment, hostility – were forgotten in the joy of finding him alive. At that moment he was simply a fellow human being whom she had managed to locate in conditions that, despite all the resources of modern technology, still bore a strong resemblance to the old saying about searching for a needle in a haystack.

But now the worst was over. Once he had inflated and launched the life raft, it would be a relatively simple matter to sail *Sea Spray* past the raft and pass him a line.

What she didn't expect was that, as soon as he had clambered on board, he would throw his arms round her and enfold her in a bear hug. The first hug of her life.

'To say that I'm glad to see you is the understatement of the century,' he said, looking down at her, unaware that this was her first experience of being held close in a man's arms...in anyone's arms, come to that!

'That makes two of us,' Maddie said, trying to sound calmer than she felt.

For the past twenty-two hours, she had been sailing on one of the world's most dangerous oceans to find him, oppressed by the awesome responsibility of being the only person who could save him from a watery grave. All the other competitors still in the Slocum race were either too far away or grappling with serious problems of their own.

'You made good time. I knew it would be a while before you got here so I was catching up on sleep,' he told her, smiling.

Amazed that anyone, however exhausted, could sleep while their life was at risk – he must have nerves of steel – Maddie said, 'Were you so sure I would get here?'

'Of course. That's the great thing about sailing...we can depend on each other to come to the rescue if need be.'

This was not the moment to remind him of his comments to the radio interviewer. A more pressing concern was to report by satcom, as they all called their satellite communications links to the outside world, that he was safe.

That done, the next priority was to get *Sea Spray* back on course for Cape Horn.

Scott's capsize had happened nearly two thousand miles west of the Horn so they still had a long way to go to get out of the Southern Ocean with its horrendous weather and other hazards. These now included the floating wreckage of his expensive boat.

Maddie wondered what he had felt as he watched the yacht's upturned hull disappearing astern and, with it, his hope of winning the prestigious race.

It wasn't until they went below for a hot drink that she realised the rescue was going to have repercussions that hadn't occurred to her when she heard he was in trouble.

While she was heating some soup, he shed his foul-weather gear – and with it the anonymity conferred by all unisex garments designed for practical purposes. Despite their previous encounters, she was unprepared for the sheer impact of his size and overwhelming masculinity in the cramped, tightly-confined space of the cabin.

Watching him out of the corner of her eye as he removed the protective clothing, Maddie remembered reading how, in another single-handed race, he'd lost his rudder in rough weather off Newport, Rhode Island.

Rather than put out a distress call, Scott had apparently ripped off the companionway sliding hatch to improvise a rudder. And, almost unbelievably, it had worked well until the boat's keel had become entangled with a lobster pot line. With a safety line tied to the rail and a knife between his teeth, he had then dived into a freezing-cold sea and cut his boat free. Unfortunately, Scott had eventually lost the race, but he had won an award for outstanding seamanship from the United States Navy.

Reading about the award in a yachting magazine and, of course, never expecting to meet him in person, Maddie had been deeply impressed by both his resourcefulness and bravery. However, she was now beginning to wonder if sharing these closely confined quarters with such a strong, larger-than-life personality, might prove to be more of an ordeal than the nerve-racking hours which she had spent searching for his boat.

Undressed down to his thermals, he seemed a more alien

being than the yachtsman who, a short time ago, had stepped aboard and embraced her. She was suddenly full of unease, deeply apprehensive at being forced to share the boat with a companion possessing such an abundance of raw masculinity. It felt like being in a cage with an untamed tiger, who wasn't behaving aggressively at the moment — but easily might do so if she made a wrong move. And they were going to be stuck with each other from now until early April.

How on earth was she going to cope with this man for two long months, and in a space which allowed them virtually no privacy?

Shortly after the rescue, the weather moderated and, back on course for the Cape, the boat became relatively comfortable.

Seeing Scott taking in his surroundings, she said, 'I expect *Sea Spray* seems rather primitive compared with your boat.'

'*Sea Spray* is still the right way up,' he said dryly. 'All my advanced technology didn't help when it came to the crunch.'

'What happened?'

'Good question.' He raked a hand through his thick black hair. 'I'm not sure myself what happened. Basically *Aquamarine* was knocked over, but that's a commonplace in these latitudes."

He used his other hand to demonstrate that the boat had crash-gibed with ninety degrees of heel. 'Why she kept going until she was fully inverted, I can't tell you...except that there was a problem with the autopilot. I barely had time to get below. Later on the mast broke up.'

Visualising herself in the same situation, Maddie knew she would have been terrified. Being scared was only bearable when there were things to be done that might reduce the danger. To spend almost twenty-four hours confined in an overturned boat, as he had, and even manage to sleep, showed courage of a high order. Or an extraordinary lack of imagination. But nothing about him suggested a pea-sized brain. He looked as if his mental powers were as well-developed as his body.

'I don't think you need to worry that saving me will ruin your chances. I'm sure the international jury who decide on such matters will award you a time compensation,' he said.

'I don't care if they don't,' Maddie said, shrugging. 'A life is more important than a race. I was never in the running to win it...but you might have done.'

'Competing is the important thing...not winning.'

Did he really mean that? she wondered. A yachting correspondent had once divided the people who competed in the Slocum into three groups: the *Formula One Drivers* like himself, with costly boats and rich sponsors, the *Boy Racers*, young men full of enthusiasm and aggression but with no money, and the *Adventurers and Eccentrics*.

If Maddie fitted in any of those categories, it could only be with the *Eccentrics*. Strictly speaking she wasn't here on her own account, but as Pierre Sardrette's granddaughter. Or, more accurately, the grandson he would have liked her to be. Could anything be more eccentric than taking part in a race to fulfil someone else's dream?

But she wasn't about to reveal her real motivation to her passenger. As far as he was concerned she was one of the unnatural women who wanted to play men's games. Let him continue to think that. Judging by the interview, he had fixed opinions and wasn't likely to change them.

'You do realise, I hope,' she said firmly, 'that having you on board could jeopardise my position if it was thought you were helping me? I'd like your assurance that you'll leave everything to me and won't interfere in any way."

'You're the skipper, ma'am,' he said, smiling.

After what he had been through, he should have looked

ready to drop, his eyelids heavy with fatigue, his skin grey under the tan. Instead he emanated vitality. She had never seen eyes of a deeper, more intense blue.

'You say that...but do you mean it? You may have forgotten the unfavourable comments you made about women skippers during the New Zealand layover. But I haven't.'

'In the light of our last encounter, it was magnanimous of you to come and find me.'

'I had no option. I couldn't let you drown without at least trying to pick you up.' Naturally your comments annoyed me. You must have known they would when you made them.'

His shoulders, moulded by the skin-tight thermal top, moved in a casual shrug. 'I was asked a question. I answered it. Maybe it's an old-fashioned view but I don't think women have any place in front-line-combat or other high risk activities. They're as brave as men...perhaps braver. Nobody would argue with that. I just don't like to think of you, or any woman, being in the situation I was in a while back.'

The thought of what he had been through made her shudder inwardly, but she wasn't going to admit it. Changing the subject, she said, 'I should think you're in need of a meal. It's a long time since I've eaten. I'll get something hot organised. Please make yourself at home.'

'If it's OK with you, I'll shave. Most of the guys grow beards but I'm not comfortable with whiskers.'

He rubbed a hand over what, anywhere else, she would have taken for the start of designer stubble. The dark bristles covering his chin and the lower parts of his lean cheeks served to emphasise the sensual shape and humorous set of his mouth. A disturbing mouth, she thought, looking away.

Maddie wondered if he was about to ask for the loan of a razor, which she didn't have. The few fair hairs on her legs were visible only in strong sunlight, but even if they had been dark she wouldn't have bothered to shave them while sailing. Personal grooming, apart from basic cleanliess, was the last thing on her mind. She had read about male sailors who carefully examined their hands every day and creamed them to keep them supple for the tasks they had to do. But her own grooming consisted of a once-a-week all-over wash in hot water and the daily use of wet wipes.

To her relief, Scott did not ask for a razor. He must have one in the survival bag he had brought on board with him.

'Sure...do whatever you want,' she said. 'If our routines conflict, we'll adjust them.'

All solo yachtsmen on races of this duration lived by routines carefully worked out to make the best possible use of their physical and mental reserves. Often they had to adapt them to changing weather conditions but the basic pattern of sleeping, eating and cleaning was a necessary link with normality in an abnormal situation.

The most abnormal thing about solo voyages was the isolation. Although nowadays it was not as complete as it had been in the days when the American mariner, Captain Joshua Slocum, from whom the race took its name, had left Boston, Massachusetts, in the spring of 1895 and sailed, on his own, round the world, returning to Newport, Rhode Island, a little more than three years later.

Nowadays Slocum contestants were linked to the race headquarters and to each other by a multiplicity of electronic devices. But although Maddie kept in contact with the race office, she had not been in touch with the other competitors and had no family to send encouraging messages. Between the layovers, her only companionship, apart from Bertie, her bear, had been a solitary cockroach and the occasional seabird passing overhead.

To have someone on board was a novelty it would take time to adjust to. She couldn't help wishing her unexpected passenger had been another woman. Then there would have been no question of having to assert her authority, and less risk of embarrassment.

Scott had come to terms with the loss of his boat while he was holed up inside her.

His grandfather, Ethan Randall, who had only recently died, had been apt to quote Dr Samuel Johnson. A little earlier than Noah Webster of Webster's Dictionary fame, Johnson had spent eight years compiling a dictionary. Many times Scott had heard Grandpa Randall repeating one of Johnson's most famous sayings. "Depend upon it, Sir, when a man knows he is to be hanged in a fortnight, it concentrates his mind wonderfully."

From the recent perspective of a man who might be spending his final hours listening to the waves battering the hull of his wrecked boat, nothing had seemed as important as survival. He had been reasonably confident that someone would try to save him. But the last person he had expected to be his rescuer was this weird British girl.

As far as he was concerned none of the Class 2 boats were serious contenders. Maddie Sardrette's 40 foot cutter, *Sea Spray*, was the smallest and oldest boat in the race. For a kid who looked barely out of her teens to be sailing such an unseaworthy craft across the Southern Ocean seemed insanity to him. She had had to have more guts than sense, and her family had to be crazy to let her attempt it.

Remembering how wooden she had felt when he had hugged her, he wondered if she disliked all men. He could understand her disliking him after what he had said to the Kiwi journalist in Auckland. But it might go deeper than that. Competitive sports, especially the really tough ones, always attracted some women who had problems with their sexual orientation. They didn't bother him. Live and let live was his motto. But it would have suited him better to spend however long it took them to reach Punta del Este, the next layover, with one of the guys in the race. Or with a girl who liked being a girl and hadn't found it necessary to put him in his place before he'd showed any inclination to step out of it.

It might save them both a lot of hassle if he asked her to drop him off when they reached the Horn. There was a lighthouse there. Although it wasn't necessarily a manned light, it would have to be serviced. Somewhere nearby there might be a small airstrip or a helicopter landing pad. Even if the only way out was by a dirt road, it had to be a better option than going the whole way to Punta with an unfriendly female determined to show who was boss around here.

By the time he had shaved and washed up, she had prepared their meal. She might be an excellent sailor, but she was no cook, he thought wryly, surveying the unappetising stuff they were about to eat.

It was reckoned that solo yachtsmen needed around five thousand calories a day to fuel them against cold, lack of sleep and the energy output involved in keeping their boats on course in taxing conditions. Being about six inches shorter than his six foot three, Maddie wouldn't need as much food. But if this was the best she could do, he would have to take over the cooking, Scott thought, as he ploughed his way through a dish of reconstituted freeze-dried fish and vegetables without any redeeming seasoning.

She ate looking down at her dish, making no attempt at conversation. But, to be fair, she must be feeling worn out after what she had been through coming to find him.

Suddenly it struck him that, on the two previous occasions when he had noticed her, she hadn't looked the way she did now. Back in Charleston, she had resembled a teenage boy with a serious weight problem. In the months they had been at sea, the hedgehog crop had grown to a length that reminded him of the thick short blond mane he had seen on an Icelandic pony at a horse farm in the States that specialised in that tough breed. At the moment her hair was tangled and sticky with salt spray and, even when clean, would still be shaggy and unflattering.

At a guess, all her vital statistics were down by at least six inches, and her face was no longer podgy. He could actually see her cheekbones now and her eyes looked larger. If she smiled and relaxed, she might even be quite attractive.

Aware that he was studying her and finding his scrutiny unnerving, Maddie raised her head and looked him squarely in the eyes. By now she ought to be used to those blue, blue eyes, but each time the colour of his irises gave her an odd little shock.

'We were going to compare our routines,' she said. 'Not that you need to keep to yours any longer. I hope you're not going to be bored. Are you a reader?'

'I like reading and listening to music, other things permitting. Are you on polyphasic sleep strategy?' he asked.

Maddie nodded. 'I'm a morning person so I like to take lots of twenty-minute naps. How about you?'

'I'm a night person. I go for longer naps around forty-five minutes...when the situation permits. If I've been ashore for a while I can sleep the full eight hours. At sea I can get by on four.'

It was on the tip of her tongue to say, 'I wish I could. I need at least five and a half,' but she decided against any admission of being less resilient than he was. Instead, she said, 'Now, weather permitting, you can sleep as long as you like. Luckily *Sea Spray* has two bunks from the time when my father and grandfather used to sail her together. She was built in my grandfather's boatyard.'

'So you've grown up around boats. How old are you exactly?' he asked.

That he had to ask showed that, if he had read her CV, which like those of all the competitors was on the race office website, he had not been sufficiently interested to remember any details. Not that her CV gave much away. Deliberately she disclosed as little as possible about herself and her background.

She debated advancing her age by two or three years, but lying didn't come easily. 'Old enough to know what I'm doing. I've been sailing since I was that high' – her gesture indicating how small she had been when she started.

'Me too,' he said. 'At seven I was racing dinghies and at thirteen I did my first Newport to Bermuda race. When school was out I virtually lived offshore. Was it the same for you?'

She nodded. In the sense that boats and sailing had dominated her life, it probably had been. But not, she guessed, in any other way. He had grown up in the world's richest country, she on a tiny island where, until offshore banking had brought about its current prosperity, the islanders had seen severe fluctuations in their economy.

The gulf between Scott and herself was as wide as the difference between their boats. That she might complete the race and he wouldn't was merely bad luck. It didn't alter the fact that, apart from being forced by circumstance to live together for a while, they had as little in common as the solitary cockroach that shared the boat with her had with the huge white wandering albatrosses that inhabited the Southern Ocean but which she had not yet seen...

Before the Slocum race started, like all the other contestants, Maddie had been supplied with a state-of-the-art digital camera in order to take pictures of herself and her boat to send to the race headquarters in the United States.

As well as providing the world's press with information

and photographs, the race office had a website on the Internet where millions of armchair sailors around the world could follow the race on their computers.

Up to now, even though she was the only woman competing, few of her photographs had appeared in the website's gallery which, understandably, had concentrated on the leading contenders, especially those in Class I.

Within a short time of Scott's safety being reported, the race office was sending urgent email requests for pictures of the two of them together, not only to show on the website but to satisfy the demands of the international media.

'Let's open a bottle of wine and take a shot of us celebrating the occasion,' Scott suggested, when they had finished eating.

'I don't have any wine.'

His eyebrows shot up. 'You're not serious?'

'I don't drink it...I'm sorry' – this in response to the appalled look on his face.

He said something in a language she didn't understand. His expression suggested it was as well that she didn't.

Then, reverting to English and a tone of half-amused resignation, he said, 'I'm beginning to think I should have stayed where I was and waited for someone with more sensitive tastebuds and a stock of alcohol to come by.'

Before she had fully taken in what he meant by the reference to tastebuds, he went on, 'In that case we'll have to pretend to be drinking coffee. Do you want to put on some lipstick before we do the photo shoot?'

Having by now understood that he hadn't thought much of the meal she had provided, she said brusquely, 'I don't have a lipstick either.'

This time only one dark eyebrow rose. 'You never use it?'

'Sometimes...when I'm ashore. It's hardly an essential item when I'm on my own in the middle of nowhere.'

'I guess not. Then the best you can do is to bite your lips, the way girls did before lipstick was invented.'

As he spoke, he was looking at Maddie's mouth in a way that started a flutter in the pit of her stomach. Even more unnerving was when he suddenly reached out to smooth her hair with his fingers, then tuck it behind her ears. The almost caressing touch of his fingertips against the tops of her ears and the sensitive skin behind them that came close to making her recoil in shock from the surge of sensation it induced. She only just managed to control the reaction.

'You do have a comb, I presume?'

'Of course,' she said curtly, turning away to find it.

He didn't like her cooking. He thought she looked a mess. It would have served him right if she had left him to drown. But even as she thought it she knew she didn't really mean it.

Cape Horn
www.nautica.it/charter/capehorn.htm
and
http://www.bobwebb.net/capehorn.html
and
www.victory-cruises.com/cape_horn.html
and
http://website.lineone.net/~dave_reay/highseas.htm

Conquerors of the High Seas
www.didyouknow.cd/aroundtheworld/sailing.htm

Captain Joshua Slocum
www.arthur-ransome.org/ar/literary/slocum2.htm

(At the site above you can read Captain Slocum's SAILING ALONE AROUND THE WORLD of which Sir Arthur Ransome said, "Boys who do not like this book ought to be drowned at once".)
and
http://mmbc.bc.ca/source/schoolnet/adventure/slocum.html

chapter four

Later, while Maddie gave her attention to the boat, Scott occupied himself sending reassuring emails to his family and close friends.

Fortunately the weather had calmed down since his capsize. There was now a steady wind which, as long as it didn't strengthen or shift, left Maddie with little to do. Leaving *Sea Spray* on autopilot, she could take a nap and make up for the long period of sleeplessness while she was searching for Scott.

When she woke up, he told her the pictures they had taken earlier were already on the race office website.

'Take a look.' He clicked on one of the thumbnail-sized pictures to bring it up to full size. 'What do you think?'

Her first thought was what attractive teeth he had: their whiteness and evenness exposed by his cheerful grin for the benefit of the camera. They were both holding the empty mugs out in front of them and looking on top of the world. Maddie hardly recognised herself. She would never be pretty but she looked far more presentable than she ever had before. Perhaps it had something to do with her hair being longer, or with the euphoria she still felt at having successfully accomplished the task that, if she had failed, would have haunted her all her life.

'It's OK, isn't it?' she said, pleased that, in the company of such a good-looking man, she hadn't come out looking a complete potato.

'Better than OK. You're naturally photogenic. This picture is going to make a lot of guys who wouldn't have cared to be in my shoes a few hours ago wish they could change places now.'

He said it so nicely that she could almost believe he really meant it and was not merely being kind.

Not many hours later the press coverage of the incident began to come through.

During the 1998-99 Around Alone race, the media had given a lot of coverage to the rescue by a leading Italian yachtsman of a famous French yachtswoman. That, this time, the situation had been reversed, appealed to them even more.

Maddie makes Scott eat his words was the headline on a UK press story by a tabloid journalist who had obviously picked up the Auckland interview. She would have expected this to annoy Scott, but he only laughed and shrugged. Whether he was angry inwardly it was impossible to tell.

Then came a story by a famous woman columnist headed *The sea-wolf and the virgin*. The story began – *The rescue of Scott Randall, 30, by Maddie Sardrette, 21, brings into intimate propinquity a man who, when on land, has the reputation of being a determined and successful skirt-chaser, and a girl who may be one of the last survivors of a now almost extinct species, the twenty-something virgin.*

Maddie has the reputation of being dedicated to sailing, to the exclusion of everything that her age group is normally interested in. "She has always held aloof from the rest of us," I was told by one of her former classmates at Guernsey's Ladies College (founded 1872) where Sardrette was educated.

Rumour says she has never had a steady boyfriend or even, as far as is known, a date with a young man.

By the time she had read the whole piece she was steaming with impotent rage at the invasion of her privacy. What her grandfather would think if he read it, she couldn't imagine. The only paper he took was the local one. But someone was sure to bring the article to his attention. Its prurient tone would disgust him even more than it did her. He was a strait-laced man with no time for what he considered the lax moral values of contemporary society.

'And are you?' asked Scott, who had been reading the article at the same time. 'One of the last surviving virgins,' he added.

For once in her life Maddie was prepared to lie rather than to admit to this worldly man, who now knew how old she was, that her experience of men was in inverse ratio to his knowledge of women.

'Of course not,' she said dismissively. 'Are you the way she describes you?'

'I've had a few pleasant relationships. I don't think the women who shared them would describe me the way she does'– with a gesture at the screen where the end of the columnist's story was still on view. 'I would hope not,' he added dryly. 'You have to learn to ignore a lot of what's written about you. It's not important. People read all that stuff but forget it five minutes later.'

Perhaps they did where he came from. Maddie had an uneasy feeling that where she came from the gossip would take much longer to subside.

Scott surprised her by saying, 'I've been to the Channel Islands. It was a long time ago. One of my sisters was dating an English guy whose parents had a summer place on Sark. Their youngest son was my age, seventeen, so I got invited to keep him company. We had a great time sailing and rock-climbing. We flew in to your island, Guernsey, and then caught the ferry to Sark. Guernsey looked great from the air, but we didn't spend time there.'

'The island has changed,' she said, relieved that the conversation had veered away from personal matters. 'St Peter Port, the main town, has had the marina extended and there are a lot more cars on the roads. Visitors used to bicycle everywhere, but our roads are narrow and getting around on a bike can be hazardous now.'

'Sardrette is a Guernsey name by the sound of it. How long has your family lived there?'

'Oh, hundreds of years,' Maddie said vaguely.

She had had her grandfather's ancestry drummed into her since childhood, but had never been allowed to forget she was not a true Guernsey woman, her blood being tainted by that of an incomer, and a worthless incomer at that. Pierre Sardrette saw all incomers as a corrupting influence, but his contempt for his vanished daughter-in-law was even more virulent than his feelings about the rich outsiders who now occupied many of the island's finest houses.

'Where are you from?' she asked, playing tit-for-tat with his ignorance of her background.

'That's hard to answer. I'm an American citizen but I was born in Italy. I've lived in a lot of places. I guess I feel more at home on the ocean than anywhere on land. But even on land, the Internet is making people forget about old-fashioned frontiers and boundaries.' He switched the conversation in a new direction by asking, 'What did you do about funding?'

Before she could answer, he added, 'I would have thought you'd have gotten some hefty sponsorship from the offshore banking industry in Guernsey. But I guess you didn't take that route or they would be getting their pound of flesh with logos all over your sails, and the boat would have a promotional name.'

'I was lucky...I didn't need to ask for that kind of sponsorship,' said Maddie. 'It would have involved a lot of publicity and I wanted to avoid all that and get away as quietly as possible. I know some people enjoy being in the news and on TV. But I would have hated it.'

'Would you still hate it...looking the way you do now?' he asked.

'Yes, I would,' she said curtly. 'I'm not doing this because I want to be famous. I don't think fame is important. It seems to me more of a punishment than a prize.'

Amused by her vehemence, he said, 'You have strong opinions, don't you?'

'On some things – yes. Don't you?'

'Sure, and I agree about the media. They can be a pain; intruding in people's lives at times when they need to be left alone. But then I don't have much time for people who let them do that. Nobody can be forced to give a press conference within hours of a tragedy hitting them,' he added dryly.

After a pause, he went on, 'But a certain amount of media attention is inevitable if you're involved in sports that interest the public. Getting back to your funding, was the whole tab picked up by your family's boat business?'

'Not all of it. They did the work on the boat, but all the expensive electronic stuff, and the new sails and provisioning, was covered by a bequest from an elderly neighbour. If Miss Lake hadn't left me a legacy, I couldn't have entered for the race.'

'Tell me about her?'

'She came to the island when I was small. Her family and another family used to spend bucket-and-spade holidays in Guernsey when their children were young. Miss Lake was the eldest daughter and the other family had a son two years older. When they grew up they fell in love and were engaged to be married. He was killed in an accident; she never married. When she retired from her job as a hospital administrator, she decided to come to Guernsey, the scene of all her happiest memories. Our cleaning lady worked for her and, when Miss Lake's eyesight deteriorated, I used to go round and read *The Times* newspaper to her. Then she asked me to read her favourite books. Looking back, I think she was doing me a favour and only pretending I was being useful to her.'

'Not many teenagers would be willing to spend time reading to an old lady,' said Scott.

'I enjoyed it. She was interesting. She'd spent her holidays travelling and she told me about New York and Paris and Venice. She hadn't led a dull life.'

'But she never found another guy to suit her?'

'The way she talked about John, he was an exceptional person. I think she preferred to remember their time together than to have a humdrum relationship with somebody ordinary.'

'Life goes on for a long time. Most people don't find memories very sustaining.'

'Miss Lake wasn't "most people". She was special,' said Maddie. 'She believed that she and John would be reunited in another life. I'm not convinced about that...but, for her sake, I hope she was right.'

'It's a nice idea but it doesn't hold water,' Scott said dismissively. 'This life is all we have and we're crazy if we don't make the most of it.'

'You're very dogmatic...writing off other people's opinions as if what you think must be right.'

'It's a view supported by science and logic.'

'Millions of intelligent people wouldn't agree with you.'

He shrugged. 'I would express my views more diplomatically if we were in a group with people who might be sensitive about their beliefs. But there's only the two of us here, and we're sailing an ocean that constantly reminds us how puny and unimportant human beings are. Anyway, you just said yourself that you had doubts about the Pearly Gates.'

'I certainly don't think much of *your* chances of passing through them,' Maddie retorted. 'Anyone as arrogant as you is more likely to find himself being roasted on a griddle by someone with horns and a forked tail.'

Scott smiled at her. 'I'm not arrogant, Maddie. I'm paying you the compliment of confiding my most private views to you. In the situation we're in, it seems pointless to make polite conversation. It makes more sense to be open and honest with each other rather than exchanging the bromides that people dish out most of the time.'

The annoying thing was that she knew he was right. In any high-risk situation, it didn't make sense to talk in platitudes, skirting the thin-ice subjects which were avoided in everyday life for fear of upsetting other people's sensibilities. When he had been close to death, and both of them were still at risk, why not say what they meant and discuss their deepest beliefs?

It had been Miss Lake who had once warned her about the four taboo topics: politics, religion, money and sex. But Miss Lake had been elderly and out of touch with the modern world. In any case only one of those four interested Maddie.

Politics left her cold. She was only marginally less indifferent to religion and money. But sex, in all its mysterious ramifications, was intensely interesting. She would have liked to discuss it with someone who knew what they were talking about – as, by the sound of it, Scott did.

But how could she say, 'OK, let's talk about sex. I know next to nothing. You seem to know everything. Enlighten me.'

He might take it as an oblique invitation to demonstrate his prowess.

The thought made her flush and say gruffly, 'I haven't time to talk. There are things to do. If you're bored, you'd better read a book.'

Sailors' saying: *Below 40° South there is no law, below 50° south there is no God.*
www.railriders.com/adventures/seas.html

Sea Change 51

Sark
www.sark-tourism.com/introduction/index.htm
and
www.stocks-sark.com/Gallery.html

chapter five

When Scott looked at Maddie's books, it was his first intimation that the girl who had saved his life might be more congenial company than he had first thought.

A title that caught his eye was *Beyond The Reefs*, a classic real-life adventure by a man who had switched from piloting aircraft to shark fishing in the Indian Ocean.

'I see you're a fan of William Travis,' he said, when Maddie reappeared.

She glanced at the book he was holding. 'Yes,' she said brusquely, preoccupied with checking the barometer and wind indicator.

When she had gone back on deck, he checked through the rest of her library. Most of the books, he noticed, had second hand prices on their fly-leaves, and some were stamped *Withdrawn from the Guille-Allès Public Library*.

He remembered, on his holiday in Sark, being told that the library in Guernsey had been founded in Victorian times by two Guernseymen, Thomas Guille and Frederick Allès, who had gone to New York as apprentices, and there explored libraries and developed a love of books that, in later life, when they were prosperous businessmen, had led them to found a library on the island they came from.

Scott's father was a man of similarly bookish inclinations. From their twelfth birthdays, he had allowed his children to charge any books they wanted to his accounts with bookshops in New York, London, Paris and everywhere else he maintained a residence. Scott had grown up in houses and apartments with their own libraries where shiny-jacketed copies of notable new books were placed on the night tables in the guest rooms.

But at school and especially at college he had been friendly with people for whom books were a luxury, as appeared to be the case with Maddie. Had he known she was a bookworm, with reading tastes similar to his own, he could have offered her the books he had turfed out at Cape Town and Auckland, replacing them with new ones.

Thinking about several irreplaceable books lost with his boat, he frowned.

Hunched in the cockpit when, without a stranger on board, she would have been in the cabin, Maddie glowered morosely at the white caps blown up by the rising wind.

She knew it was unreasonable to resent Scott handling her books when she herself had suggested he read. But she couldn't help feeling possessive about them.

Suddenly she remembered Bertie. If Scott noticed him, what an idiot he would think her, sharing her bunk with a shabby stuffed toy.

Appraising his new living quarters, Scott's glance took in the bear on the lower bunk without surprise. That females were heavily into anthropomorphism was something he had accepted from an early age when his sisters cluttered their beds with a variety of toy animals as real to them as people.

One of his sisters – an otherwise sane woman – had taken a grey plush ape on her honeymoon, on the grounds that, having slept with her since she was six, the toy would be miserable if left behind. Sensibly, her bridegroom had banned it from the connubial bed but, having sisters himself, had known better than to chuck it out of the window or deliberately lose it.

When Maddie came below, Scott had opened a storage locker and was looking at a piece of paper she had taped to the inside of the door.

'Did you write this?' he asked.

Before she could answer, he read the words aloud. '"The beauty about my life at sea alone is that my limits are the extent of my physical and psychological make-up. I succeed or fail by my own endeavours without any influence from the outside world. I like being a free agent and an individual which is perhaps why I am against all religion and political doctrines which try and impose their will on mankind."'

'It was written by one of my heroines,' said Maddie. 'Dame Naomi James.' In case the name didn't mean as much to him as it did to her, she added, 'She was the first woman to sail single-handed round the globe via Cape Horn. She had never handled a boat by herself before, but she set a new record time and made sailing history.'

Scott closed the locker. 'I've read about her. She must be getting on now, but at the time she was a good-looking chick...and not long married, I seem to remember.'

'That's right. It was her husband who taught her to sail. It must have been difficult for him to encourage her do it, knowing she wasn't anything like as expert as he was and, even if things went well, he wouldn't see her again for nine months.'

'She must have been a little crazy to want to do it when the odds were stacked against her making it,' said Scott.

'She wanted to prove herself,' said Maddie. 'She had grown up on a remote dairy farm in New Zealand. They were a close family with hardly any contact with the outside world. She was mad about riding when she small... riding and books. They didn't have television in New Zealand in those days. She was bored at school and spent all her time day-dreaming.' She broke off, wondering if he was bored by her enthusiasm for Dame Naomi.

'Do you identify with her?'

He didn't look bored. He seemed interested.

'Not really. I grew up in a busy little seaport, not the depths of the country. I didn't have any brothers or sisters.

I liked my lessons.' She didn't tell him that, like Dame Naomi, she had been a loner at school, both of them spending more time in the school library than being chummy with other girls.

'But she was, in a way, my mentor,' Maddie went on. 'Her example convinced me I could do it.'

'Why did she want to do it? Why did you?'

'I told you...to prove herself. She had left school early to be a hairdressing apprentice, but after a while the job bored her so she decided to travel. Other girls of her age were getting married and having babies, but she didn't want to do that. She wanted to do something different – but she didn't know what.'

'That's a common dilemma,' said Scott. 'I'd say fewer than ten per cent of school-leavers have their future clearly mapped out in their own minds. It may sometimes be mapped out for them,' he added, his eyes suddenly sombre.

She wasn't sure what he meant by that but hesitated to question him because, if she probed into his life, he would feel free to probe into hers, and she didn't want that.

It was safer to go on talking about Dame Naomi. 'Anyway she knocked about Europe for several years, learning German and doing various jobs. Then one day she was in the French port, St Malo, and a young Frenchman picked her up. They were walking along a quay when a woman on a moored yacht called out "Anyone for coffee?" She was speaking to the boat's crew, but the Frenchman pretended to think the invitation was aimed at him and Naomi. The boat was the famous *British Steel* and the skipper was Rob James, who became her husband. That was how, completely by chance, she found her purpose in life and someone to share it with.'

Scott made no comment on that. After a moment or two, he said, 'A few years ago my father was at a public dinner-lecture at The Explorers Club in New York. The speaker was a Russian, Captain Krystina Liskiewicz. She was billed as the first woman to sail round the world but maybe, at the time, the American and British press weren't taking much notice. She was a much older woman when she did it. She'd been sailing for twenty-five years.'

'I've been sailing for fifteen years,' said Maddie.

'Not in these conditions', he said dryly.

At that moment, as if on cue, they both felt the wind shift and Maddie pushed past him, heading for the cockpit to see what was happening.

Controlling his own instinctive reaction was still hard for Scott to do. He didn't think he would ever get used to it. It would have been easier if Maddie had been his own age or older.

Or would it? Even if it had been Captain Krystina who had rescued him, he might still have had a problem stopping himself from wanting to take control.

The fact was that although men might have to bow to political correctness and pay lip service to equality, deep down most of them felt that in situations like this they would rather be in command, or at least sharing the responsibility and able to take charge if circumstances demanded it.

Maddie's competence was not in doubt. But for her courage and skill, he would have had to choose between a slow death or a quick one by drowning.

That said, a lifetime of conditioning had made it almost impossible for him to stand by and do nothing while she coped with whatever the weather and the sea threw at them. Had she been a man, he could have borne it more easily. Not because a man would necessarily have been more capable than she was. That wasn't, he realised, the core of the issue. What really bugged him was that she might be hurt while he stood around doing nothing.

The lack of privacy that Maddie had dreaded in the

immediate aftermath of the rescue turned out to be less of an embarrassment than she had feared.

This was partly because *Sea Spray*'s amenities were not quite as brutally basic as those on the Class One boats built for maximum speed. But also, she had to admit, it was due to Scott being a far more considerate passenger than she would have expected.

Even so, in such a restricted space, it was inevitable that a big man and a tall girl would come into fairly frequent physical contact. But that situation wasn't nearly as fraught as she had anticipated, or as it might have been with someone else.

One day they were eating together when Scott surprised her by asking, 'What do you think of Prince William?'

'He seems OK. I've never thought much about him. Why?'

'Supposing he didn't like being a future heir to the throne and wanted to do his own thing? Do you think he'd be justified in refusing to toe the royal line?'

Maddie considered the question. After a bit, she said, 'Yes, I think he would. It must be an awful life…endlessly shaking hands with and being nice to people you're not really interested in. I don't know how the Queen stands it. Would you accept it as your destiny if you were William?'

'Tradition is a powerful force. There would be a lot of pressure on him to conform,' said Scott.

'Some people don't think the monarchy will last much longer anyway. They think we'll have an elected head of state like America.'

'Maybe…who knows.'

Scott's expression reminded her of a previous remark he had made that had piqued her curiosity, something about people's futures being mapped out for them.

Before she could ask him about it, a bleep alerted her to the arrival of a warning that a storm front was coming through. Moments later she was on deck; their conversation forgotten as she prepared for the next battle with the weather.

Though it had its hairy moments, the front turned out to be much less severe than the weather preceding the rescue. Or maybe it was that the presence of another person on board reduced the stress, thought Maddie, when it was over.

Considering the frustration he must have felt at being stuck in the cabin where the noise level, always high, was enough to drive an unoccupied person insane, Scott had been surprisingly even-tempered.

It was during the next lull that he asked her, 'Do you have a boyfriend, Maddie?'

'Not at the moment.'

'But you have had one?'

The implication touched her on the raw. 'Are you saying that I'm such a disaster that you can't imagine anyone looking at me twice?' she asked curtly.

She didn't succeed in embarrassing him. 'You're an attractive girl...now,' he said easily. 'But at the start of this voyage you were carrying a lot of surplus pounds, and you didn't present yourself in a way that was likely to appeal to guys in their teens who mostly go for superficial attractions.'

'My...boyfriend wasn't in his teens.'

'How old was he?'

'Twenty...and if you're thinking he was only interested in me because he was a disaster too and couldn't get anyone better, you're mistaken,' she told him hotly. 'He was gorgeous. He could have had anyone he wanted.'

'Tell me about him. How did you meet him?'

'He was...is a scaffolder.'

'A scaffolder?' Scott sounded as if he were not sure what the term implied.

'Because of the island's climate – mild, but wet and windy in the winter – the houses need a lot of maintenance, especially the old ones,' she explained. 'You hardly ever see a street without at least one building surrounded by scaffolding. Some of the large family houses, built with fortunes made by privateering, have a basement and three or four storeys. It would be impossible to paint and repair them without scaffolds.'

Knowing that a lot of people confused privateers with pirates, she added, 'Privateers were armed ships, belonging to private owners, commissioned for war service by a government; in this case the British government who were fighting Napoleon.'

Scott nodded. 'The South used privateers in the American civil war. When I was a boy, I fantasised about making my fortune as master of a privateer. I did the pirate fantasy sometimes as well...capturing merchant ships for their cargoes...and any beautiful maidens who happened to be on board.' His eyes glinted with amusement. 'Now I'm a captive myself.'

'Hardly a captive,' said Maddie.

'I can't walk away.'

She gave a slight shrug. 'That makes two of us.'

'Tell me more about your scaffolder. What was his name?'

She had hoped he wouldn't revert to that subject. 'Tom.'

'And how old were you?'

'Eighteen.'

'Were you at college?'

'I didn't go to college. I was working.'

Scott was not to be put off by the brevity of her answers. 'Doing what?' he asked.

'Office stuff.'

The office had been at her grandfather's boatyard where Maddie had been working part-time because she was also running the house while his housekeeper was in hospital. Islanders who wanted university degrees had to go to the mainland and, although he had paid for her schooling, her grandfather would not have paid college fees. He thought universities were rife with drug-taking and licentious behaviour.

'I can't see you sticking an office job for too long. How long did that last?' asked Scott.

'About a year.'

'Then what happened?'

'I was able to switch to ocean racing. I'd needed a backer and it hadn't been easy to find one. A lot of people take your view that it's a man's sport and women have no place in it...even in the shorter races. Or have you changed your mind now?'

'I've changed it in relation to your capabilities, obviously. If you hadn't been in this race, I'd be a goner,' he said. 'But it would be dishonest to say I've changed my mind about women doing seriously dangerous things like free rock climbing or going into action with the military. That women have equal courage and equal powers of endurance is a given. But instincts are hard to change. Most males are born with an instinct to shield females from harm, if they can. They feel more deeply disturbed if a woman is smashed to pieces falling off a mountain, or shot and killed in a battle.'

'I have to agree about fighting,' said Maddie. 'Of course it depends on circumstances. In a siege situation, there might be no chance of survival if women didn't help to beat off attackers. But I don't think women – or children – should be recruited as combat soldiers. But if we want to risk our lives climbing, or whatever, I think men should suffer in silence...the way wives and girlfriends do when their menfolk do dangerous things because it gives them a buzz.'

'Maybe.' Scott didn't look convinced. 'Anyway tell me more about Tom. He isn't your boyfriend any longer, right?'

Maddie shook her head.

'What went wrong?'

The truthful answer was 'I was forbidden to see him', but she wasn't going to tell Scott that. He wouldn't be able to comprehend a situation where an eighteen-year-old girl could be forced to give up a friendship that had meant a great deal to her.

As clearly as if it were yesterday, she remembered the morning the lorry piled high with planks and poles had drawn up outside the house where she was clearing the table after her grandfather's early breakfast. He had already left for the boatyard and, a few minutes later, she was able to lurk beside one of the bedroom windows and watch the three young men in matching T-shirts and denim shorts unloading.

They handled the heavy materials of their trade as if they weighed nothing. The one to whom her gaze returned most frequently was tall and blond. The seam along the top of one broad shoulder had torn open, exposing his sun-burned skin. For a reason she didn't understand, that glimpse of taut bare flesh had triggered sensations Maddie had never experienced before.

'It just didn't work out,' she said. 'He wanted to go to the cinema and discos and I needed to spend my evenings working on the boat.'

'So you weren't in love with him?'

'No.' But she could have been, very easily.

Despite – or perhaps because of – his formidable strength, Tom had been a gentle person. On their one and only date, he had treated her in an almost brotherly way. Whether he would have kissed her goodnight she would never know. While they were talking on her doorstep – she had thought her grandfather was out until late – Pierre Sardrette had opened the door, sent Tom packing and read the riot act to her.

She had seen Tom a few times after that. The first time he had shouted down to her while he and the others were erecting scaffolding round a church tower. He had come down to street level to speak to her. Though it was her fault, not his, he had apologised for getting her told off. But he hadn't suggested seeing her again.

According to her grandfather, Tom had only wanted to have his way with her a few times and then he would have dropped her. But Maddie didn't believe that. She felt sure Tom had really liked her, but not enough to stand up to the fierce old man who ruled her life.

For her part, Maddie had been more concerned about keeping the concessions she had won than in fighting to continue a relationship that had barely begun.

'Relationships can be tricky for people like us,' Scott said thoughtfully. 'They're easier for land-based people.'

A day or two later he caught sight of her giving an involuntary wince as an unguarded movement activated the pain caused by banging her ribcage during the squall.

'What's wrong? Have you hurt yourself?' he asked.

'It's nothing...only a bruise,' she said, shrugging.

Inevitably, even the most sure-footed sailors suffered many falls and knocks during a long voyage, and now she was no longer as well-cushioned as she had been.

'Let me see it,' he demanded.

'Certainly not,' she shot back.

'This is no time for false modesty, Maddie. Even a bruise needs to be checked.'

'I have checked it ...and used arnica ointment. That's the only treatment for bruises.'

'Maybe you've cracked a rib."

'If I had, there'd be nothing you could do about it. The only thing that mends cracked ribs is time. You know that as well as I do. Anyway, it isn't cracked. That would be hellishly painful. This hardly hurts at all.'

'Judging by your expression a moment ago, it's hurting

a lot. I'd still like to take a look. I'm not asking you to strip off...only to pull out your shirt.'

'Well, I'm not going to,' she said obstinately. 'You're making a fuss about nothing.'

'It's you who's making a fuss. Show me.' His tone had the ring of command.

A sharp retort was on the tip of her tongue, but she changed her mind about uttering it. Part of her would have liked to defy him, but her common sense told her that, in a clash of wills, she was unlikely to win. Besides, he had a point. The bruise wasn't anywhere embarrassing. It was at the bottom of her ribcage.

'Oh, for God's sake,' he said impatiently. 'If I were a groper, you'd have found it out before now, don't you think?'

To her annoyance, Maddie felt herself blushing. 'I never thought you were,' she said crossly. 'But you'd certainly win a prize for thinking you know what's best. Talk about bossy...' She tugged her thermal top free of her foul weather trousers and exposed the place where the bruise was.

Scott bent to examine it. 'Hmm...you took quite a clout. When did this happen?'

'Some time during the squall. I lost my balance for a moment. I've had worse knocks and so have you.'

'Mm...but even contusions can be a problem if people are under par – as most of us are after a long time at sea. How often are you using the arnica?'

'Every day.'

'Good. OK, you can cover up now.'

Sometimes it seemed to Maddie they were never going to reach Cape Horn which marked the end of the worst stretch of the voyage. But eventually they rounded that inhospitable cape.

'If I'd had the sense to bring some booze on board, we

could have had a party,' said Scott. 'But my "cellar", such as it was, will now be several miles down on the ocean floor.'

She had wondered if he might want to be put ashore, but he had not suggested it and by now she was finding his company less of an intrusion and more of a comfort. If anything terrible happened, she would not have to face it alone.

After they passed the Horn, she had a long sleep. When she woke, she was surprised to find Scott standing beside her bunk. He was frowning. For the first time since they met, he was looking worried.

She sat up in a hurry. 'What's the matter? What's wrong?'

With visible reluctance, he said, 'I'm afraid there's been some bad news while you were sleeping.'

William Travis
www.seychelles.net/hundel/Pages/BOOK.htm

Guille-Allès Library
www.gov.gg/Guille-Alles/
and
www.guernseypostcards.com/town/town13.html

Dame Naomi James
www.jolttrust.org.uk

St Malo
http://arch.ced.berkeley.edu/kap/gallery/gal185.html
(slow download but worth the wait)

chapter six

Someone's been lost, she thought. Somebody else has capsized, but they haven't survived.

'Who? What happened?' she asked. 'It's not Rex, is it?'

Rex, a gutsy eighteen-year-old, was too young to compete in the race. He was following the course unofficially. At times they had been close enough to talk to each other on the radio. She couldn't bear it if anything had happened to Rex.

'Rex is OK,' said Scott. 'It's not any of us. It's a member of your family, Maddie.'

Her expression changed from worry to bewilderment. 'I don't have a family...only my grandfather.'

'You didn't know he was sick?'

'Sick?' It took her a moment to remember that 'sick' was American for the English term ill. 'He wasn't sick when I left. He's never been ill in his life. What's wrong with him?'

'I guess he didn't want you to know...and hoped that he could hang on until you got home.' Scott paused for a moment, his tanned face full of concern. 'It's too bad he didn't make it. He spent his last weeks in hospital. He died there during the night.'

Maddie couldn't believe what she was hearing. Her strong, tough, indestructible grandparent...dead? It didn't make sense. He was only in his sixties. Her great-grandfather had lived to be ninety-something. She had taken it for granted that Pierre would do the same.

As, scarcely knowing what she was doing, she swung her legs to the deck and rose to her feet, Scott put out his hands and took her gently by the shoulders. 'It's a bad shock...a terrible shock. Especially if he was your closest relation.'

'I can't believe it...I just can't believe it. What was wrong with him? What did he die of?'

'I don't know. I don't have any details yet. Just this very sad news that he's died. The race office thought you should be told as soon as possible. I'm sure they'll send more information when they have it.'

He drew her towards him, his arms enfolding her in a brotherly hug. 'If you want to howl, don't mind me. I know how it feels to have something like this knock you sideways. Forget about stiff upper lips...just do what comes naturally...cry.'

But at first Maddie didn't want to cry. She buried her face in his shoulder, but she didn't weep. The emotions churning inside her were closer to rage than sorrow. It was not grief she was feeling but a furious sense of betrayal.

By dying before she got back, Pierre had denied her the chance to win his respect. By not telling her he was ill, he had avoided a situation that, in most relationships, brought people closer together. He had not kept it from her in a spirit of noble self-sacrifice, of that she felt sure. That was not, and had never been, his nature. He hadn't told her because he had never wanted to be close to her.

The realisation that she had spent her whole life striving to win the respect and affection of a man who begrudged her the first and was incapable of feeling the second was a revelation so painful that a muffled wail of misery burst from her.

'Poor Maddie...poor baby...' Scott was patting and stroking her as if he were comforting a child.

It was the first time in her life that anyone had soothed and petted her in this fashion. It broke down emotional defences built up since the long ago day when, as a little girl, after falling and hurting herself she had run, sobbing, into the house, to be told by Pierre not to be a cry-baby. He had dealt with her badly grazed arm, but he hadn't dried her tears or lifted her onto his lap for a soothing cuddle.

Over the years she had learnt not to mind his coldness, or brainwashed herself into believing that she didn't. Until now, when the demonstrative sympathy of someone who was almost a stranger made her achingly aware of how much she had missed.

Suddenly the dam burst. All the tears that, growing up in a normal environment, she would have shed whenever things went badly for her, forced their way through the wall of unnatural self-control she had had to erect.

Scott had told her to howl, and howl she did, her tears soaking his T-shirt, her whole body shuddering with the overwhelming force of her feelings.

When the flood had finally spent itself, leaving her too drained to feel embarrassment, Scott suggested she wash her face while he made her a mug of tea.

Knowing she must look a mess, but too exhausted to care, Maddie drank the hot tea in small sips while he checked for more messages from the race office. But for the time being there was no further information to explain why Pierre Sardrette who, as far as she knew, had never been near their neighbourhood medical practice, had ended his life in the island's Princess Elizabeth Hospital.

'I take it your grandmother's not alive?' said Scott.

She shook her head. 'I never knew her. She died before I was born.'

'And your parents?'

'My father was killed in an accident when I was three, so I don't remember him either. My mother came from the mainland. She wasn't happy on the island. She went back to where she came from. I'm not even sure where that was. My grandfather never talked about her. I only know a few things I was told by the person who kept house for him when I was at school. She told me he blamed my mother for his only son's death. It couldn't have been her fault. It was a motorbike crash. But without a son to inherit the business, Pierre felt his life's work was wasted.'

'He had you to carry on from where he left off,' said Scott.

'Being a girl, I didn't count. Pierre thought women should stick to housekeeping and having babies. He wasn't in favour of equal opportunities.'

'Is that why you're here?' he asked. 'To prove to him that anything men can do women can do as well if not better?'

'You could put it like that.' After a pause, she added, 'But mostly I think I wanted to prove to myself that his opinions – his prejudices – were wrong. At the beginning I wasn't sure I could cope. I wasn't nearly as confident as I pretended to be.'

'Every sane person has doubts,' he said. 'Oceans and mountains are unpredictable forces of nature. Things can go wrong that no human being, however tough, can survive. It's always a risk...a gamble. But if you can pull it off, it makes you feel more alive than you ever felt before. It gives you a better perspective on life. Even if he couldn't bring himself to tell you, Maddie, I'm sure your grandfather must have been proud of you. It's just a shame he's missed the chance to make amends for being less than supportive in the past.'

Maddie was silent. She knew he was trying to comfort her, but she also knew what he said wasn't true. If Pierre *had* cared about her, he wouldn't have been able to see her off on such a perilous enterprise without some show of feeling. No one with a warm heart could have done that.

But he was...or had been a man without normal feelings. The loss of an only son was a terrible blow to any parent, but surely a warm-hearted man would have found some solace in raising his orphaned grandchild? For an orphan was what, effectively, she had been.

'I don't know,' she said, in a low voice. 'Anyway it's over now. I don't have to try any more. I only have to please myself.' Then her lips began to tremble uncontrollably and she sank her chin on her chest, starting to cry again.

After she had gone to sleep, worn out by emotional stress, Scott spent some time studying her unconscious face while remaining, as always, alert to any change in the boat's progress. But that had long since become second nature to him; just as good drivers could think about other matters while at the wheel of a car but still keep part of their minds on the road and any signs of hazards ahead.

When her eyes were closed and her mouth relaxed, Maddie looked different from when she was awake and on her guard. Asleep, there was something vulnerable about her. The causes of that usually concealed vulnerability were becoming clearer. Bereft of parents, and left in the care of a man who sounded as cranky and cussed as they came, she had obviously had a bad start in life, poor kid. Which made her achievement all the more remarkable.

Perhaps she was dreaming for suddenly she made a sound like the plaintive mew of a kitten either shut out or shut in.

Scott rose from his seat and went down on his haunches beside the bunk. Her lashes were still wet and sticking together instead of lying on her cheeks like miniature fans. Very lightly, he stroked her cheek with the back of his forefinger, hoping the touch might be enough to stop her dreaming without disturbing her.

She shifted slightly and gave a deep sigh, drawing his attention to her lips. Because, most of the time, her eyes and the obstinate jut of her chin were her dominant features, he hadn't noticed before that her lips, when not sternly compressed, were unexpectedly voluptuous. They reminded him of the luscious lips he had seen in cosmetics ads in his sisters' magazines; except that those lips, while alluring in shape, were spoiled, from a male point of view, by being too brightly coloured and also covered with shiny stuff. Why women allowed themselves to be brainwashed into thinking all that goo made them more kissable was one of the many incomprehensible things about their sex as a whole.

The most kissable kind of mouth, as far as a man was concerned, was the one he was looking at now; as natural and inviting to the touch as the petals on the old-fashioned roses that filled the rooms of his father's houses in summer.

Maddie had a beautiful skin. Despite a restricted diet for months past, her complexion was smooth and unblemished. He found himself wondering, if he put his nose close to the soft skin under her jawline, what her natural scent would be like. He had grown up among women who used expensive French scents and left drifts of delicious perfume lingering in the air behind them.

Later, experience had taught him that the most erotic scent in the world came, not from costly crystal bottles from the great *parfum* houses, but from clean, warm, feminine skin. It varied from woman to woman. Some had a merely pleasant natural fragrance and others, like certain flowers, exuded a heady aroma that was as sensual and provocative as the scent of the white *Lilium regale* which grew in pots on the loggias of the house in Italy which his father had bought for his mother.

He had also learnt that, when women were excited, their natural scents intensified and became even more erotic. He wondered if Maddie knew that. He had the feeling that, although she knew a lot about boats and the sea, she knew almost nothing about people, or about sex.

In his world, girls of her age had usually had several relationships and he couldn't believe that prevailing standards were all that different on the island she came from.

But the way Maddie had looked the first time they met would have put most guys off. Heavy women could be as attractive as slim ones – in his view some superfluous flesh was a better option than being supermodel-skinny – but not if they had a prickly touch-me-not manner.

It was difficult now to remember exactly how she had been at the eve-of-race party in Charleston. Her new look: slimmed down, with swathes of silky hair in place of the punk rock crop, had superimposed itself on the unattractive image he had had in his mind for the first part of the voyage. The intervening months had transformed her into someone any guy would fancy, particularly someone forced by circumstance into the kind of intimacy they were sharing at present.

Strongly tempted to bend closer and find out what those tender rose-coloured lips felt like under his own, Scott forced himself to resist. This was neither the time nor the place to start something with her. Maybe when they reached Punta. But not now, not yet. Apart from other considerations, there was nowhere to make love in comfort and, even more off-putting, at any second the boat could demand her instant attention. Could there be any conditions less conducive to great sex than the incessant noise of the sea slamming into the hull and the cramped confines of a boat in the middle of the ocean?

And apart from all those factors, Maddie was in the throes of a personal trauma and didn't need any additional complications.

Last but by no means least, he had never been careless in his relationships with women and didn't intend to relax those principles now. Taking chances was a fool's game. Both sexes did it, and often they got away with it. But chancing his luck was not his style, either when racing or in amorous pursuits.

Flexing his thigh muscles he rose and moved away to check whether any more information had come through.

Maddie was woken by the appetising smell of an onion frying.

'How long have I been asleep?' she asked, pushing herself up on her elbows.

'About four hours...do you good,' Scott told her. 'Everything's running smoothly. Like some coffee?'

'Yes, please.'

When she started to leave the bunk, he said, 'Stay where you are, babe. Relax. I'll bring it to you.'

The casual endearment gave her an odd little jolt somewhere inside. Feeling it was time to pull herself together, she got up and stretched. Then memory clicked in and the reason for her long nap came back to her.

'Has there been any more news from the race office?'

'Yes, several things have come through...including a message from Tom,' said Scott.

'From Tom?' Her forehead puckered. She was about to ask, 'Who's Tom?' when she remembered who he was and telling Scott about him. But as she had not expected to have anything more to do with Tom, certainly not in these circumstances, it had taken a moment or two for her to make the connection.

'I hope you don't mind, I've read the messages,' said Scott.

'Of course not.'

The race office staff had gone to some trouble to amplify the bare fact of her grandfather's death. Apparently they had been given the news by the police and had then themselves got in touch with the local press, the boatyard and the hospital.

When she had read the information they had compiled, Maddie turned to Tom's message. It seemed that, since she knew him, he had become a computer enthusiast and was following the race reports online.

His e-mail to her continued, 'It was on the radio this morning that Mr Sardrette had died in hospital and that you had been notified. I'm glad you've got the guy you rescued with you. To hear the news on your own would have been a lot worse. I just wanted to let you know I'm proud to know you. I'd be dead scared to do what you've done. So would all the guys I work with. We're all keeping our fingers crossed that you don't have any more trouble. I bet there'll be a huge crowd to welcome you back to the island. Take care. Tom.'

'Sounds as if Tom will be at the front of the crowd on the quayside,' said Scott, when she had finished reading and was ready to take the mug of coffee he had made for her.

Up to this point it hadn't crossed Maddie's mind that, although she had never stood a serious chance of winning the race, the mere fact of completing the circumnavigation might be a cause for celebration on the island. The idea of sailing into St Peter Port to be met by a large crowd and perhaps having to go through a lengthy official reception was far more daunting to her than anything the voyage had produced. By nature quiet and retiring, she shrank from the thought of being in the limelight.

'Is there always a crowd when people get back from a race...even if they were only also-rans?' she asked anxiously.

'You won't be an also-ran. You'll be the heroine of the hour for saving my life,' said Scott. 'But yes, all the competitors get a warm welcome in their home ports, and in your case it's a special achievement because you're so young, and a woman.'

'But I don't want a lot of hoo-ha. I hate being on show,' she said, remembering an occasion at school when she had to stand up in class and read a poem.

'I think you'll find that you've changed and can take most things in your stride,' said Scott. 'It's no big deal answering questions and shaking hands.'

Not for you perhaps. It would be for me, thought Maddie. But she didn't argue the point with him. Despite her long sleep, she still felt curiously drained.

A few days later, while she was in the cockpit, after putting a reef in the mainsail, Maddie found tears pouring down her cheeks. She supposed it was delayed reaction to the strain of the rescue and the news from Guernsey. Before she could recover herself and remove the tell-tale traces from her face, she was joined by Scott.

He took one look and, without saying anything, put his arms round her, as he had before. But, this time, instead of hiding her face against him, she said, 'Please...pay no attention. I'm OK...just a bit tired.'

'Then why not let me take over for a few hours...catch up some proper sleep.'

'You know I can't do that. Please...let me go.' Her hands flat against his chest, she tried to push herself free.

For a second his hold on her tightened, perhaps in a brief spurt of annoyance at having his advice rejected. Then something else sparked between them and, to her astonishment, Scott bent his head and kissed her.

She had read about kisses and imagined them, but the touch of his lips was different from anything she had daydreamed. It was the most extraordinary sensation she had ever experienced: sending ripples of pleasure down nerves she hadn't known were there.

Instinctively, she relaxed, her wish to disengage herself swept aside by a new imperative. All that mattered was this moment...these delicious feelings.

It was an impulsive action that Scott brought to an end before it could get out of hand. He kept hold of her arms until she opened her eyes and recovered her balance, then he let her go.

'I'll get you some tea,' he said, disappearing.

Powerfully aroused after a long period of enforced celibacy, he was beginning to find the situation intolerable. He had not meant to kiss her. It had been a natural consequence of his wish to comfort her in a situation he had been through himself, a long time ago.

But the feel of her in his arms had stirred other emotions, and the softness of her mouth had sent a sudden hot surge of desire coursing through him.

To be forced to batten down all his masculine attitudes and obey her order to stay below, leaving her to handle whatever was happening on deck, went against all his instincts. He wasn't comfortable being a passenger but would have found it less irksome had the skipper of *Sea Spray* been a guy.

To stand idly by while a girl made the decisions was even harder. It wasn't that he doubted her competence. He owed his life to her seamanship skills. But right now she had other things on her mind. How could she concentrate on doing the right thing while still dazed by the shock of her grandfather's unexpected death?

Or, if she could, what kind of woman was she?

On deck, Maddie was wishing she *could* let Scott take charge. Already drained of energy, she now had something else to contend with.

It was months since she had seen her grandfather and the boatyard. The island and everyone she knew there seemed infinitely remote from where she was now, alone in the middle of the ocean with a man who had stirred up feelings she didn't know how to deal with.

For years she had been wondering when, if ever, someone would kiss her. But because of the way she had been before setting out on this voyage, men hadn't found her attractive. They hadn't even noticed her, let alone attempted to make contact. And she hadn't tried to change that situation. There had never been anyone who had made her want to break out. The only person she had been desperate to please had been her grandfather and he had preferred her the way she was when she left the island. He wouldn't have liked the way she was now with her body slimmed down and her hair no longer cropped short.

Why had Scott kissed her? If only she had the courage to ask him.

Women in sailing: sea tales
www.schoonerman.com/book/womsail.htm
and
www.sailboattips.co.uk

chapter seven

In the weeks that followed, Maddie could almost believe that brief kiss had been a figment of her imagination. Nothing in Scott's manner towards her went beyond the comradeship of sailors sharing a difficult passage.

All she knew about their next landfall, Uruguay, was that it was a small country tucked between Brazil and Argentina on the eastern side of South America.

Scott had been to Punta del Este before. 'For rich Argentineans, Punta is the Cannes of the Uruguayan Rivera,' he told her. 'The season starts just after Christmas and ends early in March. For the rest of the year the place is virtually deserted. My cousins have a beach house at La Barra, a village up the coast from Punta. If the media get out of hand, we can take refuge there. You do realise it's going to be like a sharks' feeding frenzy from the moment we hit Punta?'

She gave him an anxious glance. 'What do you mean...a feeding frenzy?'

His mouth turned down at the corners in a cynical grimace. 'The media aren't renowned for their nice manners when they're competing for a story. When Pete Goss rescued Raphael Dinelli in the 96-97 Vendée Globe race and they headed for Tasmania, Dinelli's girlfriend – now his wife – was waiting for him at Hobart. It's not hard to imagine what she had been through, waiting for news that Dinelli was safe. But she wasn't allowed to be on the dock to welcome him because there was an "exclusive" on the photos of their reunion.'

Maddie looked shocked. She remembered the race he was talking about. A non-stop circumnavigation; it was considered by many sailors to be the toughest of all. For his bravery in rescuing the Frenchman, Goss, an Englishman, had been presented with the *Légion d'honneur* by the President of France.

'That's horrible,' she said. 'I wouldn't have stood for it. I'd have told them to go to hell.'

Scott gave her thoughtful look. 'Maybe...or maybe not if the money they offered would help to settle some big debts. A lot of the people in this game have serious financial problems. If you don't, count yourself lucky.'

She remembered things she had read suggesting he came from a wealthy background. 'You don't have money worries, do you?'

'Nope...but I have buddies who do. I can empathise with people who sell their souls to the media, or to rich sponsors. Race sailing is an expensive sport, and getting more so every year.'

He reached out and tucked a stray lock of hair behind her ear, unaware that the gesture had almost as disturbing an effect as his kiss. Well, no, that was an exaggeration, she conceded inwardly. But the fleeting brush of his fingertips revealed something she hadn't known: that the skin behind her ears was acutely sensitive.

'Don't worry, Maddie. I'll steer you through the mayhem. I've been through it before. I won't let them tear you to pieces,' he assured her.

'Thank you.' She wondered how she would have coped with the ordeal ahead without his protective presence.

At sea they were equals. On land she had none of his sophisticated knowledge of the world and its ruthless ways.

The first intimation of the nature of the reception awaiting them was the distant drone of an aircraft that before long was recognisable as the sound of a helicopter.

They were both on deck when they saw it coming their

way. 'The first wave of photographers. I'll go below,' said Scott. Seeing her look of dismay, he added, 'All you have to do is smile and wave.'

'Why can't you smile and wave with me?'

'I'll join you later.' With his hand clenched, his touched the impact surface of his fist lightly against her chin. 'You're the heroine of the hour...the one they want to see.'

Minutes later the helicopter was circling *Sea Spray* at a height which made Maddie want to stuff her fingers in her ears to muffle the din made by the rotors. The sea could be noisy, but this was an alien clangour which she wanted to blot out. In the open doorway at the side of the chopper several men with cameras were jockeying for position and looked in danger of plummeting into the water.

Remembering Scott's instruction, Maddie pinned on a Cheshire Cat grin and waved first one arm, then the other. Today the weather was moderate. They were cruising at a steady 12 knots under mainsail and staysail. Presently the chopper took up a position some way astern of *Sea Spray*. Then, in the distance ahead, Maddie saw signs that a flotilla of vessels was coming to meet her. Scott had warned her this would happen, but she had hoped he was exaggerating public interest in their arrival.

'Scott...Scott...' she shouted, feeling an urgent need for moral support in a situation which was the last thing she wanted.

He reappeared, bringing a mug of coffee or tea for her before returning to fetch one for himself. 'This is where a shot of Dutch courage would come in handy,' he said. 'Don't look so apprehensive. Nobody's going to eat you.'

'You're used to this sort of thing. I'm not. I don't want any part of it,' she told him, scowling.

'You don't have any say in the matter,' was Scott's dry comment. 'They want you, and they'll swarm round you until the next big story breaks. All you can do is smile and cooperate.'

He put an arm round her shoulders and gave her a brief hug. 'It's only for a few days and then you'll be back at sea...on your own...with no hassle from the press, or me, and the two most taxing legs behind you.'

'You haven't been any hassle,' said Maddie. 'All things considered – ' She left the rest unspoken.

Scott laughed, giving her a glimpse of the excellent teeth which for a reason she could not analyse, always gave her a curious jolt in the pit of her stomach. 'Not as much as you expected from your preconceptions about me...is that what you mean?' he asked. 'What are you going to say if a reporter asks you what you thought of that radio interview in Auckland?'

'What ought I to say?'

'If you like, you can lob the ball into my court by suggesting they ask me if I still hold those views.'

'And do you?'

'Are you crazy? If women had been excluded from this race, I'd be a waterlogged corpse.'

His casual reference to the grim fate he had so narrowly missed sent a thrust of horror through Maddie. She found it unbearable to think of what would have happened to him if she hadn't found him. It deepened her understanding of what her grandfather must have suffered over the death of her father.

'Don't!' she said, with a shiver.

But Scott had already switched his attention to the fleet of craft now converging on them.

Maddie would have much preferred to complete the leg in the same way she had finished the previous two, with no one paying any attention to her. She was appalled when she realised that the Punta del Estate yacht club marina had been invaded by trucks and trailers bearing satellite dishes to send live TV feeds to news centres around the world.

A press conference attended by many important dignitaries had been set up, with batteries of dazzling lights and microphones and all the paraphernalia of a major event. Without Scott's support, she felt sure she would have panicked and made a fool of herself. This, from her point of view, was a much worse ordeal than climbing the mast. Much as she disliked that, she would rather do it ten times over than go through this kind of ordeal.

With him there to parry some of the questions for her, and to jump in and fill the gap should she find herself completely tongue-tied, she acquitted herself less badly than she had feared. At least the reporters were not out to savage her. They were on her side.

When Scott proposed a standing ovation for "the gutsiest girl I've ever met", many of the reporters joined in the hearty applause.

But although Maddie did her best to receive it gracefully, she was happier when the spotlight was focused on him as he dealt with questions about what had happened and how he had felt during the hours before he was rescued.

Watching him as he answered, Maddie was again made aware of her shortcomings in terms of confidence and charm. She envied him his charisma and wit, but recognised that they were inborn qualities to which she could not aspire. Nor did she really need them, for today was a one-off unlikely ever to be repeated.

'What are you going to do now, Scott?' somebody asked.

'As soon as possible, I'm going to fly to the UK where one of my sisters and her English husband are celebrating the birth of their third baby. He'll be my seventh godchild, and he's going to be christened with water from the Southern Ocean. After that…I don't know.'

If the media and the local dignitaries had had their way, the press conference would have been followed by a succession of individual interviews and then an official dinner party. To Maddie's relief, Scott announced firmly that she needed to rest but would be available tomorrow. He also suggested a postponement of the dinner party.

'We'll have a quiet dinner *à deux*, if that's OK with you?' he said, in the car taking them to a hotel where accommodation had been arranged for them.

'It's fine by me. Thank you for coping with everything. Without you, I'd have been a lamb to the slaughter.'

'You were fine. When you see a video re-run, you'll be surprised by how well you did for a first-timer. The Slocum has changed you, Maddie. You're not the same person you were in Charleston last fall. A tough race changes everyone who takes part in it. It puts the world and everything in it in a new perspective. You must have read what Robin Knox-Johnston said when someone asked him how his first circumnavigation had affected him.'

'Remind me.'

'He told the interviewer "You wouldn't have liked me before I went – I was a bloody aggressive young man and not very nice. I came back from my trip much more mellow and at ease with myself."'

'Did your first big race change you?' she asked. It was impossible to imagine him as being immature and lacking confidence, even as a teenager. He struck her as someone born with a high degree of self-possession.

'I'm sure it did, but it's a long time ago. A lot of ocean has passed under my keel since then.'

They were side by side in the back of the chauffeur-driven limousine provided for them and he was looking ahead as he spoke. But, even though she was seeing his face in profile, it seemed to her that she caught a fleeting glimpse of some kind of concern there. Perhaps his remark had reminded him that his last keel was now a piece of irretrievable wreckage.

Maddie wanted to put out her hand and place it over his. But she wasn't sure the gesture was appropriate so she didn't make it.

After living aboard *Sea Spray* for more than six months, she found the hotel room provided for her incredibly luxurious. Scott came in to have a look at it and it was he who noticed the bottle of champagne in an ice bucket.

'Shall I open it for you?'

'I can't possibly drink a whole bottle by myself.'

'I'll help you. There are two glasses. Have a glass now and another in your bath. Then lie down and have a long nap till I give you a wake-up call in time to get ready for dinner. How does that sound?'

'Great,' said Maddie, watching him expertly remove the little cage of gold wire enclosing the cork.

'Champagne corks can be dangerous,' said Scott. 'If they're not handled carefully, they can fly and do a lot of damage. The trick is to hold the cork still and turn the bottle so that the cork comes out gently and none of the wine is wasted. All that spraying that goes on after football games and other sports events is vandalism. Whoever started that fashion was an idiot.'

A small wisp of white vapour escaped from the neck of the bottle as the cork came away from the glass. He filled the glasses with the pale golden wine.

'Have you really never had a drink before?'

'I sometimes had a glass of sherry with Miss Lake, and whisky and lemon when I've had a cold.'

He handed one glass to her and picked up the other. 'To your health and happiness, Maddie Sardrette. Wherever we sail in the future, however long we live, I think we'll both always remember this passage we've just completed.'

Maddie smiled. 'All the best, Scott.' It was what she had heard the men at the boatyard say to each other when they were drinking beer to celebrate a launch. As a toast, it sounded rather mundane compared with his, but it was the best she could do.

Her first cautious mouthful of champagne made her wonder why it was considered *the* wine for special occasions. But the second mouthful tasted better and by the time she had drained the glass she was beginning to enjoy it.

'What size shoes do you take?' asked Scott.

'Six. Why?'

'Tomorrow it might be a good idea to buy a few shore-going clothes to fit your new shape.'

Maddie felt herself blushing. She wished that the day he came aboard *Sea Spray* had been their first meeting, and that he had never seen her with her hair cropped and a figure as shapeless as a seal's.

'Make sure you turn the taps off before you get in the bath. Otherwise you might fall asleep with them running. Even though you're a world class celebrity, I don't think the management would be pleased if there was an overflow.' Scott tipped the remainder of his champagne down his throat, then replaced his glass on the tray and refilled Maddie's.

'Catch you later.' With a casual pat on her shoulder, he departed to check out his own room.

It was a buzzer rather than the telephone ringing that woke Maggie some hours later. At first she couldn't think where the sound was coming from, but then realised someone was at her door.

Jumping out of bed, she grabbed the white terry robe she had found in the bathroom and left on the end of the bed when she turned back the quilted silk cover and slid between the expensive white sheets. Hurriedly shrugging on the robe and fastening the sash, she padded to the door.

'Hi. Did I wake you?' Scott walked in with an armful of parcels and a shiny carrier bag in his other hand.

In Guernsey, Maddie had sometimes seen well-dressed women emerging from the island's best clothes shops with similar carriers. Her own clothes had always come from a ships' chandler on St Peter Port's North Quay, and an old-fashioned family-owned outfitter whose serviceable and inexpensive wares had been on her grandfather's approved list.

'I've been out like a light. What time is it?' She had left her watch in the bathroom.

'Time to start thinking about dinner. What would you like to eat? Uruguay has three million people and the human inhabitants are outnumbered three to one by cattle, so steak is the national dish. But I'm sure they can rustle up whatever you fancy.'

'A salad and some fresh fruit is what I've been dreaming of,' she told him.

He dumped all the stuff he was carrying on the bed. 'I'm going to take a shower. I think everything should fit you. If not, it can be changed.' He ran a hand over his jaw. 'Need to shave again. Be back in half an hour.'

Still slightly groggy from her deep sleep, Maddie did not call him back. She stood with her hands in the pockets of the robe, looking at the packages and wondering what was in them. Before finding out, she went back to the bathroom to splash her face with cold water, dry it, and strap on her watch.

Ten minutes later, with Scott's shopping laid out on the bed, she wondered how she was going to pay him. There must be several hundred pounds' worth of clothing and she didn't have that sort of money to spare.

As well as some casual but stylish separates for day wear, he had bought her a dress; a deep red dress with no sleeves and a short swirly skirt. He had also bought underwear, sandals with heels, and a lipstick that was not as vivid a colour as the dress but toned with it.

When Scott came back, Maddie was wearing the clothes she had arrived in and the things he had bought were as he had left them. Luckily she had opened the parcels carefully and been able to re-pack them.

'What's the problem? Don't tell me the dress doesn't fit you?'

'Scott, there's no way I can pay for those things myself.'

'You don't have to. They're a gift.'

'I can't possibly accept such a lavish present.'

'Maddie, you saved my life. To refuse to allow me to provide some things you need in these unforeseen circumstances makes no sense.'

'Not to you perhaps, but I see it differently. I –'

But he didn't allow her to finish. 'OK, if you've made up your mind and won't be budged, the solution is simple. Pay me back from the fees you get for the interviews you give tomorrow.'

Her eyebrows rose in surprise. 'They'll pay me for interviews?'

'Sure. Why not? A news story is one thing. An exclusive is something else. I think you're going to need a PR person to protect you from being exploited. Let's discuss it over dinner. Neither of us has eaten since breakfast. I'm beginning to work up an appetite.' He checked his watch. 'I'll be back in fifteen minutes.'

Peter Goss
www.bbc.co.uk/devon/speakout/goss_chat.shtml
and
www.observer.co.uk/Print/0,3858,4113552,00.html

Legion of Honour
www.france-in-india.org/about/decorti.html

chapter eight

The next time Maddie opened the door to him, she was wearing the new underwear, the red dress, the sandals and the lipstick. Among the toiletries provided by the hotel, she had found a small tube of styling mousse, and had used it to restrain her hair into something approximating the styles of the women she had seen since coming ashore.

Looking at herself in the mirror a few moments earlier, she had seen the reflection of someone she could scarcely recognise as herself; a transformation of the Maddie Sardrette who had set out from Guernsey to Charleston what seemed like a lifetime ago.

They way she looked was such a boost to her confidence that when she opened the door, she flung out her other arm and sank into a theatrical curtsy, something the pre-race Maddie could never have done, except in private.

Scott smiled. 'I thought red would suit you. One of my sisters is fair and she wears it a lot. If you're ready, let's go. My room adapts to a suite and we're going to eat in the sitting room. If we dine downstairs, we may get pounced on by prowling media people. Don't forget your room key.'

Maddie fetched it from the night table, a little disappointed that he hadn't shown more reaction to her changed appearance. As she stepped into the corridor and he closed the door, she remembered his reputation as a womaniser; something she had tended to forget in their last weeks at sea. Now all her earlier reservations about him came back. How many other women had he shopped for? Most men wouldn't have a clue what size someone was just by looking at her. The bras and briefs he had selected fitted her perfectly, suggesting an intimate acquaintance with female anatomy.

The sitting room, connected to his bedroom by a door on one side with another door leading to a second bedroom opposite. It was comfortably furnished with two three-seater sofas at right angles to each other, both giving a view of a large television.

French windows led onto a balcony. Just inside them, a table for two had been prepared. Maddie had never eaten at a table with a starched damask cloth, sparkling crystal, gleaming cutlery and flowers in a silver vase.

'It's a bit different from last night's supper, isn't it?' she said, smiling.

'I hope you don't mind, I've chosen what we're going to eat,' Scott said. 'I thought you might find a long menu confusing until you've had time to adjust to living ashore.'

'Especially if it's in Spanish. Do you speak Spanish?'

'No, but I speak Italian. A lot of the words are similar.'

The door buzzer was followed by the sound of a pass-key. A moment later a waiter wheeled in a trolley and greeted them with what Maddie presumed was a polite good evening.

'Come and sit down.' Scott drew out one of the chairs for her and, when she was in position, pushed it closer to the table.

Clearly he had grown up paying these attentions to women. In her world men sat down first and expected women to attend to their needs before seating themselves. But it didn't follow that men with fancy manners were necessarily better, as people, than men who didn't have any. Whether Scott's heart was in the right place, or even if he had a heart, was something she didn't yet know and perhaps might never find out. Very soon he was leaving Punta and, apart from paying him back for the things he had bought her, that might be the end of their relationship.

The thought of never seeing him again was like a sharp

thrust of pain. She flinched and drew in her breath. Luckily Scott didn't notice; he was speaking to the waiter. In the next few minutes she had time to recover herself while their first course was being served.

But, all through the meal, while they ate and chatted, part of her mind was grappling with the startling realisation that perhaps she was falling in love with him and, for the rest of her life, would remember their time together as the high point of her existence.

That was how it had been for Miss Lake, except that her love, though never fulfilled, had at least been declared and shared. Being a realist, Maddie knew that giving her heart to Scott could never be a reciprocal condition.

She had never had any hope of winning the Slocum. To take part and survive had been the extent of her expectations. While she felt sure that Scott would never forget her, she also knew that the odds against him falling in love with her were a million to one...

When not at sea, they were beings from different planets. This room and the meal they were eating were what he was used to. To her they had an unreal feeling... like a dream from which she would soon wake up.

'You're not drinking your wine. Don't you like it?' he asked, making her aware she had not been paying proper attention to his advice about letting a public relations specialist help to manage the demands that would be made on her while she was hot news.

'Oh...yes. It's very nice,' said Maddie.

'You're still tired. Better not have coffee. It might keep you awake. Tomorrow we'll move out to my cousins' beach house. It'll be more relaxing.'

Maddie would have liked to finish the evening sitting on one of the sofas with him, watching some TV or just chatting. But, when they rose from the table, Scott said, if she would excuse him, he had some long-distance calls to make.

He walked her to the door and then, leaving it open, escorted her back to her room.

'Goodnight, Maddie. If you find you can't sleep, check the movie-guide on top of the TV. Most hotels provide some entertainment for foreign guests. There's sure to be something you can watch. See you in the morning.'

After Maddie had closed her door, Scott returned to his room aware that she was disappointed at being packed off to bed earlier than she had expected.

It was going to take both of them some time to revert to a conventional sleep pattern, and in her case there wasn't much point in trying when she would soon be at sea again. But although he would have liked to watch a movie with her, or to continue talking while sharing another bottle of wine, he knew that both those options would have been unwise.

In fact, after seeing how voluptuously beautiful she looked in the red dress, he was having second thoughts about the wisdom of spending time with her in the seclusion of his cousins' beach house.

By anyone's standards, Maddie had become a lovely girl and, for him, her allure was intensified by the fact that in every other way she was so much on his wavelength. He had known other women who shared his passion for sailing and their times together were still clear in his memory, though now the weeks in the Southern Ocean with Maddie were superimposed on the earlier memories.

From the back of his mind came the thought that if she had been five years older...if there had been no question mark hanging over his future...

He put the idea aside before it was fully formed.

The house which they moved to next morning was on a long stretch of beach to the north of a small village called La Barra. Sheltered from winter gales by a high wooden palisade, it was both very simple and very luxurious. The furnishings had been collected all over the world. It was obvious the owners were exceedingly rich but used their wealth in a discriminating way, not to show off but to create a haven of tranquillity.

On their second evening there, they went to a *parillada*, a Uruguayan form of barbecue party, at another beach house.

One of the people they met was Ana, a beautiful women in her thirties.

Up to that point, Maddie had been feeling quite pleased with her appearance. But while Scott and Ana were chatting, she realised that her new dress made her look better but not good enough to compete with the other women here, and particularly not with Ana. The older woman's immaculate grooming made Maddie acutely self-conscious about her hair, the state of her finger and toe-nails and her lack of any make-up other than lipstick.

'How incredibly brave of you to sail round the world with all those men,' said Ana, looking at Maddie with undisguised curiosity. 'When I heard about Scott's accident on the radio, and that he had been rescued by an Englishwoman, I imagined someone middle-aged and mannish. Come and meet Antonio and Luis. They're your age and a lot of fun.'

She swept Maddie off to be introduced to two good-looking young men before returning to Scott's side.

Neither of them seemed to notice anything sub-standard about Maddie's grooming. They had seen her on TV, read about her in the papers and were flatteringly delighted to meet her in person, sending her self-confidence up several notches.

'You are not a vegetarian, are you?' asked Antonio.

Maddie shook her head though, truth to tell, she liked fish and seafood better than meat, especially fresh Guernsey crab.

'Many European girls seem to be vegetarians,' said Antonio. 'But here in Uruguay we eat a lot of meat. The *parrillada,* which means grilled or barbecued meat, is our national dish. Come and see what the chefs are doing.'

A hand under her elbow, he steered her to another part of the garden where, in addition to a long buffet table ranged with cold starters and salads, several chefs with starched white toques on their heads were busy cooking hot dishes.

'Try one of these, Madeleine,' said Luis, intercepting a waiter who was carrying a salver with mussels on triangles of toast.

She took one, as did her two escorts, and smiled her thanks at the waiter who responded with an admiring look that sent her confidence up another notch. But perhaps it was the custom of the country for men to be more than usually nice to women, she thought, as she was eating the mint-flavoured mussel.

One of the chefs was preparing the largest piece of flank steak she had ever seen. It must have been a yard long.

'This is called *matambre relleno*,' Luis explained, as the chef spread red peppers and bacon on top of the steak and then swiftly and expertly rolled it up and fastened it with string before putting it on his grill.

When they arrived at the party, Scott had selected a drink for her from a tray being offered. He had told her it was called *clericó*, a mixture of white wine and fruit juice. But, when her glass was empty, Antonio and Luis insisted she try *medio y medio*, a combination of white wine and sparkling wine which, after a couple of mouthfuls, she realised had a lot more kick than her first drink.

From time to time, as they ate and chatted, she looked round to see where Scott was. Ana had not succeeded in monopolising him she noticed, with some relief. He was circulating, but mostly talking to the other male guests; their expressions suggesting that the topics they were discussing were more serious than the light-hearted stuff she was hearing from her two companions.

There were plenty of tables where people could sit to eat the main dishes and, soon after the three of them had sat down, they were joined by another young man, a friend of Antonio's, who introduced himself to Maddie as Juan, with the same sort of look the one the waiter had given her.

Even though she didn't feel the smallest spark of attraction to any of them, it was still a heady experience, having three dark-eyed Uruguayans doing what Miss Lake would have called 'paying court' to her. She hoped that Scott was aware of it, though he was never looking in her direction when she located him among the other party guests.

Dipping her spoon into a lemon sorbet, she suddenly remembered the night before they left America and how, eating alone, she had had a struggle to resist the fattening desserts in the restaurant in Charleston.

At that time it had seemed beyond the bounds of possibility that she would ever be on close terms with Scott. Or that three debonair South Americans would be competing to flirt with her.

She had almost finished her second glass of *medio y medio* and was laughing at Juan's translations of some graffiti he had seen scrawled on a wall in Montevideo, the capital, when she became aware that the other three were looking at someone behind her. Looking upwards at someone tall and starting to rise to their feet as well-brought-up young men do in the presence of a person who commands their respect.

For a moment she thought it might be their host coming by to say something affable to his younger guests.

Then a familiar voice said, 'I'm afraid it's time for *Señorita* Sardrette to say goodnight, gentlemen. She has a heavy day tomorrow, preparing for the next lap of the race, and a full night's sleep is a luxury she will have to forego after she leaves here. Will you excuse us?'

'It has been a pleasure talking to you, *señorita*,' said Antonio. 'We wish you good luck and success in the final stage.' He reached for her hand and touched his mouth to her knuckles.

Luis and Juan followed suit, kissing her hand and expressing their good wishes.

'Thank you for making the party such fun for me,' said Maddie, speaking to all of them. 'I'll remember tonight when I'm alone on the ocean. Goodnight...Antonio... Luis...Juan.'

She turned away, outwardly submitting to Scott's arbitrary decision to leave, inwardly fuming.

'I've already thanked and said goodnight to our hosts,' he told her. 'It isn't necessary for you to speak to them.'

'If you say so,' she answered coldly.

'You seemed to find those guys' company very entertaining. What was the joke you were laughing at?'

She repeated Juan's translation. 'God is not dead but alive and well and working on a less ambitious project.'

'Not as hilarious as your laughter suggested,' he said dryly. 'Maybe the *medio y medio* made it seem funnier.' After a pause, he added, 'Drinking with strangers – when you're not used to alcohol – can lead to problems, Maddie.'

By now they were on the driveway, close to the entrance to the property. There was no one around to see her swing to face him, or to hear her say indignantly. 'They weren't strangers. They were fellow guests...and I'm not drunk.'

'I'm not saying you are...but would you have refused another glass? Do you know what your limit is? I doubt it.'

Maddie said nothing. She couldn't claim that she did know, because she didn't. She only knew that she wasn't tipsy at the moment, although perhaps she might have been had she had the same amount of wine on an empty stomach.

It was only a few minutes' walk back to where they were staying and neither of them spoke again until they were inside the house.

Then, when she would have said a chilly goodnight to him, Scott said, 'I think we need to straighten this out.' Taking her by the wrist, he led her towards the living room.

The annoying thing was that, though part of her wanted to jerk her wrist free from his light clasp and tell him to go to hell, another part liked being his captive and was curious to find out what he intended to say. Her willpower had won the battle with her tastebuds in the restaurant in Charleston. But right now it was the cavewoman not the feminist who was winning the conflict.

Even while they were leaving the party, and the feminist had been resenting his failure to consult her wishes, at a deeper level the cavewoman had been responding to his authoritative decision-making.

'Do you know what your limit is?' she asked, as he let her go and took a bottle of spring water from a refrigerator concealed behind panelling.

'I found that out at college...after some mighty unpleasant hangovers.'

Maddie watched him break the seal on the bottle and unfasten the cap with those long, supple, sun-tanned fingers that she tried not to look at too often because of their disturbing effect on her.

'And you've never had a hangover since?'

'A few minor ones maybe, but I've never been out of control since then.'

'Surely people know when they're starting to lose control, don't they?'

'Some do...a lot don't, or they ignore the signs. That's why it helps to know exactly when to say no to another glass. How many have you had tonight?'

'The one you gave me – half fruit juice – and two more.'

Scott filled two tall glasses and handed one of them to

her. 'Were you hoping that one of those guys would walk you home and kiss you goodnight? Was that why you were angry with me?'

'No...I was angry because you took it for granted that I would obey you,' she said. 'I think you should have asked if I was ready to leave?'

'You could have told me to get lost.'

'How could I do that? I'm here as your guest. I was at the party as your guest.'

'So I took an unfair advantage?'

'You know you did.'

'Guys have a habit of doing that, Maddie,' he said dryly. 'If you'd had too much to drink, and any one of those young men had walked you home, the chances are he'd have kissed you...and perhaps gone further than kissing...further than you wanted to go.'

'I'm not seventeen, you know,' she said frostily, annoyed by his older-brother attitude when she wanted him to see her as a desirable woman.

A gleam of amusement lit his eyes, but he only said, 'Drink up your water and take a refill to your room. Another thing I learnt at college was that lots of water last thing makes you feel better in the morning.'

The food at the *parrillada* had been liberally salted and Maddie was thirsty. She drained her glass and held it out for a refill.

As it seemed he had finished lecturing her, she said goodnight.

To her surprise, Scott walked her to the door, at the far end of the long room, that opened into to the passage leading to her room. He had left his glass on a table and, as they reached the door, he took hold of her left hand.

'Don't think I haven't noticed the reasons why those guys were enjoying your company,' he said, looking down at her with a much warmer expression than he had had before.

As he lifted her hand she thought he was going to kiss the back of it, the way the three Uruguayans had. But it was the inside of her wrist that Scott kissed, pressing his mouth lightly, but for what seemed an endless moment, to the place where her veins were visible and her pulse could be felt.

Did his lips detect its sudden acceleration? Did he know the effect he had on her?

'Goodnight, Maddie.'

He opened the door and a few seconds later, feeling as unsteady on her feet as if she *had* drunk too much, she was alone in the corridor, her wrist still tingling, her heart pounding, her whole body consumed with longing to be in his arms and in his bed.

Why had it taken her so long to recognise that she was in love with him?

The day before Scott was due to fly to Europe, Maddie realised that she couldn't bear to have him to walk out of her life without their relationship coming to its proper conclusion. They had spent many days together. Now she wanted to spend a night with him. The nights on board hadn't counted. This last night on land would be something to remember after they had gone their separate ways.

Every instinct told her that he was a man she could trust to take her virginity in a way she wouldn't regret. She felt sure that Scott was as skilled at making love as he was at seamanship. He would know what to do in bed the same way he knew what to do when the weather turned bad. The fact that he had capsized was no reflection on his prowess as a skipper. It could have happened to any one of them. It had happened to many fine sailors, some of whom hadn't survived to tell the tale.

On his last afternoon, while he was busy with other matters, she found her way to a beauty parlour where, luckily, one of the staff spoke English and understood what Maddie meant when she asked them to glamorise her.

'But not too much,' she stressed. 'I don't want to look like the models in magazines. I only want to look prettier than I do now. How much will it cost?'

Her interpreter conferred with the manageress of the salon. Then she turned back to Maddie. 'You are the girl who rescued the man from the sea, yes?'

'Yes.'

'Then there will be no charge, but we would like some photographs of how you look now and how you look later. OK?'

'I need you to do it today...this afternoon. I can't wait for you to arrange for a photographer to come.'

'That is not necessary. We have a camera here. We often take pictures of hairstyles for special occasions.' The girl waved her hand at a screen covered with photographs of clients, some wearing bridal head-dresses.

'In that case...OK,' Maddie agreed.

Three hours later she telephoned the house to ask Paco, who, with his wife, looked after the beach house, to collect her. There was now a strong breeze blowing off the Atlantic and she didn't want her sleek new hairstyle blown into a tangle. The chauffeur didn't seem to notice any difference in her appearance but, when they got back, his wife did.

'You look beautiful, *señorita*,' she said, after taking in Maddie's hairdo, make-up and manicure. 'For tonight I have made a special dinner. But I hope you won't mind if Paco is not here to serve you. We are going to a family party at our daughter's place. We shall not be back until late.'

There was something conspiratorial in her smile. Maddie had the feeling the family party might be something arranged very recently by Maria, with her daughter's co-operation, because the housekeeper had sensed that it would be propitious for the two foreign guests to dine alone this evening. Or perhaps that was just her imagination and the party had been arranged some time ago; a fortunate chance that, hopefully, would make it easier for Maddie to achieve her objective.

Now all she had to do was to make it clear to Scott that she was his for the taking, and the rest she could leave to him.

In her room she put on the dress he had bought her. This time, set off by good grooming, it looked much better. For a long time she stood in front of the full length mirror, comparing her appearance tonight with the way she had looked at Charleston the night Scott's gaze had swept past her like the beam of a lighthouse sweeping an empty ocean. She would never forget that glance of total indifference. But it no longer smarted the way it had at the time.

After Maria's special dinner, they had coffee in the central courtyard where the still surface of the pool reflected the moonlight with diamond brilliance. The sofa where they sat was in the shadow of the covered walk, its pillars clothed with flowering creepers, which surrounded the courtyard.

'I'd like to have a house like this somewhere, someday,' said Scott. 'Where would you live if you had a free choice, Maddie?'

'I've never thought about it. I don't know as many places as you do. It's beautiful here...but a long way from Europe.'

'Do you feel rooted in Europe? Can't you imagine living anywhere but Guernsey.'

Her answer was swift and instinctive. 'I don't want to spend the rest of my life on the island.' She thought but did not say, I've been too unhappy on Guernsey ever to be properly happy there.

'But you'd want to be close to the sea?'

'Oh yes...always. I don't think I could be comfortable living somewhere a long way inland. You couldn't either...could you?'

'No, Kansas, or Chad, or Alice Springs are not where I'll settle...when I settle,' Scott said firmly. 'They must suit a lot of people, but they wouldn't suit us.'

His use of the word 'us' instead of 'me' caused her to indulge in a momentary fantasy of how it would be if the place where they finally settled was the same place.

There was an interval of silence.

Maddie ended it by saying, 'It's going to seem strange being back on board *Sea Spray* by myself. I've got used to having someone to talk to...and I'm going to miss your cooking.'

'With any luck the last leg will be easy sailing and you'll have time to improve your culinary skills.'

'I'll try.' She paused. 'Scott – ' She broke off to swallow the nervous lump in her throat.

'Mm?' He sounded as if he were listening but with part of his mind on something other than their conversation.

She started again. 'Scott, we probably won't meet again...and you've been very kind and helpful, and ...and I wonder if there's one more thing you would do for me?' The last bit came out in a rush, her tongue almost tripping over itself in her haste to say what she had to say before her courage deserted her.

'Sure...if I can. What's the problem?'

'It's not a problem. It's just that...as this is our last night together –' Her heart was thumping and her throat was threatening to close up before she got to the nub of the matter '– I think it would be nice if we spent it together...properly together...if you see what I mean?'

They weren't the words she had rehearsed. When it came to the point, like an actress struck by stage-fright, she had forgotten her lines and had to blurt out her proposition in the only words that came to mind.

To her relief, he didn't keep her in suspense. 'You mean sleep together...in both senses of the term. Right?'

She repressed a gasp of relief. He didn't sound embarrassed, as if she had put him on the spot and he couldn't believe she would make such as ass of herself. He sounded as calm as if she had said something as ordinary as a remark about the weather.

'Right,' she confirmed.

'It's a very nice idea, Maddie, but I have a better one,' he said, still in the same easy tone. 'I think we should take a rain check until you get back to Charleston. I'll be flying over for the grande finale and you'll have the race behind you and be able to relax. Tomorrow is a big day for you and I don't think a night making love is the best preparation for it. When people make love together for the first time, usually they want to repeat it several times and often they need a day to recover, which you won't have. Am I making sense?'

Was he? That she might be tired in the morning, exhausted even, had not occurred to her. If there were manuals on sex in the public library, she had never had the self-assurance to borrow them. She had learnt the basic facts of life at school, but the rest – the raptures alluded to by poets – she could only guess it.

'I didn't know you would be coming to Charleston.'

'I wouldn't miss it. In the meantime we can keep in touch by e-mail. I won't have my own laptop, but I'll be able to use my brother-in-law's computer and there will be other facilities for sending and receiving messages. I'll be sure to give you my regular e-mail address before we say goodbye tomorrow.'

Somehow, Maddie realised, the subject she had broached was closed, not to be re-opened until they were both in Charleston, and perhaps not even then. Whether, in the nicest possible way, she had been rebuffed, she wasn't certain.

Did he really believe that a night in his arms would leave her drained of energy? Or was that a gentlemanly pretext to avoid inflicting the hurtful truth that he didn't wish to make love to her?

Scott rose from the sofa. 'I'm going to stretch my legs, but I think it's time you turned in. You need to be bright-eyed and bushy-tailed for the send-off tomorrow.'

He stooped to lift the coffee tray from the table at his end of the sofa and then paused at her end while she placed her cup and saucer on it.

'Goodnight, Maddie.'

'Goodnight.'

She stayed where she was until he had had time to put the tray in the kitchen and leave the house by the door leading to the gate in the high wooden palisade. It was only then that the appalling crassness of what she had done really hit home and made her self-respect shrivel. How could she have offered herself to him in so blatant a way? She must have been out of her mind.

It was not as if he were a shy man, the kind who might need encouragement to make a move on a woman. Scott was assurance personified. If he wanted someone, he would tell them or show them, not wait to be propositioned.

Maddie lay down on the sofa and curled herself into a ball of quivering humiliation. She had heard girls at school saying they wanted to die of embarrassment and that was how she felt now.

They had been exaggerating. None of the things they had done had been in the same class as her gaffe. She must have been temporarily insane even to consider such an action.

Eventually, knowing that, if she went to bed, she wouldn't be able to sleep, she dragged herself off the sofa to clear the table and wash the dishes so that Maria and her husband could go straight to bed when they came in.

It took her less than half an hour to leave the kitchen tidy; the twin stainless steel sinks wiped dry and gleaming, the counter tops clear, everything put back in its proper place.

In her bedroom, without switching on the lights, she went to the window. Being higher than the top of the palisade, it had a wide view of the beach and the moonlit ocean.

She stood there, remembering every word she had said to him, sick with chagrin at the memory of making such a muddle of it, blurting that there was one more thing he could do for her.

It would have been better, far better, to have said nothing at all. What she ought to have done, when they said goodnight, was to reach up and kiss his cheek, leaving him to take the initiative...if he had wanted to.

Down by the sea's edge, she saw the tall familiar figure coming back in the direction of the house. But, at the point when she expected him to turn away from the water, he didn't. He went on walking, moving with that long supple stride she would recognise anywhere.

She waited a while but did not see Scott coming back. Eventually she went to the adjoining bathroom and got ready for bed.

It was just as well she had remembered to remove her make-up because, before she fell into a restless sleep, she couldn't help crying for a bit. Maria would not have been pleased to find mascara stains on the pillow-case.

Scott also had a disturbed night, dreaming about the boat he had lost and the hard choice he still had to make.

In the wakeful periods he thought about Maddie who would soon be back at sea and who, if he had wished it, would have been here in bed with him.

It was more than nine months since he had been to bed with a woman, the last time being in New York with someone he had known since they were both in their teens. At that time she had been someone else's girlfriend. Now she was a high flyer in the world of investment banking, a woman determined not to compromise her freedom by entering a long term relationship.

Louise had no time for women who let emotion rule their lives. She enjoyed sex but could take it or leave it. He had happened to be around when she was in the mood for it. They had made love before, a couple of times in their early twenties. On one of those occasions, she had said to him, 'One of my friends is getting married. She's trying to convince me that sex is better when you're emotionally committed. She says it's the difference between wine in a plastic cup and wine in a glass. I'm not convinced. What do you think?'

He remembered his shrug and his answer, 'I wouldn't know.'

But that was a long time ago when he shared Louise's wish to stay out of permanent commitments. Now he was beginning to feel it was time he settled down. But falling in love was something that happened to other people, not to him. He seemed to be immune from it.

Why, when both of them were free agents who could do as they pleased, had he rejected Maddie's offer? The reason he had given had been mainly to avoid wounding her ultra-sensitive pride. But there were other reasons that he needed time to think through...

Punta del Este
www.oceanblue.com/punta.html

chapter nine

It took all Maddie's will-power to join Scott for breakfast next morning. It didn't help that she knew she looked tired and weary, which was par for the course at sea, but more noticeable and more unflattering on land.

Although he behaved as if their relationship was on exactly the same footing as it had been twelve hours earlier, before she had invited him to share her bed or take her to his, it wasn't the same and could never be, any more than her life could revert to the way it had been before she set out from Guernsey.

She was a different person from the girl he had met in Charleston, and now their friendship was different because she had tried, and failed, to put it on a closer, more intimate plane.

'I'll drop you off at the boat and say goodbye there. There's no point in your coming to the airport,' he said, while Paco was stowing their baggage in the car.

Maddie nodded assent. She had already said goodbye to Maria, doing her best to appear cheerful and normal. It was going to be much harder to put on a light-hearted manner when the time came to part from Scott.

It wasn't possible for Paco to drive beyond a certain point. When he would have carried Maddie's belongings to *Sea Spray*'s mooring, Scott took them from him and indicated that the chauffeur should stay with the car.

The race was not resuming until the following morning and the boat had already been re-provisioned, so Maddie had plenty of time to do final checks.

Scott put her gear in the cockpit then stepped back onto the walkway. He put his hands on her shoulders and gave her a long intent look that, after last night, she found difficult to meet. She could feel her cheeks flushing an unbecoming shade of beetroot.

'Take good care of yourself, Maddie.'

'You too.'

She hoped against hope he would kiss her; instead he gave her a hug, but not as prolonged or bear-like as the hug of thanks for his rescue.

'*Arrivederci,*' he said. She knew what it meant – goodbye.

In answer she said, '*Tcheri,*' the Guernsey form of cheerio used by the few who, like her grandfather, still spoke the old Guernsey-French patois and many who, like herself, knew only a handful of words from the island's traditional tongue.

Watching him walk away, she wondered if they would ever recapture the camaraderie built up in the long weeks at sea and ruined by her own stupid folly the night before. Probably he couldn't stand women who took the initiative.

When he was out of sight, she gave a long disconsolate sigh and braced herself for the tasks she had to attend to. At least she would see him in Charleston. That was something to cling to.

On the flight to Europe, Scott wondered again why he had passed up the opportunity to get Maddie out of his system.

It would have been so easy to pick up her invitation to spend the night in her bed, taking and giving pleasure and then calling it a day until, maybe, they ran into each other again before or during some future race.

But somehow, when it came to the point, he hadn't been able to do that. Apart from the fact that he owed her his life, there was something about her that was different from any of the other women with whom he had made love.

In the time they had spent together, he and Maddie had become as intimate as a brother and sister. Despite that, he was aware there was a great deal about her that she wasn't prepared to reveal. Her mysteriousness was intriguing. She was ready to sleep with him, but not to allow him to know her in the fullest sense. She was holding things back and usually that wasn't the way women operated.

As he knew from listening to his sisters, women enjoyed pouring out their secrets in long bouts of detailed soul-searching. They were all amateur analysts, happy to listen to each others' insights for hours on end.

Maddie seemed the exception to the rule. She was as reticent as a man about her personal life. He knew little more about her background than he had at the beginning.

At London airport he would have rented a car and driven himself to his English brother-in-law's place in the county of Dorset, on the south coast. But that had to be postponed until he had given a promised interview to the sailing correspondent of a British national newspaper.

They had dinner together. Advised by his father's PR people, Scott had learned how to handle journalists a long time ago. He was adept at avoiding questions he didn't wish to answer. This time he wanted some information himself.

What he learned from the correspondent whetted his appetite for more. After spending two days in Dorset, admiring his new nephew and enjoying English country life, he drove to nearby Southampton, left the hire car in the airport parking lot, and flew across the English Channel to Guernsey.

It was not a long flight. He had scarcely finished drinking a glass of lager before, from his window seat, he saw the sea washing against the jagged crests of reefs that, in earlier times, had made navigating these waters a dangerous business for sailing vessels. Then two small islands that he knew must be Herm and Jethou appeared and, soon afterwards, Maddie's home island, a patchwork of fields threaded with winding lanes and scattered with private swimming pools and long rectangles that he knew must be the glass-houses the islanders called vineries.

The taxi drive from the airport to the main town, St Peter Port, took about twenty minutes. Scott wouldn't have been surprised if the driver had recognised him, though even on small islands not everyone took an interest in matters to do with the sea.

When the man didn't give him the searching look that would have signalled a bell ringing in his memory, Scott said, 'I suppose there'll be big celebrations here when Madeleine Sardrette gets home?'

'Who?' For a moment, meeting Scott's eyes in the rear-view mirror, the driver looked puzzled. 'Oh...you mean the girl who rescued the American fellow down South America way. For a minute I couldn't think who you were talking about. I'm into football myself, not sailing and suchlike. Yes, there's sure to be something laid on, most likely at Government House, or at the yacht club. They might give her a firework display. That's the usual thing on special occasions. Though it won't be a happy homecoming, with her granddad dying soon after the rescue.'

'Did you know him?' Scott asked.

'Never laid eyes on him. Not the sociable type, so I've heard... Kept himself to himself.'

'I heard he had a boatyard?'

'That's right. Don't know what will happen to it now. He didn't have no sons.'

'His granddaughter has proved herself the equal of any man,' said Scott.

'She may not have a head for business though. One thing's for sure, she's no looker, judging by the photo in the *Press*. A plainer girl I never saw...and built like a disco bouncer.'

'It must have been an old photo. She's not like that now,' said Scott. 'Maybe the local press hasn't bothered to get hold of an up-to-date photograph. In the one I saw she looked very attractive.'

'Is that right?'

Scott had booked a room at an hotel overlooking the harbour. Riffling through the local phone book, he noticed the large number of French-sounding names...Priaulx, Robilliard, Tostevin, Le Page, De La Mare. It didn't take him long to find the addresses of her grandfather's boatyard and his house.

At the reception desk, he studied the map produced by the girl on duty, then set out on foot. When not at sea he liked to take plenty of exercise. By the time he found the granite house where Maddie had grown up, he had decided the best way to go about his enquiries. Frequently interviewed himself, he could masquerade as a journalist without any difficulty.

When the door of a neighbouring house was opened by an elderly woman, he said, 'Good afternoon. I wonder if you can help me. I'm writing a profile of Madeleine Sardrette and looking for people who've known her since she was a child. Are you one of them, Mrs...er?'

'Mrs Vazon,' she told him affably. 'I've known Maddie all her life. You'd better come in...from the *Press,* are you?'

'No, from the mainland. I'm a freelancer, writing for various sailing publications. Have you been following the race?'

'Oh, yes...everyone has, especially since Maddie saved that poor fellow from drowning. There'll be a big celebration when she comes home.' Mrs Vazon led him through the house to a comfortable sitting room. 'I was just going to have a cup of tea. Would you like one?'

'Thank you.'

'I won't be long. Make yourself comfortable.'

When, nearly an hour later, after being pressed to eat

several slices of the buttered fruit loaf his hostess called *gâche*, an island speciality, he returned to the car he knew a great deal more about Maddie than she would ever have revealed to him.

Mrs Vazon's revelations had explained many things that had puzzled him, but he wanted to know more and she had given him several leads.

Back in town, he found an Internet café where he picked up the latest news about the race from the race office website and sent a message to Maddie. Then he explored the town before going back to the hotel for a shower before dinner.

He was in the bar, waiting to be served, when the pretty receptionist he had spoken to earlier appeared.

'Did you find your way all right, Mr Randall?' she asked.

'Yes, thanks. No problem.'

'I've found a spare copy of this, if you'd like to borrow it for tomorrow...unless you're leaving early.' She offered him a paperback collection of island road maps.

'I may stay a second night...if you have room for me?'

'I'm off duty now, but I'll check.'

'Thanks...have you time for a drink?' he added, as a steward approached.

She nodded. 'A vodka and tonic, please.'

Waiting for her to come back, Scott knew that this time last year, had he been in this situation for a different reason, he would have asked her to dine with him, and then escorted her back to wherever she lived and, given encouragement, made love to her.

But something had happened since then, though he wasn't quite sure what it was. He no longer felt comfortable with the casual relationships of his past. He could see that the girl was attractive, yet she failed to attract him. He wanted a roll in the hay, but not with her.

She returned with the information that his room wasn't

booked for tomorrow. Then she introduced herself as Fern, and their drinks came and they started chatting.

'I have this feeling I've seen you before,' she said.

Earlier, Mrs Vazon had told him he reminded her of someone. Both she and Fern had probably seen pictures of him, with longer hair and possibly several days' stubble, on the TV news about the race and the rescue. But neither had connected the unkempt seafarer with him as he looked today, close-shaven and disguised by well-pressed trousers and a smart-casual jacket. Also he had taken the precaution of booking in as S J Randall, the name on his credit card and, while on the island, was using his second name, James.

He said, 'I've never been here before. Do you belong here?'

She did, but when he asked her if she knew Maddie — she looked about the same age — it emerged that, although she couldn't avoid seeing it, Fern had no affinity with the sea. She had heard about Maddie, but wasn't much interested.

For Maddie, the last leg of the race was a period of endless speculation about whether Scott would follow up the rain check when he returned to Charleston, and what she was going to do with her life now that she was a free agent.

She felt no inclination to continue her grandfather's business. It seemed likely now that she would receive lots of sponsorship offers and could become a professional racer. But did she want to?

Pondering this question while making maddeningly slow progress in light winds, she came to the conclusion she had done enough solo sailing to last her a lifetime. With Scott on board life had been a lot more interesting, but now she was on her own again she was impatient for the race to be over.

His messages were something to look forward to, but they were too impersonal to give her any deep satisfaction.

When at last she got back to Charleston, it was a big disappointment to find Scott was not there to meet her. Nor was there any message to account for his absence. But the race organisers had made arrangements for her to stay at an hotel instead of remaining on board *Sea Spray*.

This time she had to deal with the media on her own. She found that, as Scott had forecast, it was easier second time around. Not really an ordeal at all, now she had got the hang of it.

On her second night in Charleston, rather than sit around pondering her future and wondering why Scott hadn't come back as he had promised, she accepted an invitation to have dinner with Bruce, a skipper with whom she had been in radio contact in the last phase of the race..

'But let's go Dutch,' she suggested, to make it clear she thought of him as a colleague rather than a date.

His, 'OK...if you insist,' was reassuring.

Bruce's idea of great food was a large steak accompanied by French fries. But there were some dishes on the menu that were more appealing to Maddie. In the past she had eaten for comfort. Now she had some new worries in place of her previous concerns, but she wasn't going to let them weaken her resolve never to do that again. Even without Scott's presence as an incentive, she was going to stay slim for herself. While Bruce was chomping his way through a massive T-bone, she took her time eating a seafood salad, avoiding the pile of coleslaw with its coating of mayonnaise.

While devouring his steak and large mound of French fries, Bruce didn't talk much. She couldn't help comparing his table manners, unfavourably, with Scott's. Bruce was a nice enough guy, but he didn't match up to Scott in any way. While Bruce concentrated on his food, she found herself making a mental check list of the ways he fell short of the man she was used to eating with.

Bruce's nails were not as clean and well-kept as Scott's. His hands were a clumsier shape, the fingers short and thick, not like Scott's long lean hands. Bruce had a pleasant face, but his features were undistinguished. She did not think he would age well. Scott, even when his thick black hair had turned white, and his face was seamed with the lines of a lifetime at sea, would still have something about him that made people notice him. He would be attractive to women all his life.

When his plate was empty, Bruce sat back, looking satisfied and running his tongue round his teeth. Then, not surprisingly considering how fast he had eaten, he burped and said, 'Excuse me.'

Maddie laid down her fork and touched her napkin to her lips. She wished Bruce would blot the smear of grease on his chin.

Instead he said, 'Aren't you going to eat that?' indicating the untouched coleslaw.

When she shook her head, he reached over to take her plate and tip the shredded cabbage onto his plate. 'No sense in wasting it.'

When the waiter came to ask if they wanted dessert, Maddie chose fruit salad and Bruce ordered chocolate ice cream cake. From then on he became more talkative so that, by the end of meal, she knew a lot about his background. But although he asked a few questions about hers, they struck her as perfunctory rather than genuinely interested.

By the coffee stage she was seriously bored and wishing she hadn't come. It had been a mistake.

She was glad when he called for the check. He seemed to have forgotten about dividing the cost between them and would have waved her contribution away if she hadn't insisted he take it.

'A guy likes to pick up the tab sometimes,' he told her.

'It's nice of you offer, but I like to pay my way, Bruce. You wouldn't pick up the tab for another man. Why should you pay for me? We agreed to go halves earlier.'

'OK...we won't fight about it. I know you're a feisty lady...even if you don't act that way.' He gave her an appraising glance. 'It's hard to believe you sailed that tough race. You don't look the type.'

'What type is that?'

'Oh, come on, you must have seen lady sailors who look like men. No make-up, calves like a wrestler's, their shoulders bigger than their boobs.'

'That may be the way they used to be. They're not like that any more.' His stereotyped notions about yachtswomen reminded her of Scott's early misjudgements and the hurt they had caused her.

Walking back to the hotel, Bruce told her more about himself. Clearly he was lonely. She could empathise with that, having been lonely herself.

That she wasn't lonely any more; that the feeling of isolation she had known for so long had gone away, was a discovery Maddie made as she listened to Bruce's monologue; one part of her brain tuned in to what he was saying while another part examined the change that had happened while she was too busy to notice it.

It was as if a hole at the centre of her being had been filled. The future might be uncertain, but she wasn't adrift in the way she had been before.

'I can talk to you, Maddie,' said Bruce, his tone becoming more intimate.

Guiltily, she realised that much of what he'd been saying for the past few minutes hadn't registered at all.

As she started to pay full attention, he took hold of her hand. It was a gentle grasp yet, when she tried to slip her hand free, she found that she couldn't. Not without exerting a force that was bound to offend him.

She didn't want to do that, but nor did she want to walk along hand-in-hand, suggesting a degree of rapport that, on her side, didn't exist.

'Bruce, I –' Her voice tailed off. What did one say in these circumstances? She had no experience of situations like this. How did you brush off a man without hurting his feelings?

To complicate the situation, he said, 'I've really enjoyed this evening. You're different from most girls I've dated.'

'Bruce, this wasn't a date,' she began.

'It feels like a date to me,' he interrupted. 'Maddie, I –' At which point he decided action was more effective than words.

As she realised what he was about, she said hurriedly, 'Please don't.'

Her protest was futile. He intended to kiss her and wasn't going to be put off. Perhaps he thought her objection was a matter of form, not something she really meant.

Maddie found herself held in a strong one-armed hug while his other hand positioned her face so that he could plant an unwelcome kiss on her lips, effectively stifling any more objections.

She had two choices. She could fight him off or hope that her failure to respond would make him back off without an unseemly struggle. Maddie chose the latter. She didn't want to be kissed, but nor did she want to humiliate him by behaving as if he were totally repulsive to her.

Unfortunately her passive resistance didn't have the effect she hoped for, or perhaps he thought that persistence would overcome it. He went on kissing.

What stopped him was a car drawing up alongside where they were standing, not too far from the entrance to the hotel. Maddie, who had her eyes open, was aware of this before he was.

But she didn't think the car had any connection with them until an irate voice said, 'What the hell's going on here?'

Guernsey: where is it?
www.guernseypostcards.com/satellite.html

Guernsey patois
www.societe.org.gg

chapter ten

To Maddie's relief, Bruce removed his mouth from hers. The arm round her slackened but did not let go.

'Are you talking to me?' His tone was aggressive.

As Maddie was uncomfortably aware, embracing her had aroused him to a point where he might have lost his normal sense of self-preservation. Scott was taller than Bruce, and in much better shape. But at the moment, high on testosterone, Bruce might feel his equal.

'There's nobody else here,' said Scott, slamming the door of the taxi and stepping onto the pavement.

He was ignoring Maddie, his blue gaze at its most laser-like as he concentrated its beam on the man still holding her.

Annoyed at being caught in this embarrassing predicament, and equally riled by being treated as if she were invisible, Maddie said coldly, 'We were saying goodnight. Wasn't that obvious? It would have been to most people,' she added acidly.

At this Scott deigned to glance at her. 'I wasn't aware that you two were on kissing terms.'

'It's none of your damned business what terms I'm on with anyone. You're not my keeper.'

The hostile words came out before she could stop them. Why was she flaring at him when it was Bruce she was angry with?

'Maddie's right. It's not your business.' Bruce was flushed and resentful, but his aggression was subsiding.

Scott looked intently at Maddie. 'Did you want him to kiss you?'

The truthful answer was a vehement no, but that would

humiliate Bruce and she couldn't bring herself to do that. 'Yes, I did,' she said defiantly.

'How much have you had to drink?' Scott asked.

'Are you suggesting I'm smashed?'

'It's the usual reason, at this time of day, for people acting stupidly.'

'Are you calling her stupid?' Bruce demanded, his aggression level rising again.

'Do you want to make an issue of it?' Scott did not trouble to hide his contempt for him. 'If I were you I'd bow out gracefully. You'll be glad you did in the morning.'

For a moment or two Bruce couldn't make up his mind. Maggie held her breath, willing him to forget about pride and be sensible. She was certain that, if he took a swing at Scott, he would find himself flat on his back in the flowerbed on the other side of the low hedge edging the sidewalk.

Eventually, to her infinite relief, he backed down. 'For your information Maddie had one glass of wine. If she had saved *my* life, I'd be nice to her...not bully her. If you ask me, it's a pity she didn't leave you where you were. Goodnight, Maddie. Thanks for a great evening.'

He turned and walked off, his clenched fists thrust into the pockets of his pants.

It was the right thing to do to avert a fracas in the street. But she could guess the cost to his pride and felt sorry for him and furious with Scott for causing the wound to Bruce's dignity.

Scott watched him for a moment, then shrugged and turned to pay the taxi driver who had been an interested spectator.

Maddie seized the chance the make her escape, stepping quickly over the low hedge onto the grass between the flower beds in the hope of being out of reach before Scott realised she had gone.

She might have known she wouldn't make it. She hadn't gone five yards before a hard hand grabbed her by the elbow.

'I want an explanation, Maddie.'

'I don't have to explain my behaviour to you, Scott. I've already told you it's none of your business.'

'I think it is. I feel responsible for you...like you felt responsible for me when I upside down in the Southern Ocean and nobody else could get me out of the jam I was in.'

'The difference being that I'm not in a jam and I don't need to be rescued.'

'You were lying when you said you wanted him to kiss you. My guess is you were hating every second of it. You were, weren't you? Tell the truth this time. You lied before to spare his feelings.'

It was both uncanny and infuriating the way he could read her mind.

'Unlike you, I don't enjoy hurting people,' she retorted. 'I wasn't expecting him to kiss me, but he didn't mean any harm. It's what most people do after spending an evening together.'

'Exactly, so it wasn't being fair to him to have dinner with him without making clear that it wasn't a regular date.'

'I did make that clear...I thought I had. Anyway one goodnight kiss isn't something to make a fuss about. It's you who've made a huge drama out of it. If you hadn't shown up –'

'If I hadn't shown up, he'd have his tongue down your throat and his hands all over you, and you wouldn't know how to stop him,' Scott told her curtly.

Still gripping her arm, he marched her into the building and across the lobby to the elevators. Only when the door closed, trapping her with him in the confined space, did he release his hold.

'Why were you with him anyway?'

'I was with him because I like him...on a friendly basis,' she added. 'What have you got against him?'

A peculiar expression crossed his face, one she hadn't seen before and couldn't interpret. It was as if he had switched off and his mind was now somewhere else, not in the lift with her. She wasn't sure that he had heard her question.

The door of the elevator opened and she saw that Scott had returned from wherever he had been.

'It's been a long day. I'm tired. We'll finish this at breakfast,' he said. 'Goodnight, Maddie.'

Indicating that she should step out of the lift ahead of him, he followed her into the corridor and strode off in the direction of a room he must have booked by e-mail.

Five minutes later, having dumped his grip, stripped down to his undershorts and taken a bottle of chilled spring water from the mini-bar, Scott flung himself on the bed and wondered why he had nearly lost it back there in the elevator.

Only by exerting maximum will-power had he managed to batten down his temper which, up to that point, had been under pretty good control, given the provocation of coming back to find Maddie in a public clinch with the gutless buffoon she claimed to like.

The sight of her, locked in that ape's arms, had been, in rapid succession, astonishing, exasperating and...but the third reaction was something he couldn't quite pinpoint except that it had manifested itself as an almost overwhelming urge to take Bruce apart.

Losing his temper was something that Scott didn't do any more...or hadn't for a lot of years. Even at the age when a certain amount of hotheadedness was excusable, he had never gotten into fist fights. Other kinds of youthful scrapes, yes. But mostly they had involved taking risks with his own person, not attempting to black the eyes and bloody the noses of other guys.

So why had he felt a strong desire to beat up Bruce, to the extent of asking him if he wanted to make an issue of Scott calling Maddie stupid?

Had Bruce had the nerve to accept that ridiculous challenge, they could both have been in trouble. Being involved in a public affray – with the attendant risk that it would be picked up by the media – was the last thing Scott needed. Other people's experience had taught him that a lot of taxi drivers, and at least one person in every police station and hospital accident and emergency department, were in league with the local press, and the local press had a hot line to more important newsrooms. This was the scuttlebutt mechanism that brought all kinds of major and minor misdemeanours to light.

He knew that, yet, momentarily, he had forgotten his normal caution because…because…

As he wrestled to make sense of his reasons, Scott remembered asking Maddie how much she had had to drink. Now he asked himself what mind-bending chemical influence he had been under to step out of character as he had done.

Not alcohol, that was for sure. He'd drunk wine with his meal on the flight over, but mostly he had drunk water to counteract the dehydration of air travel.

Could jet lag have made him uncharacteristically inflammable? It never had up to now, and he'd flown a helluva lot of air miles and many much longer flights than the one that had brought him here.

Maybe it was a delayed bout of air rage, he thought sardonically, tipping the bottle of water against his mouth and swallowing the last of its contents. Rage had certainly been a component of his aberrant behaviour which, now that he had calmed down, seemed a lot like the outbreaks of truculent conduct in mid-air he had read about but never witnessed.

Deciding that it would be better to take a shower and hit the sack rather than attempting to clarify an incident that might make more sense in the morning, he hauled himself to his feet. Heading for the bathroom, he closed his mind to the fact that tomorrow he would also have to make sense of it to Maddie.

Maddie had already started her breakfast when he joined her.

As on their last night at the beach house in Uruguay, she had slept badly, wakeful periods being interspersed with confused dreams.

Scott looked as if his night had been more restful. Freshly shaved, his hair damp from a shower, he looked refreshed and alert. As if nothing untoward had happened the night before.

'Good morning.' He drew out the chair on the other side of the table.

'Good morning.' Did this mean that last night's local crisis was not going to be mentioned? she wondered.

She was having her usual post-voyage breakfast of cereal, yoghurt, whole grain toast and fruit. She had never much liked them before, but now she was trying to have a kiwi fruit every day. A book she had bought on achieving peak sports performance claimed that one of the furry fruit supplied the total recommended daily intake of vitamin C. Improving her health was not her only objective. She hoped to enhance her looks.

Scott ordered a similar breakfast. Her grandfather had always breakfasted on bacon and eggs with plenty of Guernsey butter on his bread and full cream milk from the island's famous cows in his tea. Thinking of him, she felt sorrow, not for the embittered old man, but for the loss of the close relationship that could have existed between them had he been a different person.

'Did you have a good time with your family?' she asked. 'They must have been thrilled to see you safe and sound.'

'Yes, we had a lot to talk about,' he agreed. 'The person they want to see is you, Maddie. They want to thank you for rescuing me and they'd like it if you would take a vacation with them. They have a place in Italy where they go every summer. They would like it if we joined them there. How does that sound to you?'

The contrast between his angry attitude last night and the affability of his manner this morning was confusing. As for the invitation, at first she could hardly believe it. Could his family really want to meet her?

But then it struck her that if the situation had been reversed, and it was she who had been rescued by him, her family – if she had had a normal background – would certainly have wanted to meet him.

'It's very...*very* kind of them,' she began. 'But –'

'If you're worrying about the expense of getting there – don't,' said Scott. To her surprise, he said, 'I have a note for you from my father.' He put a hand behind him and produced an envelope slightly the worse for time spent in the back pocket of his jeans.

Maddie opened it and extracted a single sheet of expensive notepaper. The text of the letter was a word processor print out but *Dear Maddie* and *Sincerely, Jack Randall* had been written with a fountain pen using brown ink.

The letter invited her to spend a relaxing holiday with the writer and his wife at their summer place in Italy. They were most anxious to meet her and thank her for saving Scott's life. ...*though no words can express the depth of our gratitude for your courageous act*, his father had written.

Maddie read the letter twice then looked up to find Scott watching her.

'It's terribly kind of your parents. I appreciate the invitation –'

'But you don't want to go,' he finished for her.

'I'd like to go...very much,' she corrected him. 'But I need to go back to Guernsey to sort out my grandfather's affairs. I don't know how long that might take.'

'OK, we'll do that first. I'll come to the island with you. I'd like to see it again and it could be that having a lawyer with you, even an American lawyer, could be useful. I can recognise a con. You might not.'

'What makes you think anyone will try to con me?'

'Because when people die and leave assets – or, in some cases, liabilities – it's a law of life that someone will be sniffing round, trying to make a fast buck. Sometimes it's a family member. You tell me you have no relatives. Maybe you haven't...or maybe you'll get back to find some long-lost cousins have caught the scent of a legacy.'

'I'm sure that won't happen in this case. But I would be glad of your advice if any problems do arise. But don't you have more important things to do?'

Scott drained his glass of juice, the upward tilt of his chin drawing her attention to the strong column of his neck and the lighter colour of his throat.

'Nope...nothing more important,' he said.

Then he smiled and his eyes were warm again, last night's rift dismissed and forgotten.

'You'll like my parents. They're good fun, and Italy is a great place to chill out. They spend a lot of time there and so do I...when I can. As soon as I've finished breakfast I'll call them, and then we can spend the rest of the day taking a look round Charleston. You don't want to leave without seeing a few of the sights.'

After a long day exploring the city, they returned to

the hotel to shower and change before going out for dinner.

Maddie was so different from any of his previous girlfriends that Scott wasn't sure whether she had changed her mind about the rain check or was playing with him.

At times she seemed to be flirting, at others to be sheering off. He was not used to being unsure where he stood with a woman.

During dinner he persuaded her to postpone her return to the island until after the Italian holiday. He suggested that, in the morning, she should call her grandfather's attorney to let him know her immediate plans.

'He'll be able to tell you roughly how the land lies with regard to your grandfather's property,' he told her.

Removing their empty dessert plates, the waiter asked, 'Would you like coffee?'

Scott looked at her. 'Would you?' He hoped she would shake her head and they could get out of the restaurant and go someplace where, by kissing her, he could find out for sure whether they were going to spend the night together.

Instead, she said, 'Yes, thanks...white for me, please' – this with a smile for the waiter who was about her age with his hair fashionably styled.

'And for you, sir?'

How old does he think I am? Scott thought sourly as he said, 'Black, please.'

Maybe the boy thought he was cradle-snatching. Maybe he was. Nine years was a big gap. When he had been her age, she had been twelve years old. There were times when she still had an air of adolescent uncertainty about her, and others when she seemed all woman, the way she had that last night at the beach house.

After dinner they went for a stroll. Tomorrow was the day set for the end-of-race ceremony, after which all the competitors would be returning to their bases.

'You'll have to leave *Sea Spray* here for the time being,' said Scott. 'I think you've spent enough time at sea without crossing the Atlantic right now. Later, you can either get someone to take her across for you – there are plenty of competent people who would jump at the chance – or maybe we could take her across together. Let's see how things work out?'

When they returned to the hotel, he escorted her to her door, making her wonder if he was going to come in. But he said goodnight in the corridor, bending to brush a light kiss on her cheek before walking away.

Fortunately she knew the name of Pierre Sardrette's advocate, as a lawyer was called on the island, and, next day, was able to get the telephone number from the international operator.

'Apparently there is somebody interested in buying the boatyard,' she told Scott, after the phone call. 'So that solves that problem. I wouldn't be comfortable closing it down and leaving the men who have worked for us in the lurch. Why are you looking like that?'

'Your concern for them does you credit,' he said dryly. 'I wonder if they would feel equally uncomfortable about suing you for compensation?'

'You're too cynical,' she protested.

He shrugged. 'Maybe.' Then, after glancing at his watch, 'It's time you were getting ready to face the cameras again.

This time she wasn't nervous. She knew she would never welcome the limelight, or seek it, the way some people did, but from now on she could cope with the questions and the flashbulbs.

Scott had told her the race would change her, and it had. Or had it been knowing him that had changed her?

Maddie had not expected to fly to Europe in a private jet

owned by the company of which Scott's father was president. This discovery was her first intimation that her visit to Italy might be as fraught with hazards, although of a different nature, as the passage through the Southern Ocean. Perhaps, if his father was very rich, Scott had reason to be cynical, she thought as they boarded the aircraft.

The Romantic Love Test
www.tc.umn.edu/~parkx032/RLT-WEB.html

chapter eleven

At Genoa airport they were met by a uniformed driver. Scott introduced him as Luigi before he took charge of their baggage and led the way to a luxurious car with its soft top folded down behind the rear passenger seat.

'This was found in an outhouse when Dad bought the house here,' Scott explained, as they waited for Luigi to finish stowing the luggage. 'Dad is keen on vintage cars so he had it refurbished for collecting and despatching visitors.'

The last lap of the journey took an hour. As they drew near their destination, Maddie grew increasingly jittery. Although they might not show it, she couldn't believe that Scott's family would welcome a stranger from a totally different milieu.

'Why are you nervous?' Scott reached for her hand and held it in his larger one.

It surprised her that he knew how she was feeling inwardly. She had been trying not to show it.

'Your parents might prefer to have you to themselves,' she said.

'Are you crazy? If it weren't for you, they wouldn't be having me at all. You're already at Number One on their favourite people list...and they haven't even met you met. When they do...' He made an expressive gesture with his free hand, at the same time squeezing her hand. 'So just relax and enjoy your first time in Italy.'

He surprised her by starting to sing a lilting Italian song in an attractive tenor, placing his hand on his heart and gazing at her with an expression that, had it been genuine, would have rocketed her to heaven. But of course it was only a teasing way of jollying her out of her nervousness. She knew that, but even so it made her heart beat faster, her pulse race.

'You have a good voice,' she said calmly, when he stopped.

'*Grazie, signorina.*' He lifted her fingers to brush his lips across her knuckles, before replacing her hand on her lap. 'Maybe one day I'll take you to Milan to hear some really good voices. The Opera House there is a place everyone should go once in a lifetime.

When he said things like that, suggesting she would always have a place in his life, it made her spirits soar. Yet common sense told her that, in the nature of things, they were bound to drift apart. The only way they could stay friends forever was if he fell in love with her. And how likely was that?

He had everything going for him: looks, charm, brains, background, the lot. She didn't underrate herself, but she knew she wasn't in Scott's league. She didn't belong in this glamorous old limousine with a liveried driver at the wheel. Her place was in a family saloon with a nice ordinary man who would never amount to much in the world's eyes but who would be a kind and loving husband and father. In the days ahead, living the high life with Scott and his family, it would be important to keep reminding herself that this was only an interlude. Not real life.

Unbeknown to her grandfather, Maddie had visited several of the great houses on Guernsey. With a group of holidaymakers she had paid for a tour of Sausmarez Manor. In her teens she had spent happy hours in the garden at Castle Carey, then open to the public on certain days. Sometimes she had talked to the lonely old man who had owned it at that time.

But when they arrived at the Randalls' holiday home, it proved to be grander by far than anything the island had to offer.

Evidently Scott's parents had been warned of their arrival by the gate-keeper. When the car turned the final bend of the long drive, two people were standing on the steps of the imposing mansion.

Moments later Maddie was shaking hands with an elegant dark-haired woman and a man who was an older edition of Scott, with white hair, a deeply lined face and eyes that were blue-grey instead of the brilliant blue of his son's eyes.

Having clasped her hand between both of his, Mr Randall said, 'To hell with formality. If it weren't for you, my son wouldn't be here today. I'm going to give you a big hug.' Which he did, kissing her on both cheeks before folding her in a bear hug.

He then hugged Scott even more vigorously, drawing back from the embrace with his eyes full of tears that he blinked back, saying, 'I hope you're not going to give us any more scares like that. Not that I want to cramp your style, but you had us seriously worried for a while there.'

'For a while I was worried myself,' Scott told him, smiling but obviously moved by his father's visible emotion.

They kept an arm round each other as they mounted the steps to enter the house.

Tucking her hand through the crook of Maddie's arm, Mrs Randall said, 'I can't tell you how delighted we are that you're able to spend some time with us. I'm sure you must need a rest after being at sea for months. We want you to feel at home and free to do just as you please.'

'Thank you. You're very kind.'

'My dear, there is nothing we can say or do to express the warmth of our feelings.' She lowered her voice so the two men walking ahead of them wouldn't overhear her. 'Jack has already known great grief in his life. To lose Scott would have broken his heart...mine too. But, thanks to you, the adventure has ended happily.'

A little later she took Maddie up to a large bedroom with a balcony and a sea view. 'I think you'll find everything you need but, if not, you have only to ask.'

As she was saying this, Scott joined them. 'Maddie needs some clothes, Francesca. Perhaps tomorrow or the next day you could take her shopping.'

'I'd be delighted. I love shopping and this season there are some really lovely things to chose from,' said his stepmother, before she left them together.

'Are you going to be comfortable here?' Scott asked, glancing round the room furnished with pale woods and pale neutral colours to create a peaceful atmosphere. In one corner was a sculpture of a naked girl with her head thrown back and her arms supporting the baby curled over her shoulder.

Noticing Maddie looking at it – to avoid looking at him – Scott said, 'That's a piece by Benno Schotz called *The Thanks Offering*. Dad bought it for my mother after I was born.'

'It's beautiful. As for being comfortable...how could anyone not be? It's the loveliest room I've ever been in.'

He had strolled across to the statue and now ran his hand down the women's sleek marble side from below her arm to the lovely line of her hip. 'It feels almost like flesh except that it's cold instead of warm,' he said, turning to look at Maddie.

Was it his intention to make her imagine him running his hand down her side? Whether or not he meant to send a tremor through her, he did. It was impossible for her to be in a bedroom with Scott without longing to be on the bed in his arms. Did he know that? Probably. If only she could read his mind as easily as he seemed to read hers.

'When you've unpacked it will be time for a drink before lunch,' he said. 'It will be just the four of us, very informal. Have you stopped being nervous now that you've met them?'

'Yes.'

'I told you there was nothing to worry about. Trust me.'

'I do.'

Walking towards her, Scott smiled. 'When we've digested our lunch, we might go for a swim.' On the way past, he pinched her chin. 'Come down when you're ready. When you get to the bottom of the stairs, you'll see a door to the garden. We'll be on the terrace.'

The following day, while they were having a coffee break during the shopping expedition, Francesca told Maddie about Scott's mother. The two men had stayed at home for Mr Randall to bring his son up to date on some business matters.

'Scott inherits his passion for sailing from his mother,' said Francesca. 'It was she who taught him to sail. He could handle a dinghy by the time he was six. When he was eight, she was sailing alone, as she often did, and a freak squall caught her. She drowned. Jack was devastated. When we heard about Scott being in danger, I could see all that old pain reviving. I know that now Jack loves me as deeply as he loved Sofia. But a tragedy like that leaves a scar on the soul. For him to lose Scott to the sea would have been unbearable.'

Loving Scott, it was easy for Maddie to empathise with their feelings during those endless hours between the news of the capsize and the rescue.

'I've sometimes thought,' said Francesca, 'that Scott's attitude to women, during his twenties, was the result of losing his mother at an age when it's hard to cope with the worst things that happen to people. I suspect that he may have felt as if she had deserted him. His intelligence would have accepted that it was an accident. But in his eight-year-old heart he may have blamed her for leaving him and decided that loving someone was a risk he was not going to take.'

'I can understand that,' said Maddie. 'My mother walked out on my father when I was two. I don't know what went wrong with their marriage. My grandfather never had a good word to say for her...partly because she was an incomer, not Guernsey-born. Perhaps she couldn't stand sharing a house with him. He could be very difficult. But, whatever happened, I've never been able to understand her walking out on me.'

She paused before adding, 'If she ever hears that he's dead and tries to make contact, I don't want to meet her. So perhaps you're right. Even though he knows it's irrational, Scott may have the same sense of betrayal that I have. But what exactly do you mean by his attitude to women?'

'He has never taken anyone seriously. Most young men lose their heart a few times before they commit themselves to marriage. Scott never has. Which is strange because in all the other areas of his life he does care about people. How does he strike you?'

'He's been very kind to me. We've had a few heated arguments but mostly because, on a boat, we both want to be skipper,' Maddie told her, smiling.

She didn't want Francesca to guess how she really felt about Scott.

Although the race office had released the news that Maddie was visiting Scott's family, it was a surprise when, a few days later, she received a letter addressed to her care of the *palazzo*. The envelope had a London postmark and the name of a limited company which meant nothing to Maddie until she opened it. The letter-heading told her that the firm was a literary agency founded before she was born. The first paragraph congratulated her on finishing the race. The second suggested she should write a book about the experience.

'If you feel unequal to the task, we could introduce you to a professional ghost writer to handle that side of the project. We are confident that, given appropriate promotion, the book would have very substantial sales. We would expect to secure a high six-figure advance.'

When she had read it, Maddie passed it over to Scott. 'Can they be serious? Six figures...that's a hundred thousand pounds.'

'They're serious,' he said emphatically. 'Promotable authors – young, attractive, articulate – are worth a lot of money to publishers.'

'But I'm not very articulate...and I had a hard time writing essays at school.'

'Maybe because you weren't interested in the subjects they set,' he suggested. 'Writing on a subject you know inside out is much easier than writing about Shakespeare's sonnets or the Industrial Revolution. The logs you wrote during the race were excellent...far better than anything the guys wrote.'

'Were they? I didn't know you'd read them.'

'During the last lap from Punta back to Charleston, I read them as soon as they were posted on the race office website...and looked up your earlier logs in the archive. Someone at this literacy agency may have done the same thing...although if they had done that they wouldn't be suggesting using a ghost writer,' he added.

At this point his father made a comment. 'Before Maddie accepts any offers, it would be wise to check out the people they're coming from,' he advised. 'A top New York agent is a member of one of my clubs. He'll be able to give an informed opinion of the company that has written to you, Maddie. He may also be interested in representing you himself. The more people who are interested, the better the final deal is likely to be.'

It was Mr Randall who, a few days later, suggested that, as he and his wife had been invited to spend a few days with friends in Paris, and Maddie's home island was only a short hop by air from the French capital, it would be a good opportunity for her to confer with her grandfather's legal advisors about the future of the boatyard.

'Scott can go with you for moral support,' he added.

'That's what I was planning to do,' said his son. 'How long are you staying with the Whitakers?'

'Only for three nights. Our friends spent their honeymoon in Paris,' he explained to Maddie. 'Now they're celebrating their fortieth wedding anniversary and, as I was Ben Whitaker's best man, we've been invited to the party.'

The Whitakers, Maddie concluded, were as rich and cosmopolitan as the Randalls. She felt she would never adjust to the mindset of people who used private planes the way ordinary people used buses. But she had to admit that going back to Guernsey with Scott as her escort was less daunting than going back alone.

Seeing the island from the air reinforced Maddie's feeling that to return would be a mistake. Wherever her future lay, it was not here.

Having had a light lunch on the plane, they were able to go straight to the advocate's office to pick up the keys and confirm the appointment to see him early the following morning.

It was a strange sensation, returning to the house that was the only home she had known yet so unlike the safe haven that a home was supposed to be. With all its internal shutters closed, it looked even more unwelcoming than her memory of it.

Scott unlocked the front door for her, pushed it open and stood back. She wondered if he had ever been in a house as lacking in comfort or elegance as the one he was about to enter. At sea, he was used to the discomforts all sailors took in their stride. But, if his father's other houses were as luxurious and beautiful as the *palazzo*, he was bound to be surprised to discover that the mod cons here did not even include a refrigerator.

Despite his housekeeper's urgings, her grandfather had felt that a pantry with stone shelves on the north side of the house was perfectly adequate cold storage even in the hottest summer. Disapproving of married women working outside the home, he had regarded freezers as an extravagance that encouraged them to neglect their traditional skills and shop at the supermarkets whose popularity he deplored.

Pressing a light switch, Maddie discovered that the electricity was off. She thought it likely her grandfather had turned it off before he was admitted to hospital. If he had realised he was going to die there, it would have been entirely in character for him to arrange for the power to be disconnected until such time as she returned to the island.

'How musty it smells. I'll open some windows,' she said, opening the door of the sitting room that had never been used since her grandmother's death.

She had opened the top and bottom shutters that, being hinged in the middle, folded neatly back against the reveals formed by the thick granite walls, and was gripping the china-knobbed catch that locked the sash window when Scott said, 'Let me do that.'

Standing close behind her, he reached his arms over her shoulders and their hands brushed for a second as she stopped struggling with the catch and let his long brown fingers take over.

Even for him it wasn't easy to budge the part that, in regular use, would slide out from under the catch screwed to the frame of the lower sash. While he grappled with it, Maddie tried to ignore the sensations aroused by having him close behind her, so close that she had only to sway slightly for her back to be in contact with his chest. How would he react if she did lean against him?

Before she could put it to the test – and she wasn't sure she had the courage after the humiliating rebuff in Uruguay – he succeeded in moving the catch and, using the heels of both hands, pushed the lower sash upwards, admitting the breezy outer air into the stale atmosphere of a room furnished in the style of a long-gone era.

Whatever he was thinking as he glanced round it, Scott made no comment.

'We never used this room. In winter, we sat in the kitchen,' said Maddie, leading the way there. 'The whole house needs a lot of modernisation. Goodness knows what it will cost to make it habitable by most people's standards.'

'A lot of people would rather buy a house that needs a total make-over than one that's already been upgraded in a way they don't like,' said Scott.

The kitchen overlooked the long granite-walled garden at the rear of the property. 'What are those trees…and the tall blue spire-shaped plants?' he asked.

'The trees are myrtles. The tall things are echiums. Every year they come up somewhere different, sometimes in the neighbours' gardens, sometimes in ours. The plants that do really well here are fuchsias…and the little Mexican daisies that grow between the stones in the walls.'

She was about to tell him the history of the daisies but thought better of it, not wanting to bore him with details unlikely to interest him.

'The garden looks in good shape. The lawn has obviously been cut since your grandfather went into hospital,' said Scott. 'Did he employ a gardener.'

'An old man who used to work at the boatyard cuts the grass and clips the hedge at the front. I shall have to go and see him…explain that I'm not going to stay here.'

'If he's willing, it would be a good idea to have him keep it in order while it's on the market,' said Scott.

'Maybe the next owners will want to retain his services. How many bedrooms are there?'

Maddie took him upstairs, opening a window in her grandfather's spartan bedroom and then in her own. Once, when she was about sixteen, she had wanted to replace the dark unattractive wallpaper with something paler and prettier, but her grandfather had vetoed the idea as a needless extravagance.

Looking back, it annoyed her to remember how spinelessly she had accepted his arbitrary decisions on everything except entering the Slocum. Had he lived, he would have found her more adversarial now. The voyage had given her the confidence to stand out for what she wanted...except in the case of the thing she wanted most. But that was not something that could be achieved by force of will. Love was a reciprocal thing. She could not make Scott love her.

Looking round Maddie's bedroom, and remembering his sisters' rooms, Scott was struck by the absence of pinboards, posters and all the paraphernalia that he associated with girlhood. Here there was no TV set or even a radio.

The old-fashioned pictures, one in the centre of each wall, were clearly not of Maddie's choosing. The wallpaper and curtains looked as if they had been there for fifty years or more.

The heavy white cotton cover on the high single bed with its polished mahogany headboard and footboard had a Victorian air very different from the divans covered with brightly patterned duvets that Alicia and Gaia had slept in.

'Where's Bertie?' he asked. 'Did you bring him, or leave him in Italy?'

'I left him on *Sea Spray*,' she said. 'He was company during the race, before I had you to talk to, but it's not exactly normal for a grown-up person to have a toy bear around, is it?'

'He was your mascot. Lots of people have them,' said Scott. He told her about the toy ape his sister had taken on her honeymoon.

They were staying at an hotel in the centre of the small seaport. Before dinner they walked past the castle at the mouth of the harbour and along the causeway to the lighthouse.

As they turned back Scott looked at the buildings arranged in tiers on the steep hill behind the waterfront. 'This is a nice town. Are you sure you don't want to keep at least a foothold here, Maddie?'

'Quite sure. I've had plenty of time of think about it. Even if I don't know where I do want to be, I know it isn't here,' she said firmly.

In the Italian restaurant where they had supper, every time the door opened to admit other diners Maddie half-expected to see someone she knew. Although she didn't want to run into anyone from her past, she couldn't help being curious about whether she would be recognised in her new persona.

Next morning they spent about forty minutes with the advocate. Afterwards Maddie said she had some bits of shopping to do and Scott said he would like to visit the public library. They arranged to meet in an hour's time at an outdoor café with a view of the other islands.

They walked down Smith Street together, pausing to look in the windows of the two bookshops where she had often browsed but, in her teens, had never had the money to buy. At the bottom of the hill they separated, Maddie turning left and Scott right.

Apart from buying shampoo and tissues, there was

nothing she needed. After shopping in Italy with Francesca, the shops here seemed much less tempting than they had in the years when her peers were spending their seemingly lavish allowances on the latest fashions. After half an hour's window-shopping, she had had enough.

She was heading in the direction of the café when, coming towards her, she saw Tom. She recognised him immediately, but doubted if he would recognise her; many pounds lighter than she had been when he knew her. Also she was wearing a floaty Italian skirt and clingy cotton top in place of the unisex sailing rig of any end-of-race photographs that he might have seen in the press, and today her hair was loose, tucked behind her ears but not tied back as it had been when she and Scott arrived at Punta.

When he was about twenty feet away, Tom noticed her. Perhaps his attention was caught by the vivid colours of her skirt, or perhaps by her legs which had always been a better shape than the rest of her and now, when not hidden by trousers, attracted quite a lot of male attention.

As the gap between them narrowed, Maddie saw Tom appraising her figure with an openness that, had he been a stranger, she might not have liked.

He was only a few steps away when his gaze reached her face. For a second or two, she saw no sign of recognition and intended to let him walk past without showing that she knew him. Then, at the very last moment, when he was about to pass, something about her obviously rang a bell in his mind and he checked his pace and said uncertainly, 'Maddie?'

Sausmarez Manor
www.guernsey.org/sausmarez/main.asp
and
www.gardenvisit.com/g/sau2.htm

Guernsey
www.images-of-britain.freeserve.co.uk/isle/is00004.htm
and
http://user.itl.net/~glen/description.html

The Pollet
www.visitguernsey.com/shop.shtml

chapter twelve

'Hello, Tom. How are you?'

They stood in the middle of the crowded street, where motor traffic was restricted to delivery vans and security vehicles, and the passers-by flowed around them, the locals moving briskly while the tourists dawdled and window-shopped.

'I'm fine...and you're looking great. How long have you been back? There's been nothing in the press or on the radio. I would have heard if there had been.'

'I didn't want any publicity. I'm only back for a short time.' After a pause, she added, 'I'm surprised you knew who I was. I've changed since the last time you saw me.'

'Yes...but your eyes haven't changed. You always had beautiful eyes.'

It was said with such patent seriousness and sincerity that Maddie was taken aback. Recovering herself, she said, 'Thank you. Well...tell me about yourself. What's been going on in your life?'

'Nothing much. I'm still in the same job. I suppose, if I was ambitious, I'd switch to being a financial adviser. But working in a bank wouldn't suit me,' he said, with a grin.

Maddie laughed. Now that Guernsey's traditional resources, agriculture and tourism, were slowly being superseded by offshore banking, it wasn't difficult for any reasonably numerate islander to get a job in the finance industry. In fact there was such a shortage of local candidates that some of the banking employees came from the mainland, on licence, in the same way that the island's hospital depended on foreign nurses to make up the number required.

'No, I can't see you driving a desk,' she agreed. 'I couldn't do it either. It would bore me out of my mind. I guess we're both outdoor people.'

'Have you time for a coffee?' he asked.

'I'm meeting someone for coffee. Why don't you join us?'

'OK...if your friend won't mind.'

'Of course not. I told him about you. He'd be interested to meet you.'

They started walking towards the old granite-built town church which dominated the lower end of High Street.

'You told him about me?' Tom queried.

'I've been staying with Scott Randall's family and he offered to come here with me to help sort out the problems to do with the house and the boat yard,' she explained. 'When you e-mailed me after my grandfather died, Scott asked who you were. I told him you were my first date...my only date,' she added, smiling.

'Are you and Scott an item now?' he asked.

'No, no...just very good friends,' Maddie assured him.

'It wouldn't be surprising, after all you've been through together, if you'd fallen in love with each other. He's certainly never going to find a girl with more guts,' said Tom. 'I've often regretted being so gutless the night your grandfather opened the door and told me to get lost. I should have stood my ground, not left you to face the music.'

'If you had, it would only have made him angrier...and it wouldn't have changed anything,' she said. 'I wasn't ready to challenge his authority then. I was still hanging on to an impossible dream that someday he would turn into the kindly Father Christmas grandfather everyone would like to have. It was only when he died that I realised that could never have happened.'

'He must have given you a really hard time. I talked to my mother about it. She used to be a home help and she knows a lot about families and why some are happy and others aren't,' said Tom. 'She reckons that people like your granddad had a tough time when they were kids and it sort of stunted their emotions, stopping them ever being happy. I'm not sure I buy that theory. Some people can survive a rotten childhood. A couple of people I was at school with had the lousiest possible starts in life. But once they left home everything changed and got better for them.'

'It's certainly got better for me,' she said.' The race has changed my life. I feel a different person from the Maddie who left here.'

Tom curled his hand lightly round her arm just above the elbow. 'I liked the Maddie you were.'

'Even though I was like this?' She spread her hands in a gesture indicative of the size she had been at the time they were speaking of.

He shrugged. 'So you were overweight. You were still a nice person where it counts...in your heart and your head.'

They walked round one side of the church, crossed the end of Fountain Street and climbed a flight of stone steps whose sweeping curves always reminded her of a wave. A short distance up the hill that led to Hauteville, the street where Victor Hugo had spent his exile from France and where Maddie had once dreamed of living some time in the future, they entered the gateway to the café that was her rendezvous with Scott.

He was sitting on the upper level of the café's garden which had a panoramic view of the harbour and the islands of Herm, Jethou, Sark and, in the distance, Jersey.

When he saw her coming, he rose, ducking his head under the edge of the umbrella which shaded the table from the sun, where a cup and saucer and a glass of red stood on a tin tray.

'Hello...I ran into Tom and suggested he join us,' she said. 'It was Tom who e-mailed me after my grandfather died,' she added, in case Scott had forgotten being told about him.

'Hi, Tom. I'm Scott…the guy Maddie rescued from the fishes. Glad to know you.'

As the two men shook hands, she couldn't help thinking what splendid examples of the male sex they were: both tall and well-built and fit, but one strikingly dark and the other eye-catchingly blond.

And in that moment she knew that, if she had never met Scott, she could have loved Tom and perhaps been reconciled to Guernsey and learned to live happily here with the sorrows of the past forgotten, or at least only rarely remembered.

But she *had* met Scott, so loving Tom was impossible and anyway, for all she knew, he might be engaged now, or married, or living with a partner. But somehow she didn't think so. The things he had said in the High Street, the way he had touched her, had suggested he was still heart-free.

'Maddie, what would you like? Coffee and wine?' Scott asked.

'Yes, please. White wine for me.'

'What about you, Tom? The same…or would you rather have a beer?'

'I'll go to the counter,' said Tom. 'There's a bit of a queue and your coffee might go cold before you got back' – with a gesture at the half-full cup.

Scott didn't argue. When Tom had gone, he pulled out the chair next to his and waited for Maddie to sit down. 'Did you get your shopping done?'

'No, I ran into Tom before I got as far as Boots. Did you find the library?'

'I got as far as the entrance and then decided I'd rather sit in the sun. This place has a fabulous view.'

'Yes,…doesn't it. When I was at school, I wanted to live in a house with a view like Victor Hugo and his mistress

Juliette Drouet – she lived in another house near his – had from their windows higher up the hill in Hauteville.'

'Victor Hugo...the guy who wrote the novel *Les Misérables* that the stage show was based on, right?'

Maddie nodded. 'In 1870 he planted an oak in his garden at Hauteville House and said that when it was mature, in a hundred years' time, Europe would be united? That was pretty far-sighted of him, considering all the major and minor wars there've been in between then and now.'

'If you've always wanted to live there, maybe now you can,' said Scott. 'Together, your grandfather's house and the boatyard should fetch a good price; enough to buy another property. It could be a wise move to keep a foothold here. Retaining your status as an islander would be a big advantage if your book is a bestseller and you make a pile of money.'

'I shouldn't think that's very likely and I want to get away from Guernsey.'

'Now you do. Later you may think differently. You need to have a base somewhere...at least until you get married.'

Maddie saw Tom coming back. 'I'd rather have a base in France...or live on the boat and be a completely free agent.'

To her relief, Scott let the subject drop and made himself pleasant to Tom with the same easy warmth of manner that Mr and Mrs Randall had shown towards her. Had Tom been awkward with strangers, Scott would have drawn him out.

But in fact Tom was perfectly at ease. He was not as well-educated as Scott, and his family background was totally different. But he had the innate assurance of a man who, without any chips on his own shoulders, sees through other people's pretensions and is neither intimidated or impressed except by achievements he values.

As she listened to their conversation, she was struck by

their similarities rather than the differences between them. They were both men who, in a bad situation, she would trust to do whatever was best.

Presently, when his own glass was empty and Tom had only a little of his beer left, Scott said, 'Let's have another drink,' and went off to fetch them.

'You said you weren't staying long. When are you leaving, Maddie?' Tom asked.

'The day after tomorrow. I'm going back to Italy for a bit. Scott has another short race coming up soon. His parents are pressing me to stay until he comes back from that.' She told him about the book she had been asked to write and the offers of sponsorship from firms who wanted her to compete under their banners.

'I'm very undecided about the future. A long race like the Slocum leaves you feeling...a bit bushed.'

Tom gave her a thoughtful look. 'You said you were only friends, but you've fallen for him, haven't you?'

Alarmed that what was obvious to him might be equally obvious to Scott, Maddie said, 'What makes you say that?'

He shrugged. 'Nothing specific...just instinct. He's the type most girls would fancy, and he seems a nice bloke as well.'

'He is...but the only thing we have in common is sailing. In every other way we're poles apart. He's coming back,' she added, lowering her voice.

As Scott returned to the table, there was a loud booming sound from the direction of the sea.

'What was that?' he asked, looking round.

'It's the twelve o'clock gun being fired from the ramparts of Castle Cornet,' Maddie told him, pointing to where men in the scarlet uniforms worn when the castle was a military garrison had been carrying out the daily ceremony.

'That's a nice piece of living history,' said Scott. He

looked at Tom. 'It's a great place…your island. Tom, do you have a girlfriend? And, if so, what time is her lunch break?'

'I'm not involved with anyone special,' said Tom. 'Why did you ask?'

'I thought it might be fun to make up a foursome and have lunch at the hotel on Herm,' said Scott. 'If we've missed the regular ferry, we could find someone to take us across in a motorboat, couldn't we?'

Maddie would have preferred to have Scott to herself, but before she could comment on the suggestion, Tom said, 'I know someone who will run us over, and fetch us when you want to come back. My sister works near here. I can call them both on their mobiles.'

'Great…you do that,' said Scott, taking Maddie's compliance for granted.

Within an hour of the noon gun's reverberation, they were crossing the deep water channel called Little Russel to one of the two small islands lying close to Guernsey, with a table at the White House Hotel booked and waiting for them.

Tom's older sister Alice worked in a dress shop and was visibly delighted to find herself in a party that included a personable American who, clearly, she did not regard as Maddie's property. Alice knew about the race and the rescue, but probably because Tom had talked about it rather than because she had any personal interest in sailing races.

She was good company and Maddie wondered why she was unattached, for surely she wouldn't have been so flirtatious if she had a partner or a serious boyfriend. Maddie could see that Tom was slightly embarrassed by his sister's manner. Perhaps he regretted inviting her. He concentrated on his food and didn't say much. Maddie tried to focus on her lunch and not think about Scott's insistence that she shouldn't cut all her ties with Guernsey.

Why would he advise that if he had any long-term interest in her?

Later, when they had returned to St Peter Port and said goodbye to Tom and Alice, Scott gave Maddie a searching look. 'You're not feeling under the weather, are you? You were very quiet at lunch.'

'I'm fine,' she assured him, a little heartened that he had noticed her silence when she had thought that Alice had his full attention.

'Tom's sister ought to get herself a job as a disc jockey,' he said. 'All that vivacious patter must be wasted in a dress shop.' After a pause, he added, 'Thank God you're not a non-stop chatterbox.'

The remark made her spirits soar. She spent the rest of the day in what she knew was a fool's paradise, but she couldn't help herself. She had to snatch all the happiness she could to sustain her in the bleak time ahead when he was no longer in her life.

The day after their return to the *palazzo*, Scott's sister Gaia and her husband, Richard, and their two young children arrived. They wanted to spend time with Scott before he left to crew on a friend's boat in a short race to which he had committed himself before the Slocum.

Maddie enjoyed taking part in family activities. It made her regret even more that she had no brothers or sisters. Having them obviously gave life an extra dimension.

It wasn't until the day before his departure that she had Scott to herself while the rest of the family went on a visit to friends who lived about fifty kilometres inland. Scott opted out of this trip, saying that he and Maddie had things to discuss. It had already been agreed that she would remain in Italy during his absence.

For much of the morning he was busy on the telephone, making international calls. Shortly before lunch he joined her in the airy pavilion where she had retreated from the noonday heat which burned down on the paving surrounding the shining surface of the *palazzo*'s swimming pool.

'What are these things we have to discuss?' she asked, thinking they must have to do with her grandfather's boatyard.

'They come later. First you have to answer a question.' He paused. 'Will you marry me, Maddie?'

Moments ago she had been relaxing – not that she was ever totally relaxed when Scott was around – on a luxurious sunbed in the shade of the white pavilion's blue-lined canopy. Now she was sitting bolt upright, gaping at him in speechless astonishment.

'But you don't love me,' she protested.

He smiled at her. As it always did, Scott's smile made her insides flip. 'Anyone who has been married to the same person for a long time will tell you that successful marriages are based on friendship. Everything else is extraneous to that key element : friendship. We have it, don't we?'

Did they? She wasn't sure. Circumstances had thrown them together in conditions that revealed every facet of a person's character. But could she honestly describe this tall man with his splendid physique, highly educated mind and sophisticated outlook as her friend?

They were different beings from different worlds. Chance had thrown them together and now, astonishingly, he wanted them to embark on the most intimate relationship of all. Marriage.

'We have something else,' he added, watching her with that slightly narrowed blue gaze that always stirred embarrassingly earthy feelings in her.

'What else?'

'I want you in my bed...and you want to be there. That's the basic reason why most people get married. They dress it up in emotional trappings. Falling in love and so on. But basically it's the animal urge to mate. If we weren't civilised people, we'd do it here and now...or somewhere slightly less public,' he added dryly. 'Our lunch is arriving. Do you want another quick swim before we eat?'

His brain, not numbed by shock as hers was, had picked up the signals that their secluded tête-à-tête was about to end. Moments later she saw several members of the *palazzo*'s large staff arriving to lay a table in the permanent pavilion which housed the changing rooms and which had a large veranda where meals were served.

The pool and both pavilions were enclosed by a high wall clad with various flowering creepers and climbing roses. At the foot of the walls were carefully tended beds of sun-loving Mediterranean shrubs edged by fragrant clumps of herbs such as lemon thyme spilling onto the flagstones.

To Maddie it was like a corner of paradise. She could not imagine a more beautiful place than *Il Balcone,* the ancient but discreetly modernised *palazzo* surrounded by lovely grounds and overlooking a sea that, since her arrival, had been flat calm and as blue as Scott's eyes.

'I'll wait till later,' she said, as he rose from his lounger.

'OK...whatever suits you.' Dipping his head to avoid brushing the overhanging edge of the canopy, he stepped out into the sunlight.

He was built like a god. In Maddie's estimation that had nothing to do with the over-developed musculature of an iron-pumper. Scott's proportions and his lithe, long-legged stride were what people noticed. The strong muscles under the tanned skin only came into play when he was exerting himself. As they did a few seconds later when he crossed the paving, swung up his arms and took a neat unsplashy header into the deep end of the pool. For fleeting seconds all the muscles between his broad shoulders and lean waist rippled into life. Then he was under the water and out of view, reappearing as a long dark shape gliding along the bottom.

Watching him after he surfaced near the far end and began to swim back and forth with a leisurely graceful crawl, Maddie could almost believe she had just woken up from dream and the words *I think we should get married…as soon as possible* had never been spoken but were merely a figment of her romantic imagination.

It didn't make sense. Why should Scott want to marry her?

The reasons he had given – friendship and physical desire – were not enough to justify an alliance between a man like him and a woman like herself. If a virgin could claim the title woman. Even though she was twenty-one, 'girl' still seemed more appropriate. Either way she was light years behind Scott in experience and knowledge of the world.

His Italian step-mother had helped her to refine her appearance. She looked a lot more presentable than she had when he first brought her here. But there was a long way to go and many things to learn before she could move in this milieu without mentally holding her breath in case she did or said something that showed her up as an outsider, an interloper.

Not that any of them were snobs. Never for an instant had they made her feel she didn't belong here. As accustomed to money and luxury as she was accustomed to penny-pinching, the Randalls, as a family, were the nicest, most gracious people she had ever encountered. But probably they would be as stunned by Scott's proposal as she was. It was one thing for him to bring home a girl who had no family of her own and, for the time being, nowhere else to go.

Marriage was a very different proposition. Maddie felt sure they had never envisaged that Scott was considering marrying her.

His long brown fingers with their well-kept square-ish nails appeared on the rim of the pool. With another brief play of powerful muscles he swung himself out of the water, his arms and chest glistening, his black hair plastered to his skull until with a practised flick of his head he sent a sparkling halo of crystal drops spinning through the bright air.

While he rough-towelled his head, Maddie rose from her lounger and reached for the wrap she had dropped over the back of it. Her bikini and the matching cover-up had been picked out by Francesca, Scott's step-mother, on a shopping trip to Genoa, the nearest large city. Maddie didn't know what the things had cost, but the shops where Mrs Randall was a valued customer catered to women of fastidious taste whose clothes' budgets had no limits. Maddie could recognise quality even if she had never been able to afford it herself.

As she slipped her feet into sandals and reached for the wrap of cool blue and white cotton voile, she became aware that Scott had stopped rubbing the thick black hair that now was expensively barbered but, when their lives had impacted, had been several inches longer and following its natural inclination to curl.

Instead of continuing to dry himself, he was looking at her nearly nude body in a way that made her wish she had chosen to wear a more discreet swimsuit than the skimpy bikini cut to display her curves more freely than she was comfortable with…at least in his presence.

Appraising her figure with his usual openness, he said, 'If I didn't know you, I'd suspect that your breasts owed something to silicone. Girls with handspan waists usually have tiny breasts.'

To her annoyance, Maddie found herself blushing. Quickly she slipped her arms into the loose kimono-style sleeves, drawing the wrap around her and tying the belt in a slip-knot. Did he think her breasts were too large? She was now a 36B. Once her bras had been larger, but that had been in the days when eating had been her only solace. She didn't need food as a comforter any more. Now she was as slim and firm-fleshed as the girls she had envied in her teens.

'You have a beautiful body, Maddie.' Scott had lowered his voice so that he wouldn't be heard by the manservant and maid busying themselves on the veranda.

'Thank you...but I think people's brains are more important than their bodies. I'd like to be a lot better educated than I am at the moment. Excuse me. I'm going to tidy up before lunch.'

Leaving him to finish drying, she walked the length of the pool, smiled at the staff and went into the women's changing room.

Today was the first whole day she had spent alone with Scott since their arrival. The rest of the time there had always been other family members with them, either his parents, or his two sisters and their husbands and children.

The Randalls were close in a way she had only dreamed of. They took an interest in each other, had a fund of shared jokes and were casually and freely demonstrative. Scott cuddled his nephew and niece as lovingly as if they were his own children. His tenderness with them touched her deeply. He would be a wonderful father.

But there were plenty of men who were good to their children and not so good to their wives. What Scott would be like as a husband was a matter for conjecture. The fact that he could propose marriage to someone he didn't love was proof that, in some respects, his heart was *not* in the right place.

In the changing room, she shed her clothes and stepped into the shower compartment. The water in the pool was purified by the most advanced non-chemical technique. She didn't really need to wash off any residue. However to lather herself with delicately-scented soap, or use the top quality bath gel provided, was a pleasure that hadn't yet palled.

Standing under the power-jet of warm water, she visualised taking a shower with Scott. A long tremor ran through her at the thought of his being in here with her, placing his hands on her waist and drawing her against him.

A soft groan of longing escaped her. More than anything in the world she wanted him to be her first and only lover. But she knew that she couldn't bear it if, after a few years, he tired of her and looked elsewhere for his pleasures.

Many people would think her mad even to hesitate. Scott was the heir to a vast pharmaceutical empire established by his great-grandfather who, escaping from poverty in Europe, had gone to America and made his fortune there.

The company he had founded was now one of the global giants though most of the stock was still owned by family members. In time Scott, the only son, would step into his father's shoes, inheriting Il Balcone and several other properties.

Did he really believe she could cope with all that was involved in being the future chairman's wife? His mother, like Francesca his step-mother, had been an Italian aristocrat. Their upbringing had prepared them for marriage to an American merchant prince. Hers had not. Could she cope with the responsibilities and the pressures when all she really wanted was the relatively undemanding life of the wife of an ordinary man?

Tormented by unanswerable questions, she finished her shower and towelled her head as vigorously as Scott had dried his. Francesca's hair stylist, who had cut it for her, had complimented her on the healthy state of her hair despite the fact that the highlights were natural sun streaks, not the result of time spent in a salon. After combing conditioning mousse through the swingy chin-length bob that had replaced the long hair she had arrived with, she used the electric dryer to complete her hairdo.

When she returned to the veranda, Scott was leaning a shoulder against one of the tall white columns supporting the roof. He had put on a dark blue cotton shirt, and very short white drill shorts.

Turning to greet her, he said, 'A glass of champagne... fruit juice...what's your pleasure, *signorina*?'

'Some peach juice, please.'

Usually the drinks were served by Benito, the butler, but Scott must have sent him away.

'Have you made up your mind?' he asked, on his way to the refrigerator built into the wall.

'I still think you're out of your mind to suggest such a thing,' Maddie replied in a low voice.

She had put on a simple loose cotton sun-dress, the fabric a lighter tone of the dark grey of her eyes. According to Francesca, her eyes were her most striking feature.

'On the contrary, I'm in full possession of my senses...which most guys are not when they ask someone to marry them. Shakespeare was right...love *is* blind,' he said, fixing her drink. 'I've been best man at eight weddings since I left college. In my opinion, only the last two couples have a chance of staying the course. The first two have already split. They teamed up too young. I wouldn't bet serious money on the other four pairs being together for their tenth anniversary.'

'But you don't think I'm too young to get married?' she said, as he brought her a crystal goblet of chilled juice. 'Thank you.'

Instead of going back to fix his own drink, Scott stayed looking down at her. 'Most girls of twenty-one are too young. In general I don't think anyone should marry before twenty-five, though I know a few elderly people who have been together since they were very young. But their generation didn't have the same pressures ours does. Brides were virgins. Most of the men didn't know too much about sex. Also they were conditioned to stay in the marriage even it wasn't perfect. All that has changed.'

'Why don't you think I'm too young to marry you?'

'Because you've been tested in ways that most people aren't. You've had a tough life and you've come through it, colours flying. I want a wife who's my equal: not a slave, or a pet, or a dead-weight, the way some wives are. An equal. I know that you are.'

She knew he was speaking seriously and sincerely. He really meant what he said. Fortunately, having said it, he turned away to get his drink. He didn't see the sheen of tears in her eyes or the quiver of her lips. By the time he had poured himself a lager, she was in control of the emotions aroused by his tribute.

Whatever happened, whatever decision she made, she would treasure those words all her life. If only he had added *and I love you with all my heart*. How joyfully, then, she would have said yes.

'Let's have our drinks here, shall we?' He indicated a group of natural came armchairs with linen-covered cushions. 'The soup is cold today. It won't spoil if we don't start lunch yet.'

Maddie sat down and tried to relax. 'I need time to think about this, Scott. I'm still in shock. It's the last thing I expected.'

'Then you're a lot less intuitive than Dad and Francesca,' he said, leaning back in a characteristic posture, one ankle resting on his other knee.

He was still barefoot. Despite the fact that she had never been to bed with anyone, she had seen a lot of bare male feet. Not many were as pleasing as Scott's. If, as a growing boy he had resembled a puppy in having the large paws that indicated a big dog in the making, now that he was full grown his hands and feet were relatively small for his size.

There was nothing gross or hulking about him.

'What do you mean?' she asked.

'Last night, after you went to bed, they asked my intentions. I told them I was going to ask you to marry me. They're hoping, by the time they get back this evening, it will be settled and Francesca can start organising the wedding. Parents like to see their children settled in stable relationships.'

'Yes, but I'm surprised they think I'm a suitable wife for you.'

'They think you're the only possible wife for me,' he said dryly. 'I'm not everyone's idea of an ideal husband you know.'

'You come pretty close, I should think. You're good looking, famous in your field, well-connected, the heir to a fortune —'

'You don't include "nice", I notice.' His expression was teasing.

'There are women who would think your first four assets were enough.'

'But my first four assets, as you call them, aren't important to you?'

'Not important enough to make me commit my whole future to you without even thinking about it.'

'Hadn't it crossed your mind that this was where things were leading?'

Only as wishful thinking, she thought. But she didn't tell him that. 'When the time came, I assumed you would marry someone from Francesca's orbit, or perhaps an American...one of your sisters' school or college friends. But I felt you preferred your freedom and playing the field.'

'Playing the field is for young studs. I'm long past that phase. At thirty it's time to put down roots, at least domestically. That's why my parents think you're the ideal wife for me. Because you understand my lifestyle.

Because no other woman would tolerate my being away a lot.'

Maddie said, 'If she truly loved you, a woman would want you to do whatever you wanted, even if sometimes it was hard on her.'

'That's the theory,' he agreed. 'But I don't see it happening a lot in practice. Women are nesters. Their instinct is to tie a man down. They want him always around, protecting the nest. They also think they can change men. Sometimes they do, but it never works out that well. People don't want to be changed. They resent it, if only unconsciously. You understand all that. You know the score from the start.'

She had already finished her juice. He drained his glass and rose. 'Let's eat now, shall we?'

As he moved to the glass-topped oval dining table, now laid with fresh linen place mats, bamboo-handled cutlery, sapphire-stemmed wine glasses and all the other trimmings of what passed for an informal meal at Il Balcone, Maddie wondered if his parents realised she was in love with him.

Scott drew out a chair for her, pushing it in at exactly the right moment. It had taken her some time to get used to his perfect manners. Her grandfather had had no social graces. She did not think the difference was solely to do with their very different backgrounds. Some people seemed born with an instinct for gracious behaviour and Scott was one of them. He was as courteous to the staff as to his family. He would always be, she felt sure, an unfailingly courteous husband.

But were courtesy and creature comforts enough to sustain her through their marriage after his present desire for her had died down?

There was another factor that worried her. What was his fundamental motive for this proposal? Was it prompted, in part, by the fact that she had saved his life?

Love and relationships
www.cyberparent.com/love

What is romantic love?
http://65.107.211.206/trollope/rhbromance.html

chapter thirteen

In the centre of the table a colourful majolica tureen was set in a matching bowl of crushed ice to keep its contents chilled. Removing the lid, Scott said, 'This is one of Maria's specialities...spiced *zuppa di cetriolo*. Can you translate?'

'Going by the colour, I'd guess cucumber soup.'

'Correct.' Using a china ladle, he filled a bowl and passed it to her.

The meals at the *palazzo* had been a revelation to Maddie. She hadn't known that food could taste so delicious or be arranged with such artistry.

When Scott had served himself, he sat down, opened his napkin and then folded back the napkin covering some crusty rolls that gave off the delicious aroma of bread freshly baked. He offered the basket to her.

'Thank you.' By closely watching how Francesca did things, Maddie had learned not to cut her roll but to break off small pieces.

She sensed that it wouldn't matter to Scott how she behaved, but the women of his world might be more critical of her lapses of etiquette. For her own sake she wanted to conform, to fit in.

She passed him the butter. She didn't eat it herself. Having, at long last, fined down, she had no intention of letting the pounds creep back on. He *would* mind her losing her figure.

They drank the creamy-textured soup in silence. Maddie declined a second helping but Scott refilled his bowl. He had a big appetite. He also used a lot of energy. Early that morning she had seen him striding down through the garden on his way to the private beach. The bay was visible from her balcony. Some time later she had glimpsed him swimming the distance between the headlands, not once but many times. He must have swum for the better part of an hour, surging through the water like someone in training for the Olympics. That sort of exercise used up a lot of calories.

Deciding to voice the question that had been on her mind since before they sat down, she said, 'Scott, does your proposal have anything to do with the rescue? Do you feel under some kind of obligation to me?'

She had hoped that he would deny it, immediately and with vigour. But he finished the last few spoonfuls of soup, then touched his napkin to his lips.

In a measured tone that reminded her he was a qualified lawyer, even though he didn't practise law, he said, 'If it weren't for you, I wouldn't be alive. That puts us in a special relationship. If, afterwards, our paths had diverged, we would always remember each other. Or perhaps the rescuer forgets...but the person they saved never does.'

He paused to reach for her bowl and place it inside his own before tilting back his chair and stretching a long arm to put both bowls on the side table behind him.

Straightening, he went on, 'But an obligation...no, I don't feel that. What you did that night is beyond any kind of repayment. Asking you to marry me has nothing to do with what happened, except in the sense that it brought us together and, in a few weeks, showed us aspects of each other that normally take a long time to find out. I think we should marry simply because we're well-suited...and strongly attracted.'

Maddie had been toying with the stem of her wine glass. Now he put his hand on her wrist and caressed the smooth skin of her arm with the ball of his thumb. 'And whether you say yes or no to marriage, tonight I shall come to your room and make love to you,' he told her quietly. 'You want it as much as I do. Don't try to deny it, Maddie. Every time I come near you, your body betrays you. Your response is more subtle than mine '– with an amused downwards glance – 'but we both know it's mutual.'

He released her wrist and rose to investigate the main course in the dish with a silver dome covering it.

'This is another of Maria's specialities...her black olive terrine.'

'What are the white stripes?' she asked, as he placed a slice of the terrine on a plate and added a dramatic red sauce that she recognised as a combination of tomato and red pepper.

It was a relief to have something impersonal to talk about. Although they had known each other for some time now, she still wasn't used to the open way he talked about matters that with her grandfather had been strictly taboo. Sex had been a forbidden subject. With Scott, nothing was off limits. He was at ease with his body and all its functions. She knew it might be difficult for her to overcome her inhibitions.

'The stripes are made from ricotta cheese, Parmesan and egg yolks,' he told her.. 'The dark part is polenta mixed with black olive paste. When I was small, I used to go to the kitchen and watch Maria cooking. She'd give me titbits to taste and let me stir things. Polenta has to be simmered until it's thick. If it isn't stirred, it will burn.'

'What exactly is polenta?' She had wanted to ask on several occasions before but hadn't liked to display her ignorance in front of the others.

'In America we call it cornmeal. It's ground from maize. You won't need to add any salt. The olives and Parmesan make it salty enough.'

There was also a bowl of salad to be eaten from kidney-shaped side plates. Scott filled their water glasses and lifted a bottle of white wine from a cooler. It had already been uncorked and had its own miniature linen neckerchief to catch any drips.

'*Buon appetito*,' he said, as he picked up his fork.

'*Buon appetito*,' she echoed.

He was the first person she had met who seemed equally at home in two cultures, adapting himself to wherever he happened to be. She knew that his mother had died when he and his sisters were small. There had been an interval of five years before his father married again. No doubt it was during those years that Scott had spent time in the kitchen with Maria, a woman with a motherly manner but no children of her own, so Francesca had told Maddie. Francesca was also childless but clearly devoted to her step-children and they to her.

Before coming here, Maddie had always believed that the super-rich were rarely if ever happy. Her grandfather had resented rich people, although those who had been his customers had not been in the same billionaire category as the Randalls.

Although his business had depended on them, Pierre Sardrette's manner had always been surly, reflecting his deep-rooted dislike of people better off than himself. He had made Maddie believe that, spiritually, the rich were mean and miserable people who over-indulged their children and sent them to the devil. It had been a surprise to her to find so much happiness and loving kindness in Scott's family.

The puzzle was why did Scott himself take such a cynical view of marriage. His sisters appeared to be happy with their husbands. His father had grieved for Scott's mother for a long time before falling in love with Francesca.

Their lunch concluded with small pots of home-made custard topped with a crisp golden layers of caramelised sugar. All round the outside of the white porcelain pots,

Maria had tucked small sprigs of rosemary through a circlet of wire.

'How pretty!' Maddie exclaimed, when Scott produced the pots from the ice box.

As a child, she had detested the thin glutinous custard served with school meals, forcing it down as fast as possible. But this was a totally different taste experience. Maria's smooth creamy custard, delicately flavoured with vanilla and rosemary, and the contrasting crunchiness of the topping made each spoonful a pleasure to linger over.

'For someone who has put up with some tough privations, you're a sensual being when you get the chance, aren't you?' Scott remarked.

Intent on the pleasurable messages from her taste-buds, she hadn't realised how closely he had been watching her.

'You're used to food like this. I'm not,' she reminded him. 'Don't you think it tastes wonderful?'

'Not as good as some things I can think of.' His eyes were focused on her mouth.

Her pulses began to race. She knew that he hadn't been teasing when he said that, tonight, he would come to her room and make love to her.

Tomorrow he was going away. He wouldn't be back for some weeks. There was always the slight possibility that something would go wrong and he might never come back. Even though the risk was small, the chance that she might spend the rest of her life without knowing what it would have been like to spend a night in his arms was not one she could take.

Going to bed with him wasn't something she had to think about. She wanted it as much as he did. But saying yes or no to marriage...that was another matter, a decision needing deep thought without the distraction of his presence.

It surprised her a little that he wasn't planning to make love to her this afternoon.

With disconcerting intuitiveness, he said, 'I would like to whisk you upstairs as soon as we finish our coffee, but during the day nothing goes on in this house without the staff knowing about it. Francesca is rather strait-laced. She warned me the other night to be careful of your reputation. Tonight, after the dinner party, the staff won't be around. They'll have gone back to their flats or the village.'

As Maddie knew, several of the senior household and outdoor staff lived in the grounds in converted stables and carriage houses.

'This afternoon I should like to go for a walk...alone,' she said. 'Walking helps me to think.'

'Is it really such a difficult decision? It's seems straightforward to me.' Scott rose to deal with the electric coffee pot he had switched on earlier. 'Where's the problem?' he asked, over his shoulder.

'The problem is that you're not...we're not in love,' she amended. 'I think that's important even if you don't. Supposing we married and, a few months later, one of us met someone we could love...then what?'

'We won't be looking around for other people. Couples content with each other don't do that. It's only the discontented ones who have wandering eyes.'

'That's probably true if people are always together. But we'll be apart a lot because of your commitments.'

He brought the coffee tray to the table and waited while she made a space for it.

As he filled the demitasse cups, he said, 'You're a worrier, that's your trouble. Forget all the hypothetical negatives and look at the positives. You need a man in your life and I need a woman. I could suggest living together but it's an arrangement that's never appealed to me. I've had a few affairs in my time, none of them serious. I've never had or wanted a living-in partner. Now what I want is a wife. But I only recognised that fact after being holed up with you and realising, to my surprise, that I liked it. I thought you felt the same way.'

She wondered how he would react if she admitted to being passionately, desperately in love with him. There was no way she could do that unless every instinct told her he felt the same way. There were woman strong-minded enough to take that initiative. She wasn't one of them. And knowing that she loved him *would* put him under an obligation. She didn't want that.

Instead, she said, 'You said you wanted a wife who was your equal. But you and I aren't equal, Scott. We couldn't be more unequal...socially, financially, intellectually... every which way. Basically you're a prince and I'm a beggar-maid.'

The two little fans of sun-lines at the outer corners of his eyes became more pronounced as he smiled at her. 'But it seems to be the least of your worries that I'm planning to exercise my *droit de seigneur* as soon as we've seen off the guests at tonight's dinner party.' Before she could answer, he went on, 'There are more important things than social status, money and college degrees. I'd rate courage a whole lot higher and you have courage in spades, physical and moral.'

'Not really...I did what I did because it was the only thing to do.'

'I don't buy that, Maddie.' He placed her coffee in front of her, then replenished her wine glass. 'Your grandfather couldn't have made you do it. You could have backed out, but you didn't. You gritted your teeth and saw it through. That takes a lot of guts. It tells me that whatever goes wrong in my life, if you're my wife you'll stand by me.'

'But nothing is likely to go wrong and I can't give you other things that someone in your position needs. I'm never going to be the kind of accomplished hostess that someone who's had an Ivy League education would be.'

'I don't want an accomplished hostess. I want someone whose eyes won't glaze over when I ride my hobbyhorse and who is creative in bed...which judging by the way you savoured that *crème brûlée* I feel sure you will be. Women who relish good food are usually enthusiastic about all the pleasures of the senses.'

'What do you mean by creative?'

She found it hard to speak calmly about matters that for most of her life had been off limits. She had never had any close friends to discuss such things with and not enough pocket money to buy the teenage magazines that, judging by the articles listed on their covers, taught girls like herself what they needed to know if they didn't have a mother or sisters to enlighten them.

'Imaginative...playful...generous. Nothing kinky so don't start worrying about that,' he said, with a smile.

Leaning across the table, he made one of those gestures that raised her hopes that one day he might come to love her. He touched the back of his forefinger to the side of her cheek and moved it up and down. She had seen him give the same caress to the children, but when he did it to her it made her heart turn over.

'It wouldn't surprise me if you don't know what kinky means in that context,' he said teasingly.

'I do...of course I do.'

His smile faded to an expression she couldn't interpret. 'If you didn't, it wouldn't matter. Innocence isn't something to be ashamed of, Maddie. In a world awash with corruption, someone untouched by it is a very special person. I ought not to tease you. It's one of your most attractive qualities.'

'Really?'

'Yes, really. Girls who know all the answers are a dime a dozen. Girls your age who have never been to bed with anyone, never got drunk, never inhaled are as rare as swans in the Southern Ocean.'

'That's saying they're non-existent. I don't believe it. Maybe it's just that being...worldly is fashionable now so that's the way people pretend to be, whether they are or not.'

He raised a sceptical eyebrow. 'Maybe.'

'Anyway I expect I would have done all those things if I'd had the chance. I never had the opportunity. You keep telling me how gutsy I am, but I never stood up to my grandfather...never told him I wanted to go to parties and have boyfriends and fun like other girls.'

But even as she said it, she knew it hadn't been cowardice that had prevented her from defying her grandfather. There had been something she had wanted more than her freedom. His love. His good opinion.

'Not because you're a natural doormat, that's for sure,' said Scott. 'You've stood up to me a few times.'

But that was before I fell in love with you, she thought. I was weak with my grandfather because I loved him. I don't want to repeat that experience by letting you rule my life.

Aloud, she said, 'I'm not afraid of you. I wasn't scared of him in a physical sense. He never raised his hand to me. His anger took other forms. Sometimes he wouldn't speak for days at a time. I couldn't bear that. It was easier to do what he wanted than to have to endure those terrible silences.'

Scott drank some coffee, looking thoughtfully at her over the top of the cup.

'I know my father was concerned about my sisters when they were growing up. It's hard having daughters when you've been a young guy yourself and know how randy they are. I guess in his day it wasn't that easy to persuade girls into bed. But he didn't have any illusions about the pressure there would be on Alicia and Gaia. Dad's admitted he was worried about all of us getting into the drug scene. Your grandfather had the same concerns. That was why he was tough on you. I don't like to think of you being unhappy, but his being over-protective was better than the other extreme. You wouldn't be how you are if he hadn't been a disciplinarian, and I like the way you are.'

But did he like the way she was because there was something of her grandfather's autocratic temperament in Scott's own nature, she wondered?

Despite his claim that he wanted a wife who was his equal, in the absence of love on his side, might their relationship eventually deteriorate into something resembling the years she had spent hoping to win her grandfather's love?

Finishing her coffee, she stood up. 'I need time alone to think this out, Scott. I'll see you later.'

He rose. For a moment she thought he was going to reach for her. Instead he put his hands in the pockets of his shorts.

'OK...if you must deprive me of your company. I'd prefer we spend our last afternoon together, but if I stop you thinking straight I guess that's a good sign. Don't get lost.'

'I won't.'

As she stepped off the veranda, heading for the *palazzo* to change into clothes more suitable for country walking, Scott said quietly, 'Whatever conclusions you come to, we're still going to be spending the night together.'

Maddie walked away as if she hadn't heard him..

The *palazzo* was a few kilometres from the nearest village by way of a tarred road on which there was never much traffic.

The village, far off the beaten tourist track, had only one *caffè*. Maddie sat at an outside table and drank a *limonata*, probably the first of the Randalls' guests to patronise the establishment.

On the way back she tried to sort out her thoughts, but

they were still in a muddle when she arrived at the imposing stone gateway bearing the carved escutcheon of the original owners of the estate. From what she had heard, the place had been in a bad way when Scott's father had rescued it from dereliction.

She had half a mind to seek out Francesca and ask her advice. But she knew that pride would prevent her from admitting her love for Scott. It might be that Francesca suspected the way things were with her, although she had done her best not to reveal her feelings. Anyway the Randalls would not be back from their outing yet.

Not wanting to go back to the pool, she went up to her bedroom to wash her hair and re-do her nails for the evening.

The day she had had her hair styled, she had also had her first manicure. The manicurist, recognising that Maddie's nails had never received any attention other than being cut and scrubbed, had given her a kindly lecture on taking more care of them.

Maddie might have disregarded her advice except that the same evening Scott had noticed her clear-varnished nails, taken her hand to examine them and concluded his inspection by kissing the back of her palm.

Since then she had taken trouble to maintain the improvement achieved by the manicurist. Now, as she worked on her cuticles, her mind continued to grapple with the momentous decision of whether to accept or refuse Scott's extraordinary proposal.

Her heart wanted to say yes. Her head counselled caution.

She went down to join the others for drinks before dinner wearing one of the new dresses Francesca had insisted on buying for her. When Maddie had protested, Scott's stepmother had said, 'Oh, please...let me spoil you a little. I always longed for a daughter, you know. Alicia and Gaia were only at home for a short time after Jack and I married, and the things on Scott's wish list were wet-suits and equipment for his boats. Teenage boys are no fun to go shopping with.'

The dress she had persuaded Maddie to accept was a simple tunic of soft clinging material in a subtle shade of blue with a hint of shimmer about it. The fine straps showed off her tan and the fluid fabric displayed her figure.

In the shop, she had not been sure that her figure was up to this degree of display. Francesca and the saleswoman had been adamant that it was, and Scott's comments today by the pool had confirmed their opinion.

The others were assembled in a *salotto* with a lofty carved wood ceiling and deep coral-coloured walls hung with Chinese glass paintings and Venetian sconces. Two 15th century carved figures stood in front of a large windows, but the feather-cushioned sofas and chairs offered 21st century comfort.

Maddie paused on the threshold, watching everyone listening to an anecdote told by Jack Randall. His son, who was standing with his back to her, seemed to sense her presence and swung round.

As Scott came to where she was standing, his vividly blue eyes swept over the paler blue dress and the smooth brown flesh revealed by its low-cut top and narrow straps. By the time he reached her, the heat in his eyes made her heart lurch with excitement.

'You look gorgeous. To see you now, no one would believe you can go up a mast with a gale blowing. We're drinking champagne. Is that OK?'

As a burst of laughter broke out from the group behind him, he turned and put his arm lightly round her, his hand resting on her waist. His fingers and palm were warm and firm through the thin material of her dress. As they moved forward he drew her against him, so that her shoulder was touching his chest. All the men were wearing lightweight linen or cotton blazers over their open-necked shirts. This, Francesca had explained, was what Americans wore to be 'smart casual'.

'Champagne would be lovely.'

'Over here,' said Scott, steering her to an antique gilded side table which was probably of museum quality. He filled a crystal flute for her. As he put it into her hand, he gave her a searching look, but he did not ask if she had made up her mind.

Instead he took her round the room, introducing her to the people she hadn't met.

When dinner was announced and everyone moved to the *sala da pranzo*, Maddie found that she and Scott had been placed next to each other in a central position at the long table where Jack Randall sat at one end and Francesca at the other.

Throughout the meal, although he did not neglect the woman on his other side, Scott gave most of his attention to Maddie. He didn't flirt with her verbally. But in subtle ways he conveyed that this party was only a prelude to a private party for two that would take place later.

Between the main course and the pudding, when her hands were lying on her lap and she was attending to an exchange of cross-table views between the man on her left and the man seated opposite him, she was suddenly distracted by Scott's fingers closing over hers.

He held her hand for only a moment or two, but it was long enough to throw her entire nervous system into a flutter. Somehow, the knowledge that his hand was capable of feats she could never emulate – reefing sails twice as fast – made it doubly disturbing when those long brown fingers were gentle.

Coffee was taken in the *salotto* where Scott talked to other people, making himself agreeable to his parents' guests. Maddie tried to keep her attention on the people she was with and not to watch him. But she couldn't help an occasional glance in his direction, and every time he caught her at it and his eyes would send a signal that made her cheeks burn with swift colour.

Part of her longed for the guests to go home and the family to retire to bed. Part of her wanted the party to go on and on. Because when it was over...

Droit de seigneur (Charlton Heston in The War Lord)
www.unf.edu/classes/medieval/film/site/www/mcallister/warlord.html
and
www.bartleby.com/61/49/D0394950.html

chapter fourteen

It was after midnight when the last of the guests departed.

'It's a good thing you don't have to catch an early flight, Scott,' said Francesca, as her husband closed and bolted the massive front door, the staff having gone off duty some time ago.

'Yes, I'd rather have a leisurely breakfast before leaving for the airport,' he agreed.

'I shall sleep late and have breakfast in bed,' said his sister. 'So I'll say *buon viaggio* now. Take care and have fun, Scott.'

They exchanged a farewell embrace and Scott shook hands with his brother-in-law who was also planning to lie in.

'I think we should all go to bed, not sit up discussing the party. We can do that tomorrow,' said Francesca. Her smile included her husband and her step-son. 'You two have had plenty of time to talk. You don't need another chinwag… and you definitely don't need any more alcohol,' she added, linking her arm with her husband's. 'I know what you are when you get together. Scott's liver can take that punishment. Yours can't, my dearest.'

'My carousing days are over,' said Scott. 'I've drunk a good deal less than most of our guests tonight.'

If asked, Maddie could have confirmed that at dinner he had drunk more water than wine, several times placing his hand over his wineglass to prevent it being refilled.

'But bed is a good idea,' he added. 'After tomorrow night I shall have to forego the luxury of eight hours' shut-eye, so I may as well make the most of my last night here.'

The four of them followed the others upstairs, Francesca and Maddie leading, the two men behind them. At the top of the staircase, Francesca kissed her goodnight, Jack blew her a kiss, 'Goodnight, honey,'

Scott said, 'Sweet dreams, Maddie,' before all three of them went in the direction of the family wing while she headed for the guest wing.

In her room, Maddie hurried to the bathroom. She was not sure how much grace she had before he joined her. Would he shave again? Probably not. He looked as if he had shaved before dinner, but of course that was more than five hours ago so perhaps he would.

Automatically she took off her makeup. Only when she had done so did it occur to her that perhaps she should have left it on. But then he had seen her many times without any. Her naked face would not come as a surprise to him.

Brushing her teeth, she wondered if the reason he had not drunk much this evening was because he was going to make love to her. She couldn't think of any other reason. Perhaps making love was like driving and sailing, requiring a clear head and swift reactions.

She found herself starting to shake. Not from nervousness. From anticipatory excitement. In a different way, this was like sailing into the Southern Ocean: an unknown territory.

Instead of putting on the pretty filmy night-gown Francesca had insisted on buying for her, she wrapped herself in a monogrammed towel, folding it firmly round herself and tucking the loose end in at the side of her left breast.

Then, barefoot, she padded across the bedroom where most of the floor was covered by a thick cream carpet and the original tiles with their patina of beeswax showed only round the edges of the room. She had switched on the lights when she came in, but now she went to the window and felt for the cords that controlled the heavy interlined curtains. As they swept apart, moonlight flooded in.

Maddie turned out the lights, then went to sit down in a comfortable chair near the tall windows. It was hard – impossible – to relax! She had felt some measure of this tension in Charleston, the night before the race. But nothing like as much as she was feeling now, waiting for Scott to come to her.

There was no warning knock. The door opened and he entered, closing it quietly behind him. For a moment he stayed there, motionless, looking at her across the expanse of pale carpet, the hard planes of his face accentuated by the moonlight.

He was wearing a dark silk robe and, like hers, his feet were bare. As he came towards her she rose, her heart thumping against her ribs as violently as it had in the hairiest moments of the passage through the high latitudes.

'Have you made up your mind?' he asked.

'Yes...I have,' she said, in a low voice. 'I will marry you, Scott.'

He reached out and drew her to him. 'You looked beautiful this evening, but I like you better as you are now.'

His arms closed round her and he kissed her, softly at first and then, as she slid her arms round his neck and responded, with increasing ardour.

After such long uncertainty, Maddie could hardly believe she was finally where she longed to be and, this time, there was nothing to go wrong. Under her left hand she felt the powerful muscles cladding his broad shoulders. The fingers of her right hand were exploring the back of his neck and discovering that his thick dark hair was slightly damp. He would have showered before dinner but must have showered again before coming to her. Her eyes closed, she was aware of the lemony tang of his shaving lotion. But her dominant sensation was the feel of his mouth on her parted lips.

When he broke off the kiss and relaxed his embrace, she opened her eyes in surprise. But Scott had only let her go in order to untie the sash of his robe and shrug it off, letting it drop on the floor. As she gazed at his naked torso, often glimpsed before but never in situations where she could feast her eyes, he reached for the tucked in corner of her towel and gently pulled it free.

Maddie lifted her upper arms away from her sides to let the towel fall round her feet. Scott's hands closed on her waist and he drew her against him, her softness melding with his harder flesh.

For a moment they stood like that, gazing deep into each other's eyes. Then he steered her towards the wide bed.

Some time during the evening it had been prepared for the night by one of the housemaids. The quilted cover that Americans called a 'comforter' had been removed, and the linen top sheet and satin-bound light wool blanket folded back at an angle of forty-five degrees from the centre of the bed to the outside edge.

Leaning down, Scott took hold of them both and, with a one powerful yank flung the uppermost bedclothes aside exposing the taut undersheet. Then he swung her up in his arms and laid her on it, far enough from the edge for him to lie down alongside her.

Maddie's heart was beating so wildly she could hardly breathe. It was happening at last : the climactic experience she had dreamed of and wondered about for so long. She closed her eyes, waiting for him to kiss her again.

The click of a switch and the sudden awareness of golden light against her eyelids startled her and made her open them.

'Why have you turned on the light?' she asked, her voice close to a whisper.

'Because I want to look at you...all of you.' He, too, was

speaking very quietly, in a tender, playful tone something like the one he used with the children, but even softer and more intimate. 'All evening I've been wanting to undress you...to see every detail of this beautiful body.'

He swept a slow, caressing look from her throat to her thighs, and his look was followed by his palm and his fingertips. They touched her skin as lightly as a breath of wind but ignited a turmoil of hot sensation as he reached her breasts and slowly explored them. She could almost believe that she was the first woman he had ever touched in this way and that it was as strange and wonderful for him as it was for her. And when he bent his head and she felt his warm mouth following the passage of his hand, and his hand moving on down her body, she couldn't stop herself gasping as if he had hurt her, when in fact the feeling induced was a thrill of the most exquisite pleasure.

Or so she thought at that moment, only to discover soon afterwards that the pleasure had barely begun. Before long she was making sounds she had never made before: wordless exclamations of delight and soft, smothered cries of bliss that came from the deepest and most primitive part of her being.

'You sound as if you're being tortured,' he murmured, close to her ear.

'Oh no...it's lovely...*lovely*,' she breathed, her forearms flung above her head, her body quivering in response to his touch.

Scott was having a hard time battening down his own responses. But he knew it was vital to keep them under control. There was no doubt in his mind that, for reasons he could understand, she had lied to him about not being a virgin. That being so, it was crucial that he made this, her first experience of love-making, as good as it could be given the limitations imposed by her virginity.

They had the whole night ahead and he wasn't planning

to sleep much, or to let her sleep. There would be time to release his impatience later, but right now his primary concern was making it easy for her to accept his invasion of her body.

Not that she was showing any maidenly reluctance to give him the freedom of it. That mean old bastard who had raised her had messed up her life for a long time, but he obviously hadn't succeeded in repressing her most basic instincts. At least not up to the stage they were at. Whether she had inhibitions that would spring into action when, in a few minutes' time, Scott took things a stage or two further, remained to be seen.

Stroking her silky thighs, he moved them gently apart.

When she felt him making a space between her legs, Maddie's heart began to beat in the same way it did when she was at the top of *Sea Spray*'s mast. Except that up there it was fear that caused it to hammer. Here it was the excitement – and yes, a tiny element of apprehension – of expecting that very soon she would feel him covering her body with his and suffer the unavoidable pain that the first time always involved. But all women had to go through it and, when it was someone you loved with all your heart, it was worth a few moments of agony to experience the joy of becoming 'one flesh', as it said in the Bible.

Determined to stay relaxed and not to spoil the pleasure for him by revealing any sign of discomfort, she concentrated on the enjoyable tingles induced by the touch of his fingertips up and down the insides of her thighs. Although he kept his nails short, she could just feel them brushing the ultra-sensitive skin and part of her wished this moment could go on forever and what came next could be postponed for a while.

What came next was not what she was expecting. She felt him move from where he had been beside her, and she felt an impact on the mattress which she thought must be his knees landing between her spread legs. But, as she braced herself for the first sword-like thrust, what she actually felt was a touch as precise and delicate as a cat lapping cream.

For a moment it didn't make sense. And then, as she grasped what was happening, she felt an instant of shock, and another of wild uncertainty, before all coherent thought was driven from her mind by waves of ecstatic sensation that went on...and on...and on...like one of those endless rollers down in the Southern Ocean.

When it was over, and she was slowly recovering the power of thought, she heard Scott say, 'That, in case you weren't sure, was an orgasm. But there are other kinds and we'll work our way through them all.'

Dazedly, she looked down the length of her body to where he was lying with his cheek resting on her limp thigh.

At some point in the time – how long had it lasted – when she had been out of her mind, he had changed her position on the bed. At the beginning, she had had her head on a pillow and her feet somewhere near the footboard. Now they were both lying in a diagonal line across it.

She pushed herself up on her elbows. 'You haven't...why didn't...?' She wasn't sure how to put what she wanted to know.

'Because it will be better for me...for both of us...if you're totally relaxed. Lie down and stop thinking. It will be your turn later.'

In the end when, after she had experienced that incredible sensation again, and then a third time, he finally did what she had expected at first. But by then, as he had promised, she was so melted by pleasure that the final fusion of their bodies hardly hurt at all and it was he whose body was racked by shudders.

Afterwards, when she wasn't sure what happened next, he prevented the weight of his torso from being too heavy on her by propping himself on his elbows. For a while he stayed like that, motionless, and she wondered what he was thinking...if he was thinking at all.

Their bodies were locked in the closest possible intimacy but their minds were like planets set far apart in space.

After a while he kissed her cheeks and her forehead and, very lightly, her lips. Then he withdrew his body and, watching him, she realised that, while she had been totally out of her mind, he had remembered to ensure that nothing happened as a result of their coupling.

'Time you were asleep,' he said, leaning across her to switch off the bedside lamp. 'I'll be back in a minute.'

She felt him spring off the bed and, seconds later, heard the click of the bathroom's light switch and saw, for less than a second, his tall frame silhouetted in the doorway.

In his absence she moved back to where she had been at the beginning with her head on the pillow. But however long ago that had been, perhaps an hour, perhaps less, she felt a different person...her reason for being completed, the mystery revealed, her love for him reinforced by the way he had put her pleasure before his own.

When he came back, he retrieved the discarded bedclothes and drew her against him. 'Perhaps we'll do that again, but right now we both need some shuteye.' He turned her onto her side and arranged her to fit against him, his right hand closing lightly over her left breast.

She felt him brush a kiss on the nape of her neck and then he expelled a satisfied breath and was still.

Some time in the early hours, Scott woke up. He would normally have checked his watch, but he had taken it off before stepping into the shower and afterwards, his thoughts focused on making love to Maddie, had not automatically replaced it as he normally did.

The feel of her, snuggled against him, had the inevitable effect. While he was sleeping his hand had relaxed its hold on her breast. He recaptured it and began to stroke it with his thumb, listening for the change in her breathing that would signal she was waking up. But neither the movements of his hand nor soft kisses along the top of her shoulder were enough to rouse her from the deep sleep induced by what had happened earlier.

Wanting her, but reluctant to wake her if she was still exhausted, he reached a long arm to switch on the lamp behind them that would not shine directly on her. Carefully shifting his position, he looked down at her sleeping face, wishing he didn't have to leave her in a few hours' time. As matters had turned out, his commitment to the race was a bloody nuisance, but it wasn't one he could shelve, however much he wanted to stay and teach her to be as great in bed as she was in a boat.

Not that it would take long. Remembering the eager way she had embraced him even at the moment when he must have been hurting her, he felt a deep tenderness for her, and something else...something that reminded him of that dark time long ago that even now he preferred not to think about.

Switching off the past before old and disturbing memories could form, he realised that even if he hadn't been leaving in the morning, they could not have spent tomorrow in bed together...not under his parents' roof. His father had old-fashioned ideas about what was acceptable behaviour and, although like most of his generation he disapproved of the sexual freedom his daughters' generation enjoyed, he would be particularly shocked at the idea of his son 'seducing', as he would think of it, a girl like Maddie who, despite her daring exploits at sea, was patently what Jack Randall rated 'a thoroughly nice girl.'

Realising that, if he continued to lie here, he was going to break his resolve not to disturb her, Scott took a last long look at her unconscious face, imprinting every detail in his memory. Then he turned out the lamp and, careful not to disturb her, moved off the bed, retrieved his robe from the floor and left her bedroom to return to his own.

Several times in the sleepless hours that followed, he was tempted to go back. But something kept him from giving in to that urge. He did not regret his decision to marry. He knew that from every practical perspective he and Maddie were ideally suited.

So why, deep down, did he feel an indefinable uneasiness as if he were going to sea in a boat that hadn't been thoroughly checked and had a critical flaw?

When Maddie woke up she was alone, but there was a depression in the pillow alongside hers, showing that Scott had spent part of, or perhaps most of, the night with her.

Why had he left without waking her, without kissing her? Had he been disappointed with her response to his love-making? Had he changed his mind about wanting to marry her?

Assailed by doubt and uncertainty, she got up and went to the bathroom to brush her teeth. It was still early, an hour before she would have to appear at the breakfast table and behave as if nothing momentous had happened.

From what she read in books and magazines, for most people of her age making love, even for the first time, wasn't all that momentous. Providing it didn't lead to an unwanted pregnancy, it was merely the beginning of a series of trial relationships that hopefully would culminate in a long-term partnership or marriage.

But what, to others, was no big deal, to her was hugely important and life-changing. She was not the same person she had been this time yesterday. Then she had been a girl. Now she was a woman.

Perhaps, she thought, combing her hair, it was a more important transition for her because touching and hugging and kissing had never been part of her life the way they were with most people. The normal familial and social intimacies that most people took for granted were a preparation for the extreme intimacy of the man-woman relationship. She had missed out on that preparation.

Scott's invasion of her body, although wanted and welcomed, had from her point of view been like jumping off the highest diving board before learning to swim. Luckily for her, he was not a bungling amateur and had made the first time far less of an ordeal than she had imagined it would be.

What worried her was that she had failed him. Had she been too passive? Too uncreative?

'I want someone who is creative in bed...imaginative... playful...generous,' he had told her yesterday.

But I wasn't any of those things, she thought unhappily.

The whole experience had been so overwhelming that all she had done was let him do wonderful things to her. She hadn't been quite as inert as a Victorian bride lying back and thinking of England. But at no time had she taken charge and sprung astride him, or done any of the pleasurable things she had read that women did to their lovers.

She could visualise doing some of them later, when she was more accustomed to making love. In fact she felt sure that, given a bit more time, anything Scott wanted to do to her, or wanted her to do to him, would have her enthusiastic co-operation. But like everything else in life, from sailing to riding a bike, making love needed practice.

Last night she had been a totally inexperienced beginner. She had a sinking feeling that he had expected more of her than she had been able to give.

By the time she went downstairs, she had convinced

herself that, for an experienced man accustomed to far more sophisticated partners, last night must have been a disaster. There was no doubt in her mind that, before he left, Scott would extricate himself from their agreement.

In fine weather they always had breakfast on one of the loggias. The others were there ahead of her.

When Scott rose from the table to draw out a chair for her, his expression was serious, even stern. Maddie's heart sank, but she managed to pin a smile to her face as she said good morning to his parents.

They, unaware of what had happened, responded in their usual cheerful manner.

Then, as she moved round the table to take the chair next to Scott, he astonished her by saying, 'Dad...Francesca...I know you'll be delighted to hear that Maddie has agreed to marry me.' Putting his hand on her shoulder, he added, 'Unless, after sleeping on her decision, she has changed her mind. Have you, Maddie?'

For a moment she didn't know what to say. Was he announcing their engagement because he was too honourable to back out of the commitment? Somehow she couldn't see Scott putting chivalry ahead of common sense.

'Not unless you have,' she said, flushing.

'Once my mind is made up, I never change it,' he told her. Then he bent his head and kissed her lightly on the lips.

His father was already on his feet. 'This is wonderful news. Congratulations, Scott. We couldn't be more delighted that you've agreed to take him on, Maddie.'

He shook hands with his son, and kissed his future daughter-in-law on both cheeks. Then Francesca embraced first Maddie and then Scott.

'We've been hoping this would happen. We feel you're ideally suited. How lovely that a potential disaster has had such a very happy outcome.'

They said goodbye at the *palazzo*. Scott didn't want her to go to the airport with him. 'The time would be better spent making a start on your book,' he said. 'By the time I come back you should have the first draft ready for me to read.'

'I'm not even sure I can do it.'

'Sure you can. No problem.'

In their short time alone together before he was waved on his way by all the family, he made no reference to the time he had spent in her bedroom, and Maddie felt it was not the moment to mention her own disquiets.

When he kissed her goodbye, she clung to him, longing to beg him to stay, but knowing that he could not and would not.

'Take care...please take care,' she said, as he let her go.

'I always do,' he said cheerfully.

She could tell their parting did not pain him as much as it pained her and that intensified her misery, although she did not show it.

The next day, while Maddie was in the palazzo's library, sitting at one of the large writing tables and wondering how to begin the story of her sail round the world, Mr Randall came in.

'Francesca said you were here. Maddie, I'd like to talk to you. May I disturb you for ten minutes?'

'Of course. I'm not making much headway anyway...in fact none,' she said, indicating the blank sheet of paper in front of her.

'Wouldn't it be easier to write your text on the computer?' he suggested, with a nod at the desktop machine in the corner of the room. 'You're welcome to use it.'

'Thank you...I am more used to typing than writing.'

'Right, I'll set you up with a folder and a shortcut to access it quickly. Come over here and we'll do it together.'

Unlike her grandfather, with his almost paranoid aversion to the latest technology, Mr Randall, who had to be at least in his middle sixties, was obviously a practised user of computers. In a matter of minutes, the existing icons on the screen had been joined by one marked *Maddie's Book*.

'If you want to change the way the pages in the word processor are set up, and you aren't sure how, or you get in a muddle, just let me know,' he told her. 'I'll be glad to help out .'

'You're very kind...thank you.'

'My pleasure. Now, before you get started, why don't we have some coffee and I'll tell you what's on my mind.' He moved to a desk where there was a house phone and she heard him ask for coffee to be brought. Although he spoke Italian fluently, his accent had an America intonation, whereas Scott's Italian had been learnt in the nursery and was perfect.

As her prospective father-in-law moved to a comfortable leather sofa and beckoned her to join him, he said, 'Scott did outstandingly well at law school and I hoped he would practise law for some years before joining the business founded by his great-grandfather. It was a blow when he told me he didn't want to do that. But I remembered my own youth and the pressure I was under to conform to the family tradition. I offered him a compromise. He could do as he pleased until he was thirty, and I would back him financially, but after that I would expect him to toe the line as I did and my father did before me. Do you call that a fair deal?'

Maddie considered the question. 'I think there are many fathers who would have been less generous, but I'm not sure it's ever right to make anyone do something they have no aptitude for.'

'I think you mean inclination. Scott doesn't lack the ability to take over the reins when I step down. In fact I believe he has gifts that have largely been wasted in the years he's spent pitting his skills against the wind and the sea. It's been a great physical challenge, but not an intellectual one.'

At this point Benito entered the library with a tray and the conversation was shelved while the butler poured out the fragrant-smelling coffee.

As soon as the door had closed behind him, Jack Randall said, 'I discussed the future with Scott shortly before the Slocum race. He still hadn't made up his mind and I was impatient, even angry, with him. When we heard that his life was in danger, I made a bargain with God...as people do under intense stress. I promised God that, if he would spare him, I would set Scott free from all family obligations.'

Because she could understand precisely how he had felt – how she would feel if some unforeseen calamity occurred in Scott's current race – Maddie's eyes filled with tears. 'It must have been torture for you until you heard he was safe.'

Visibly moved by the memory and her response, Mr Randall nodded and patted her hand. After clearing his throat, he said, 'The irony is that I believe in evolution, not Creation, but there are no atheists in the trenches...as they used to say of the First World War,' he added, in case the allusion puzzled her.

'And now,' he went on, 'I feel irrationally guilty because I still want him to take over when I step down. I'm telling you this because, although you're so young, you have been tried and tested in a way most people never are. I think you're wiser than your years, and certainly you have far more influence on my son than I or anyone else does.'

This was so far from the truth, that Maddie could only say, 'I feel Scott must make his own decisions and do what *he* thinks is right. Whatever he decides will be fine by me...and I'll do my best to be the kind of wife he needs in whichever life he chooses...the sea, or being your successor.'

Then, prompted by curiosity, she asked, 'Who will succeed you if Scott decides not to, Mr Randall?'

'A cousin of mine has a daughter who also trained as a lawyer and has worked her way up to a senior executive position with our company entirely on her own merit. She's extremely ambitious and would like to be my successor, but I have some reservations about her suitability. If anything, she is too focused. She has no personal life and no relaxations. She is not as good with people as Scott is. He has his mother's gift for handling people...winning them over. Has he shown you the photographs of them together when he was learning to sail?'

Maddie shook her head.

'They're in the desk over there. I'll fetch them. Let's have another cup of coffee."

Presently, when she had finished re-filling their cups, he laid an expensive album on her lap. Opening it, she found that all the pictures had neatly hand-written captions. In some of them Scott was on his own, in others with a tall, slim woman with the same thick black hair.

'He was a scrawny little guy when he was that age but, like the pups of big dogs, he had big paws,' said his father, as she studied the pictures of the shaggy-haired, skinny boy who had grown up to be an outstandingly personable man.

She wondered why Scott had never shown her the album. It seemed a curious oversight for a man not to show the girl he intended to marry these pictures of the woman who had set him on the course that led to their meeting in Charleston and more fateful encounter in the Southern Ocean.

Scott had been gone for a week when Maddie realised she couldn't endure the torture of being without him for months on end. Until now, she hadn't realised how desperately she would miss him. It had been bad enough when he had flown away to Europe while she finished the race, but at least she had been fully occupied then.

She was supposed to be occupied now, working on the book. But she found that writing was much harder than sailing a boat. Try as she might to concentrate, her thoughts kept skittering off in a dozen different directions.

Also she had less incentive to write now. Before, it had seemed her only way to make some money and keep her head above water. As Scott's wife, she wouldn't have any money worries.

But could she stand being Scott's wife if much of the time he wasn't there?

It was one thing to wave goodbye to a man when you knew he loved you but needed to spend chunks of time pitting himself against the sea, or climbing a mountain, or trekking across arctic wastes. Many adventurous men's wives had to do that, and did it gladly because everything had its price and that was the price of loving that kind of man.

But when the love was all on one side, as it was in her own case, the separation was much harder to bear.

By the end of the second week, she knew that she could not bear it for the rest of her life. During a sleepless night, she drafted, re-drafted and finally finished a letter to tell Scott she had made a mistake and could not marry him after all.

Then she went down to talk to Francesca, relieved that what she had to say would be woman-to-woman. Mr Randall had flown to Spain to spend three days playing golf with a friend who had a time-share apartment at a famous course called La Manga.

Francesca listened without interrupting her. To Maddie's surprise she did not try to persuade her to change her mind. At the end of Maddie's explanation that she had been overwhelmed by Scott's magnetism but now knew they were not really suited, his step-mother said, 'Where will you go? Back to Guernsey?'

'No...*no*,' Maddie said vehemently. 'I may have to go back and attend to things, but first I'll go to London to talk things over with the literary agent, and then...well I'll see.'

'Do you have somewhere to stay?'

Maddie nodded. Pondering the problem of accommodation, she had remembered that her subscription to a British yachting association included associate membership of a private club with room rates far below those of central London hotels.

She said, 'I'll give you my address and telephone number, but please don't let on that you have it, Francesca. Scott might take it into his head to come chasing after me, and I don't want that. It's better that we don't meet again.'

'It's your decision, but I must say I'm very sorry that you feel this way. Both Jack and I felt you two were ideally suited,' said Francesca.

But she did not say that Scott would be broken-hearted, Maddie noticed. Perhaps she knew that he wouldn't be, that he was incapable of love as Maddie defined it.

'I'd like to leave as soon as possible...before Mr Randall gets back. That's cowardly of me, I know, but I don't feel that I can face him,' Maddie admitted.

'My dear, cowardly is the last word anyone would apply to you,' said Francesca. 'I'll explain it to Jack. He'll be upset because he hoped that marriage to you would make Scott settle down. He would like Scott to give up racing and involve himself in the business. Jack wants to hand over the reins to him, but I can't see Scott wanting to take control. It's not that he isn't capable of it. He is. But his spirit is too adventurous to be contained in a boardroom. It would be like caging an albatross.'

For the first few days of the race, Scott enjoyed being back at sea in the company of men he had sailed with before. But it wasn't long before the enjoyment wore off and he wished he were doing this alone; or, if not alone, with someone quieter than these guys.

At first he ascribed his flashes of irritation to the fact that he was basically a loner. Not ashore, but here on the ocean. But, at the back of his mind, he knew that he hadn't felt like this on previous group races. What he was feeling was different from anything felt before : to the extent that when he should have been sleeping, he found himself lying awake, unable to settle, unable to rest.

It was after he got into an argument with one of the others, and damn nearly lost his temper, that he was forced to recognise what was wrong.

He didn't want to be here. He couldn't wait for the race to be over and done with, leaving him free to go back and complete the unfinished business he had left behind.

If Maddie hadn't been so unhappy, she might have enjoyed exploring London. In her present state of despair, its magic eluded her. Even lunch at a fashionable restaurant with the effusive literary agent, who seemed to think the world was now Maddie's oyster, did little to boost her morale.

'In France, their two top women sailors, Isabelle Autissier and Catherine Chabaud, are national stars,' the agent enthused. 'You can be a star here...a Number One best-seller.'

But what was the good of that, Maddie thought dully, if you didn't have the only thing that mattered...someone to love who loved you.

She did her best not to show how down she felt because she did need the money. But the other trappings of success she was being offered – media attention and public acclaim – seemed shoddy achievements to her. Love was life's only real prize, and it didn't come twice in a lifetime.

One morning, during breakfast at the club, she was called to the telephone.

After saying, 'Hello...it's Francesca,' Scott's stepmother added quickly, 'Don't panic. There's nothing wrong. Everyone's fine...including Scott. He got back last night and is now on his way to London. I should warn you he's in a towering rage.'

Maddie's stomach turned over. 'You've given him my address? Oh, Francesca – why? It won't do a bit of good. I explained how I felt in the letter. I'm not going to change my mind.'

'He hasn't seen your letter,' Francesca said calmly. 'I decided not to give it to him. I think it's better you sort out your differences face to face.'

'*What?*' Maddie couldn't believed that the woman she had liked and trusted had betrayed that trust.

'If you can face the Southern Ocean, you are certainly up to facing Scott in a temper,' Francesca said blandly. 'I expect he'll have calmed down a bit by the time he gets there. His flight lands at Gatwick at ten minutes to twelve your time. It might not be a bad idea to be there to meet him.'

'Certainly not!' Maddie said angrily. 'I shouldn't dream of going to meet him...and I won't be here when he shows up. I'll have checked out and gone.'

'If you do, you'll be making a big mistake. Stay there and face the music. It might turn out to be your song,' Francesca said quietly.

Without saying goodbye, she rang off.

Maddie replaced the receiver. What had Francesca meant by her parting shot? It didn't make any sense. She was tempted to call her back and insist on knowing exactly what his step-mother had told him to make Scott lose his temper and come belting over to London in pursuit.

The way Francesca had acted, taking the law into her own hands, wasn't fair to either of them. Scott would be exhausted after the race and not properly re-orientated, and the hours Maddie had spent composing her farewell letter to him had been a waste of time.

She couldn't even remember the precise words she had used to explain her feelings to him. Now it was more than likely that, in the heat of the moment, both of them would say things they would later regret. Instead of having their night together as their final memory of each other, it would be their first serious row that they would recall in the lonely years ahead.

Not that they were likely to be lonely for Scott. Sooner or later, he would find someone else. Maddie never would. She knew that as surely as she knew that day must end in night and life must end in death. She was a one-man woman. After all she had shared with him, she could never hold another man in her arms or her heart.

She went to her room and the tears she thought had dried up began to seep slowly between her closed eyelids.

Isabelle Autissier photos
www.sevenoceans.com/SoloAroundTheWorld/AroundAlone98-99/Autissier.htm

Catherine Chabaud interview
www.nationalgeographic.com/adventure/0011/q_html

Harvard University virtual tour
www.harvard.edu/about

chapter fifteen

'What's wrong with the passenger in 5A, I wonder?' an air stewardess who had been serving champagne before take-off on Flight 316 from Genoa to London Heathrow asked the senior stewardess on duty in the First Class cabin. 'I smiled at him and he looked as if he'd like to kill me.'

She was an exceptionally pretty girl and not used to male passengers glowering at her, though she sometimes got hostile looks from the women. 'You don't think he's a nutter, do you?' she added anxiously.

'I doubt it. He's just in a bad mood,' the senior stewardess reassured her, remembering the frigid response she had received from the occupant of seat 5A when welcoming the passengers on board. 'Maybe he's been made redundant, or his Internet start-up has gone bust, or his shares have taken a dive. There are all kinds of reason why businessmen have that grim-death expression.'

'You can't have looked at him closely. That guy isn't driving a desk,' her colleague informed her. 'He's got shoulders like a boxer's and his belt isn't hiding under an expensive account paunch. He looks more like a top tennis player, or a commando, than a boardroom type. Also he refused the champagne and asked for water.'

'I'm sure he'll mellow if you work at it,' the senior stewardess replied, with a touch of acid in her tone.

She was married to an air traffic controller and didn't approve of the avaricious attitudes of some of her younger colleagues who would let anyone pick them up if he looked rich.

When they had landed at Heathrow and she had pinned on her professional smile to bid the first class passengers goodbye, she noticed that 5A still wore a preoccupied scowl, though he gave her a civil 'Thank you...goodbye,' on his way past.

Even scowling he looked more attractive than the corporate executives who occupied ninety per cent of the airline's first class seats, she thought.

'Mr Randall is in reception for you, Miss Sardrette.'

'I'll be right down.' Maddie had recovered her self-control by the time the expected call came.

Instead of taking the lift to the ground floor, she went down by the stairs. They led directly to the reception hall where she expected to find Scott pacing the black and white marble floor. But he wasn't there.

'I showed Mr Randall to the drawing room,' the receptionist told her, her smile a tacit acknowledgement that Maddie's visitor was a man any woman would be pleased to have calling on her.

'Thank you.' Maddie turned towards the elaborately architraved doorway where the solid mahogany door was always open. Pausing on the threshold of the large room furnished in the style of a old-fashioned upper crust town house, she saw at a glance that the only person there was the tall man standing with his hands behind his back, his attention apparently fixed on the view from one of the three long windows.

'Hello, Scott,' she said quietly, moving into the room.

Immediately he swung round, his dark brows drawing together in a forbidding frown. But it wasn't his scowl that struck her most forcibly. It was the change in his appearance. Not only had he lost a lot more weight than she would have expected in the time he had been away, but he looked as if he hadn't slept for a week. She had never seen him like this: dark stains under his eyes, his cheeks no longer those of a naturally lean man but as hollow as if he were ill.

Dodging the sofas and tables in his way, he strode towards her but stopped short a yard away. 'Why have you walked out on me? What the hell are you playing at?'

'I left a letter with Francesca. It's not my fault if she chose to withhold it. She rang me this morning to say you were on your way. I'm furious with her. The letter explained everything.'

'You had no right to leave. If you wanted to go, you should have waited and told me. I had some things to tell you.'

His gaze shifted from her face to a point behind her. Glancing over her shoulder, Maddie saw that an elderly man had come quietly into the room and was looking at a selection of newspapers and magazines laid out on a side table, apparently unaware of the altercation going on nearby. Perhaps he was hard of hearing.

'We can't talk here,' said Scott. 'Isn't there somewhere private?'

'There's a small library along the corridor. It's usually empty.'

Turning, she began to lead the way. As she returned to the hall, Scott gripped her arm. 'We'll go to your room,' he said, in an undertone.

'Visitors aren't allowed upstairs.' She attempted to shake off his hand but only succeeded in making him tighten his fingers. 'You have no right to bully me like this,' she protested in a low voice, knowing that she couldn't break free without making a fuss that might attract attention. The last thing she wanted was a public scene on top of everything else. But nor did she want him in her room where most of the limited space was taken up by the bed and raised voices would be heard by the chambermaids who would still be working in some of the rooms on her floor.

In tense silence, she led him to the library. On their way there, one of the Portuguese maids came out of the ladies' cloakroom, carrying cleaning equipment. She gave them a smiling, 'Good morning.'

Maddie replied. Scott didn't. It was a measure of his mood that he ignored her. It wasn't like him to be discourteous to anyone, least of all staff.

In the library, he released her arm. She moved away to lean on the radiator sited beneath the window. Scott remained near the door, glowering as fiercely as before.

'I would have bet serious money you would never run out on anyone.'

'I didn't run out. I've told you...I left a letter. If you had read it you'd realise how long and hard I thought about my final decision.'

'You reached that decision on insufficient evidence.'

'I don't understand what you mean by that.'

'I've done some hard thinking too. The time that we've spent apart has finally opened my eyes to what should have been obvious almost from the beginning. I've been falling in love with you. Head over heels...hook, line and sinker in love with you.'

It was said in the tone of someone announcing they had a chronic condition which could never be cured and might worsen. The way he spoke made her feel she must have misunderstood him. Nobody declared their love in that glum tone. Did they?

Scott didn't move. He went on, 'For the first time in my life I didn't want to race...not unless you were with me. I couldn't wait for it to be over so that I could get back to you. Then I found you had gone...and, according to Francesca, you didn't intend coming back. When I thought you had disappeared without leaving an address, I nearly went berserk. The thought of not being able to find you... losing you forever...was unbearable. Finally Francesca relented and told me she knew where you were. But she warned me not to phone you. She said if I did that you might really vanish.'

Maddie listened to this outburst with mounting incredulity. This was a new Scott, one she had never even glimpsed before. Previously he had always seemed the one in control of the situation. Now, suddenly, it seemed to be she who had power over him.

'I suppose it's hard for you to understand why I didn't tell you I loved you before I left,' he continued. 'Now that I've sorted my head out, I don't understand it myself. But I guess if we don't want to face something, we're good at dodging the issue that we're not comfortable with. Almost the first thing I learnt about life was that loving someone doesn't guarantee they love you to the same degree.'

'Do you mean you were in love with someone who didn't return your feelings?'

He shook his head. 'I've never been in love before. Not like this. Not knowing it was forever. But as a small boy I loved my mother very much. After she drowned in a sailing accident, I heard people talking about it, saying that she shouldn't have taken those risks when she had three young children. I understood that to mean that she hadn't loved us as deeply as we had loved her. Now that I'm seeing it from an adult perspective, I haven't changed my mind. Life is a series of choices. If you choose to have children, you should be prepared to give up taking risks which could be fatal.'

The thought of him as a small boy, having to come to terms with the fact that his mother was dead, wrung her heart.

'Oh, Scott...I'm sure she adored you. Her death was a freak accident. She wasn't competing in a race. She was out sailing and a squall blew up without warning. Francesca told me about it. It was wrong and cruel of people to suggest that she didn't love you. When she realised she wasn't going to make it, it must have broken her heart to know she would never see you again, never hug you. If it were not for her, you wouldn't be the person you are. Your courage, your daring, your spirit of adventure come from her.'

Scott looked only partially convinced. 'She shouldn't have been sailing on her own. If the two of us are together...OK, we'll take our chances. But I'm never going to put you in the position of hearing bad news about me...and I'm sure as hell not going to stand for you sailing anywhere without me,' he told her adamantly. 'If we can't agree on that, then I'd rather call it quits right now.'

Maddie looked at him for a moment. 'Who's arguing?'

The blue eyes blazed. He covered the space between them like a leopard springing on its prey, except that, once she was safely captive in his arms, the fierceness in him abated.

'Oh, Maddie, I'm crazy about you...tell me you love me. I want to hear you say it.'

'I love you,' she told him, smiling. 'The night you made love to me, I had to bite the words back. But it started long before that. It started in the Southern Ocean, but I didn't want to admit it because it seemed hopeless.'

'Why hopeless? We were made for each other.'

'Yes, I know that...now,' she agreed. 'But it didn't seem like it as first. I thought you wanted to marry me as a convenience...that the love was all on my side.'

'You were wrong,' he said softly, his lips brushing her cheek.

Then he tilted her chin up and kissed her, and for the first time Maddie was able not only to let down her guard, but to cast it from her forever. To relax into his embrace, to kiss him with all the ardour of which she was capable was a delight beyond all her previous experience.

Some minutes later, she said, 'If you like we could go to my room.'

Scott's eyes glinted. 'A short while ago you told me visitors weren't allowed upstairs.'

'They aren't...but I don't mind breaking the rules if you don't.'

'I would break every rule in the book for you, and you know it.'

Scott would have liked to get married as quickly and informally as possible.

'But if you want a traditional wedding that's OK with me,' he told Maddie, when they got around to discussing the immediate future.

She had never given any thought to the kind of wedding she would like. Until very recently love and marriage had seemed out of reach. She was happy to go along with whatever he wanted, although now she *was* thinking about it, a brief and businesslike function in a registry office did sound much less romantic than a traditional ceremony.

Before they had made any firm plans, his parents arrived in London and came down heavily on the side of tradition.

'Why not get married from Alicia's house in Dorset,' Francesca suggested. 'Their village has one of the prettiest parish churches I've even seen.'

'It's likely to be the last big family get-together in my lifetime,' said his father. 'I enjoy seeing you girls dressed up. I don't mind dressing up myself. Never pass up the chance to have a great party, that's my motto. But yours is the casting vote, Maddie.'

She looked questioningly at Scott. He responded with the loving smile that still made her heart leap with joy.

'You choose the wedding. I'll choose the honeymoon. I think that's a fair allocation of the major decisions.'

Maddie turned to his step-mother. 'Won't a wedding from Alicia's house make a lot of extra work for her when she has only just had a baby?'

Francesca shook her head. 'I'll take care of all the organisation. I've done it for both our girls and helped my sisters with their children's weddings. I can do it on my head. All the rest of you will have to worry about is what to wear and that's no problem for the men. They already have morning suits.'

Maddie looked at a number of wedding dresses but finally chose the one with a skirt that reminded her of a lazy summer wave frothing gently over a smooth beach. With its modestly low neckline and long sleeves, the dress looked as virginal as she had been until the night in Italy.

She decided against a head-dress, her gauzy veil to be held in place by three pearl-tipped pins pushed into the coils of her hair which was going to be arranged in an upswept style by a local hairdresser on the morning of The Day.

When that morning arrived, she felt unexpectedly calm: a different person from the nervous girl at the party in Uruguay. How long ago that seemed.

Her hair had been done, and she was having a cup of coffee when her soon-to-be sister-in-law delivered a flat package wrapped in white paper and tied with curling silver ribbons.

'A present from the bridegroom,' said Alicia.

Maddie opened it. A satin-lined jeweller's box revealed a necklace made from several graduated circlets of almost invisible thread, rather like fishing line, on which, spaced at irregular intervals, were small pearls and silver and crystal beads.

On the card that came with the necklace, drawn with a fountain pen and black ink, was a heart and, over it and larger, the single sweeping initial *S*.

Maddie was wearing a silk robe over her bridal underwear, a lacy white bra with a white silk-chiffon camisole and lace-trimmed French knickers.

She undid the robe, shrugged it off and tried the necklace on. 'Could you fasten it for me, please, Alicia? Have you already seen it?'

'No, we asked Scott what he was giving you, but he wouldn't say. But he's always had excellent taste and this is just perfect for you, not only today but for all kinds of occasions.'

'It's lovely,' Maddie agreed.

The pearl drops she was wearing in her ears were a present given to her the night before by Scott's father. They had belonged to Scott's mother, all of whose jewellery Jack Randall had put aside for his son's future bride, knowing that this was what his first wife would have wished.

The ceremony was starting at noon and, all the time she was getting ready, Maddie was longing to see Scott in his wedding finery. She knew that he would look marvellous in it; not, like some bridegrooms, rather uneasy in a rented outfit that felt like fancy dress to them. Scott's morning dress was his own because he had been best man at numerous formal weddings, and she had no doubt he would wear it with the easy distinction he gave to all his clothes by virtue of his fine physique and inherent assurance.

When, at last, the moment came and she walked down the aisle on his father's arm and saw Scott waiting for her at the far end, she was unaware of the heads being turned towards her and the murmurs of approbation.

She saw only the tall, dark-haired man with the white carnation in his button-hole and the piercing blue gaze that had once swept past her and now looked mesmerised by her.

As he introduced his bride to relations and friends she hadn't yet met, Scott was aware that her confidence, once confined to practical matters, now permeated her whole personality. She was charming everyone who met her with her glowing smile and her friendliness.

From the day at the club in London when, for the first

time, he had told her how much he loved her, she had been metamorphosing into someone far more assured and carefree than the lovely but mixed-up being she had been when they met.

Although it still made him angry to think how her grandfather had dominated her life and restricted her freedom, the fact remained that, but for her strange upbringing, it was extremely unlikely they would be man and wife.

Now, with her standing beside him, the most beautiful woman in the room, so lovely it was an effort to take his eyes off her to make the small-talk expected of him, it was hard to remember the way she had been the first few times he had seen her.

Even today when, as she came down the aisle to join him, her radiant looks had caused a concerted murmur of admiration, it was not her beauty that moved him most. During the first part of the ceremony, before they made their vows, Scott had been wondering if anyone else at their wedding was fully aware how lucky he was to have Maddie to share his life.

Although hopefully it would be a long time before his father died, when that day came a load of responsibilities would be transferred to his shoulders. He had no doubts about his ability to handle them, but having Maddie beside him would make it a hell of a lot easier. She had already proved her courage and determination. No matter what they had to face in the years ahead, and it was too much to hope that their lives would always be trouble-free, he knew his wife would never let him down.

When the people they had been talking to moved away and they had a few moments to themselves, Maddie said, 'You were looking very serious just now. You aren't having second thoughts, are you?'

Her eyes were twinkling as she spoke, but she was

curious to know what had been on his mind while his thoughts were elsewhere. The others would not have noticed those twenty or thirty seconds of inattention, but she was becoming increasingly attuned to him. Compared with their previous relationship, it was like being in a territory where before she had been unable to speak the language and now she could.

'I was thinking how lucky I am to have found you,' he told her quietly. 'It's a needle-in-a-haystack business, finding the right person to share life with. Not many people do, but I have.'

'We both have.'

For a moment they looked deep into each other's eyes. Then a middle-aged couple approached to congratulate Scott and wish them both every happiness.

'Where are you going for your honeymoon, or is that a secret?' the wife asked.

'Even the bride doesn't know,' Maddie answered, smiling. 'When I asked Scott what clothes I'd need, he said two bikinis and something cool and informal to dance in. So I gather it's going to be hot, but that doesn't narrow it down much.'

What Is Love?
www.crystalinks.com/lovevideo.html

Love
www.tc.umn.edu/~parkx032/LVindex.html

Famous Love Letters
www.theromantic.com/LoveLetters/main.htm

chapter sixteen

Having made only a few air journeys, Maddie had a hard time guessing where they were heading when, about half an hour into the flight, she looked out of the window of John Randall's private jet.

Up to that point, Scott had been holding her hand and talking about the wedding. Then, suddenly, he had said, 'Time for a cat nap, don't you think?' and, leaning towards her had brushed a light kiss on her cheek before releasing her hand, reclining his seat, and folding his arms across his chest.

Watching him as, with closed eyes, he took a deep breath, exhaled it in a contented sigh and appeared to fall asleep immediately, Maddie wondered how long it would take her to accustom herself to the idea that for the rest of her life she would be able to watch him re-charging his batteries.

Scott opened one eye. 'Rest while you have the chance, Maddie. You're going to need a lot of energy before this day's over.' The shadow of a smile showed at both corners of his mouth as he closed that eye again.

She didn't ask why. She could guess, and her insides fluttered with anticipatory excitement. They had not slept together since their reunion in London. Perhaps in deference to their parents' views on such matters, his sister had put them in separate bedrooms.

Not that the arrangement would have stopped Scott sharing Maddie's bed if he had wanted to. But for whatever reason – she hadn't asked him that yet – he had chosen not to come to her. So tonight, wherever the bed was which they would be sleeping in, they would both be eager to resume the delights they had begun to share in Italy and London.

She didn't count Italy as her bridal night because she had thought it a one-off, and that, from her point of view, had prevented it from being perfect. In London, it had been different – a million times better – because then she had known that he loved her and they had a future together. But the anguish she had experienced between those two occasions had left her emotionally exhausted. Tonight, when they made love, she would be able to respond with her whole being, body and soul.

Before she followed Scott's example, she took a quick look out of the window. From her limited experience of aerial views, they could have been anywhere in northern Europe which had fields, woods, country roads and scattered villages. That ruled out all the over-urbanised places but included a large number of others.

Putting her curiosity on hold, she lay back and relaxed, closing her mind to everything but the intense happiness of being with the man who was now her husband.

When she woke, he was still deeply asleep. Maddie watched him for a while. Would she ever tire of studying the details of what, to her, was the most attractive face in the world? She didn't think so.

In London she had noticed that a lot of businessmen's faces looked as if they were mass produced. A few moments after passing them in the street, you couldn't remember what they looked like except that they all had the same fleshy cheeks and necks, the same office pallor, the same worried expressions. None of them looked like men who could sweep you up in their arms, or defend you, or make you forget the last shreds of your inhibitions. It seemed to her that most men had been emasculated by the world they lived in.

Scott wasn't like that. Even though, most of the time, he

behaved in a civilised way, he had not lost his essential maleness. It was under control, but there was a wildness in him to which something in her responded.

In case, even in his sleep, he sensed he was being watched, she turned away to the window. The view had changed. Now, in place of the fields and villages she had seen earlier, there were soaring mountain peaks and inaccessible valleys which still had snow in them. Could they be the Alps which stretched across southern Europe from France to Austria and beyond? Or could they be that other great mountain barrier, the Pyrenees? If they were, the aircraft must be heading for Spain.

It was not a country Maddie knew much about, except that it was home to huge numbers of expatriate sun-seekers and had lots of mass-tourism resorts all along its coasts. It didn't sound Scott's sort of place, unless they were heading for somewhere in the untouristy interior, perhaps an ancient castle now converted into a hotel.

If they were, she felt sure it would be both comfortable and romantic, and she wouldn't seriously miss the sea, the way she had in London and, a little, at his sister's house. Just because she had grown up with a view of the sea from her window didn't mean that she couldn't live without it. She might have to if Scott's future responsibilities meant they had to live in a city part of the time.

A drowsy sound from behind her made her turn. Scott was waking up, unfolding his arms and stretching them above his head.

He looked at his watch. 'Did you get some shut-eye?'

'Yes...I've not been awake very long. We're over some mountains.'

'That means we haven't far to go. Maybe twenty or thirty minutes more flying time and then, from the airport, it's about a forty minute drive to where we can unpack our bags and start relaxing properly.' As he spoke, he put out his hand and caressed her mouth with his thumb. 'I think the first thing we should do is to take a shower...together. How does that strike you?'

'As probably the most brilliant idea I've ever heard,' she said, smiling. 'Somehow it seems like a week ago that your sister brought me a breakfast tray and then came to tell me she had run a divinely scented bath for me to wallow in. Bridegrooms don't get those treats. I suppose, for you, the day started just like a normal day.'

He returned his seat to its upright position, then rose to cross to the bulkhead and open a refrigerator. Maddie caught a glimpse of bottles of champagne and white wine and cartons of fruit juice. But it was a bottle of chilled spring water and two tall glasses which Scott brought to where they were sitting.

'It started that way,' he agreed, filling the glasses, 'I spent fifteen minutes shaving and having a shower, and then I went down and found Pete was fixing breakfast. We read the papers until it was time to get changed. Then Pete drove me to the church and I stood around, wondering how you were feeling...if you had changed your mind.'

'You *didn't seriously* think that, did you? Why would I change my mind, for heaven's sake?'

'A large family can be a bit overwhelming if you're not used to it. You haven't had much time to yourself since the preparations started. I thought there were moments when you looked kind of trapped.'

'Oh no, Scott, I never felt that...not for an instant. I love your family. They couldn't have been kinder to me if I'd been the perfect wife for you.'

'You *are* the perfect wife for me. They know it as well as I do. How long will it take to convince you of that simple fact?'

'As a matter of fact I've always thought I was perfect for you...from the moment I realised you were perfect for me,' Maddie told him, grinning. 'But that was just *my* opinion. I could see that, from a worldly point of view, I wouldn't be most people's choice for Scott Randall's bride.'

'To hell with most people. What do they know about anything?' Scott clinked his glass against hers and took a long swig of the water. 'Every time I read the papers I think how few people understand the realities of life,' he went on. 'Then I remember that the press and TV show the world through a distorting lens. It's too bad they have so much influence. They try to make people believe that money and fame and power are worthwhile objectives. But all that really matters is love and friendship...and I've found both in one person...you.'

There had been a time when Maddie could not imagine him opening his heart to her like this. She had not been sure he had a heart. Now she knew for certain that he did and, even better, was willing to put his feelings into words in a way that, by all accounts, not many men could or did.

Now that there was no need to control and conceal her emotions, his tenderness brought a lump to her throat and the shimmer of tears to her eyes.

The pilot's voice came over the intercom, informing them that the plane had begun its descent and they would be landing shortly.

'Landing where?' she asked. 'I'm bound to find out as soon as we're in the airport.'

'I doubt if you'll be any wiser if I tell you. As airports go, Gerona's not in the front rank.'

Maddie called up a mind's eye view of a map of Spain. She could pinpoint quite a few places but Gerona wasn't one of them. 'I've never heard of it,' she admitted.

'It's a cathedral city between the frontier and Barcelona. Maybe we'll take a look round one day...if we get bored where we're staying.'

'Have you been there before?' she asked.

'Only once, as a guest of some friends of Dad's at their

holiday place. They won't be around this time. We won't need to do any socialising. I want you all to myself...the way we were at the beginning...but on more intimate terms this time around.'

He gave her one of the looks that never failed to excite her.

Had she had to take the wheel of the open-topped sports car Scott had rented for the last lap of the journey, Maddie, who had no experience of left hand drive cars, would have been less at ease than her husband for whom driving on the right was the norm and the UK's rule of the road the exception.

Having always thought of Spain as sun-scorched and arid, she was surprised to find that, at least in this north-eastern part of the country, it was unexpectedly green and wooded.

'Not at all how I imagined it,' she said, as they drove through a rural landscape of low hills sheltering isolated colour-washed farmhouses. 'Though I knew you wouldn't bring me anywhere that wasn't lovely.'

'Peace and quiet in a good climate are not too easy to find these days,' said Scott. 'They must have a lot of rain at other times of year to be this green now, and I'm told that the winds blowing down from the Pyrenees can be cutting in winter. You can see those high peaks in the distance.' He took one hand off the wheel to point them out.

He drove as ably as he sailed, she had noticed. In control but relaxed, not like the young bankers and other show-offs who had made her island's once quiet roads a perilous place for cyclists. Scott had no need to drive fast to advertise his machismo.

When she was beginning to think they must be near journey's end, he turned the car off the road up a narrower lane that followed the rise of a hill with trees at the top. At the point where the lane started to dip down the other side, a cluster of Roman-tiled roofs was visible. Beyond it, to her delight, was a calm blue sea..

'One of the last unspoilt bays on the Costa Brava,' said Scott. 'We shall be sleeping down there on the Harrisons' boat but having lunch at the house. It's looked after, in their absence, by a Catalan couple. Rosa, the wife, loves to cook. The Harrisons think she would leave if they didn't lend the place to people. The larger the house party, the better she likes it.'

While they were having drinks before dinner on a veranda with a sea view, Maddie said, 'In Guernsey there's a small cemetery on a hill overlooking the sea and the other islands. I was wandering about there one day and I came across a small rough granite headstone. Part of the front had been smoothed and on it was engraved a line drawing of two hands...a man's and a woman's...'

She took Scott's hand from the table between their chairs and lifted it until his forearm was upright. Then she placed her fingers between his thumb and forefinger. '...like this.'

She paused for a moment, looking at their clasped hands, his the larger and stronger but both somehow matched in their general appearance.

'Below the drawing were two sets of initials,' Maddie went on, 'two dates, eighteen-ninety and nineteen fifty-one, and some blank verse. *From life's troubles there is no escape. But with my heart safe in your keeping nothing daunts me.* The words 'safe in your keeping' rang a bell. I thought it must be a quotation. But when I went to the Guille-Allès public library to look it up, one of the librarians found a whole batch of references for me. The words 'safe in your keeping' are part of a prayer to be used at weddings, and part of a ceremony admitting new members to the Rotary Club. The phrase crops up all over the place, but we drew a blank with the actual words on the gravestone. Perhaps they were written by one of the people buried there.'

'Did you find out who they were?'

'I tried, but I didn't get anywhere. Nobody seemed very interested. After a bit I decided I'd rather not know anything more about them than that they were together for sixty-one years and loved each other as much at the end as they did at the beginning.'

'*But with my heart safe in your keeping nothing daunts me*,' Scott quoted softly. He turned their locked hands in order to press a kiss on the back of her palm. 'Presumably eighteen-ninety is when they met, or married, and nineteen fifty-one was when one them died. Sixty-one years is a long time. I hope we shall be as lucky as they were.'

Maddie's eyes filled with sudden tears. 'Even now, at the very beginning, I can't bear to think of it ending...as it must...eventually.'

He didn't laugh, or pooh-pooh such a melancholy thought. 'I can't bear it either,' he told her. 'Having found you, I want to spend eternity with you. And who knows – maybe, by the time we reach our diamond wedding, science will have found a way to extend our lifespans and we'll be together for a century or more.'

'I hope so,' Maddie said fervently.

After dinner they said goodnight to Rosa and Paco, and followed the path and steep steps leading down to the beach. A rubber dinghy was moored to a small jetty. The Mediterranean was flat calm.

Minutes later, as she stepped onto the sun-bleached teak deck of the old timber-built schooner that had been discovered and restored by the owners of the property, Maddie said, 'What a perfect place to spend our wedding night.'

'I thought you'd like it.' Scott put his arms round her from behind and kissed the side of her neck.

For a while they stayed watching the last rosy traces of sunset fade from the clear sky that promised a fine day tomorrow. Then, as the horizon vanished, sky merging with sea, they went below.

The between decks accommodation was far more luxurious than any she had seen before. The master's cabin had a double bed, not as large as the one she and Scott had shared in Italy but more than adequate for two people who would be sleeping close together.

They had made love earlier, up at the house, soon after their arrival and the shared shower. But now they had the whole night ahead of them and, despite the excitements of the day, Maddie had never felt less like sleeping.

'What time do you think we should go to bed?' she asked demurely.

'Right this minute,' said Scott, beginning to unbutton his shirt.

Laughing, she unzipped her skirt.

Winning the race to strip off, Scott whipped off the white cotton quilt and vaulted onto the bed, waiting with open arms for her to join him. Maddie stepped out of her panties and made a running jump, knowing that he would have no problem fielding her. One of the many nice things about being his woman was that – even though she wasn't and never would be fragile – he made her feel the epitome of desirable femininity.

He rolled her onto her back and leaned over her.

'Back where I belong...in your arms,' she said happily. 'And back where we both belong ...on the sea.'

Costa Brava photographs
www.planetware.com/photos/E/ECB3.HTM

The parador on the Costa Brava
www.spanishparadores.com/aiguablava.htm

Spain in 86 clicks
www.parador.es/ingles/85clicks/buscador.html

All About Spain
www.red2000.com/spain

Forthcoming titles from HEARTLINE:

OPPOSITES ATTRACT by Kay Gregory
Although *he* doesn't realise it, Venetia Quinn has been in love with her boss, Caleb, ever since he hired her. To Caleb, she's just one of the boys...but a passion filled night has consequences which neither of them could have anticipated...

DECEPTION by June Ann Monks
As a result of his childhood, Ben has always taken a serious approach to life, so 'Kathy Lam's' arrival – she faints in his arms – makes him realise what he's been missing. 'Kathy' has loved Ben all of her life, but what will happen when he discovers that she's been deceiving him?

TROUBLE AT THE TOP by Louise Armstrong
Highly ambitions and fast-moving Nikki has been appointed to close down a once successful business. The one man who stands in her way is gorgeous and sexy Alexander Davidson...definitely a force to be reckoned with!

APPLES FOR THE TEACHER by Steffi Gerrard
Ellie is an experienced teacher of adults, but finds it incredibly difficult to cope with Chris Martin – the most extraordinarily handsome and sexy man she's ever met. In fact, it is isn't long before Ellie is beginning to wonder if Chris Martin is all that he seems.

Why not start a new romance today with Heartline Books. We will send you an exciting Heartline romance ABSOLUTELY FREE. You can then discover the benefits of our home delivery service: Heartline Books Direct.

Each month, before they reach the shops, you will receive four brand new titles, delivered directly to your door.

All you need to do, is to fill in your details opposite – and return them to us at the Freepost address.

Please send me my free book:

Name (IN BLOCK CAPITALS)

_____

Address (IN BLOCK CAPITALS)

_____

_____

_____

_____ Postcode _____

Address:
HEARTLINE BOOKS
FREEPOST LON 16243,
Swindon SN2 8LA

We may use this information to send you offers from ourselves or selected companies, which may be of interest to you.

If you do not wish to receive further offers
from Heartline Books, please tick this box ☐

If you do not wish to receive further offers
from other companies, please tick this box ☐

Once you receive your free book, unless we hear from you otherwise, within fourteen days, we will be sending you four exciting new romantic novels at a price of £3.99 each, plus £1 p&p. Thereafter, each time you buy our books, we will send you a further pack of four titles.

You can cancel at any time! You have no obligation to ever buy a single book.

Heartline Books – romance at its best!

What do you think of this month's selection?

As we are determined to continue to offer you books which are up to the high standard we know you expect from Heartline, we need you to tell us about *your* reading likes and dislikes. So can we please ask you to spare a few moments to fill in the questionnaire on the following pages and send it back to us? And don't be shy – if you wish to send in a form for each title you have read this month, we'll be delighted to hear from you!

Questionnaire

Please tick the boxes to indicate your answers:

1 Did you enjoy reading this Heartline book?

   Title of book: _____

   A lot   ☐
   A little   ☐
   Not at all   ☐

2 What did you particularly like about this book?

   Believable characters   ☐
   Easy to read   ☐
   Enjoyable locations   ☐
   Interesting story   ☐
   Good value for money   ☐
   Favourite author   ☐
   Modern setting   ☐

3 If you didn't like this book, can you please tell us why?

   _____

   _____

4. Would you buy more Heartline Books each month if they were available?

   Yes ☐
   No – four is enough ☐

5. What other kinds of books do you enjoy reading?

   Historical fiction ☐
   Puzzle books ☐
   Crime/Detective fiction ☐
   Non-fiction ☐
   Cookery books ☐

   Other _____
   _____

6. Which magazines and/or newspapers do you read regularly?

   a) _____
   b) _____
   c) _____
   d) _____

And now a bit about you:

Name _____

Address _____

_____

_____ Postcode _____

Thank you so much for completing this questionnaire.
Now just tear it out and send it in an envelope to:

HEARTLINE BOOKS
PO Box 400
Swindon SN2 6EJ

(and if you don't want to spoil this book, please feel free
to write to us at the above address with your comments
and opinions.)

Code: SC

Have you missed any of the following books:

The Windrush Affairs *by Maxine Barry*
Soul Whispers *by Julia Wild*
Beguiled *by Kay Gregory*
Red Hot Lover *by Lucy Merritt*
Stay Very Close *by Angela Drake*
Jack of Hearts *by Emma Carter*
Destiny's Echo *by Julie Garrett*
The Truth Game *by Margaret Callaghan*
His Brother's Keeper *by Kathryn Bellamy*
Never Say Goodbye *by Clare Tyler*
Fire Storm *by Patricia Wilson*
Altered Images *by Maxine Barry*
Second Time Around *by June Ann Monks*
Running for Cover *by Harriet Wilson*
Yesterday's Man *by Natalie Fox*
Moth to the Flame *by Maxine Barry*
Dark Obsession *by Lisa Andrews*
Once Bitten…Twice Shy *by Sue Dukes*
Shadows of the Past *by Elizabeth Forsyth*
Perfect Partners *by Emma Carter*
Melting the Iceman *by Maxine Barry*
Marrying A Stranger *by Sophie Jaye*
Secrets *by Julia Wild*
Special Delivery *by June Ann Monks*
Bittersweet Memories *by Carole Somerville*
Hidden Dreams *by Jean Drew*
The Peacock House *by Clare Tyler*
Crescendo *by Patricia Wilson*
The Wrong Bride *by Susanna Carr*
Forbidden *by Megan Paul*
Playing with Fire *by Kathryn Bellamy*
Collision Course *by Joyce Halliday*
Illusions *by Julia Wild*
It Had To Be You *by Lucy Merritt*
Summer Magic *by Ann Bruce*
Imposters In Paradise *by Maxine Barry*

Complete your collection by ringing the Heartline Hotline on 0845 6000504, visiting our website www.heartlinebooks.com or writing to us at Heartline Books, PO Box 400, Swindon SN2 6EJ

WOOD NOTES WILD

Wood Notes Wild

Essays on the Poetry and Art
of Ian Hamilton Finlay

EDITED BY ALEC FINLAY

Polygon
EDINBURGH

© Editorial arrangement Polygon 1995

Pages 267–9 constitute an extension of the copyright page.

First published in 1995 by
Polygon
22 George Square
Edinburgh

Set in Fournier by Westkey Ltd, Falmouth, Cornwall and printed and bound in Great Britain by Page Bros Ltd, Norwich

Cover design by Red Letter

A CIP record for this title is available.

ISBN 0 7486 6185 9

The Publisher acknowledges subsidy from

THE SCOTTISH ARTS COUNCIL

towards the publication of this volume.

Man with Panzerschreck.
Ian Hamilton Finlay, 1993
Photo by Antonia Reeve.

List of Illustrations

v	Man with Panzerschreck
8	Ian Hamilton Finlay, Stephen Bann, Sue Finlay, Bernard Lassus
	Jessie McGuffie with Ian Hamilton Finlay
25	*Homage to Malevich*
31	*Pond Stone*; *Cloud*
38	*Westward-facing Sundial*
45	*Lugger*
54	*Emblem*, design for a medallion
80, 81	from *Heroic Emblems*
89	*Pacific*
97	from *Nature Over Again After Poussin*
115	Garden Temple, Little Sparta
123	*Elegaic Inscription*
148	Saint-Just
151	*Idylls*
176	'A model of order . . .'
	A View to the Temple
205	Ehrentempel model
219	*Flock*; *Aphrodite herm*, Stockwood Park, Luton
258	*Small is quite beautiful* (*Trophies of War*)

Contents

Acknowledgements	xii
Editor's Foreword	xiv
Notes for the Reader	xxiv
Introduction	1
Duncan Macmillan	
Poem: To Ian Hamilton Finlay	6
Edwin Morgan	
Man of Sparta	9
Sue Innes	
Early Finlay	16
Edwin Morgan	
Poor. Old. Tired. Horse.	26
Edwin Morgan	
Concrete Poetry	28
Stephen Bann	
The Aesthetic of Ian Hamilton Finlay	32
Simon Cutts	
Poem: Stonypath	36
Kathleen Raine	
Ian Hamilton Finlay	39
R.C. Kenedy	
Versed in Vessels: An Appreciation of Ian Hamilton Finlay's Fleet	46
Ian Stephen	
Ian Hamilton Finlay: An Imaginary Portrait	55
Stephen Bann	

Armis et Litteris: Ian Hamilton Finlay's Heroic Emblems	82
Cleo McNelly Kearns	
Poe and the Poetics of PACIFIC	90
Miles Orvell	
Nature Over Again After Poussin: Some Discovered Landscapes	98
Stephen Bann	
Aphorisms on the Garden of an Aphorist	107
Charles Jencks	
On the Contemplative and Spiritual Use of the Temple at Little Sparta	116
Michael Charlesworth	
Wood Notes Wild: A Tale of Claude	124
Murdo MacDonald	
The Idiom of the Universe	131
Thomas A. Clark	
Finlay in the 70s and 80s	137
Edwin Morgan	
Terror is the Piety of the Revolution	149
Alexander Stoddart	
Pastoral	152
Thomas A. Clark	
Eye, Judgement and Imagination: Words and Images from the French Revolution in the work of Ian Hamilton Finlay	156
Yves Abrioux	
Models of Order	177
Stephen Scobie	
Wild Flowers	206
Patrick Eyres	

Contents   xi

Features in the Park: Ian Hamilton Finlay's Garden at Luton	215
Lucius Burkhardt	
A Luton Arcadia: Ian Hamilton Finlay's Contribution to the English Neo-Classical Tradition	220
Stephen Bann	
Ian Hamilton Finlay	234
Tom Lubbock	
Appendix A	
Poor. Old. Tired. Horse.: Contributors 1961–67	246
Appendix B	
Ian Hamilton Finlay: Serpentine Gallery Exhibition 1977: List of Works	250
Appendix C	
Spartan Defence: Ian Hamilton Finlay in conversation with Peter Hill	259
Copyright Acknowledgments	267
Notes on Contributors	270
Index	273

Acknowledgements

I would like to thank the Scottish Arts Council for a grant that allowed me to travel to the United States of America in the early part of 1993, where I was able to research parts of this book. I should also like to take this opportunity to thank all of the individuals and institutions who made my stay there so enjoyable, particularly the Poetry/Rare Books Collection, at S.U.N.Y. Buffalo, and the Getty Archive at the Getty Center Resource Collection, Santa Monica.

Other institutions whose assistance has been invaluable are the Scottish Poetry Library; the Fine Art Department of Edinburgh City Library; the National Library of Scotland; the Little Magazines Collection, UCL Library, London, the Archive at workfortheeyetodo, London; Graeme Murray, Edinburgh; and the Wild Hawthorn Press, Little Sparta.

Many people helped and guided me in the making of this book. Particular thanks are due to Stephen Bann, of whom Ian Hamilton Finlay recently wrote that 'his comradely explications of my projects have been of the greatest encouragement to me since the long-ago day when he described "shaded paths" in an infant garden where the only verticals were rhubarb'. Thanks are also due to Pia Simig and Ian Hamilton Finlay for their contributions and advice.

Notable for their support, or for conversations and correspondence which clarified and encouraged, were Sue Finlay, Ian and Gerlinde McKeever, Robert and Penelope Creeley, David Levi Strauss, Norma Cole, Susan Howe, David Connearn, Tom Lubbock, David Miller, Robert Bertholf, Murdo MacDonald, Tom Clark, Harry Gilonis and Hamish Henderson. For others, for their sustaining kindness throughout, I thank them dearly.

I would like to thank all of the contributors for their co-operation, and Kathryn Maclean and Marion Sinclair at Polygon for their good humour and careful guidance.

Whatever is mine in this book I dedicate to my mother, my father, and to my sister Ailie.

Editor's Foreword

ALEC FINLAY

> O tell us, poet, what do you do? – I praise. [...]
> How have you the right, in every disguise,
> beneath every mask, still to be true? – I praise.
> How can the calm and the violent,
> star and storm, both know you?:- because I praise.
>   Rainer Maria Rilke (1921; translated by Harry Gilonis)

The essays collected here present a comprehensive survey of Ian Hamilton Finlay's poetry and art, from 1958 to the present day. Although attention has often focused on the diversity of forms and media that Finlay has employed, and the practice of collaboration which has made this possible, the essays gathered here argue convincingly for the continuity of his vision. It is rather the range of poetic expression, from profound lyricism to the confrontation of force and conflict, that seems to me the most insistently challenging aspect of his work.

    Finlay first came to prominence as a lively member of the international poetry avant-garde, most famously as a concrete poet, and later aligned himself with the artistic traditions of neo-classicism and the landscape garden; however, the continuity of vision these essays describe stands firmly against any separation of these activities. Considered as a whole his work challenges the conventional oppositions between avant-garde and tradition and between poetry and the visual arts (as it also avoids easy political characterisation). 'Poet' he still calls himself: an understanding of his personal vision of the role,

Editor's Foreword

and the duties it carries, will illuminate our enquiry. There is after all a tradition of poet-artists and artist-poets, stretching from the Renaissance to modernism, from Michelangelo to Kurt Schwitters.

As Hamish Henderson has said, Finlay is by nature a poet of the 'rebel' party. Alongside Hugh MacDiarmid he is our modern master of the flyting. Finlay's determination to be in perpetual opposition to the times inspires his most persistent conceit, the presentation of his allegiance to tradition as dissident; 'Reverence is the Dada of the 1980's as irreverence was the Dada of 1918'.[1]

This allegiance to tradition came about as a direct result of his in some ways unique activities as a poet — which is to say, as a poet-gardener — and the origins of his aesthetic, philosophical and political positions over the past three decades can all, in one way or another, be traced back to this essential physical and artistic activity. 'I am like the Greeks, in that I have to imagine everything in terms of a Solid Place'.[2]

The eighteenth-century poetic garden once held a position equivalent to what we now term the avant-garde. Immersing himself in this tradition, amongst others, Finlay discovered an existing body of knowledge which allowed him to fulfil the possibilities for a new poetics, first revealed in concrete poetry. Foremost amongst the values that he held in common with the landscape garden tradition was the belief that art and the natural world shared a spiritual dimension, made manifest in the relation between the two; something his own lyrical sensitivity to nature insisted upon, and which the modern avant-garde appeared to shun.

One characteristic of the poetic faculty, suggests Robert Creeley, is 'a much higher tolerance for disorder than is the usual case', and the possibility of a resolution of this disorder achieved through 'an intuitive apprehension of a coherence which permits . . . a much greater apprehension of the real, the phenomenal world, than those otherwise placed can allow'. Here is a traditional vision of the poet as the communicator of privileged experience; does this also have a ring of dissidence in contemporary terms? Tradition depends upon and is defined by such hierarchies; as Finlay makes clear: 'The inscription seems out of place in the modern garden. It jars on our secularism by suggesting *the hierarchies of the word*'.[3]

The quotation from Creeley is appropriate to Finlay's work, primarily in the resonance of the conjunction of disorder and coherence; but also, as a poet-gardener Finlay not only has words at his disposal but all the elements of the 'real, the phenomenal world'. In a garden the poem not only casts meaning over the world, it draws elements of that world within it, as aspects of its content and meaning.

Finlay's primary poetic gift is composition: 'Garden art is essentially a matter of composing different elements',[4] 'the organisation of landscape . . . grass, trees, flowers, and artefacts';[5] 'the thing I am really good at is what I call the lyrical . . . every situation has its own possibilities and the poet is the person who can best see the extent of these possibilities'.[6]

In his poetry there is a fascinating reach, inward towards the spirit of a particular place, and outward, as he summons absent figures, events, or artistic visions, synthesised within the composed surroundings of the landscape garden. His faith in the spirit of place singles his work out in terms of the contemporary art world. It implies an implacable opposition to a materialistic view of art. As a whole Finlay's garden, landscape and civic projects bespeak a radical renewal of public art. It is, however, the garden at Little Sparta that is his most widely recognised achievement. If he resists this it may be because the garden is so intimately a part of his life and of his artistic battles. His other permanent works do not as markedly share Little Sparta's character as a 'hedgehog garden';[7] they seem less defended. What Little Sparta represents above all is an example of commitment to a vision: 'my work is the very opposite of making a division between the real and the idea; to me the real is the material which is to embody the idea';[8] 'What a Possibility lies in a newly dug turf!'[9]

Through his gardening Finlay made the elementary but essential discovery that 'you can change a bit of the actual world'.[10] From this his aspirant Jacobinism emerged; to understand his politics fully – for example, the conjunction of the pastoral and the sublime in his interpretations of the French Revolution – this context must be borne in mind. Thus Saint-Just represents action, the embodiment of a Yeatsian 'mask' representing revolutionary commitment to the transformation of the world: 'What I like in Saint-Just is the very close relation between the thought and the deed, whether it is a matter of storming a barricade or transforming a garden'.[11] This equivalence – this fusing of the real and the ideal – is another arch in the bridge that unites his work.

Editor's Foreword

Finlay's poetry and art bear witness to a rigorous attention to form. From his early concrete poems to his idealist interpretations of the Jacobin revolution, his art presents exemplary 'models of order'.[12] What follows is a constant interrogation of these models; as Thomas A. Clark describes; 'It is almost as if he had embarked upon a *via negativa*, discarding successive forms as unworthy of his rigorous demands of order'.[13] The religious terminology is appropriate.

A general example of this self-interrogation can be seen in the way that the years Finlay spent creating the garden at Little Sparta are paralleled by the gradual emergence of the imagery of modern warfare in his work, for example the group of works which meditate on the theme of Poussin's 'Et in Arcadia Ego'. His garden was never allowed to be a 'retreat'.[14]

In his relation to language Finlay's interrogative stance can be seen to have a philosophical origin: 'I understand language (in my work . . .) as an effort to find a mode of language which is true to the relevant mode of being. In fact . . . it always turns out that the temporary resolution of the language difficulty occurs through a temporary intuition of a suitable form'.[15] Thus concrete poetry was a resolution of an early (pre-garden) poetic crisis: 'the movement of language in me, at a physical level, was no longer there'.[16] Set this alongside his explanation of the importance of the Revolution ('the Jacobins desired to change the being of everything'[17]), and a clear continuity begins to emerge.

Stephen Bann sums up Finlay's concern as the 'simple but fundamental question: how do we confer meanings upon the world'.[18] An interesting example of this – perhaps the most insistent example of Finlay adopting a tradition that runs counter to accepted contemporary conventions, and also one in which the 'language difficulty' plays a crucial role – is the dispute over the rating of the Garden Temple at Little Sparta and the events of the Little Spartan War. The purpose of the Temple is to declare a 'mode of being': it is a concrete manifestation of the garden's spiritual dimension. Finlay relates how the dispute arose:

> I became aware of a fundamental problem. It concerns piety and the total secularisation of culture. I wanted to actualise the conflict between my own vision and that of the surrounding culture.

> At this point (*circa* 1974) I had already made the old farm building into a gallery ... The word gallery does not mean what it used to mean ... [as it] is now merely an aspect of tourism and this is a false description of [Little Sparta]. So I changed the building into a garden temple (1980) and whereas before the building existed to house works of art, now the works – permanently sited in the building – existed to define the building as a temple.[19]

Finlay forces contemporary culture, 'a culture that has become purely material and has no place for the non-secular',[20] to confront a concept and function of art that was central to the Western European tradition. 'He presents us with no more important question than this one: whether Western culture has any meaning, or destiny, whatsoever, if it is divorced from the religious intuition of being' (Bann).[21] The authority of the secular state and the poet-gardener (or as Finlay would claim, the neo-classical tradition as a whole) clash over this issue of definition, one which extends by implication to the potentiality of human experience each vision allows for. 'The secular is something that only acknowledges one level in the universe'.[22]

The highest of these levels of human experience – a word we may be more comfortable with than hierarchies – is the metaphysical. In coining the word 'non-secular' Finlay clears a space for the unknowable, the unsayable. It is only in the realm of art – 'a construction that holds', to paraphrase Edwin Morgan[23] – that the spiritual characteristic of existence can be actualised. Hence Finlay's version of Wittgenstein's dictum, 'What we cannot speak about we must pass over in silence', to a determination, 'What we cannot speak about we must construct'.[24] For Finlay the poetic is the mode of language which most truthfully reflects the disparity and the depth of experience that characterises existence – hence his avowal of prose, 'consecutive sentences are the beginning of the secular'.[25] Poetry is an act of unconcealment, one which reveals the essential unity that relates all opposites – what Heidegger refers to as '[carrying] opponents into the provenance of their unity by virtue of their common ground'.[26] This is a fundamental tenet of Finlay's Pre-Socratic faith. Words are divine: they both allow for and predicate division. *Wild*flower. 'Terror and Virtue', or the rhyming forms of guillotine and garden trellis, are images of the rift that characterises human existence, the 'temporary resolution' of which is achievable only in art.

The theme of conflict in his art operates on many levels. In the Pre-Socratic cosmological model which Finlay adheres to, 'strife' is the dominant force: 'Conflict is one of the givens of the universe. The only way it can ever be tamed or managed or civilised is within culture. You cannot pretend that it does not exist'.[27] Here again is a characteristic refusal to 'remain silent'. Finlay confronts contemporary society with the violent imagery of its own time. Encountering his work, we are forced to construct ourselves as historical subjects. Although there is a movement in these works from provocation towards resolution, Finlay also acknowledges that he derives a Blakean form of energy from his flytings; so, on one level, the imagery is a commentary on creativity – the charge born of the frisson between 'disorder' and 'coherence'. 'It seems to me that artists in general want the triumph in the world of their work ... what interests me is the triumph of beauty and order'.[28]

Finlay's disputes or 'wars' are other means to interrogate culture. In the dispute over the Garden Temple his use of the word 'war' stems, he explains, from the refusal of the authorities to enter into 'meaningful discussions', and he refers us to 'the "limitless" aspect' of the dispute, in which 'The War is simply the mode of utterance of a barbaric society'.[29] He describes the First Battle of Little Sparta as an exercise in artistic composition: 'I saw that this was a great force we could really do something with, and I made this kind of battle scenario ... I saw that one could by lyrical art make this construction'.[30] In this conflict, Little Sparta – the garden, and the spiritual vision that is actualised by the Temple – are the form of his refusal 'to accept reality simply as a given'.[31] To the phenomenal reality of place is added a collage of remembrances; the philosophy of Rousseau and Heraclitus, the Revolutionary ideology of Robespierre and Saint-Just, the painterly visions of Claude and Poussin, the poetry of Hölderlin and Virgil, the metamorphoses of Philemon and Baucis: all are called to bear witness. These many levels of culture and experience evoked in the garden – time, the fleeting or transitory effects of the natural world, the drama of history, the woven pattern of mythology, and the eternal verities – are all embodied in place. They both spring from it and give it its full significance. 'Landscapes are *ideas* as much as things'.[32] If these 'wars' involve some threat to the garden, they also measure his commitment and vision of what art can achieve and the duties it carries. 'Art that stops short at art is not enough'.[33]

The radical extension in the materials and content of his art – whether in the shadows or ripples of a poem, or in a Saint-Just Vigilante raid on the Scottish Arts Council – and his personal sense of the lyrical, which has seen him evolve from poet, to poet-gardener, to revolutionary, are all reconciled in the central educative project of creating the garden. Subsequently all his work has sought to re-create the poetic synaesthesia of the garden, a place where individual works are gathered in 'areas', themselves connected by paths, glades and views, so that the experience is in one sense unique, and in another total. Thus it is true of the garden, and of his art as a whole, that there is not one narrative or argument, but rather a series of ideas or epiphanies through which we find our own way.

Consider the way Finlay composes exhibitions, such as the crucial one held in the Serpentine Gallery in 1977, the most important of the middle part of his artistic life. Here the work was presented in five rooms, each with a distinct theme: beginning with a 'Neo-classical Room', imagined as 'a small temple opening upon a garden at Stourhead or Stowe' (note: this anticipates the Temple at Little Sparta and the dispute over its status by some three years); a 'Neon Room', presented as a reinterpretation of his fauve concrete poems of the early 1960s; the 'Midway Room', an allegorical representation of this dramatic sea-battle of the Pacific War; a room of 'Embroideries'; and an 'Outdoor Room', containing slides of Finlay's own garden, as well as examples of his garden poems. The garden is presented as the crucial context for his work as a whole.

Finally, if we compare this with a crucial exhibition of his later work, 'Wildwachsende Blumen' ('Wild Flowers') in the Lenbachhaus, Munich (1993–4), we discover similar precepts. Where at the Serpentine Finlay had infiltrated the garden (specific gardens) into the gallery space -- because these distant places were a crucial context for the exhibition as a whole – at the Lenbachhaus place is insistently present in the historical charge of the Ehrentempel site[34], which is visible from the gallery windows. This is Finlay's chosen place to review his most important artistic statements on the themes of culture and politics,

Editor's Foreword

specifically the histories of the Third Reich and the French Revolution. In this exhibition we see the different keys to his lyricism: the panorama of epic history, terror, tragedy, loss, remembrance, spirit of place, and finally, in the central image of the wildflower – symbol of an endurance greater than that of empire – his lyrical sensitivity to nature. A reconciliation may be achieved here in terms of art; one which is denied us in the realms of history or politics.

In Finlay's work, meaning is ultimately dependent upon context. His art explores the limits of what can be said, and it returns us to the daily act of re-creating or re-composing our 'mode of being'. He speaks of his work as a series of 'temporary resolutions'; paradoxically these achieve a lasting character, in their material form, enduring sensitivity to place, admission of many levels of meaning and complexities of experience, and a sense of measure that is essentially metaphysical.[35] His work urgently demands that we attend, as individuals and as a culture, to the necessary task of 'endlessly interpolating' our own world.[36]

Notes

1. IHF, from *The Little Critic* 4 (Victoria Miro Gallery, London, 1988).
2. IHF, from a letter to R.C. Kenedy, quoted in Kenedy's essay 'Ian Hamilton Finlay', first published in *Art International*, vol. XVII/3, March 1973; reprinted in this volume.
3. IHF, from 'More Detached Sentences on Gardening in the Manner of Shenstone'. *P.N. Review* no. 42, 1982
4. IHF, interview with Everett Potter, 'A Forgotten Art'. *Arts Magazine*, vol. 62, no. 1, September 1987.
5. IHF, interview with Paul Crowther, 'Classicism, Piety and Nature', *Art & Design* Profile no. 36, Autumn 1994.
6. *Ibid.*
7. 'Many English gardens have been hedgehog gardens, enclaves standing for one kind of culture against a surrounding culture'. IHF, interview with Everett Potter (see note 4). See also Patrick Eyres' essay, ' 'Hedgehog' Stonypath & the Little Spartan War', *Cencrastus*, no. 22, Winter 1986.
8. IHF, interview with Paul Crowther (see note 5).
9. IHF, *Domestic Pensées* (unpublished).
10. IHF, interview with Everett Potter (see note 4).
11. IHF, interview with Tom Lubbock, *Independent on Sunday*, 9 February 1992.
12. IHF, letter to Pierre Garnier, 1963; see also Stephen Scobie's essay 'Models of Order' in this volume.

13. From 'The Idiom of the Universe', first published *P N Review* 47, vol. 12, no. 3, 1985; reprinted in this volume.
14. 'Certain gardens are described as retreats when they are really attacks'. IHF, from 'Unconnected Sentences on Gardening'. *Nature Over Again After Poussin*, Collins Exhibition Hall, Glasgow.
15. IHF, interview with Peter Hill, 'Spartan Defence', *Studio International*, vol 196, no. 1004, 1984. Reprinted in this volume as Appendix C.
16. IHF, letter to Pierre Garnier (see note 12).
17. IHF, quoted in John B. Ravenal and Andrea Miller-Keller, 'Ian Hamilton Finlay: The Garden and the Revolution', Philadelphia Museum of Art, 1991.
18. Stephen Bann, 'Ian Hamilton Finlay: An Imaginary Portrait', Serpentine Gallery, London 1977; reprinted in this volume.
19. IHF, interview with Paul Crowther (see note 5).
20. IHF, interview with Everett Potter (see note 4).
21. Stephen Bann, from his essay in 'Nature Over Again After Poussin', exhibition catalogue; reprinted in this volume.
22. IHF, quoted in 'Ian Hamilton Finlay: The Garden and the Revolution' (see note 17).
23. Edwin Morgan, 'To Ian Hamilton Finlay', in *Collected Poems* (Carcanet Press, Manchester, 1990); reprinted in this volume.
24. IHF, *7.01* (Wild Hawthorn Press, 1993); also in *Interpolations in Hegel* (Wild Hawthorn Press, 1984).
25. *Interpolations in Hegel*. Table Talk of Ian Hamilton Finlay, Barbarian Press, Vancouver, Canada 1981.
26. Martin Heidegger, 'The Origin of the Work of Art', *Basic Writings* (Harper Collins, San Francisco, 1977).
27. IHF, quoted in Malise Ruthven, 'Gardens, Politics of Little Sparta', *Architectural Digest*, July 1989.
28. IHF, interview with Everett Potter (see note 4).
29. IHF, interview with Peter Hill (see Appendix C).
30. IHF, interview with Paul Crowther (see note 5).
31. *Ibid.*
32. IHF, quoted in Patrick Eyres, 'A People's Arcadia', *New Arcadians' Journal*, no. 33–34, 1992.
33. IHF, interview with Everett Potter (see note 4).
34. See Patrick Eyres' essay 'Wild Flowers' (reprinted in this volume) for a detailed consideration of Finlay's Ehrentempel project.
35. 'Every eternity is a measure of things eternal, and every time of things in time; and these two are the only measures of life and movement in things'. Proclus, *The Elements of Theology*, quoted by Ian Hamilton Finlay in the catalogue of his exhibition *Unnatural Pebbles*, Graeme Murray Gallery, Edinburgh, 1981.
36. The phrase is Walter Benjamin's.

Notes for the Reader

The following brief notes may clarify some points.

For a biographical survey of Ian Hamilton Finlay's life and work, see *Ian Hamilton Finlay: A Visual Primer* by Yves Abrioux (Reaktion Books), and also the various essays, reminiscences and letters published in *Chapman* 78–9.

The Wild Hawthorn Press was founded by Finlay, with Jessie McGuffie, in 1961. During the early 1960s the press published poets and artists such as Lorine Niedecker, Louis Zukofsky, Gael Turnbull, Robert Lax, and Victor Vasarely. Subsequently it published Finlay's work exclusively.

In common with many contemporary artists Finlay works with collaborators. It has remained his practice to credit these collaborators in the catalogues of his exhibitions, as, for example, in Appendix B.

From 1966 to 1989 Finlay's primary collaborator was his wife Sue Finlay. Together they created the garden at Stonypath, Little Sparta. She also collaborated on the realisation of his exhibitions and permanent landscape, garden, and civic projects. Since 1989 Finlay's exhibitions and permanent landscape, garden, and civic projects have been realised in collaboration with his associate Pia Simig.

The Finlay family moved to Stonypath in 1966. Their new home was a shepherd's cottage lying at the end of the Pentland Hills, twenty-five miles south-west of Edinburgh. The land around the cottage had returned to moorland, and it was here that Ian and Sue Finlay set about creating the garden, of which Finlay has recently said 'I became quite inspired, not so much from inside but from outside . . . I became obsessed with the vision of a classical garden, which was absolutely absurd considering this was just a moorland and I had only a spade' (interview with Paul Crowther, *Art & Design*, 1994). The name Little Sparta was given to the garden in 1978, as part of Finlay's 'Five Year Hellenisation Plan'. The original name Stonypath is still used to refer to the house.

The garden at Little Sparta is open to the public between June and September, by appointment only.

All references to Yves Abrioux's *Ian Hamilton Finlay: A Visual Primer* are to the first edition (Reaktion Books, Edinburgh, 1985). This book is an essential companion to Finlay's work. It includes illustrations of many of the printed works, the garden at Little Sparta, and other garden and landscape projects, as well as a substantial essay by Yves Abrioux, and introductory notes and commentaries by Stephen Bann. The book is now available in a revised and expanded second edition (Reaktion, London, 1992), including over 400 illustrations and a revised and updated bibliography by Pia Simig. It is available in paper and hardback, (ISBN 0 948462 40 X). A co-publication in the USA is also available from MIT Press, Cambridge, MA. (ISBN 0 262 01129 8).

Unless otherwise specified, all publications by Ian Hamilton Finlay are published by the Wild Hawthorn Press, Little Sparta. They are distributed by the Worthington Miro Archive. All enquiries should be made to Greville Worthington, Saint Paulinus, Brough Park, Richmond, North Yorkshire DL10 7PJ. A complete catalogue will be available in 1995.

A catalogue raisonné of all of Ian Hamilton Finlay's permanent art works, gardens and landscape projects in Europe is currently in preparation. This will be published on the occasion of a major exhibition of his work in the Deichtorhallen, Hamburg in Autumn 1995.

Finally, the title of this book is taken from Milton's *L'Allegro* as it was quoted by Robert Burns in the emblem he designed for himself.

Introduction

DUNCAN MACMILLAN

If you enter Scotland over the Cheviot Hills, at the top of Carter Bar a breathtaking landscape opens before you. After the barren moors of north Northumberland, especially if it is a summer's evening, as you look down on the lush Border countryside, it is as though Scotland is a garden that you are entering and you seem to encompass the whole country in a single glance. You apprehend in a second what you can study for a lifetime and still understand only imperfectly. Ian Hamilton Finlay's art is like this. It is simple in form and yet wide in its references and rich in its meaning. His greatest single work *is* a garden, too, complex in its unity.

Through his work on his garden – certainly, as a unit, the most important work of art produced in Scotland for a long time – Ian Hamilton Finlay is a landscape artist and Claude, the father of landscape painting and of landscape gardening, is one of his great heroes. It was, however, not just Finlay's approach to landscape, but his whole approach to classicism that originally grew out of the inspiration of Claude. When he turned to installing sculpture in the garden that he had begun to create at Stonypath, Dunsyre, and which he later called Little Sparta, he turned naturally to Claudian classicism.

Claude paints the real landscape of the Roman Campagna in all the glory of trees and water and in the freshness of the morning sun. He paints the wilderness and the life of its pastoral inhabitants among the ruins of ancient Rome. Without disjunction, however, he introduces into this world the people who inhabit the poetry written when these great buildings still stood, the poetry above all of Ovid and of Virgil. Thus, in one of Claude's last and most magical paintings, in the age of heroes before the dawn of history Ascanius shoots the stag of Silvia in a world where Rome is already in ruins. The result in such a picture is not a sense of anachronism, but of permanence, of the constant relevance of history and of the heroic, and the perpetual struggle between nature and order and the violence that it entails. By innocently shooting the stag, Ascanius, son of Aeneas, brought discord to Italy. Out of this Rome rose, but also fell. The ruined temple stands for the completion of the cycle that his action began.

An important part of the inspiration of these poets was the pastoral life itself and, in Ovid especially, its beliefs: memories handed down in myths already ancient even then. In these myths the divine and the human inhabit the same world. In metamorphosis they personify the inseparable presence of the metaphysical in the physical, our awareness of it, but also of the gap between the ideal and the real. In one of Finlay's works, a homage to Claude's great contemporary Bernini, this is identified as the tension between the eternal, divine beauty of Apollo, god of the ideal, forever pursuing, and the fugitive beauty in nature personified in Daphne, forever escaping. Such classicism is not something dry and formal; as Finlay presents it it is human and profoundly poetic.

The idea of the pastoral as the simplest and most unadorned relationship of man to the natural world and so to nature in himself is central to Finlay's art, just as it was to the thought of another of his heroes, Jean-Jacques Rousseau. In Finlay's art, fishing-boats are one of the most frequent symbols of this. Still, in the twentieth century, the vehicles of the hunter-gatherer, in their search they make their tracks across the trackless oceans looking to the perfect order of the stars to guide them through the imperfection of this world. Like words, identified in their serial numbers by typography, they stand for focused meaning in the sea of unmeaning, just as the garden does at Little Sparta.

A key work in Finlay's oeuvre is the *Battle of Midway*, a sea-battle understood as a kind of garden, the achievement of order in the face of disorder. The garden at Little Sparta is just such a site of struggle, a battlefield between order and disorder. Since what is at stake is human order, the struggle is not just that of the gardener, battling heroically against the hostile environment a thousand feet up in the Lanarkshire hills, or against its equally hostile bureaucratic enemies: it is also and at the same time an ethical struggle, as exemplified by the Little Sparta wars. It is on that single premise that all Ian Hamilton Finlay's art stands. Art and ethics are indivisible.

If this seems an unfamiliar premise in modern art, it is not because we are being offered something new. It is because of what we have lost. Ian Hamilton Finlay belongs in a very long tradition which incorporates much that is best in Western art. At the very beginning of the modern era, Pieter Brueghel painted a picture of the blind leading the blind in which he proposed directly the identity of moral vision with the actual vision of the painter. In the eighteenth century this was made explicit by the empirical philosophers in Scotland, and among artists by Hogarth and Blake. In the nineteenth century, Ruskin developed it to make a passionate defence of the identity of moral and visual truth and, incidentally, based this initially on an analysis of landscape painting.

Ruskin was not alone, nor was his legacy sterile. Although the conventional image of modernism is of a non-moral art concerned above all with itself and indeed with the artist's self – with ego – there were many who thought and acted differently. This has been passed down through two lines of tradition which are reunited and flow together strongly once again in Finlay's art and in his struggle on our behalf against the secularisation of art and of society. One line comes through Malevich, Dada and the radical modernists who sought a reconstruction of our ways of seeing from first principles. The other line, native to Britain, descends directly from Ruskin through the Arts and Crafts movement. In Scotland its spokesman was Patrick Geddes who stood for the central importance of art in maintaining the moral discourse on whose vitality and constant renewal the health of society depends. Geddes' own vision of society derived not only from Ruskin, but directly from the thinkers of the Enlightenment; before them it had been formulated during the Reformation in the Calvinist vision of society itself as enshrining a metaphysical ideal.

Ian Hamilton Finlay belongs, therefore, in a very long tradition of Scottish thought: of thought, but also of action, for to make art is to act.

The identity of thought and action and the belief in principle lies behind his admiration for the great Jacobins, Saint-Just and Robespierre. In his struggle to assert the indivisible supremacy of principle, identified at Little Sparta in the Temple of Apollo, Finlay is a true classicist, but one can equally see his passionate defence of principle and the way it has led, without regard for comfort or consequence, to heroic action anticipated in the events of the Disruption in 1843, when more than a third of the ministers of the Scottish Kirk marched out of their livings and their livelihoods to defend the idea of a metaphysical society based on a belief in principle.

A few decades later, a similar idea of society was central to the ideology of the Arts and Crafts movement. In it the artist plays a social role. Far from constituting a strenuous declaration of the artist's uniqueness, if necessary apart from society, art should therefore be anonymous, even the product of co-operative labour. This is of course a feature of Ian Hamilton Finlay's art. He works with other artists and craftsmen in collaboration in his larger works; in smaller works he favours the anonymous surface and the multiple production of the printed page. So deeply ingrained is the romantic/modernist aesthetic of the artist as creator in the mind of many people, however, that this withdrawal of self from the art work actually constitutes an obstacle to people's understanding of his art. It is, nevertheless, a declaration of his dedication to their interest, not his own, and that the struggle in which art is engaged is one in which the ego is no more than a transient, a hireling whose concern is for his wage, not the welfare of the flock. Such an image returns us to the pastoral, not of Claude, but of another great contemporary, Milton. For him such hireling shepherds are

> Blind mouthes! that scarce themselves know how to hold
> A sheep-hook, or have learnt aught else the least
> That to the faithful herdman's art belongs.

It is fitting to quote *Lycidas* here. Ian Hamilton Finlay began as a poet and he is still a poet as well as an artist. In that poem, too, Milton makes it clear that for him, as it is for Finlay, the pastoral was a deeply serious form and one that focused the moral role of the artist. In this Finlay is his heir and in the essays that follow we are led through an exploration not just of a body of art, but of a moral vision that is complex, lucid, sometimes uncomfortable as true morality must be, but always guided by the artist's passionate commitment to the service of society through the high calling of his art.

To Ian Hamilton Finlay

EDWIN MORGAN

Maker of boats,
earthships,
the white cradle
with its patchwork quilt,
toys of wood
painted bright as
the zebras' muzic
in your carousel,
patiently cut
space cleanly!
There's dark earth
underneath, not far
the North Sea,
a beach goes out
greyer than Dover's
for ignorant armies.
Scotland is
the little bonfires
in cold mist,
with stubbornness,
the woman knits
late by a window,
a man repairing
nets, a man carv-

To Ian Hamilton Finlay

ing steady glass,
hears the world,
bends to his work.
You give the pleasure
of made things,
the construction holds
like a net, or it
unfolds in waves
a certain measure,
of affection.
Native, familiar as
apples, tugs,
girls, lettres from
your moulin,
but
drinking tea
you set for Albers
his saucer of milk.

(1966)

Stonypath, 1976
From left to right: Ian Hamilton Finlay, Stephen Bann, Sue Finlay, Bernard Lassus.
Photo by Michael Conan.

Jessie McGuffie (co-founder of the Wild Hawthorn Press) and Ian Hamilton Finlay, Edinburgh, early 1960s.

Man of Sparta

SUE INNES

He is very direct but also unexpectedly diffident. Why, I asked, is he so interested in the French Revolution? 'Because I am a revolutionary', he replies, looking at me sharply, then adding, 'at least I hope so'. And then, 'because it is the prime example of neo-classical art in action'.

Sitting in the porch-cum-greenhouse of the cottage he shares with Sue, his wife and chief collaborator, surrounded by wellie boots, spades, watering-cans and a pile of catalogue photographs to be checked, Ian Hamilton Finlay confounds stereotypes of the Great Artist. You could mistake him for the gardener around here, but then he *is* the gardener around here ... nor does he fit the Hamilton Finlay myth of some sort of wild man of the hills. He is friendly and courteous and self-questioning. A passion-flower plant grows luxuriantly up the wall; five grey and white kittens sleep in a box.

He enjoys talking. His currency after all is meaning – often questions will set off a preamble into pure linguistic philosophy. A friend describes him as having 'a fantastic lucidity' and the phrase seems apt. He has gleaming blue eyes of remarkable intensity and humour; he is deeply analytical and very serious but with a devastating wit.

Thrawn, passionate about ideas, ascetic, concerned with the spiritual dimension of art, he is a man profoundly out of step with his time – but with a clear vision of it.

At 63, he is a prophet more honoured outwith his native land. Working in what one French critic has called 'a northerly outpost of Western civilisation', he has had an international reputation since the sixties. No other Scottish artist this century has equalled his impact in the rest of Europe, but he is better known here for his battles with Strathclyde Region than for his work.

Though few Scots seem even to know where it is, most of the curators of the important European and American art galleries have made their way along the rutted field path to Stonypath, in Little Sparta, Dunsyre. There, where the words of Saint-Just carved in broken stone confront the sky; the marvellous garden and garden temple, the romantic landscape with its grotto and broken classical columns, the lochan and pools are now seen only by those who seek them out – closed to the general public because of the dispute with Strathclyde.[1]

He has major work in Italy, Holland, Germany, Switzerland, Austria and California; the British sculpture show which opened Liverpool's Tate of the North is called *Starlit Waters* after one of the four pieces he is showing there. His guillotine arches[2] were the centrepiece of the recent Documenta – the world's largest forum for modern art – at Kassel, in Germany. The French in particular recognise his significance; last year four exhibitions of his work were held in Paris.[3]

Foremost among recent commissions is one to mark the bicentenary of the French Revolution, which has now become embroiled in a complex political row and legal action.[4]

In Scotland he has more work in progress than ever before; his memorial to Robert Louis Stevenson for Princes Street Gardens in Edinburgh should be in place later this year. He is also doing work at Preston and Swansea docks, and has exhibitions in New York, Strasbourg and Milan this autumn. Not that this greater success – if that's the word, he's not so sure – has made much difference to life.

'We've never been idle at all... always been very involved in things. Usually battles. And it is idle to suppose', he says ruefully, 'that being known will be an end to the battles'.

He stays away from the glamour and high finance of the international art world; in recent years he has left his garden only once – in an ambulance, with a heart attack. Sue represents him at the fireworks and champagne openings his work is nowadays accorded. He works in his small workshop or at his typewriter in a study so filled with books that there is scarcely room for furniture. He gardens and he walks in the hills. When there was more time he enjoyed making model boats. But his is scarcely a quiet life.

Little Sparta is created within the tradition of the poet's garden – using inscription and metaphor and provoking philosophical reflection. But it is a very modern response. A stone aircraft-carrier is a bird-table and the smooth black slate *Nuclear Sail* is silent and threatening and beautiful beside the lochan. Neoclassical gardens like Stowe and Stourhead surround stately homes and are the product of great riches; this garden surrounds a humble farm steading and has been created on a bare, exposed hillside at 1,000 feet.

This Temple to Apollo was once a byre. The temple pool is beautiful with its water lilies and poetry, but it was also dug for his children to sail on in a little boat that he made them. Now that it exists it is easy perhaps to accept and praise it – but twenty years ago there was only moorland and one battered ash tree.

It began, appropriately, as a tattie patch. Ian and Sue had moved to the abandoned croft in the Pentlands with their baby son Eck 'because where we were living had no running water, and you need that with a baby. There was the ground so we started to dig it. There was no thought then of making a garden that anyone would take seriously, or come to see. It's a question of whatever situation you are in you make the best of it. . . .'

His use of the classical – highly unfashionable until recently – grew out of working in the garden when he began to create and place inscriptions for it. 'The natural way to cut letters in stone is in classical form and obviously that influences one's manner of composing for it. And there can be no doubt that the most practical way of siting things in gardens is the classical way'.

'The fact is that what I've always been interested in in all my work has been some vision of order and I've adopted different solutions to that ... I don't really mind what means I use at all'. It has been suggested that he is afraid of the modern. 'I'm *not* afraid of the modern. I'm not afraid of any of it. They're all means of achieving an end – producing order, clarity'.

His work has great depth and resonance. It is, he says 'a cross which marks the intersection of different lines of culture and experience ... a very precise point of tension'. He has drawn on some of the most stark of modern images – tanks, the SS flash. Because of this he has been called a Nazi by sections of the French press, and his memorial to the Revolution put in jeopardy. The accusation is wide of the mark, though he is no easier to categorise politically than he is as an artist; he hates liberalism as much as fascism.

'In the same way as the Greeks used Pan to mean savage nature, I used the fighting SS. The image of Pan no longer carries any terror for us . . .' It is important, he says, to use imagery of one's time.

'I try to confront this pervasive unclear, liberal, sloppy thinking, with its decadence and lack of decision, its refusal to set up values and stand by those values. What a long way from the Greeks! A whimsical universe, without conflict, without tragedy. I don't apologise for the militaria because I hope I work across the whole range of the world. The sum of my work is tragic. But it is centred on the lyrical; so much of it is pastoral, Virgilian. . . .'

For a poet and artist, his use of collaborators to carry out his ideas – craftsmen in stone and print and other contemporary artists – is highly unusual. It also has the advantage of making him unusually prolific. 'When I wrote drama I had to rely on actors, producers and people so it wasn't an unfamiliar idea to me'. You need, he says, the basic integrity of first-rate craftsmanship. 'Either I had to learn how to do all those things myself or else I had to start and collaborate with other people. Also the nice thing about that is that it removes it from the area of self-expression'.

Equally singular is his insistence on art as an ethical practice. 'I have always had an ideological or ethical extension to what I am doing – not in terms of a message but in that I always see the particular work as being part of some general ethical or ideological concern'. Tolstoy is an influence he quotes.

This is perhaps Finlay's point of greatest divergence from the dominant trends in art this century. 'Ian for me represents the first break in the formalist attitude', says Jean de Loisy, who commissioned the Revolution monument. 'It has become eccentric to be involved in philosophy – in meaning – rather than shapes and forms only. But there is no philosophical problem that has no resonance in Ian's art'.

It also separates him from the Scottish tradition in which the artist as intellectual has (so far) no real place.

'One of the things that used to separate me very much from Scotland was the fact that I felt always so at home with art. I never felt any need to agonise over it or justify it in any way. And I've never doubted the power of art'.

He was born in the Bahamas, which is, he says, 'ridiculous, not in character at all'. It happened because his father had a schooner and had made money by boot-legging. But he lost it all, the family came back to Glasgow and poverty. Ian's schooldays were ended at 13 by war; evacuated to Perthshire, he ran wild — but also read books on cubism. A short spell at Glasgow School of Art — 'I didn't go much' — was interrupted by his call-up. After three and a half years as a sergeant in the RASC he was demobbed and went to Orkney where, working as a shepherd, he began to write — mainly short stories, which were first published in the fifties. Plays for radio and theatre followed, and then his concrete poetry in which circles he rapidly became famous — praised abroad but controversial at home.

'It would be idle to pretend that Scotland's ever been very welcoming to me', he says. 'I've always been attacked because I always did things ten years before they became acceptable. The thing that irks me now is that in all these battles you're only going to be shown to be right or wrong after ten or fifteen years and then, if you raise the subject, they say "oh, can't you forget all that?"

'I'm not complaining, I recognise the necessity of battles. It just sometimes seems to me that Scotland forgets too rapidly what attitudes it had ten years ago'.

He has had a great many disputes — with publishers, the Scottish Arts Council, and, of course, the on-going affair with Strathclyde — all characterised by intense theatricality, angry letters and pre-emptive ducking. He uses his work, wit and devastating sense of analogy to attack his critics; for example, placing heads of his enemies in guillotine baskets in the Fondation Cartier exhibition. A memorial now marks the spot where barricades against Strathclyde's sheriff's officer were raised in the 'Battle of Little Sparta'.

He will compromise neither in the face of fashion nor of need. But that shouldn't seem so strange, he says. 'Art is not a question of self-indulgence, self-expression, it's a question of certain duties

. . . I've always seen what I think is the crucial thing and stuck to that, whatever the consequences'.

And there have been consequences. Ian is happy to re-fight old battles, but doesn't dwell on the poverty which must have made life very very hard. 'But I've never thought that it would be otherwise – I'm not complaining about that. Poverty is a nuisance in so far as it stops you getting on with your work. I mean, there were times when I didn't have money for pencil and paper, but it's a long time since that. Now it's a matter of not having the £8,000 for the pyramid immediately – but I'll get it and do it. No – much more than poverty has been the amount of abuse suffered for not toeing the line. I mean, it's made quite clear to you what lines you've got to toe'.

In the art world he inspires fierce loyalty and equally vehement hostility; admiration and alarm. 'You have to understand', says the French critic Yves Abrioux, who knows him well, 'that the important thing to him is the principle – not to come to terms and make an arrangement but to clarify the issues'. And, yes, he thrives on conflict. 'The trouble is the enemy isn't usually up to it!'

'There's this extraordinary myth that people tell me about', says Finlay, 'that I'm really an absolutely impossible person. That's been done to me for thirty years now. Of course I realise that I've done things which Scotland considered outrageous but the basis of it is this thing of showing that you will stick to your own perception of the truth, whatever.

'Of course I'm difficult, if you want to side with fraud. I'm very easy if you are reliable in your principles'.

He finds people's passivity in the face of authority extraordinary – 'They say "but did you have *permission* to do that?" ' – and is contemptuous of 'respectability and safety and all that usual sort of rubbish'. His rule is that you must carry all the battles as far as you possibly can, that you don't just give up. The role of David against Goliath suits him. 'People say "you can't stand up to Strathclyde Region!" But nobody has tried it – not using the powers of art'. Of an early dispute he remembers gleefully that 'there was this conviction from the beginning that no wee bloke on a Scottish hillside could stand up to *London*'.

Although it might seem that the battles are an unfortunate distraction from making art, he insists it is all the same struggle, carried out by other means. Indeed he looks back to the first war with the Region, especially, as an energised, creative time from which a great deal of his subsequent work has grown.

Much of his time is devoted to the very 'mundane' execution of ideas. 'But I suppose that what I get in certain moments is a really wild excitement about my work and a feeling of "fantastic!" if some great clash of ideologies is occurring, or when I conceive of a new kind of work. It's those kind of moments on a tightrope that are extraordinary.

'I don't know, it's like being on the peak of two searchlights that have crossed and the feeling it's not really you but you're carrying this thing along.

'That's what the Revolution would be like – if we had it'.

(1988)

Notes

1. The garden reopened to the public in 1989.
2. *A View to the Temple*, in *Documenta 8* (1987).
3. The exhibitions were *Inter Artes et Naturam* at the Musée d'Art Moderne de la Ville de Paris; *Midway*, Bibliothèque Nationale, Paris; *Pastorales*, Galerie Clare Burrus, Paris; and *Pursuites Révolutionnaire*, Fondation Cartier, Jouy-en-Josas – all 1987.
4. The project was subsequently cancelled by the French Government. These events became known as the 'French War', 1987–89: see biographical notes in *Ian Hamilton Finlay: A Visual Primer* (Abrioux), and Angus Calder's essay 'The Wars of Ian Hamilton Finlay: A Philosophical History', *Chapman* 78–9.

Early Finlay

EDWIN MORGAN

In this essay I am taking 'early Finlay' to mean the decade of his work between 1958, when he published his first book, *The Sea-Bed and Other Stories*, and 1967, when he closed his magazine, *Poor. Old. Tired. Horse.*, establishing himself at Stonypath, and turned his attention to the evolving concept of a garden which has since become so famous. Any division of an artist's life is artificial, but in some ways the logic of Finlay's subsequent and continuous development during the 1970s and 1980s can be more clearly realised by examining the earliest phase of his work.

If one uses the broad categories of 'literature' and 'art', this is his most literary period, when he is writing short stories, plays, and both traditional and concrete poetry, as well as moving out into poster-poems, poem-prints, poem-cards, and poems as physical objects in glass or other materials. At the same time, it has to be remembered that he started off his career as an artist, and his early books, as if to acknowledge this, are nearly all illustrated, both *The Sea-Bed* and *The Dancers Inherit the Party* (his first book of poems, 1960) having woodcuts by the Yugoslav artist Zeljko Kujundzic, and *Glasgow Beasts, An a Burd, Haw, an Inseks, an, aw, a Fush* (1961) having papercuts by John Picking. An even closer marrying of text and illustration came with Picking's artwork for *Concertina* (1962). Nevertheless, in these publications, as also in his plays which although they belong to the early period were published later (1965 to 1970), the literary component remains extensive and dominant.

Early Finlay

The short stories, which have an admirable economy and simplicity of style, are more sure-footed than the plays, but there are many points of contact between the two groups. The play *The Estate Hunters* is simply another version of the story 'Straw'. Similarities between the play *Walking through Seaweed* and the story 'The Sea-Bed' are not so direct, but are clearly there: the two girls talking together, one ordinary and down-to-earth, the other imaginative and trying to describe the importance of walking barefoot with a friend through seaweed to the sea, are paralleled by the two boys in the short story, one interested merely in catching fish, the other unable to indicate his strong but strange feelings about the depth and movement of the sea. In both cases, the imagination has been stirred by something that is more an absence than a presence, something set deep into the non-human world: the girl does not know why she wants to get to the sea, the boy has been shaken by the sight of a huge cod which quickly vanished and which he did not even try to catch.

> He could feel the sea behind him, and he felt his friend at his side. Then, into his mind where the sea had been putting its cold, dark pictures, came pictures of familiar objects he saw every day without really looking at them. He saw his father's pipes (he had several pipes), his mother's knitting needles, the Libby's calendar that hung up above the mantelpiece, and his own white mug filled with brown tea. They were familiar things but now he saw them as if for the first time.

This is a very Wordsworthian kind of imaginative transformation: mysterious and refreshing, but unwitty and non-symbolic (even the cod resists symbolization), and it is different from approaches Finlay was to use later on. Perhaps a closer pointer to his future development is seen in the riddling visual transformations in the story 'The Boy and the Guess', where the ancient (classical, if you like) device of asking someone to identify a riddlingly described object is used to open up a very Finlayesque vein of metaphor. It's a pony, tied up with rope when not in use, nibbling the grass below a high dyke. It's an old-fashioned caravan with a door in two halves, so that you can lean on one and look out of the other. No, it has no wheels, no wings. It turns out, of course, to be one of Finlay's chief recurring images, a fishing-boat. His pleasure is to see it transformed into other things which he equally wants to recommend to our attention: a munching horse, an old caravan.

This, so far, is in prose, but the early (pre-concrete) verse shows the same interest in transformation, sometimes adding in an element of verbal play that might seem proper to the more intensely organised language of poetry. In an attractive love-poem, 'The Gift', the speaker opens and wonders at what appears to be the strange gift from his lover of 'a dehydrated porcupine'; he strokes it and discovers it is in fact a pine-cone, accompanied by a written message:

> I hope it did not prick you, dearest mine,
> I did not mean you to be hurt at all.

The engaging complicity, one might say, of sender and receiver is sealed not only with the visual likeness of the two objects but also by the verbal link of *-pine* and *pine-*. In a more playful poem, 'Catch', the visual similarity of a lobster ('lapster') and a helicopter is neatly exploited when a fisherman catches the one and thinks it might be a small example of the other. Why not, when the two words by their sound-link suggest a new transformation, *helicapster*.

> There's lots are caught in the sea off Scrabster.

Although Finlay did not, in his own work, push his new interest in concrete poetry in the direction of sound-poetry, his early verse is very much aware of the sound of words, whether in the spirit of play, as in 'Catch', or humorously dialectal, as in the booklet of *Glasgow Beasts*, or slyly incantational, as in the 'Poem on My Poem on Her and the Horse':

> A little horse came treading through the snow
> At which she said, Poor Horse, poor horse thou art
> Poor little horse to have that heavy cart,
> To have that cart, to have to make it go.

> And then I thought, Oho, I thought, Oho
> She's thinking of her own small saddest part.
> Poor horse. Poor horse. Poor horse. Poor cart.
> And in her eyes the snow, you know, the snow.

Perhaps the traditional, rhyme-and-metre poem which foreshadows his later interests most unmistakably is 'Scene', where the metamorphic imagination, still with the lightest touch, sets out without any argument the sense of a natural world where structure and order are inherent, if we have eyes to see:

> The fir tree stands quite still and angles
> On the hill, for green Triangles.
>
> Stewing in its billy there
> The tea is strong, and brown, and Square.
>
> The rain is Slant. Soaked fishers sup
> Sad Ellipses from a cup.

'As I am open to it, so it ripples out' was Finlay's note at the end of the altogether delightful *Concertina*, which is still a poem with illustrations and not a concrete poem, but clearly paving the way for *Rapel* in the following year, where the step into concrete had been taken. Being 'open to it' in the work produced before 1963 meant the simplicity of the stories, the atmosphere of the plays, the charm and surprise of the poetry. Associations were themselves more 'open' than defined or directed, as indeed in the *Concertina* note quoted above, which 'explains' (his own inverted commas) the words 'Barley!' and 'Keys!' as they have just been used in noon-day and night-time scenes: 'The sudden halt in a game, hush, the silence of noon-day, moon-day, barley-fields; the dark halt of night-time, a darker silence, stars, locks: keys . . .'. This romanticism may seem to be at a great distance from his more hard-edged and strongly politicised work of the 1975–85 decade, but it is important to remember that there is a Coleridge, and even a Loki, lurking in Finlay all the way through; he never becomes pure Vitruvius or Panzerman.

Nothing could be more 'open to it' than *Poor. Old. Tired. Horse.*, the magazine which Finlay edited in twenty-five numbers from 1961 to 1967. In both format and contents it was something quite fresh in the Scottish literary scene at that time, and its Scottish provenance was all the more important to Finlay because of the international range of contributors; the country of origin was put in brackets at the end of each contribution, so that for example in the first three numbers writers from Scotland rubbed shoulders with writers from England (the weasel-word Britain was not used), the USA, Russia, France, Italy, Finland, Poland, Hungary, and Japan. The first poem in the first number was a sound-poem, and the last poem in the last number was a one-word poem; yet as soon as you decided this must be an avant-garde or experimentalist magazine you discovered that its policy was also to rescue neglected poets from the past like John Gray and Hamish McLaren. And as soon as you decided that heavily portentous numbers devoted to the art theory (not even the art!) of Ad Reinhardt or Charles Biedermann implied an equally unyielding functional or abstract literary commitment, you were presented with a 'teapoth' number rich in unportentous homely fantasy and charm. Some issues were thematic, some general; some illustrated, some not; some hand-drawn, some printed; some with fine artwork and layout, some with – not so fine. Few magazines encouraged such a marked sense of anticipation from number to number. The ability to disconcert inevitably draws some flak, and Finlay, taking a leaf from Hugh MacDiarmid's book, advertised the magazine thus in *The Scotsman*:

'Utterly vicious and deplorable' – Hugh MacDiarmid

But *P.O.T.H.* flourished, and its Scottish contributors included, in addition to its editor and the present writer, George Mackay Brown, Robert Garioch, Douglas Young, Tom McGrath, Helen B. Cruickshank, R. Crombie Saunders, J. F. Hendry, and D. M. Black. The magazine did publish concrete poetry, semiotic poetry, and sound-poetry, and its reputation among those who had not seen it was that it was 'some sort of concrete poetry broadsheet'; this was not true, but perhaps it overlaps on the fact that well-crafted thing-y poetry was preferred to expressionist or confessional 'depth'. Finlay wrote in 1967 that 'the example [of using the experience of the Nazi death-camps] suggests that the whole idea – now in fashion – of "depth for depth's sake" might well be looked at critically' (letter to Stephen Scobie, 4 August 1967, quoted in *White Pelican*, Vol. I, No. 2, Edmonton, Canada, Spring 1971). There was no minimalist or even miniaturist gospel, but the magazine's title did tip its hat to Robert Creeley, from whose poem 'Please' (in *A Form of Women*, 1959) it is taken, and Creeley does stand for certain cat-like gestures and anti-large preoccupations.

> This is a poem about a horse that got tired.
> Poor. Old. Tired. Horse.
> I want to go home.
> I want you to go home.
> This is a poem which tells the story,
> which is the story.
> I don't know.

Quite unCreeleyan, however, was the magazine's inclusion of poets who dealt with the larger socio-political issues: Mayakovsky, József, Neruda, Günter Grass, and writers from Cuba and Brazil. If the result is eclecticism, it is an eclecticism that two decades later seems to belong so much to the spirit of the sixties as to have gained more unity and harmony than it appeared to possess at the time. It undoubtedly succeeded in its aim of opening Scotland out to new names and new ideas, and all at the astonishingly unelitist price of 9d (4p) which was held throughout the five years of its existence.

Concrete poems made their first appearance in *P.O.T.H.* in No. 6 (March 1963), and both Finlay and his commentators have described the mixture of acknowledgement and uneasiness with which he regarded the international concrete poetry movement. It is clear that it offered many suggestions to him in the areas of syntax, structure, metaphor, and metamorphosis. Also, under its alternative title of 'visual poetry' its possible or actual links with painting, sculpture, and architecture spoke directly to the artist in Finlay. He used it, contributed to it, learned from it, moved on. It is significant that collections of his fairly straight or mainstream concrete poetry, such as *Telegrams from My Windmill* (1964) or *Tea-Leaves and Fishes* (1966) are less fully satisfying than books which he has designed wholly round one idea, so that the book virtually becomes the poem. These two collections are (inevitably) uneven in quality, and one tends to pick out the poems one admires and neglect the others, but in the more 'designed' publications one has to grasp a much more original approach, where the poem-book or book-poem has become a halfway house to the poem-object which he developed, at Stonypath and elsewhere, beyond the period of his work being discussed in this essay. In distrusting the miscellanyism of poems-in-a-book (as, with the demise of *P.O.T.H.*, he was tacitly distrusting the miscellanyism of items-in-a-magazine), he had embarked on his more heroic attempt to relate language to the world in a three-dimensional way. The turning pages of a book, the use of blank pages, of transparent pages, of coloured paper, all this was a beginning, an adumbration of the three-dimensional 'world out there'. Eventually the words had to be on objects – carved, sandblasted, or whatever – and placed, like that old wordless jar in Tennessee, somewhere in the environment. As Finlay has himself said, it had been one of his earliest questions, back in the fifties when he was writing his short stories, 'How can one write TREE and *mean* TREE?'

In *Canal Stripe Series 4* (1964) the long horizontal pages, turned over, read 'little fields/long horizons/little fields long/for horizons/horizons long/for little fields'. The words, at the bottom of the page, suggest a boat drifting along a canal and the word-play (the l/f alliteration, the adjective/verb transformation of 'long') suggests in its sound as well as saying in its meaning that there is a natural linkage of the near and the far; and in human terms (since it is human language that is being used, not boats and fields) we are being told we must expect to oscillate, perhaps for ever, between the homely and the infinite.

The page-turning in *Ocean Stripe Series 3* (1965) enacts the biblical story of the Flood, and can do so with the utmost verbal economy because of the near-coincidence in the English language of 'ark' and 'arc'. Four times the ark is still there, on the same spot of each page, but on the fourth page you can glimpse the word 'arc', high up, showing through the paper, and finally, as you turn again and remove the cloud which is hiding the rainbow, the rainbow – overlapping pages of red, yellow, and blue – appears. The accidental sound-identity of 'ark' and 'arc' helps to clinch the *idea* of the divine covenant, but it is the sudden flash of the brightly coloured pages which shows the *joy* of the promise. As in *Rapel*, we have suprematist and fauve elements coming together.

In *Autumn Poem* (1966), perhaps the most attractive of these kinetic poems, the conception of 'turning over' which starts from turning the pages is itself moulded into the body of the poem, where a series of photographs (first a square patch of earth, later a circular patch suggesting the sphere of the whole earth) is covered by transparent pages bearing the words of the poem. 'Turning over the earth' (square patch) is followed by 'the earth turning over' (circular patch), and this in turn modulates back, in the movement of the seasons, to 'Turning over' (circular patch) 'the earth' (square patch). Here, the use of photographs taken by someone else (Audrey Walker) further objectifies the poem, and suggests also that word and world are being, if not brought into one, forced to confront each other. Nevertheless, like the token three-colour rainbow of *Ocean Stripe Series 3*, the flat globe of *Autumn Poem* is there to remind us that we are still in *mir iskusstva*, the world of art.

A further development of the confrontation, in *Ocean Stripe Series 5* (1967), is more striking but more problematic. Each page prints the photograph of a different fishing-boat (taken from *Fishing News*) above a quotation on sound-poetry or concrete poetry taken from Kurt Schwitters, Ernst Jandl, or Paul de Vree. There are few obvious connections between boat and text, beyond the fact that boats' registration-letters (indicating port of origin) have been used by Finlay in concrete poems, and that both photographs and texts do have a kind of climax at the end, when rougher seas accompany more far-reaching (but less modernist, indeed anti-modernist) statements – 'Poetic feeling is what the poet counts on' and 'It is impossible to explain the meaning of art; it is infinite'. The romanticism, or fauvism, of this (strongly underlined by the cover photograph of a choppy, boatless sea, swirling under louring cloud and a dash of light) is balanced by a 'postscript' which brings back the suprematism: a Schwitters poem consisting entirely of short groups of letters, like the letters on fishing-boats. Whether, in the voyage of this book, the good ship modernism has sunk, though not without trace, is an open question. The Aivazovskian cover certainly proclaims that *those* horizons are not longing for little fields. 'Models of order' are not in order. This is a stark ocean, and the only stripe on it is a stark zigzag of light. This tantalising, difficult, but important book is a good point at which to close. Its visibly unruly sea should be placed against the neatly distanced message of 'Pond-stone' (in *Stonechats*, from the same year, 1967):

> HIC IACET
> PARVULUM QUODDAM
> EX AQUA LONGIORE
> EXCERPTUM

An inscribed stone in a pond marks the grave of a drop in the ocean. Finlay was to go on, working with others, to make many inscribed stones, but the languageless sea is still there, very big, very challenging, full of life and death and not art.

(1986)

Note

See also 'Into the Constellation: Some Thoughts on the Origin and Nature of Concrete Poetry' in Edwin Morgan's *Essays* (Carcanet New Press, Manchester, 1974).

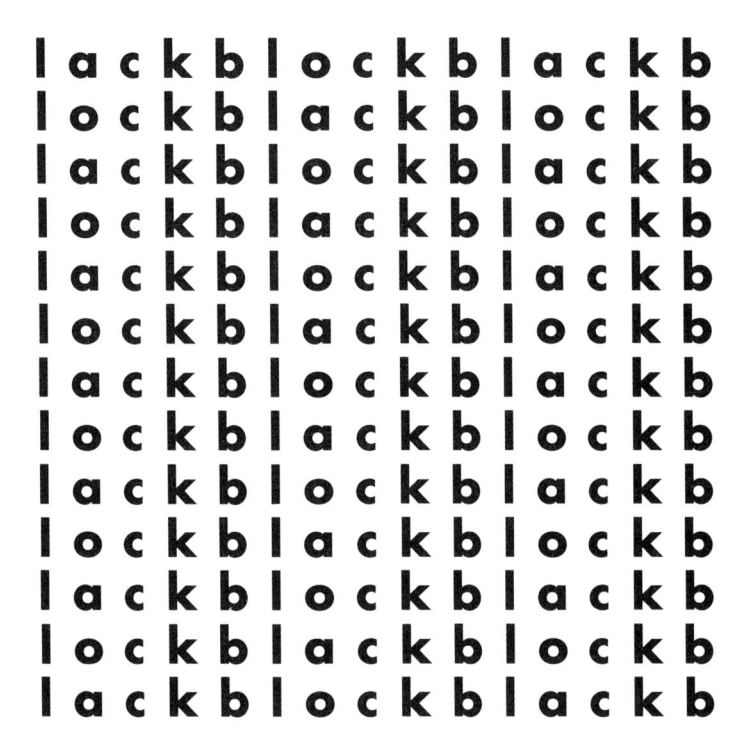

```
l a c k b l o c k b l a c k b
l o c k b l a c k b l o c k b
l a c k b l o c k b l a c k b
l o c k b l a c k b l o c k b
l a c k b l o c k b l a c k b
l o c k b l a c k b l o c k b
l a c k b l o c k b l a c k b
l o c k b l a c k b l o c k b
l a c k b l o c k b l a c k b
l o c k b l a c k b l o c k b
l a c k b l o c k b l a c k b
l o c k b l a c k b l o c k b
l a c k b l o c k b l a c k b
```

Homage to Malevich, from *Rapel*, 1963.

Poor. Old. Tired. Horse.

EDWIN MORGAN

It is sad to record that the twenty-fifth number of this magazine, which has recently appeared, is likely to be the last, owing to the ill-health of its editor, Ian Hamilton Finlay. From its beginnings in April 1961, *Poor. Old. Tired. Horse.* has pursued its own eclectic but distinctive policy, and although numbers have inevitably varied in interest and quality it has held its own with remarkable persistence over these six years.

It started off as a single folded sheet, and has never become fatter than twelve pages; the price has remained unchanged at 9d; but every bit of its space is used for creative work – there are no editorials, comments, reviews or letters. The complete absence of editorial statements has, of course, led to some misunderstandings about the aims and functions of the magazine. It is commonly thought of as a vehicle for concrete poetry, but in fact, although it introduced examples of concrete poetry in 1963, this has never been a dominant feature of its contents. Its main aims were (i) to introduce a variety of foreign poets in translation to Scottish readers, (ii) to present a selection of good poetry, mainly lyrical, wherever it came from (Scotland, England or America), and (iii) to explore aspects of the visual presentation of poetry through a series of illustrated numbers using drawings, woodcuts, calligraphy, and typographic design.

In all this, there was the desire to keep certain lines of communication open, in particular those from country to country, but also those between poet and artist, and those between present and past. Finlay himself has said that he was looking for 'connections between . . . *apparently* different categories', and he would therefore include not only representatives of what can only be called an avant-garde like Ad Reinhardt and Bridget Riley, or the Russian Constructivists of the 1920s, but also the traditional verses of Hamish MacLaren or John Gray. But even if readers would sometimes find the connections hard to see – and they are partly the connections within Finlay's own unformulated but formative view of the world of art – still, the impression one gets from *Poor. Old. Tired. Horse.* of an ability to surprise and stimulate (and simply to please) remains. Irritate it could and did, like Robert Creeley from whose poetry its title is taken; but also like Creeley, it stands for something. The series of carefully thought out special numbers, each devoting itself to a specific poet or artist or theme, has no real counterpart elsewhere, and has been widely recognised outside Scotland as a distinctive contribution to the arts. Good or bad, convincing or irritating, it will be missed.

(1968)

Note
See Appendix A for a complete list of contributors to *Poor. Old. Tired. Horse.*

Concrete Poetry

STEPHEN BANN

The term 'concrete art' was first employed by Van Doesburg in 1930 to signify a new relationship between the work of art and the natural world. The artist's function was no longer to be interpretative – concerned with reproducing the particular and the individual – but was to be constructive – concerned with achieving a harmony of simple forms. The resultant movement in painting and sculpture, which swiftly attracted some of the most prominent European artists of this generation, is the direct ancestor of concrete poetry. The actual term originated with the Swiss poet Eugen Gomringer in 1956, and Gomringer intended it as a gesture of respect to two pioneers of concrete art, Arp and Bill. It was therefore natural that concrete poetry should reflect from the start an aesthetic theory which had been developed in relation to the plastic arts, especially sculpture. Already in 1954 Gomringer had spoken of the 'constellation' poem as 'an object to be seen and used . . . a reality in itself and not a poem about something or other'. He continued to emphasise the distinct and self-sufficient quality of the poem, explaining in 1960 that he had for several years considered it as a 'functional object' (*Gebrauchsgegenstand*). This was the essential formula adopted by concrete poets throughout the world. The *noigandres* group of Brazil, who had arrived at this type of poetry by a more exclusively literary path, wrote in their 'Pilot plan for concrete poetry' of 1958 that they were investigating 'a general art of the word: the poem-product: useful object'.

Although this aesthetic of solidity and function was originally applied to describing the characteristics of the concrete poem on the page, it led inevitably to experiments with media. The German poet Franz Mon has spoken of the ideal of a poem which 'subsists by itself in a manner so powerful that anyone can penetrate into it as if into a public building'. His impressive poem-print, from a series published by the Wild Hawthorn Press, approaches this ideal, since the poem has been given the scale and immediacy of the poster. Pierre Garnier, the French poet, has recently taken the problem of scale and function to its final conclusion in his *Textes pour une architecture*. He views the poems in this collection as 'prototypes' which are no more than sketches for a wider application. Garnier's notion of a prototype which can be re-created on an architectural scale finds a close parallel in the writings of Vasarely, and Garnier clearly envisages applications of concrete poetry which correspond to the architectural projects of Vasarely and other kinetic artists.

It was, however, the Scottish poet, Ian Hamilton Finlay, who first began to experiment with the possibilities of concrete poetry in an architectural setting. In company with Dick Sheeler he has already carried out a number of projects in which the poem is given a stable structure and designed for a more or less specific context. This question of context is particularly important with the poem construction. The individual letter has an intrinsic plastic quality which allows it to stand on a purely formal level. But the combination of letters into words involves a semantic element, which may be emphasised in the overall structure of the poem. The best way to demonstrate these features is to describe some projects which Finlay has already completed.

Finlay's 'acrobats' is a relevant example. It has been printed as a poem, with the letters dispersed over a large page. Recently Finlay has mounted it on the outside wall of the farmhouse where he lives in Ross-shire. But it calls for a larger scale and a more particular context, possibly that of a children's playground. To this environment it would contribute not only the vibrancy of its overall pattern, but also the challenge to trace the key-word along the diagonals. The poem would tempt the eye to agility just as the playground invites the activity of the limbs. Similar in the use of repetition, but distinct in purpose, is Finlay's *Ajar*. The word suggests a domestic interior, and the completed version, which is 15 ft high, stands against the stair-wall in IHF's house.

Both these poem-constructions are essentially reliefs. Quite different in form is the 'column-poem' which was designed by Finlay, constructed by John Furnival, and shown in the exhibition *Between Poetry and Painting* at the Institute of Contemporary Arts (1965). This is almost a freestanding sculpture, with one side decorated by a sequence of coloured stripes, and the other side displaying a sequence of words which echoes the arrangement of the stripes. The subject of the poem is a parallel between the worlds of sea and land, which becomes most explicit in the juxtaposition of the blue-painted 'bow' and the single green word 'bough'. Finlay intends it to stand by a garden pond, where it could reflect the meeting of water and land.

Another poem construction which is also designed for a garden or park is his 'little fields', in which the letters are mounted on a triangular frame, and each face presents a different episode of the poem. Here the poem is in wood, but Finlay would prefer it to be constructed with three low brick walls and letters of wrought iron, protruding a little from the surface of the wall.

All these poem constructions are still prototypes, and the means of construction employed has been determined by limitations of money and materials. Finlay has recently given his first commission for a poem to be sandblasted on glass, an expensive technique which he has wanted to use for some time. But ultimately the potentiality of the poem construction can only be realised through the co-operation of architects and planners. Many of them have already accepted the principle that modern painting and sculpture can be used in close conjunction with architectural schemes. The poem construction can be used in the same way, but it introduces an additional standard of appropriateness to the environment. It does not mimic the forms of nature, yet it belongs intimately to a particular context. The letter is formally distinct, but the combination of letters evokes a range of images. Hence the poem is not simply a decorative project on a public scale, but also a field for private interpretation. We can trace its meaning, yet, because of its formal structure, it remains inexhaustible. The concrete poem in architecture offers us an entirely new standard of mediation between ourselves and the world in which we live.

(1966)

Pond Stone (above), by the Temple Pool, Little Sparta. Ian Hamilton Finlay, with Maxwell Allan, 1967.

Cloud, Little Sparta.

Photos by
Dave Paterson

The Aesthetic of Ian Hamilton Finlay

SIMON CUTTS

The reductive nature of Ian Hamilton Finlay's *The Dancers Inherit the Party* (Migrant Press, 1960) presupposes the move on the part of a writer to find a scheme of working more universal than the writer considers to be his function. That he seems to write poetry about certain simplified subjects is a concession to the usual idea of poetry, but in *The Dancers Inherit the Party* the real subject is the idea that poetry can be written about these subjects in all their simplicity with the rigidity and tautness of great verse. There is something ironic in his inversion of language for poetic ends, the incorporation into the verse scheme of the occasional colloquialism, in fact the seeming ease and casualness in making this handful of near-perfect poetry which, by its underlying redundance, questions the future of poetry with the syntax of speech, the old lyric notion of song. This irony is enforced by the suggestion of a folk element as an axis of the book's arrangement, Orkney folksongs. But in this work, crucial to poetry this century, it is not only one writer's discovery that narrative sequential verse will not support this degree of scrutiny and integrity, it is also that writer's search for a mode of working outside the particularisation of poetry, a generalising aesthetic asserting itself.

In his letters following *The Dancers Inherit the Party*, in the formative period of a new poetry with a visual as opposed to a narrative syntax, Finlay often repeated his concern for order as the central axis of art. In quoting Malevich in one letter – 'by means of perfected objects, man seeks to recover the divine, non-thinking state' – he repeats the recurrent search for an aesthetic for art, not merely for poetry. Poetry has often failed to see itself objectively enough to make this connection. It has been easy for poets to escape the implications of art by concerning themselves only with the most immediate meaning, as opposed to the formal possibilities of language.

The fallacy of the Institute of Contemporary Art's exhibition *Between Poetry and Painting* (1965), held in the most formative year for concrete poetry in this country, has never been corrected, and so it is possible for people to look at Finlay's work and believe that it lies somewhere between poetry and painting. Then they would be unable to place certain items of his later work without calling him a sculptor.

That impetuous exhibition allowed people to look at an early example of 'mixed media' activity, so-called, and in this writer's opinion has severely damaged an accurate concept of concrete poetry. The truth is, of course, that the only real mixture of the media occurs in the work of a particular artist working from a centralised aesthetic about art, not painting or sculpture or poetry alone. In his later work it has become obvious with Finlay that his procedure is from such a position, which to some extent then makes redundant the categories of art previously mentioned.

It is in this respect that Finlay can be compared to one other Scottish artist with whom there is a more than superficial similarity, Charles Rennie Mackintosh. Both were and are working in times and in styles that have become by and large excessive to the point of saturation, the one Art Nouveau and its immediate surround, the other concrete poetry. It is when both are examined beneath the superficialities that it is discovered that both owe less to the 'style' in which they work than at first appears. (This is not to imply that the empirical basis for concrete poetry has in any way deteriorated, only its practice.) Both were concerned with the type of aesthetic much spoken about here, a means of consistency beneath the appearance of the style. Both were concerned with some kind of perfection. It is in this sense that Magritte is distinguished from the Surrealists.

Under these circumstances, the logical move was from the printed or typographic object to a constructed solid subject, in which the texts from a continuation of typographic interest figure as the motif to be harmonised with the materials of construction. Since 1966 Finlay has been concerned with the production of works in glass, stone, and wood, and during this period it has obviously been less a question of what a poem should be made about, as what it should be made of in terms of the relationship of material to motif, which is more a question of sculptural harmony than the usual concern of the concrete poet. But whilst each item can be apprehended and understood on its own terms, its own unique system of nuance of material for idea, and the corresponding co-ordination of divergent elements into a single unifying form, the work has wider metaphorical implications. As with the width of his aesthetic, so the metaphoric system he has built deals almost entirely with an elemental structural view of the world, an order. Often this takes the form of an opposition of the basic landscape components, for instance, sea and land, sea and sky.

The NETS weathercock of 1968 consists of a flat table with solid letters for points of the compass lying flat. True to the form of a weathercock, the arrow swings in circular motion over the points of the compass, bearing upright along its back the letters NETS. Thus we have the juxtaposition NEWS/NETS. First of all we see the most simple metaphorical implication of fishing-boats and their nets all over the globe. The same simplicity of metaphor is present in the *Water Weathercock* of 1968, in which no part-literary metaphor is necessary, but only the presence of circular points of the compass anchored but floating on the surface of the water, and a central arrow or pointer likewise anchored but floating, revolving with the currents caused by the wind.

So far Finlay has not received his rightful recognition in the area in which works like those mentioned above could be used, namely in architectural and landscape planning situations. This is perhaps not easily corrected under the present circumstances, where anything like a classicism corresponding to his work is now on the wane.

For Finlay's work this concern with materials, in what previously could only be seen in a painterly or sculptural sense, is the logical plastic extension of the typographic or visually syntactical poem, and, as it becomes somewhat arbitrary to define whether or not Finlay is basically a poet or another kind of artist at this level of working, so he begins to fulfil in Britain an equivalent position to that previously occupied by artists losing faith in the plastic object and becoming involved in the

The Aesthetic of Ian Hamilton Finlay 35

less finite environment. Finlay's work still fulfils the classical premise of the finished plastic object. As stone-carving for sculptors becomes unavailable in our Colleges of Art, it becomes possible for Finlay to consider making his delicate one-word poems into solid stone tablets. In fact most of the one-word poems from *Stonechats*, a small book of his published by his own Wild Hawthorn Press in 1968, have now been transferred to stone inscriptions, some of which have been inset in his own sunken garden at his house, Stonypath, in Lanarkshire.

The carved *Cloud* board in wood (1968) again emphasises the metaphoric system most particularly, and the final shift of metaphor that takes place when the lily is open in the small pond in summer is more the concern of poetry than anything else.

Finlay has also partially pioneered the use of sandblasted glass, and the choice of this material has an obvious relationship to his concern for the pure, perfected object. *Wave Rock* was the first poem to be made in sandblasted glass in 1966. The cast concrete version (in Dunfermline Park) becomes so harmonious with its surroundings that it is remarkable to think it was produced by a claimed member of the avant-garde.

The true arbitrariness of classification for his work becomes altogether apparent in the scale of the recent exhibition at Dunfermline Park. The fishing-boat letters KY are transformed into a completely abstract work in cast concrete. This seems to be one of the perfections of Ian Hamilton Finlay's work to date, exemplifying more than anything else concrete art in Max Bill's sense.

(1969)

Stonypath
(For Ian Finlay)

KATHLEEN RAINE

To restore lost paradise, that imaginary place
Where beyond a mere wire fence
All belongs to the moles and the thistles
You have recovered a stony parcel of Lanarkshire
Where each step, up or down, hedged by sweet scotch briar
Leads to the Hour Lady's hortus conclusus;
Brought back the other-worldly birch to hills laid bare
By Knox and Calvin of sanctuary, shrine or sacred grove,
The Lamp of Lothian put out, and all profaned.
Here are sunk pool and rising grove of young aeolian pine,
Wood, water, wind, within your containing image,
Restored to mental space
Which is the world's true place.
The Moslem on his prayer-rug in the desert
Kneels in this same garden;
Jung, stone by stone with his own hands built his temenos,
Yeats found his four-storied four-sided tower, and every day
Between five rocks disposed with meaning
A monk in the Roanje garden takes the sand.
Pushed, Milton says, by the horned flood
Where Odysseus, navigator of the stormy world
All his long years sailed (or so Plotinus reads the story)

Towards his heavenly beginning, found in the end.
Here on dry land
The many names of ships, record of pride or prayer
Of men who set sail for no known shore
Across the seas of time and space
Where battleships have gone down, and submarines
In whose conning-towers you honour
An emblem of men not drowned under the *unda*,
You, who navigate with ante-diluvian charts,
Commemorate in green grove and flowery plot of every wanderer's dream.

(1977)

Westward-facing sundial, in the garden at Little Sparta. Ian Hamilton Finlay, with John R. Thorpe, 1971.
Photo by Dave Paterson.

Ian Hamilton Finlay

R.C. KENEDY

No critical task could be more difficult than the description of Ian Hamilton Finlay's achievement. Superficially, his work seems to be uncomplicated. Indeed, simpler means than his could hardly be employed to make art and to provoke thought or emotive response. It would be easy to maintain that he is a concrete poet and equally convincing to argue that he is a minimal or conceptual artist. But none of these labels fits him without leaving a large part of his impact unrepresented in any exegesis of his aims. Undoubtedly, he has been in the forefront of every renewal during the past fifteen or twenty years but he has been so independent throughout these decades that his contribution has remained unique. So individual has been his voice that demonstrable instances of his primogeniture as an artist have been wholly and perhaps excusably overlooked. His avant-gardism has never been revolution-prompted. His inventiveness has never been in the service of mere novelty; and his discoveries were superimposed on the contemporary advance (which came, as a rule, in his wake) – as though the accident had contributed more to his inspiration than design. The genuineness of his sympathies, not fashion, motivated his search for terser modes of expression; and his classical inclinations were so insistent on formal perfection that they obscured the rebellious modes of his statement. It could be argued that the tectonic nature of his thinking was so determined to use formal harmonies for stating his case that one was almost tempted to overlook the immediate originality of his oeuvre; the contemporary scene prefers disharmonies and its audiences are more attuned to cacophony than melody. Harmony, however, has played a major role in everything tackled by him and its traditional serenities removed his work from the reach of clashing sensibilities – which tend to be identified with the recognition of innovation. Hence the obstacles in accounting for Finlay's direct relevance. There are no negative gestures in his compositions. He contradicts no heritage and he rejects neither predecessors nor accepted values. His work reduces available styles and idioms to bare essentials.

Nor has he committed himself to genre or mode. The entire world of art is his happy hunting ground; and he recovers ideal-seeming objects from the whole reach of the imagination. Landscape gardening has provided no less to his ways of thought than poetry. Sculptural notions are just as important in his instance as calligraphy. Colour plays a role in his contribution to parallel the sensations evoked by the strange games of an almost Lewis-Carroll-like logic. His spirit moves among diverse possibilities after the butterfly's fashion and it gathers its nourishment from every encounter capable of taking the flower's place – at any rate, in the mind. The careless-seeming joy Finlay has in sheer, unadulterated beauty is the proof of its entirely natural character. It is in his nature to pluck the fruits of every ripe possibility. The ripeness of it has, always, been the proof of his involvement in the general advance – but, as said, discoveries came, as it were, towards him – and he progressed from victory to victory with such casualness that his pursuit seemed too effortless to be appreciated on our much more intellectually conditioned terms. His art did not reveal any laboriously obtained triumphs – because his successes were instinctively received from the generous lap of the earth itself; and we, who had been attuned to measure attainment in accordance with the critical criteria of sweat and deliberation, did not always respond to the much simpler ethos of mere liberation.

In these circumstances, we tended to consider Ian Hamilton Finlay's work as though it had to conform to labels invented after the event of his primary creative experiments. Minimalism and conceptual art provided the tenets which have helped to create our responsiveness to his aims but the canons of these movements were too narrow to accommodate more than mere aspects of his work. When troubled by inconsistencies, the spectator had to be satisfied with facile references to concrete poetry – which presupposed printed precedents for a great many of Finlay's monumental notions. The synthesising tendencies were ignored for the poorer sake of finding some sort of means to react to the grand simplicities of a classical attitude. The final conciseness of Finlay's words was made to serve as an excuse for ignoring their environmentally intended design. His devotion to tradition has served to obscure the fact that he employed the model's notion for a principle. Indeed, it has gone unrecognised that his progress was along a straight line which moved towards the model's own self-signifying symbolism. His beginnings connected his own verbal experiments with the heritage of sundial-construction and the graveyard's monumental masonry; with signwriting and with the much more mysterious profession of naming; but in all these pursuits his concern was with finding a ready-made and craft-hallowed vehicle for his personal vision. In these works the precedent served for a model, but it took only a slight leap of the logic-prompted imagination to discover that the scale-model multiplied the possibilities of such a precedent-sanctioned commitment. It spoke much more directly about the principles which stimulated Finlay's inspiration. For Finlay has seldom been prompted by precise events, by precise happenings or by individual experiences. His concern has always been with static ideas; and fundamental or generic notions are incompatible with a dynamic context. The concept of change appears only in his landscaped gardens, in the lakes he has dug with his own hands from the Scottish soil and in the trees he has planted for the pleasure of the merciless northern storms. Otherwise, his universe is still. The silence of the stone is its hallmark and the taciturnity of the engraved inscription. Finlay's work is dedicated to the concept of endurance, timelessness, and equilibrium. Tensions and romantic-seeming, unbalanced forces are excluded from his compositions. They are not without forces, but their vectorial energy is always counterbalanced. Even his predilection for the metaphor's rudimentary structure comes from this desire for an absolute and static equilibrium. He equates forces in order to still their rebelliously separate existence and in order to produce, from the suddenly engineered union, a tranquil thought, larger than its parts. (A few examples: a paving slab, inscribed 'Wave / Sheaf'; a folding card which states *'the SEA'S / WAVES' / SHEAVES*'; the poem: '*THE CLOUD'S ANCHOR / swallow*'.)

It is by no means an accident that any discussion of Finlay's art must focus on the difficulties it presents to a metropolitan public. It is very much to the point that he is, quite literally, a nature poet. He himself insists on this distinction: 'I am like the Greeks, in that I have to imagine everything in terms of a Solid Place' (letter dated 21 November 1972); and the self-evident differentiation between the city's art and the countryside's may well have to be stressed once again. Nature, of a kind, seeks to occupy a central place in every creative definition. Even the popular love-song is incomplete without the obligatory aside to moon and rose. But, in a metropolitan context, the jungle flourishes most conspicuously in men's hearts – Dostoevsky is perhaps the best example of this truism. Not so when we leave cities. Outside the labyrinthine context of streets there are permanent and independent principles which enact a dominant role. The sea and the sky provide a stage. Against them man appears in differently conceived proportions. There is a shift in scale and the emphasis becomes utterly subordinative. Individualities and psychological depth-characteristics seem irrelevant when huge surfaces are the background against which the human presence asserts itself. Man avers his place by stating his human principles when he confronts the eternal – and it should not be overlooked that essentially there is no true distinction between the violence of the storm which rends skies or that which rends the souls of Dostoevsky's heroes. But, even if there is no categorical difference, there is an irreconcilable cleavage between the internally oriented art of the psychological novel and the externally influenced acts of wonder. Ian Hamilton Finlay's craft is one of the purest instances of the outward-reaching stance. There is a grandly impersonal quality in his voice. It has the sonority of the cry in a hurricane. Even his small, private-seeming jokes carry this supra-individual quality. The memorial he places below a tree is exclusively dedicated to the sacred-seeming spirit of the forest: 'Bring Back the Birch' is its motto and its ironies are militant in their hostility to the city's ethos. Generalities take precedence in such a context over the singular and the unique. The hero finds no place in a framework such as this, which leaves room only for the principle of heroism. The individual is replaced by the moral laws which govern his conduct. The battleships and the fishing-boats lend their silhouettes in order to assert the imperatives which govern the existence of the creature. They represent the reasons of discipline and hunger which must justify action; and they are wholly uninterested in the individual's excuses for gratuitously-conceived or personal-seeming deeds. The fisherman's spirit lingers in his boats which decorate the endless series of postcard-poems, poem-prints and booklets he has produced in collaboration with other artists. Yet mistakes on this score must not be made. The conception, in every instance, is his and it is essentially pictorial. He exploits concepts and illustrates them. On the face of it, these illustrations seem genuinely naïve because they are so precise. Often they come in the form of the naval engineer's diagrams, helped along, as it were, by the allusively employed name of the craft illustrated. Yet the simple aims of description are very far from Finlay's explicit intent. Finlay's pictorial aims of description reside beyond image and sculpture. His objects are a framework for delineating ideas and it could be maintained that he is one of the very few artists alive today who has succeeded in giving a pictorial definition to abstract concepts. His works must be regarded as representing an iconography of moral principles. It would be a grave error to think of them as self-complete art objects, designed to be mere instances of creative decoration. Their passion is such that it has alienated many, but, however rare and extraordinary a component passion has been in the stuff of our contemporary inspiration, it cannot be denied that it is certainly the most powerfully intoxicant. Nor can it be debated that it has the longest and most august role in providing the promptings of the artist's utterances. Research is a very poor substitute for convictions and there is no room for it in Finlay's vision. His eyes confront the huge vistas which dwarf the hand-wrought shrines of human awe; and his work has a consequential modesty which proclaims the magnificence of his visions. Their minimal, reductive and conceptual characteristics are, in fact, acts of reverence and have only the remotest links with fashions. Nor, indeed, do they have the capacity to move the spectator unless given their proper frame in the fields or the gardens – where they belong. They are especially designed for special places. They deny the canons of abstraction by proclaiming the much more important concept of belonging. In fact, they have the inalienable air of dependence which brings them into a close relationship with altar-pieces, and which emasculates every real masterpiece once it is removed from its unique setting. In the day's pervasive terms, Finlay's is an exceptional sensitiveness to the spirit of place and for the location's. He has shown a surprising aptitude for co-operation with architectural projects – and the poems he has written for Jürgen Brenner and his Max Planck Institute in Stuttgart are excellent examples of it. No wonder that his gallery showings have failed to obtain proper recognition for the context-prompted springs of his genius. Exhibitions like his present appearance in the Scottish National Gallery of Modern Art will be slow to remedy this situation, but they will be a step in the right direction if they tempt the visitor to envisage Finlay's songs of homage in their appropriate setting.

But, it should be remembered that under God's free sky only the generic voice has real meaning.

(1973)

Lugger, Ian Hamilton Finlay.

Photo by Dave Paterson.

Versed in Vessels:
An Appreciation of Ian Hamilton
Finlay's Fleet

IAN STEPHEN

>   Maker of boats
>   ... a man repairing
>   nets, a man carv-
>   ing steady glass,
>   hears the world,
>   bends to his work.
>   You give the pleasure
>   of made things,
>   the construction holds
>   like a net, or it
>   unfolds in waves
>   ...
>   Edwin Morgan[1]

My neighbour, across the road, worked on the *Girl Norma*. My neighbour, up the road, worked on the *Girl Isabel*. Two doors away, Frank Strachan, a strayed East Coaster like my own father, had a share in the *Lilac*, which worked from Stornoway. *Daffodil* then worked from Scalpay, as recorded by Norman MacCaig. That secondary layer of allusion was not in my culture then. Nor was *The Night Fishing* nor Mackay Brown's calm fisherman sinking with his pipe still on fire; nor the squads of herring-girls moving fast through the lines of Smith, Thompson and MacDonald (N.M.)

When I drifted eastwards to Aberdeen, I learned these waypoints but before most of them came incantations of starry names, gleaners, reapers, harvesters – arranged in type and ink placed into card as surely as paint into grain broken by the steady sweep of chisel or router. Products of the Wild Hawthorn Press were arranged round the shelving and walls of a gallery which seemed to me a stone fo'c's'le entered in Old Aberdeen.

Probably because I could go to sea when it suited me but I'd not long completed a year as a forestry labourer on Mull, I reached out for the comfort of familiarity. Names I knew, or cousins of them. Then I was unsettled, having to puzzle how the leafy package worked with the salty stuff. Maybe not harmonies, but I was left with chiming in the language of these worlds, with the boat-names bolder.

It took a while to realise that the imagery and language of sea, wood, garden, revolution, classical, neo-classical, neo-neo allusions and references all coexisted in the work of IHF. I suppose I'd assumed that the artist had moved from 'earlier' boat stuff to 'later' columns. I was helped to a better understanding by Hamish Henderson (whom I knew initially through the first and already scuffed reissue of *Elegies for the Dead in Cyrenaica* by Polygon, encountered in the front shop of *Aberdeen People's Press* and later as a tall man who introduced everyone floating down the streets of Keith to everyone else). He advised me of the relaunch of Tambimuttu's *Poetry London*. I ordered and received a copy. The back cover was a full-colour printing of the language of navigation-lights which brought me back to the IHF I'd encountered in Old Aberdeen. But the relationship between fishing-boats, architecture and warships still seemed distant. It was years later that I walked through the gate into Little Sparta to sense that the fishing-boat names, language of trees, columns, and warships were part of a fully integrated attack on the expected. They shared wit and craft.

Finlay has recorded that his earliest childhood memory is of sitting on the deck of a schooner. From his first published works to those of the present time he has returned again and again to the imagery and the names of sailing-boats, fishing-boats and ships. Studying a fleet of cards, booklets, bookmarks, prints, and three-dimensional constructions of this poet's obsession, it seems impossible to identify any chronology. His language and imagery of vessels spans more than a quarter of a century.

There seems perhaps to be an assumption by many that the boat-works are earlier, perhaps even lesser, than works which use the dramatic imagery of classicism, neo-classicism, neo-classicism and the French Revolution.

A close look at 'Lemons' – a boat-metaphor often used by Finlay – will cut through any suggestion that works which share this fruit's shape can be fitted to a period of time in the poet's creative life. In *The Dancers Inherit the Party* (Migrant Press, 1960), 'An English Colonel Explains an Orkney Boat' has the narrator resort to the lemon as a device for explaining the amazing hollowness which permits the thing to float. As the happy owner of an Orkney Yole which has maintained its ability to float since 1912, I can respond to that appropriate jump in the language. Fishing-boats are graceful things but the wit of their build is held together by sound structural principles. The hull-shape of the wherry, sgoth, Fifie, Scottish Zulu or Stroma Yole was not so much designed to create charm as developed to enable its crew to accomplish specific hunting operations. These hulls had to carry appropriate gear and be fashioned to survive an extreme range of conditions encountered within the vessel's sphere of navigation.

So we move on now to a group of lemons, nestled (temporarily) in the 'tidal bowl' of a harbour. These double-enders, particularly good in a following sea, could have raked sterns (Zulu) or straight (Fifie) with comparative advantages and disadvantages in load-carrying capability, and built of larch or oak to a designer's blueprint or half-model. But even vessels produced in the same yard at the same time will have variations, as anyone who has tried to transfer a pattern for a sawn frame from the port to starboard side will testify. Hulls take knocks, so a particular vessel will, in use, collect its own bumps and bulges in its skin. Finlay's berthed shapes are harmonic but the references are specific. The wit is accurate and bursts in squalls across these harbour scenes. The vessels are not toys, but the word-play of their names, registration, sails, or surroundings retains the playfulness, shown in Finlay's own model boats, captured in verse or photography. Consider the Mediterranean colour-schemes of boats tied to grey

Peterhead and likely to trawl the North Sea or north-west of the Butt of Lewis.

A 1968 card, '3 Blue Lemons', lets these names chime into a poem:

> ANCHOR OF HOPE
> DAISY
> GOOD DESIGN

A 1970 card shows a net of lemons (the catchers caught), this time with the Kirkcaldy, Aberdeen, Lerwick, and Peterhead registrations visible on the fruit. For someone from a fishing town or whose work connects them with the fishing community, the network of registrations is a cultural reference as valid as a classical column.

I assumed that a blueprint card (with Michael Harvey) providing a builder's plan for a planked lemon must have been made in the same years as those mentioned above – but no, this is just off the stocks. The yard's own nameplate is Wild Hawthorn Press.

Finlay maps a series of explorations *Ocean Stripe Series 3* (1965) or *Ocean Stripe Series 5* (Tarasque Press, 1967), just as a dynasty of skippers will carry a name forward. A random browse through the current Olsen's (a fisherman's almanac which has annual supplements to summarise details of registered vessels over a certain tonnage) produces *Three Fevers III* and *Argonaut IV*.

The patterns are satisfying in themselves. A visual order stems from the 1968 card *Sea Poppy 1* built only of port letters and fishing numbers. *Sea Poppy 2* has stars for petals and is an allusion to a whole genre of naming. I think it is enough to recognise a design of this nature as a homage. An allusive chiming of syllables combines with the visual pattern to give pleasure. For me it is like recognising the structural strength in a light clinker hull. The shapes of the individual planks amount to the shape of the vessel. Those cards were my first voyaging with IHF, fixed to boards in my room in Aberdeen and sent out to anyone I knew would link the starsights to those nameplates seen when down for a fry, or when on the almost nightly pilgrimage to see what and who were coming off the ferry.

Finlay describes his enjoyment of a visitor to Little Sparta focusing on her own family picture of a vessel revealed in a sculpture only as a name and registration. Again it is a recognition of what is shared between people.

This is Ian Hamilton Finlay on art as showing a liking for things:

> I sometimes think that the things which are most important to me never get mentioned, far less discussed. Of course it is difficult to know what to say, or more difficult than writing about 'controversial' things. A lot of my work is to do with straight-forward affection (liking, appreciation), and it always amazes me how little affection for ANYTHING there is in art today.[2]

The 1993 Christmas book *A Harbour of Roses* (with Gary Hincks) is a visual and aural celebration. Simple drawings of varieties and stages of bloom meet with a series of boat-names, all including the word 'rose' and following registrations from implied harbour to harbour. The roses are seasonal by name or by the associated Festival or refer to history or geography. This is a sequence to be enjoyed. Its purpose is surely to share the artist's and poet's liking for the subject. Many publications, over the years, detailing specific types of vessel and rig, share this aim.

Sailing craft made particular by build, rig, or name are also remembered. Woods and Moor(e) are linked with the last Norfolk Wherry as the names of the owners (a bit like the name Reekie, over a fish-curer's shed in Torry, Aberdeen). The essential primer is Eric McKee's *Working Boats of the British Isles* (Conway Maritime Press, London, 1983) which traces varieties of hull design evolved to confront the prevailing winds, seas, and shallows of home waters from Shetland to Cornwall. Here are the scantlings of the Nobby, the Lugger, the Jolly Boat. Demands on vessels capable of carrying out ring-netting, pair-trawling, or drift-netting are specified.

The coupling of pair trawlers, each towing a warp to a shared net, enables distinct names to join in a shared effect:

> LEA RIG
> HAZEL GROVE

That first name has a pun in each word, gently emphasising the joining of land and sea imagery. The second name furthers this with the woodland echo but also brings the boats together, like lovers, allowing the allusion to a Burns love-song to work.

The boats' timbers make another link between land and sea, but one made long before Finlay. He is again tapping a genre of naming. Without moving outwith Lewis, I can quote *Sea-Harvest* and *Golden Sheaf*. One Wild Hawthorn Press card chants a group of names of trees framed between the words 'CLINKER' and 'BUILT'. The reverse is, of course, another incantation of tree-names from carvel (flush-planked) vessels.

Yet you cannot relax into a notion that the sailing-boat and fishing-boat works are always purely celebratory. Further names and numbers coupled as pair-trawlers continue through many collaborations, for example with Margot Sandeman in *Peterhead Fragments* and with several others in *Seven Bollards*. The latter carries forward 'Odysseus PD 294' with 'Traveller PD 301' from the former. This association gives the bones of a narrative. But the former work also links 'Salamis' with 'Harvest Hope'. Here the pastoral is reached only after the name of a great sea-battle. An association of the fishers' vessel with the heroic achieving the pastoral is thus accomplished, but lightly. A classical allusion was already present in the first name but the juxtaposition with the second provides another layer.

Quoted names of stars are often taken from Greek myth. But was the skipper-owner referring to the star or the myth or to the other vessels gone before, bearing that name? The sea-poppy image, with its layers of petals within petals, looks even more appropriate now. Names are a legacy.

If the sailing-boat and fishing-boats cannot be segregated from the widest ripples of cultural reference, neither can they be said to be always on a different course to IHF's warships or images from modern battle. In *Silhouettes* (with Laurie Clark), an elegy for the last sailing-vessel of a class moves from 'petrel' to '*petrol*' to an unstated word like 'napalm'. The next silhouette in the sequence is 'Transitional Work – armed trawler', linking fishing-boat with warship but surely also a self-reference to a movement within his own art.

With a shudder, you realise that the fishing-boat, beautiful, heroic, pastoral, or all of these, but at any rate to be admired, is never so very far away from the nuclear submarine. And some contemporary vessels bearing names with traditions behind them come bristling with electronics far more sophisticated than on any Second World War warship. Catching-power is itself fearsome. And knowledge of the inherent terrible nature of *HMS Vanguard*, created to carry Trident, cannot alter the perception that the shape is a refined sculpture.

In *The Old Stonypath Hoy* (with Gary Hincks, 1991) the reader is ambushed by verse and image that collides with the expectations stemming from a dainty cover. An epitaph for a schooner, 'The LITTLE SECRET', finds her torpedoed:

> Here, a tin-fish in her hold,
> Lies the Little Secret, told.

In terms of style, the poetry is close to that of *The Dancers*. This is often Stevenson-like and full of fun, but the linking of sea-creature and mechanical thing was already present in that early work, 'Lobstercopter'.

Looking through all these arrangements of words, in so many formal expressions, with so many collaborators, I am convinced that Finlay's use and re-use of language amounts to something way beyond the quantifiable skills shown by many accomplished poets who are much less engaging. In his ear and eye for words which nudge against each other, Ian Hamilton Finlay has what seems to me a unique gift for poetry which is often underestimated when attention is devoted to more dramatic or controversial works. In 'diamond-studded fishnet', the lightness of touch is a way to resonance, but it is also working on a tradition of wit and word-play in the maritime world. A 'CQR' pattern anchor is so called, they say, because it is secure. An aircraft becomes a 'paraffin-budgie'. The taboo word 'rabbit' is transmuted to 'underground chicken'. And my ex-navy watchmate, RTW, glancing at the portable computer on which this was written, termed it a 'thwarttop'.

Analysis of wit and craft can, however, only take us so far. Finlay's own application of the word 'eery' to his sea-poems seems to me especially helpful: a one-word navigation-mark. Wit is seldom excluded but it meets with eeriness. I think of that moment when the auxiliary engine is cut and the dynamics of the hull are propelled by oar or sail. The strange appeal of such combinations of words defies explanation as in another work realised in many forms, but using the same few words: 'Evening will come They will sew the blue sail'. Trying to rationalise the mysterious 'they' and the changing light/colour/time risks killing the effect. Finlay uses the word 'eery' again, in a letter accompanying a selection of sea-poems ending with:

$$\frac{\text{WAVE}}{\text{av}\bar{\text{e}}}$$

– 'the last one is a kind of blessing for the eery ones'.[3]

These maritime poems are no minor aspect of the large range of the poet-artist, Ian Hamilton Finlay. They are concurrent with and overlap with other works which are more overtly challenging. Each piece needs to be approached in a spirit of openness. They are integral planks of the whole ship.

(1994)

Notes

1. Edwin Morgan, 'To Ian Hamilton Finlay', in *Collected Poems* (Carcanet Press, Manchester, 1990); reprinted in this volume.
2. Letter from Ian Hamilton Finlay to Ian Stephen, September 1994.
3. Letter from Ian Hamilton Finlay to Jessie McGuffie, 1967.

Medallion. Ian Hamilton Finlay, with Ron Costley; commentary by Stephen Bann.

Finlay's long-standing pre-occupation with the fishing-boat and its attendant imagery has within the last few years largely given place to a concern with the modern warship, and the panorama of recent sea warfare. Here he cites the Battle of Midway, which took place in June 1942 between the fleets of America and Japan and marked the turning point of the Pacific War in America's favour. The motto picks up the famous opening lines of Dante's *Divine Comedy*: 'In the middle of the journey of our life ('Midway'), I come to myself in a dark wood'. The 'dark wood' of Dante's allegory is recreated in the bursts of anti-aircraft fire which cover the sky in surviving photographs of the battle.

From *Twentieth Century Studies*, No 12, December 1972.

Ian Hamilton Finlay: An Imaginary Portrait

STEPHEN BANN

> To Apollo, praying that he would come to us from Italy, bringing his lyre with him: Ad Apollinem, ut ab Italis cum lyra ad Germanos veniat.
>
> Walter Pater, *Duke Carl of Rosenmold*

Almost twenty years have passed since the publication of Ian Hamilton Finlay's first book, *The Sea-Bed and Other Stories*, in 1958. For anyone who tries to make sense of the volume and variety of the work which stands between that group of short stories and the present exhibition,[1] there are two false tracks to be avoided. One is the biographical approach, which is a matter of stringing individual books, booklets, cards, and so forth along the ideal continuity of the artist's career. Actually this is a temptation which Finlay himself has effectively barred by the sheer plurality of his production: whenever a complete catalogue raisonné of his work succeeds in being produced, it will doubtless seem an effect not of reason but of delirium. The other false track is the systematic, synchronic approach. Taking an overall sample of what he has produced, we might attempt to distribute it across a chart of ideal locations, achieving in the end a constructed schema of the artist's 'poetic universe'. Finlay's work undoubtedly lends itself to this kind of quasi-anthropological treatment, articulated as it is upon a series of binary oppositions (land/sea, garden/ocean) which are mediated by the effect of metaphor. But the fault lies in the fact that this schema, in so far as it is constructed synchronically, is necessarily inert. No account can be taken of the dynamic transformations through which one type of language use has passed into another, one medium supplanted its predecessor. For the would-be biographer, we might say, Finlay has provided the obstacle of the intractably small – the card/fragment that is a minimal unit of information and yet seems oddly recalcitrant when we attempt to adjust it to the circumstances of the artist's 'life'. For the critic turned structuralist, he provides the obstacle of the inconveniently large – the earth, sky, or ocean as a timeless alibi.

To steer between Scylla and Charybdis is therefore the aim of this essay. It will attempt to demonstrate how, through a sequence of stages which must to some extent be arbitrarily chosen, a particular poetic practice emerges. The very unexpectedness of such an exhibition as this, which seems to bear only a tangential connection to the work of any other living artist, makes such an element of recapitulation necessary. But once again, this is less a matter of trying to fit every available link into a plausible chain, than of tracing a series of movements which are irreversible. In many ways, these 'movements' are the most extraordinary feature of Finlay's development. How far he has travelled (or voyaged, if the more appropriate metaphor were taken) is visible not merely in the shift of medium from the printed page to the stone inscription, but in the irreducible cognitive stages through which such a shift has been prepared and consolidated.

It is because of the need to trace stages in cognition, and sensation, that the context of Pater's 'imaginary portraits' has been evoked. Obviously this implies a certain obliquity as far as the biographical basis is concerned – an obliquity which might well imply the birth of our subject not (as is reliably reported) in the West Indies in the 1920s, but in Orkney after the Second World War. But this is not the only implication of the reference. In the course of this essay, it will become evident that another subject is concerned – a mythic subject invoked in his absence through indirect appellation, through the trope of *transumption* or *far-fetching* which Harold Bloom has qualified as the distinctive mark of our post-romantic culture in its relationship to the past. In Pater's terms:

... the hyperborean Apollo, sojourning, in the revolutions of time, in the sluggish north for a season, yet Apollo still, prompting art, music, poetry, and the philosophy which interprets man's life, making a sort of intercalary day amid the natural darkness; not meridian day, but a soft derivative daylight, good enough for us.

Apollo, with his lyre, sojourning among us – yet (as Pater well knew) the prospect is not so much an idyll as a threat of violence. 'Apollo in Picardy' shows the transplantation of the Greek spirit to the mediaeval French province, with its inevitable concomitants of madness and violent death. Finlay's 'Lyre' – the Oerlikon gun – is an evocation of the distant god, a *transumption*, which is brought to the pitch of violence by the very distance which it has travelled. It serves to translate the classical symbol in the very measure in which it is excessive, hyperbolic: 'Apollo in Picardy' as the First World War gun which helped to devastate that province – the 'lyre' coming *ad Germanos* with deadly effect:

> They came as a Boom and a Biff to the Hun
> The Bofors, the Bren and the Oerlikon Gun.
>   from *The Old Stonypath Hoy*[2]

But this is to anticipate Finlay's point of arrival. If he has now acquired the right to a transumptive mode, this is because of the solid preparation of his earlier work. Such work may now, in retrospect, seem to have quite a different significance from what appeared at the time. But such revisions are forced upon us by the continuing drama of Finlay's achievement.

To begin with, at any rate, it is a question of 'concrete poetry'. The label which still adheres persistently to Finlay, 'the leading British concrete poet', at least serves to remind us of his decision, around 1962, to break with traditional discursive forms in his poetry. Such a decision has indeed proved irreversible. But it is precisely in this designation, and in the folklore that has gathered around it, that we risk being misdirected from the start. When Finlay became a concrete poet – when he adopted the non-discursive poetic forms already employed by

Eugen Gomringer and the Brazilian noigandres group – he was not following a style, but responding to the ontological insistance of language. The distinction becomes completely clear in the much quoted letter which he sent to the French poet, Pierre Garnier, on 17 September 1963:

> I wonder if we are not all a little in the dark still as to the real significance of 'concrete' . . . For myself I cannot derive from the poems I have written any 'method' which can be applied to the writing of the next poem; it comes back, after each poem, to a level of 'being', to an almost physical intuition of the time, or of a form . . . to which I try, with huge uncertainty, to be 'true'. Just so, 'concrete' began for me with the extraordinary (since wholly unexpected) sense that the syntax I had been using, *the movement* of language in me, at a physical level, was no longer there – so it had to be replaced with something else, with a syntax and movement that would be true of the new feeling (which existed in only the vaguest way, since I had, then, no form for it . . .). So that I see the theory as a very essential (because we are people, and people think, or should think, or should TRY to think) part of our life and art; and yet I also feel that it is a construction, very haphazard, uncertain, and by no means as yet to be taken as definitive.

This remarkable statement deserves to be quoted at length, if only for the reason that the rhythmic patterns so closely mirror the process of searching 'with huge uncertainty' which Finlay describes. It is altogether evident that concrete poetry represented for him not so much a new technique, a 'grammar' of non-discursive syntax, as the intimation of a form which fulfilled (at least from time to time) an ontological need. Just as the need – which sprang from a growing sense of a changed relationship to language – preceded the discovery, so it might be expected to continue its insistence, over and beyond the objective formulations of 'theory'.

This helps to explain, of course, why Finlay subsequently drew apart from 'concrete poetry', in so far as it represented an orthodoxy which had already begun to degenerate. In retrospect, the entire development of the phenomenon in Britain (and elsewhere) throughout the mid 1960s can be seen to have perpetuated a strange illusion: the notion that concrete poetry was a novel artistic or poetic form, still in its primary stages, which would acquire its basic 'grammar' and then proceed to the task of large-scale achievement. Thus the concrete epic might be expected to succeed in due time, in the same way as Pound's *Cantos* or Williams' *Paterson* have been seen as the epics of Imagism. In effect, it would be more realistic to stress the fact that, from the outset, concrete poetry could be characterised not as a beginning but as an ending (or at least the beginning of an ending) – not as a grammar but as a mannerism. The concrete poets were completing a cycle of linguistic experimentation which had begun in the early days of the Modern Movement. It would indeed be possible to argue that Gomringer and the Noigandres group succeeded in producing a modernist poetry of high achievement precisely because of their acceptance of the constraints of late-coming. They offered a 'mythic' resolution to the enterprise of fragmentation proclaimed by the Futurists and Dadaists.

Finlay himself was never unaware of this historical dimension. Indeed his need to make it explicit will be seen as a necessary stage in his further development. But it must not be supposed that he was alone in seeing the problem of ontology, in its implications for poetic form, as much more crucial than the generalised questions of method. When he explained his scepticism about the adequacy of 'theory' in his letter to Garnier, he was nonetheless defining his relation to language in terms that were particularly appropriate to Gomringer and his German antecedents. He was touching – perhaps quite unconsciously – that vein of philosophy of language which in German culture (and in the German rediscovery of Greek culture) had run in parallel to the stream of poetry. At a later point in the same letter, he offered a formula which lucidly defined the ontology of the concrete poem: 'It is a model of order, even if set in a space which is full of doubt'. Surely this definition comes close to Hölderlin's celebrated formula: 'Poetically man inhabits'? Finlay articulates in his own terms a view of poetic language which emerges from German classicism and German metaphysics in the eighteenth-century – a view which Michel Deguy has traced through paraphrasing its point of arrival in the philosophy of Heidegger:

> Every act of making has habitation in view; preservation, protection; no violence that does not propose conservation, the 'making of a world' (Heidegger) . . . What man makes: shelter. And language, 'Shelter of being', to shelter there from it; as one shelters with earth from earth.

This therefore is the purpose of the 'violence' done upon discursive language in Finlay's first collection of concrete poems, *Rapel* (1963). The sense of the loss of syntax is compensated by the enterprise of founding syntax *in another place*. The world is, as he reminds Garnier, 'to be made by man into his *home*'. But man's strategy for the domestication of the Other can only thrive through the colonising project of language. Symptomatic more than any other poem in *Rapel* of this equivocal 'Shelter of being' is the 'Homage to Malevich'. Here it is a question of the equivocal status of the edge, the bordering limit which both separates language formally from the surrounding 'blank' space and also (as it were) bisects the semantic units 'black' and 'block', leaving an oscillation of the resolved and the unresolved in the terms 'lack' and 'lock'. Finlay expresses a tension which will prove crucial to his further development as an artist: that of form and non-form, language and non-language, being set not merely in opposition, but *in a dialectical relationship*. If Malevich, in his 'Square' series, achieves dialectical expression of the painter's problem of figure and ground, Finlay carefully avoids the implication that such a problem can simply be transposed into poetic terms. For language is in itself presence and absence, in terms of Saussure's distinction it comprises both *signifier* and *signified*. In 'Homage to Malevich', the space 'of doubt' is not simply the white page, but the dimension of meaning whose incompatible signs (lack/lock) are in contrast with the certainty of typographic structure.

Indeed, whether or not we trace it through these honorary German antecedents, or whether we relate it to common ground in the Pre-Socratics, whom Finlay was subsequently to discover, the assumption of a dialectical tension is the early guarantee that concrete poetry will not, for Finlay, become a barren, formalistic practice. The function of Finlay's poetic is differentiated even at this early stage from that of Gomringer, or the Brazilians, in so far as it enshrines the principle of

Ian Hamilton Finlay: An Imaginary Portrait 61

conflict – a conflict made evident by the very title of *Rapel*, which announces a division between 'Fauve and Suprematist poems' (and carried over in the context of this very exhibition with reference to the 'fauve' neon poems and the adjoining room of neo-classical inscriptions). As 'Homage to Malevich' indicates, the principle of conflict animates the very formal structure of the poem. But it is also a force that will break open the framework of syntax's new shelter on the printed page, making Finlay's career a continual transcendence of medium.

Appropriately Michel Deguy, the translator of Heidegger into French poetic culture, defines the poet's quest in a way that sums up Finlay's initial predicament:

> But the pretension of exposing oneself to risk, to experience in language . . . the pretension of daring with it and of running into it as if into a specific element, a sortie comparable to that of the Navigators, appears exorbitant. How to avoid being simply a profiteer, under cover of the boldness of others . . . but to enter into relation with the possibility of growth in the language.

Rapel had been published in 1963. By the end of 1965, the concrete poetry movement had risen quickly and unexpectedly to a certain degree of fame. Finlay contributed both to the first International Exhibition of Concrete and Kinetic Poetry at Cambridge in December 1964, and to the extensive display of work *Between Poetry and Painting* at the ICA, London, in the following year. Among his contributions were the first 'Standing Poem' (1963) and the splendidly vivacious poem-print 'Le Circus' (1964). However, the critical response to these exhibitions was on the whole disconcerting. A review of the ICA show in *The Times* appeared under the title 'Purity and Thinness in Concrete Poetry': such terms as 'refined', 'bloodless', 'pastoral', and 'Georgian' were used to describe Finlay's exhibits – however anomalous this may have appeared with reference to 'Homage to Malevich'. Finlay was well aware by this stage that what had generally come to be called 'concrete' designated an artistic approach in many ways the very opposite of his own intentions. He began to speculate on the need for what he called a 'new classicism'.

In the course of this period of reflection, which coincided with his move out of Edinburgh to a farmhouse in Ross-shire, Finlay began to pose two problems which were to dominate the immediate course of his work and have indeed remained implicit in it up to the present day. These might be defined as the problem of *inscription* and the problem of the *sign*. To separate them one from another may appear to some extent arbitrary, since they are often raised in conjunction in the same work. But they nonetheless remain distinct on the level of analysis. Inscription is the problem of the relation of the work to the world, the problem of its *material* embodiment. The problem of the sign (or of 'sign and supersign') involves on the other hand the relation of part to whole within the work considered as a structure. Both are integrally connected with the question of classicism, as an overall aesthetic stance.

Indeed it is hardly accidental that the concern with a 'new classicism' voiced in the autumn of 1965 should have coincided with a technical discovery which was to offer exciting new possibilities of inscription. Disappointed in his attempts to gain technical assistance from Edinburgh College of Art, Finlay had located by post a glass factory in London which was willing to experiment in the sandblasting of poems on sheets of glass. Already he had begun to move away from the habitual constraints of the printed page. For example the 'le Circus' poster-poem (one of a series of poster-poems by various authors published by Finlay's Wild Hawthorn Press) could be said to be set in social space rather than in the private space of the printed book. But the inscription on glass went much further than this, since it formed a material imprint upon the hard, intractable surface. Finlay had begun to explore, in a further dimension, the dialectical insights of his letter to Garnier. The poem as object could be abandoned, up to a point, in the material world. Yet as a balancing compensation, the poet's act of inscription – his projection of symbolic order upon the real – acquired intensified force.

The first sandblasted poem, *Wave Rock*, finely demonstrates this newly acquired situation of balance. The letters appear (and are confirmed by the touch) as being deeply gouged into the thick glass panel. But of countervailing effect is the relationship to 'atmospheric' conditions which this material embodiment implies. In accordance with circumambient light conditions, the relationship of 'poem' to 'page' –

or figure to ground – undergoes a constant process of transformation. With intense oblique sunlight, the letters appear to have a deep black shading, and project a further image of the poem on to an adjacent wall. In the open air, on the other hand, the letters are virtually absorbed in the opacity of the dark glass sheet. Of course this continual physical variation has its semantic counterpart in the opposition of terms which is the poem. 'Rock' is the massive aggregation of its own letter constituents to form a solid structure, whilst 'wave' is the dynamic charge which contests this structure, distributing 'v's and 'w's along its implied crest.

Wave Rock has remained for Finlay an ideal test of the possibilities of inscription. A now destroyed version, which was exhibited at Dunfermline in 1966, served as a prototype for the notion of the permanent garden poem which has since become so important an aspect of his work. A ceramic version, built up of separately cast tiles, is still projected for the side of the loch at his present home, Stonypath. But *Wave Rock* is also important in relation to the other chief problem of this period, that of sign and supersign. Briefly, this is a question of the relation of the individual units of sense and structure in relation to the overall concept and form of the poem. In *Rapel*, this relationship had been asserted largely through use of the metaphor of pictorial space. Poems like 'to the painter, Juan Gris', 'a peach/an apple', and indeed 'Homage to Malevich' evoked specific painterly parallels, in the light of which the space of the blank page could be seen as a notional canvas. In *Wave Rock*, however, a different principle is in play. The individual signs (letters, words) combine into an aggregated supersign: this supersign *is* the rock assaulted by waves.

That Finlay's thoughts were moving in this direction becomes clear from a letter written in the early months of 1966, when he gave his definition of 'the real present problem in concrete': 'to start with it was a problem of syntax but now it's one of keeping the simplicity without abandoning metaphor'. The word, or at least the meaningful assemblage of letters, had to remain the basic constituent of his poetry, but ways of achieving 'metaphor', or the overall form as a transformation and transcendence of its parts, could be more ambitious and various. One possibility can be glimpsed in the new version of the 'Homage to Malevich', which was published in 1967: still an extension of the words 'black block' into cubic form, it was extended in this version to form five cubes and an overall cross. Here, undoubtedly, a new thematic charge (equally faithful to Malevich but absorbing a more general reference) was added, though the sense of dynamic interaction between the form and the surrounding space was necessarily diminished. However, the work from this period which most clearly pointed to the new possibilities of metaphorical transformation was the two-page spread (later a freestanding poem and a glass poem) entitled 'Four Sails', which was first published in the *Beloit Poetry Journal*, Fall 1966. Here Finlay's rhetorical range is exploited to a greater degree than in any earlier poem. Borrowing the conventional Homeric metonymy of 'sails' for 'ships', he brilliantly transfers the figure of speech into typographic terms by dividing the two pages into triangular areas ('sails') with a thin line rule. Within these four demarcated areas, there appear not simply the successive adjectives qualifying the four sails (ships), but capitalised letters emerging from the adjectives which signify ports of origin (e.g. KY for Kirkcaldy). It would be hard to think of a more effective way of combining 'metaphor' with 'simplicity'. Finlay introduces a fertile tension between the free, expressive use of language (the adjectival qualifiers which signal modes, or moods, of being) and the pre-constrained formulae (letter combinations which 'name' the fishing-boat). Indeed it could be said that it is the fishing-boat – for the next few years the poetic vehicle of his linguistic discovery – which resolves for a while the initial antagonism between 'fauve' and 'suprematist' principles. Through the use of this privileged symbol, Finlay is enabled to make his 'sortie comparable to that of the Navigators'.

Although an interesting parallel can be made between 'Four Sails' and Gomringer's 'I konstellation: 15' (published 1969), it is the difference between these two works which is most significant. Gomringer uses the closed form of the grid, and the aggregation of simple words over fifteen successive pages, to accentuate the concrete, coded character of the printed message: his expressive effects come as a local disruption of the symmetries and regularities of the ludic combinatory, in accordance with the strictest principles of the aesthetics of information. For Finlay, on the other hand, the 'grid' is simultaneously a closed form and a rhetorical figure (as a 'sail'): typographical coding is not simply accepted as the concrete manifestation of language, but worked for its possibilities of double meaning. Gomringer's work stands, no doubt, with the *Poemobiles* of Augusto de Campos as the late, but unsurpassed emergence of a concrete poetry consistent with the reductive postulates of the Modern Movement. Finlay is by contrast visibly estranged from the tendency which, in its more vulgar applications, he had already begun to condemn.

The years 1965–67 therefore see a further process of reappraisal, building upon the ontological insights of the period in which *Rapel* was composed. Under the general rubric of a 'new classicism', Finlay began to investigate both the inscription of the poem in the world, and the transcendence of the sign through metaphor. Both of these areas of investigation were, in a sense, no more than the index of Finlay's total commitment to 'the possibility of growth in the language'. Through the refinement of the problem of metaphor obtained in 'Four Sails', he was obliging himself to confront yet another aspect of the poet's dialectic. How to secure the transformation of a language that offers itself simultaneously as expressive and inert? How to emphasise its public character, its status as the common change of everyday communication, whilst simultaneously conferring upon it a private, poetic meaning? For Finlay, the problem seems always to have presented itself in terms of this impossible project of resolution. Consequently, from 1966 onwards, every variety of pre-constrained linguistic formula – cliché, proverb, riddle, headline, title, registration sign – has been welcomed in his work. But recognition of this public, pre-constrained quality has been simply the prelude to poetic rehabilitation. It is as if the distance travelled by the formula – its initial estrangement from any freshness of meaning or vision – were an integral factor in our awareness of its final and realised poetic form.

It is *Homo significans* – man the maker of signs – who emerges clearly as the persona governing Finlay's work in the previous section. The problems of the sign, and of the inscription of the sign, involve him in the last resort in the simple but fundamental question: how do we confer meanings upon the world? Yet there is another person who must also be taken into account even in this early period – the apparently more humble one of *Homo faber*, man the craftsman. For Finlay, a concern with the poem as object in effect preceded his emergence as a concrete poet. In 1962, he published his 'Concertina' poem as one of the first productions of his own Wild Hawthorn Press. This experiment with folded paper led to the series of 'Standing Poems' (1963–65), and finally to the elaborate construction of *Earthship* (1965) which required the stapling of sections of card in order to obtain a series of curved surfaces for the poetic text. By this stage he had also begun to make toys in wood, using simple reductive forms as in the *Fish* strung between pegs which dates from 1964. On moving from Edinburgh to Gledfield Farm, Easter Ross, at the end of the same year, he immediately found a strong stimulus to construction in the availability of natural and architectural settings which could be adapted to take poem-objects. With the help of Dick Sheeler, he completed a series of much larger wooden structures based on recent poems like *Ajar* and *Canal Stripe Series 3*, the former for placing against the stair-wall of the house and the latter to be freestanding in the adjacent field. At the same stage, a construction based on the poem 'Ark/arc' was built onto the wall of the farmhouse, facing the road. Finlay also used the outside wall of the farmhouse for a most effective version of the 'Acrobats' poem, soon to be published as a poem-print but already, at this stage, destined ideally for some public site such as a school playground.

Finlay's concern with the poem-object must not, however, be seen as antagonistic to the ontological position in which we have based his work from 1963 onwards, – quite the opposite: he has testified recently that this inclination could be explained with the aid of Gombrich's philosophical distinctions in the essay 'Icones Symbolicae', where the 'free-floating' quality of the emblem is seen as an index of its metaphysical status. In a real sense, the emblem – to an even greater extent, the emblem engraved on a medallion – is the successor to the 'toys' and poem-objects of the earlier period. But there is a further, crucial point to be made about the gradual transition towards the object – one which recalls to a central importance the dialectical element already traced. With the commission for the sandblasting of *Wave Rock*, Finlay had clearly reached a stage where he was relinquishing control over the technical processes of fabrication, to a much greater extent than with the customary processes of typesetting. The work when complete would almost necessarily come as a surprise to him, however scrupulous his concern to supervise the process of realisation and however clear the idea for which he was aiming. In the same way, the collaboration with Dick Sheeler, however closely it was carried on, suggested a reliance on the individual capabilities of a craftsman which might itself be a determining factor in the type of realisation selected. Just as the finished work was intended to stand in the semi-public space of farmyard or garden, so the fabrication of the work could be said to give it an irreducible distance from the poet/originator.

There is no more crucial point to make in connection with Finlay's work than the one which arises from this assumption of distance – this voluntary alienation of the poet's proprietary right over his language. Instead of presuming that Finlay's innumerable essays in 'collaboration' represent an unfortunate (if necessary) relinquishment of the artist's plenary powers, we should recognise that such a strategy is integral to his dialectical approach. It is, quite simply, the recognition and assumption of the 'Other'. Arguments which try to sort out the importance of such and such a collaborator in such and such a project therefore fall into mere irrelevance. The only point worth bearing in mind is the fact that, for Finlay, the 'otherness' of a craft or style as represented in its practitioners is a means of growth through dialectical interchange. (Whether Finlay can in the same way represent 'otherness' for his collaborators is an interesting question, but one which is obviously subsidiary to the problem of assessing his work.) Perhaps it is unduly misleading to insist on the word 'collaborations' (incidentally the title of Finlay's most recent exhibition)[3] to describe this unusual relationship. One would in any case be hard put to find a term which more accurately conveyed the sense of Finlay's strategy, precisely because of its unfamiliarity within the context of artistic psychology, as it is generally understood today. In a period when the French theorist Jean Baudrillard can argue convincingly that the artist's signature is the only necessary guarantee of the status of an art work (with a consequent, and unprecedented, notoriety for the 'fake'), Finlay's procedure is determinedly iconoclastic. It is an interesting, and undoubtedly significant, fact that the present exhibition[4] amounts to a kind of consecration of Finlay's strategy, at a time when its implications are only imperfectly understood. We can hardly predict the effect that it will have, once these implications become more obvious.

Yet if we are stressing the unique and challenging aspect of Finlay's method of working, we must be clear that this is only so in relation to present-day assumptions in the realm of the plastic arts – in a period when, as Gustav Metzger has wittily pointed out, Picasso has perpetrated the 'Hiroshima' of modern painting. If we look more extensively into the history of the arts in the post-romantic period, we can find important parallels for Finlay's strategy. In his masterly work on Mahler, Theodor Adorno refers to the poetry of Heine (the writer from whom Pater took the myth of the Hyperborean Apollo) in terms of its openness to the ready-made phrase, even the cliché. Verbal formulae occur in Heine's poetry (and indeed the same could be said of Baudelaire) not as artfully concealed commonplaces, but as artefacts of language which do not claim their origin in the soul of the poet Heine. Such a stage (Adorno claims) is characteristic of late romanticism: it is the sign of its mannerist phase. Clearly there is a parallel here with Finlay's approach, as described in the last section – with his deliberate cultivation of the pre-constrained verbal (or letter-based) formula. But there is an even closer connection in Adorno's account, when he goes on to stress the importance for Mahler's music of the conductor. In his view, it is precisely the state of musical expression in Mahler's period that impels him to grant to the conductor a greater liberty of interpretation than any of his predecessors. Music, in so far as it is a language which has undergone specific and highly organised development from the time of Mozart and Beethoven onwards, reaches a point where the fiction of personal expression must be contraverted: the conductor takes up his baton.

However indirect this comparison, it surely makes manifest the essential feature of Finlay's 'collaborations'. For Finlay, the collaborator serves a purpose reminiscent of both the examples just quoted. In the less ambitious sense, he can offer the same relation of 'otherness' as the cliché or formula: a style which is set within a particular convention of (say) lettering or carving and can be used as such. In the more ambitious case, he takes the risk of performance – of conducting the project in a virtuoso style which draws a large measure of attention to his own deliberate extension of the possibilities latent in the score. Perhaps Jud Fine's recent collaborations with Finlay, to which Douglas Hall[5] has rightly drawn attention, are the clearest examples of this possibility to date. All the same, it is important to bear in mind the fundamental issue which lies beneath the analogies from Adorno. Finlay's collaborative projects do not simply amount to a capricious gesture, or even a necessary method for putting ambitious schemes into practice (though they are that as well). They arise from what is both a stage in the late development of post-romantic poetics, and a dialectical attitude which attempts to circumscribe that stage: they postulate the recognition, and retrieval of 'otherness', in circumstances where the victory of the 'Other' is sometimes the unexpected outcome.

A final word must be said about an equally important strategy which accompanies, indeed is inseparable from, Finlay's strategy of collaboration. Although the opportunities provided by Gledfield were more propitious than those of Edinburgh to the planning of poem-constructions, they did not offer any prospect of permanence. It was only in 1967, when Ian and Sue Finlay moved to the farm of Stonypath, near Dunsyre in Lanarkshire, that it became possible to think of a permanent site for poem-objects in a natural setting. In the ten years that have elapsed between the move to Stonypath and the present exhibition, the garden at Stonypath has been continually elaborated and extended: artificial ponds have been created, and the number and variety of works installed has grown from year to year. This is not the place to make a detailed survey of the stages of the garden's preparation, which are described elsewhere. Nor does it seem necessary to enumerate the various garden works as such: the present exhibition contains a superb slide documentation of Stonypath by the photographer Dave Paterson, while the West Coast Poetry Review publication, *Selected Ponds*, includes his fine black and white photographs from a previous year. In the line of the present argument – which is concerned not with documentation but with an 'imaginary portrait' – it is simply necessary to extend the point which has been made about Finlay's collaborations. Once the work, or an important proportion of the work, is retrieved from the stone-carver, carpenter or ceramicist who has realised it, the garden serves as a location in which it can take its own place. It still stands in antithesis to nature – a projection of the symbolic upon the real – but it mediates this antithesis through the meanings which it proposes for nature, and through the effect of its generic reference – lyric or heroic, elegiac or pastoral. As Robert Kenedy concludes in an essay on Finlay for *Art International*, 'it should be remembered that under God's free sky only the generic voice has real meaning'.

Stonypath the garden also provides the most profound invocation of the 'Other', as a domain which cannot be conquered except by symbols. Beyond the garden itself, as a location for poem-objects, there is implied the presence of the Ocean. Indeed one of the first inscriptions on stone to be installed, as early as 1967, was the text which implied the connection of the small pond in the farmyard with the source which made it possible: 'Hic jacet parvulum quoddam ex acqua longiore excerptum' (Here lies a small excerpt from a longer stretch of water). As the sequence of ponds has been extended, the reference has been magnified. *Nuclear Sail*, the image in slate of the conning tower of a nuclear submarine, now stands beside the artificially constructed loch, transforming its rippling surface into Ocean by simple analogy of proportions with the adjacent work. The Ocean is therefore the alibi of Finlay's garden: even its bird-tables take the form of aircraft-carriers, whilst the sundials evoke the seasons in terms of the names of fishing-boats. However tentatively we may wish to establish a point which becomes merely banal through crude statement, we must trace this logic of displacement through to its conclusion. If the Ocean is the alibi of the Garden, the alibi of the Ocean is Death. The Other as a final, irreducible term is the point beyond which no further symbolic conversions are possible.

It is not difficult to see that, from this aspect, the garden at Stonypath can hardly be taken as the summation of Finlay's achievement. As a garden, it already represents a modern equivalent to the philosophical gardens of the eighteenth-century, to The Leasowes and Ermenonville. As such, it already serves as a prototype for new inflections in the landscape planning of our period: the set of poems designed by Finlay for the garden of the Max Planck Institute, Stuttgart, is the clearest index of his influence in this domain to date, but it will certainly not be the last. Yet, as the argument of this essay has tried to demonstrate, it would be inconsistent with Finlay's original project to imagine any definitive point of arrival, marked by an acquired body of work. What Deguy describes as 'running into [the language], as if into a specific element, a sortie comparable to that of the Navigators', is still the keynote of his activity. And this commitment clearly precludes any

Ian Hamilton Finlay: An Imaginary Portrait 71

stage of rest. I have attempted to show how, consistent with the dialectical insight of his earliest concrete poems, Finlay has adopted the strategies of collaboration and garden planning, these being not merely a matter of context or technique but on a more profound level of keeping otherness in play. To continue to make this wager is still the purpose of his work.

Yet it is doubtful whether Finlay could have sustained his remarkable development after 1967 if he had not recognised the need to come to terms with a further dimension of otherness – one more subtly but no less insistently connected with his strategy as a poet. This was the dimension of History – the cultural and historical dimension in which he was obliged to find his own stance through defining the stance of others. Even in 'Homage to Malevich', the acknowledgement to the Russian painter suggested a point of reference in the Modern Movement, one which was further extended by the Fauve and Cubist reminiscences of the other poems. 'Homage' has indeed remained a recurrent theme in Finlay's work, culminating in the 'Homage to Watteau' exhibition (Graeme Murray Gallery, Edinburgh, 1976) and the recreation of Salvator's *terribiltà* with a dead tree which presides melodramatically over the rubbish dump at Stonypath, achieving an imaginative triumph over the initial anomaly. But these single examples, though indicative of a general attitude, are not enough to define a historical and cultural position. The issue is well understood by Marcelin Pleynet who, though he is in effect writing about young contemporary painters tracing their affiliation to Cubism and Cézanne, expresses the psychological truth of any present-day coming to terms with the past:

> These cultural stages cannot be seen as points of rest (nor indeed as points of reference) if they are to be constitutive: they are before all else cross-roads of influences, which have hardly been understood at all if the interplay of forces working upon them has not been understood. What we need to raise upon the strength of them does not serve as a form of accumulation, in necessarily quantitative terms, but as a form of obstacle, in qualitative terms. To put it briefly, there would be no chance of the subject constituting itself in the gesture of appropriating acquired riches: in

effect the subject would take its own measure in the moment of a threatened loss of subjectivity.

The deliberately psychoanalytic cast of Pleynet's judgement should not blind us to the fact that such a distinction undoubtedly holds. However much we may like to picture cultural history as a rich crop which is ours for the picking – however much we wish to see ourselves as tourists of the many-splendoured past – it is obvious that the artist cannot afford to take such an illusion for reality. For the artist, to assert a position in the continuous development of cultural forms is not to tap a vein of inexhaustible richness, but to encounter and wrestle with the problem of self-definition. Only at this price will he be able to articulate his own historical position in such a way that the 'stages' are seen to be genuinely 'constitutive', rather than mere effects of his retrospective vision.

In so far as they have tackled this problem of cultural tradition, different contemporary artists have come to terms with it in different ways. In the context of Pleynet's argument, it would be worth stressing that the modern painter (specifically the modern American painter) celebrates an extreme state of the development of his art, in which 'history' exists as a series of constitutive stages beginning with the formulation of post-Renaissance representational systems in Alberti's *De Pictura*. Finlay, of course, starts not from the *exclusive* position of the painter, but from the *inclusive* integrative stance of a poet who must absorb into his present reference the cultural tissue of the past (which itself includes painting, in so far as painting is an aspect of culture). He must therefore come to terms not merely with the Modern Movement and the Renaissance (stage of the mythic birth of painting for an artist like Brice Marden), but also with the ancient world, before and after its codification of aesthetic and philosophical principles in the works of Plato and Aristotle. However excessive this claim may seem (but is it excessive if we think of Joyce, or Pound, or Stevens?), it is the claim which Finlay obliges us to investigate.

In the first instance, obviously, it is a matter of coming to terms with the Modern Movement. Finlay's early references to modernism – which were in any case inescapable at a time when the relation of concrete poetry to (say) the calligrammes of Apollinaire was a lively

Ian Hamilton Finlay: An Imaginary Portrait 73

subject of debate – had to be subsumed in a work which was at the same time a manifesto, or *traité de méthode*. This was surely the function of *Ocean Stripe Series 5*, a poem-booklet produced in 1967. As I have already analysed this poem in a degree of detail which would be inappropriate here, I shall present simply the main features of this extraordinary work, which are themselves sufficiently various. *Ocean Stripe Series 5*, (Tarasque Press) consists of fourteen successive right-hand pages: the last of these is a 'Postscript', while each of the previous ones juxtaposes the photographic image of a fishing-boat with a short (unattributed) text. In effect the textual material is all drawn from a series of manifestos reprinted in the magazine *Form*, manifestos which spanned a range from the pioneering 'sound-poet' of the Modern Movement, Kurt Schwitters, to his recent successors, the Austrian Ernst Jandl and the Belgian Paul de Vree. The photographic images, incidentally, were all taken from the publication *Fishing News*.

The basic scheme of *Ocean Stripe Series 5* thus involves two binary oppositions: the first, obviously historical, between Schwitters' manifesto and those of our contemporaries within the same 'tradition'; the second, not historical at first sight, between the text and the image. Finlay uses these two possibilities of interplay to achieve what is at first perceptible as an ironic distance from all levels of meaning: the very phrase 'sound-poetry' which opens the first text acquires the ambiguity of association with the sea (or 'sound'), as well as posing the ironic question – is this bizarre montage-poem *sound*? Gradually, however, this level of irony becomes less easy to sustain. After an initial group of three pages concerned with *definition*, and the more or less static image of the fishing-boat, we move to dynamic indications of poetic procedure, with the fishing-boats under way ('a sortie comparable to that of the Navigators'). In the final section of five pages, irony is altogether abandoned. The fine images of the boats complement texts in which we are offered the promise of 'a kind of rehabilitation' after the reductive feats of the modernist poetic. The final image of (in Finlay's words) a 'white boat, lit by the sun, setting off into a dark firth' splendidly fulfils Schwitters' pronouncement: 'It is impossible to explain the meaning of art; it is infinite'.

It might have been tempting to conclude at the time that Finlay was establishing a kind of distance from the modernist aesthetic, in so far as it was still associated with the revivalist manifestations of concrete and 'phonic' poetry in the 1960s. This is true up to a point. And it is also clear that Finlay's strategy of confuting (or complementing) Schwitters with the image of traditional beauty was a way of claiming access to the aesthetic domain of Symbolism – the very domain before which modernism interposed as an 'obstacle'. But it is necessary to point out that this symbolic treatment of the fishing-boat – this access to the Symbolist world which so many of his works were to assume in the next few years – was not in any way in nostalgic retreat from the modernist situation. Symbolism was itself to lead to the investigation of Renaissance Neo-Platonism: Neo-Platonism to prompt a sustained investigation of the Pre-Socratics. In close parallel, the image and symbol of the fishing-boat was to be supplanted by that of the modern warship. Finlay had therefore embarked on a deconstruction of Western aesthetic systems, a reconstitution of cultural stages, in which the placing of the Modern Movement in parenthesis, as it were, formed a necessary point of departure.

Nor was this process unrelated to the other aspects of Finlay's development as an artist. *Ocean Stripe Series 5* ends, as has been mentioned, with a 'Postscript' which is a phonic poem by Schwitters, employing only the letters of the alphabet in isolation. Its promised 'rehabilitation' is in terms of the codes set up by the registration signs of the fishing boats, which enable the otherwise bare capital letters to be seen as the possible signs of imaginary boats deriving from figmentary ports. Against this transformation of the Schwitters poem into an imaginary Finlay text, we have in the same year as *Ocean Stripe Series 5* the first rendering of a fishing-boat name in painted, wooden, freestanding letters, *Starlit Waters*. This work, which by its entry into the collection of the Tate Gallery in 1976 obviously marks a crucial stage in Finlay's acceptance as an artist, seems to arise directly from the preparatory exercise of *Ocean Stripe Series 5* – as if the establishment of that historical dimension were a necessary prerequisite to his self-recognition as an artist.

The same is true if we consider the entire development of Finlay's work from 1967 onwards in the light of his aesthetic and philosophical preoccupations. Although it has been necessary in this essay to set up a series of converging arguments which establish the different aspects of Finlay's procedure, it must be clear that they cannot in the last resort be taken as separate – least of all the philosophical intuition which is here represented as prior to them all. Just as the first fishing-boat name constructions – soon to be followed by the fine series involving port names and numbers – took for granted the expanded claims of the poet who had completed *Ocean Stripe Series 5*, so many subsequent new departures in poetic mode or material technique have had their foundation in a wider cognitive grasp of the issues of Western cultural history. Finlay does not in any way abandon earlier concepts, but it is nonetheless possible to pick out at every stage of his career works which he could not have completed at an earlier stage – works which thus represent irreducible new stages in his process of discovery.

This is certainly the case with two poem-inscriptions which were installed at Stonypath in 1975 and subsequently appeared in *Selected Ponds* in photographic form. The one can be identified by its simple inscribed text, '*See* Poussin/*Hear* Lorrain', whilst the other bears a title from Albrecht Dürer, 'The Great Piece of Turf'. As we have seen at an earlier stage in this essay, *inscription* was originally Finlay's response to the challenge of a 'new classicism': the act of inscribing signalled the poem as an object which could be incorporated in the material world, or more specifically at a later point in the garden. These two works from 1975 clearly relate to the same procedure, but there is in one respect a decisive break. In both cases, the inscription – which is recorded on a stone hardly larger than the inscribed text – does not so much signal the poem as an object, as serve in the capacity of a *shifter*. That is to say, it converts the natural milieu into the terms of a pictorial analogy. '*See* Poussin/*Hear* Lorrain' is thus the ambivalent 'signature' of an elegiac classical landscape, perceived in miniature across Finlay's constructed pond: according to the degree of serenity of the prospect, we can interpret what we see through the medium of Poussin's calm stillness or Claude's more animated atmospheric effects. The monogram 'AD', used as the signature of Dürer's works, identifies the carefully tailored block of flowering turf with one of the artist's most famous watercolours.

It is fascinating to note the correspondence of these works with the original collection discussed here, *Rapel*. In a sense, Finlay is using an imaginary pictorial space to place the natural world in parenthesis, just as he once used an imaginary pictorial space to transform the printed page. But the development between these stages could only have taken place through the constant refinement of procedures, the constant exploration of dialectical relations, the exposure to 'risk', which I have attempted to trace. With these two works, we come full circle, in the sense that they are not simply recorded by the photographer: they actually reach in the photograph, and in the poem-card, a form of concision within the rectangular format which they could not possibly achieve in their natural setting. They are conceived, one might say, with the photograph in view, as only the photograph will restore the original purity of the conception. And yet, as we look at the photograph, we make the detour through inscription, through implantation, which has been necessary to the end product. We trace the multiple interaction between the work and the world.

And of course, part of that detour is through history – through those constitutive stages of Western culture marked by Poussin and Claude, the supreme French classical painters, as well as by Dürer, whom Pater indeed qualifies in terms of the Apollonian myth: 'himself, all German as he was, like a gleam of real day amid that hyperborean German darkness'. That Finlay should assume these references is in part, at least, a polemical retort to the modernist devaluation of cultural history. Lionel Trilling even went so far as to say of 'The Modern Element in Modern Literature', 'I can identify it by calling it the disenchantment of culture with culture itself'. To Trilling's diagnosis of 'the bitter line of hostility to civilisation that runs through' modernism, Finlay replies with his systematic retrieval of cultural stages, his *parti pris* for culture. Yet his project is not to be identified with the humanist ideal of Trilling, which smacks too much of 'appropriating acquired riches' (or lamenting the fact that they are capriciously neglected, which comes to the same thing). For Finlay, it should once again be emphasised, there is no store of cultural treasures to which the modern artist has, if he wishes, an automatic right of access. Each stage which he selects is already in itself a displacement – Poussin as the displacement of the classical ideal in French culture, Dürer as the harbinger of the Renaissance in Germany. Finlay observes a myth of recurrence which is uncannily like that of Pater (or Heine), in which his own Scotland is the unstated location of the further displacement:

Ian Hamilton Finlay: An Imaginary Portrait

> ... the hyperborean Apollo, sojourning, in the revolutions of time, in the sluggish north for a season, yet Apollo still, prompting art, music, poetry, and the philosophy which interprets man's life, making a sort of intercalary day amid the natural darkness; not meridian day, of course, but a soft derivative daylight, good enough for us.

This reference to the 'sluggish north' would, perhaps, seem unduly pejorative, were it not for the quite inordinate reluctance of Scottish critics and commentators to treat Finlay's work with the serious attention which it deserves – and which it has long since achieved in the world outside. Maurice Lindsay's recent, and in intention authoritative, survey of the history of Scottish literature refers disparagingly to 'some Scottish purveying of concrete verse' without so much as mentioning a name. He goes on to predict: 'this seems unlikely to be of lasting interest or significance, since the overtones of poetry must ripple outwards, and not attempt to turn impossibly back upon themselves'. Even supposing that Mr Lindsay is speaking allegorically, it is not irrelevant to point out that the 'overtones' of Finlay's poetry have 'rippled' as far as the East and West coasts of America, where he has books both published and in the process of publication; that a French Professor of Architecture recently spoke on his work at the international 'Habitat' conference at Vancouver, whilst a group of enthusiasts in the Faculty of Letters at the University of Liège are planning an exhibition, a conference bearing on his poetry, and a permanent installation of one of his sundials on their campus. These random examples could be multiplied many times, and the Scottish critic has in any case to go no further than the Scottish National Gallery of Modern Art, or Livingston New Town, to observe the outgoing character of Finlay's recent productions. Since Finlay is, beyond reasonable doubt, one of the most internationally well-known Scottish poets and artists of his generation, there is more than a touch of the grotesque in Mr Lindsay's stricture on genres of poetry which 'turn impossibly back upon themselves'. Or perhaps it is his intention to revive the ritual of exorcising one of Scotland's most distinguished artists – for the benefit of a generation that knows not Charles Rennie Mackintosh?

A final question remains, and it is a measure of Finlay's maturity that it can now be posed and answered. The recent works under discussion re-create (as indeed is the aim of this essay) the sense of the displacement of the classical ideal through French and German mutations – the infinite refractions of an original Sun. Yet the ontological problem, the problem of Hölderlin and Heidegger, is a question of *being*: of an origin which is not so much historical as metaphysical, yet has its cultural location in the Greek world. Finlay is indebted to an extraordinary coincidence which has enabled him to draw two strands of enquiry into one celebratory work. For five years or so, he has been increasingly concerned with the modern warship as the contemporary, hyperbolic symbol of classical heroism: beside the purity and simplicity of the fishing-boat, it has signalled the ultimate metaphor of elemental conflict. Thus the US Navy's nuclear carrier *Enterprise* could be seen, because of its functions and forces, as a 'Celebration of Earth, Air, Fire and Water'. At the same time, he has become passionately interested in the genre of the emblem, an interest which will soon result in the publication of an entire collection of *Heroic Emblems*[6] which place the classical text beside the modern intimation of heroic achievement. Beyond the treatises which interpret the significance of the emblem for the post-Renaissance world, he has been led to the origins of enigma and device and hieroglyph in the ancient world, and the techniques of interpretation used for elucidating these mysterious texts.

Within the last year, he has become aware of the fascinating convergence between the motif of the *Enterprise*, whose predecessor, the Second World War carrier bearing the same name, was known commonly as the 'Big E', and Plutarch's essay 'On the E at Delphi', which could be regarded as a classic statement of the problem of interpretation. Confronted with the enigma of the 'E' at Delphi – an inscribed stone fragment of immemorial origin placed near the shrine of Apollo – Plutarch's participants offer diverse and ingenious explanations. The sign may stand for the number 5 (E being the fifth letter of the alphabet) and thus signify the self-assertion of the Five Sages, who wished to exclude all pretended sages from their company. Alternatively it may be an ideograph representing the Three Graces, or the Sumerian symbol for a temple. More plausible is the suggestion that it does duty for the Greek 'If' (Ei), and so prefigures the mode of address customarily used for the oracle – one asks *if* one will be victorious, *if* the gods are propitious to a certain course of action. But the final explanation acquires, by virtue of its position and its solemnity, priority of attention. 'E' (Ei) is the second person singular of the verb 'to be' – Thou art. Thus Apollo is named at the entry to his shrine in his quality of pure being, 'and we in turn reply to him "Thou art", as rendering unto him a form of address which is truthful, free from deception, and the only one befitting him only, the assertion of Being'.

Finlay's 'Big E' series, the Second World War *Enterprise* inscribed with the E of Delphi, is therefore a coincidental meeting of the two extreme boundaries of his cultural field: the immemorial inscription and the modern warship. But it also serves to remind us, as Apollo is from a distance evoked, that the recognition of being is the necessary myth of art.

(1977)

Notes

1. *Ian Hamilton Finlay*, Serpentine Gallery, London, 17 September to 16 October 1977; see Appendix B for list of works in this exhibition.
2. This poem first appeared in *New Poetry* No. 20 (1973), and was reprinted in *The Old Stonypath Hoy* (Wild Hawthorn Press, Christmas 1991).
3. *Collaborations*, Kettle's Yard Gallery, Cambridge, 13 April to 8 May 1977.
4. See note 1 above.
5. See Douglas Hall's essay 'The Finlay/Fine Collaborations', *Collaborations* exhibition catalogue.
6. *Heroic Emblems*, Z Press, Calais, VT, USA, 1977.

ET IN ARCADIA EGO

Heroic Emblems, Ian Hamilton Finlay, with Ron Costley; commentary by Stephen Bann. Z Press, Calais, VT, 1977.

One of Panofsky's most justly celebrated essays in iconology (the term he takes directly from Cesare Ripa) is concerned with Poussin's painting *Et in Arcadia Ego*. Contemporary disputes about the significance of this enigmatic work lead him back to Greek pastoral poetry and the progressive formulation of the cultural concept of 'Arcady', with its almost infinite tissue of poetic references converging upon the point that even here, in the ideal pastoral world, death is present. But Panofsky has not checked the speculation about the inner meaning of Poussin's picture, which may indeed be bound up with a hermetic interpretation of the golden section and might even lead (it has been suggested) to the rediscovery of the lost treasure of the Albigensian heretics in a particular part of southwestern France.

The metaphorical presentation of the tank *as* Poussin's inscribed monument, within the Arcadian setting, offers us not so much an emblem as an enigma. Estienne describes the role of Enigma as that of serving 'as a Rind or Bark to conserve all the mysteries of our Ancestors wisdome'. We are not immediately tempted to generalise or extend the implications that we see, as in the 'moral' emblem. The treasure, such as it is, is necessarily remote from us, and we have no foolproof method of lifting the hermetic seal (an oblique comment on the fact that here, particularly, Finlay's adoption of a pre-existent motif has proved a stumbling-block to those who would deny the relevance of wide-ranging cultural reference, Estienne's 'ignoramusses').

Virgil, *Eclogues*; John Sparrow, *Visible Words*; E. Panofsky, *Meaning in the Visual Arts*; Walter Friedlaender, *Nicolas Poussin*; Elizabeth Wheeler Manwaring, *Italian Landscape in Eigthteenth Century England*; F. M. von Senger und Etterlin, *Die deutschen Panzer 1926–45*; *Wenn alle Brüder schweigen* (foreword by Colonel-General Paul Hausser).

The U.S.S. *Enterprise* appears by name as the final, evolved exemplar of the modern warship. It also unites in itself the different elements of the cosmology of Heraclitus: earth being represented in the landing ground offered by the carrier deck, air by the element in which its aircraft move, fire by the dynamic and destructive character of its nuclear capacity and water by the surrounding ocean. Modern physics has set up a progressively more accurate picture of the material world which is analogous in imaginative terms to the world of the pre-Socratics. In the same way, the nuclear-powered carrier embodies in intimate and terrifying conjunction the power released by the splitting of the atom, and the poetic message of union of elements.

One may well wish to meditate further upon the purpose of this invocation of Heraclitean cosmology in relation to modern nuclear warfare. It is as if this vicarious presence in the age which immediately preceded the establishment of the Western aesthetic codex, with Plato, were a method of gaining priority over the Platonic system. As if, on the other hand, the references to the modern fighting fleet were intended to bracket off the codes of warfare – the epic, the chivalric and indeed the romantic view of sea-faring being radically foreclosed in the elemental heroism of the nuclear confrontation. In a sense, the operation of these two brackets (the first anticipating Platonic and Aristotelian aesthetics, and the second demarcating the codes of the past) places the Western cultural tradition in parenthesis. And the self-contained form of the medallion seems to be the precise correlative to this poetic act.

Furley and Allen (eds.), *Studies in Presocratic Philosophy*, Vol. 1; Plato, *Timaeus*; R. D. Hicks, *Stoic & Epicurean*; Sandbach, *The Stoics*; Edward Hussey, *The Presocratics*; G. S. Kirk and J. E. Raven, *The Presocratic Philosophers*; F. Nietzsche, *The Birth of Tragedy*; Simone Weil, *Gateway to God*; Gareth L. Pawlowski, *Flat-Tops and Fledglings*; Commander W. H. Cracknell, *USS Enterprise (CVAN 65)*.

Armis et Litteris: Ian Hamilton Finlay's Heroic Emblems

CLEO MCNELLY KEARNS

About ten years ago, Ian Hamilton Finlay, working in collaboration with Ron Costley, published a collection of black and white line drawings with accompanying mottoes and prose called *Heroic Emblems*, clear little black and white images in the classic tradition of Renaissance emblem books, with extensive authorised commentaries by Stephen Bann (Finlay and Costley, with Bann, *Heroic Emblems*, Z Press, Calais, Vermont, 1977). Some of the emblems are usefully reproduced, along with pictures of much of Finlay's remarkable work, in Yves Abrioux's *Ian Hamilton Finlay* (Reaktion Books, 1985.) Finlay's emblem project, both reminiscent of and different from the Renaissance and Victorian emblem books of the past, serves the double purpose of helping to establish a 'visual primer' – the term is Bann's – for his own work and of bringing to our attention one of those relatively forgotten art forms which anticipate, in an almost uncanny way, the aesthetic concerns of our own moment. I cannot possibly do justice to these lucid and disturbing postmodern emblems in so short a time, but I hope to indicate a little, at least, of their impact and the historical associations they bring to mind.

These associations include, as Bann points out in his introduction, some rather profound and deliberate connections with the theory and practice of the Renaissance emblematists. (I have drawn, in discussing these, not only on Bann's commentary and on the work of Mario Praz and Ernst Gombrich, but also and especially on that of Robert Clements, whose *Picta Poesis* (Rome, 1960) makes stimulating reading in the context of Finlay's work.) Like those of his Renaissance predecessors, Finlay's emblems consist of a scrutable, if sometimes hermetic, visual image, a motto, often in Latin, sometimes in French or English, and then a lengthy commentary, which takes us through an elaborate network of analogies and allusions, some obvious, others more arcane.

These emblems, like their precursors, encourage meditation on such traditional classical or neo-classical themes as the relation between the devices of nature and those of human invention, the differences, if any, between art and artifice, and the inevitable conflicts of value between original works and their massively reproduced and disseminated replications. Like some Renaissance exemplars, Finlay's emblems also gain much of their uncanny effect by juxtaposing ancient heraldic devices with the weapons of modern warfare. Certainly, too, they maintain the traditional and hybrid conjunction of word and image in old emblem books, a conjunction which, as Bann points out, disturbs a long-established taste in the West for keeping text and picture apart (viii).

Finlay's emblems and those of Renaissance tradition also share a sometimes didactic and even pedantic interest in conveying at least a smattering of classical learning and elite culture to a relatively unlearned and popular audience. 'I shall have to learn a little greek to keep up with this/but so will you, drratt you' Pound provoked his audience in Canto 105. Likewise, Finlay dares his audience to pursue, through winding paths nonetheless clearly laid out in the commentaries, the resonances of the Pre-Socratics and the echoes of the Augustans. For Finlay, of course, coming late in the Western tradition as he does, these resonances and echoes must include an acknowledgement of the way the classics have been mediated to us, not only through the Renaissance, but through various neo-classical revivals since that time. Hence his work in general is full of allusions not only to Homer and Virgil but also to the classicism revived of the eighteenth century and the French Revolution, just as his garden at Little Sparta makes conscious reference to Poussin and Claude Lorrain. In expressing this concern for the classics and their revival, Finlay reiterates the Renaissance desire to preserve at least the vestige of certain antique values of personal honour, integrity, courage and craftsmanship in the midst of a new, commercial and highly mechanised culture. In this respect, as Bann points out, his work takes after that of Thomas Blount, who translated Henry Estienne's *Art of Making Devices* into English, drawing on heraldry from both sides in the civil war in self-conscious celebration of an old ideal of heroism transcending, he thought, the current issues at stake (ix).

The emblem tradition is curiously, if not always wisely, suited to such gestures, for it has always sought to fight fire with fire, to maintain a humanist culture by means of the very forces that appear to threaten it. Hence it supports an ancient tradition in part by making use, ironically enough, of the very media – printing, multiple reproduction, and mass distribution – which have supplanted it. This willingness to engage the enemy with his own weapons extends in Finlay's case to the content of the images themselves. As even a cursory glance will show, Finlay's major preoccupation in these works is with the arsenal of the Second World War, with the battleships, armoured tanks, parachutes, guns and radar screens of battles from the Pacific Basin to the Rhine, and to some extent with the newer, nuclear, technologies that 'protect' our increasingly fictive national and cultural boundaries. These giant artefacts of war, so impersonal, so collective and so apparently outside of individual human control, consort oddly with the benign and playful mottos Finlay has given them, as well as with the leafy camouflage, sweet and tender, that often twines them about. The weapons seem to present an intrinsic challenge to all that classical humanism holds dear – civility, individuality, wit, beauty of form and elevation of purpose – and yet in their metamorphosis into art they are clearly being mobilised in real if ambivalent support of these values.

In terms of their historical associations, I would argue, these emblems of war and camouflage might be seen as a series of illustrations or comments on the ancient and dignified Renaissance trope of *armis et litteris*, arms and letters. (The fullest treatment of this topic, Clements (p. 138) tells us, is to be found in the *Emblemata politica* of Juan de Solorzano, whose emblem for this motto shows Athena in armour with weapons in one hand and books in the other.) The usual point of this juxtaposition is that letters, if not exactly mightier than weapons, are at least their equals in power and must be associated with them if either is to hold its due place. *Non solum armis* is another expression of this sentiment, which may be traced back, though emblematists do not often say so, to the eighth book of Plato's Republic (Clements, p. 138). A change is often rung on this theme which reverses the normal priority of weapons and art by suggesting, with Montaigne, that the pen is mightier than the sword. The familiar Renaissance motif of the helmet taken over by bees illustrates this revised notion and enjoys a certain recurrence in Finlay's warship/hives of buzzing fighter planes. Bees are also often frequent emblems for the muses in Renaissance iconography (Clements, p. 248), another allusion crucial to Finlay's work, particularly to some of his more recent installations.

Clements proposes some motives for the exploitation of this ancient topos which might well apply to Finlay's (and our own) situation. He suggests that in a time when art is threatened and seen as effeminate, inessential or even counterproductive in the face of demands for new technologies and new forms of social organisation, some interface between arms and letters may be of strategic benefit to both. The arts, particularly the classics, may lend to the warrior a little much-needed cultural legitimation, while the warrior donates, by association, a certain glamour and a certain connection with the central powers that be. (Is this, we may ask ourselves, why so many nuclear weapons bear wonderfully classical names, why we have our Tritons and Neptunes and Plutos? One understands why we do not have weapons with Old Norse names, names like Blood-Hungry or Killer-Axe or Skull-Muncher or whatever, but why not, as with cars, some animalistic-sounding Cougars, Mustangs, Thunderbirds or Cobras?)

The mutual strategic advantage of the association between arms and letters is, I am sure, consciously at work in Finlay's emblem book, just as it is consciously at work in much of his art. His garden temple at Little Sparta, for instance, bears the dedication 'To Apollo, His Music, His Missiles, His Muses', stating the connection between art and weaponry in no uncertain terms, and much of his later work suggests a profound and acerbic critique of the marginalised status of the artist or poet today. To see the heroic emblems as simple illustrations of the *armis et litteris* trope, however, does not, I think, entirely do them justice, not at least in the terms so far proposed. There is a quality deliberately arch, deliberately self-conscious, even deliberately parodic or sinister about these wood armaments and armoured woods which calls this ancient topos into question. Something more disturbing and more authentic is going on here, I would posit, than a simple self-promoting attempt to co-opt the sensationalistic impact of a nuclear arsenal or borrow the prestige of an antique form.

But what is this 'something more'? In his way of taking up the practice of the emblem book, Finlay has suggested, I think, a deeper appreciation of and a different attitude towards the neo-classical alliance between arms and letters than the one to which either Renaissance emblem tradition or modern usage have accustomed us. He has suggested that the conjunction of art and weapons in many aesthetic contexts is not simply ornamental, or even ironic, but expressive of a link between them that is far from adventitious. This link is grounded in a perpetual human thirst for the absolute, a thirst in art as in politics unquenched even by the recognition that it colludes always, at least *in potentia*, with the celebration of totalitarian order. (This connection, by the way, has already been realised in the history of the emblem, as Finlay is well aware. Emblems apparently enjoyed a brief revival in Nazi Germany in the form of stamps issued for the tenth anniversary of the Fascist Regime (Bann, vii).)

Through his *armis et litteris* emblems Finlay forces us to confront this thirst for the absolute and its emergence in neo-classical aesthetics, and to confront as well some of its political consequences. In particular, Finlay wishes to remind us that the very shapes and forms, what we might call the aesthetics of modern weaponry, have in their symmetries and streamlined silhouettes as firm an origin in ancient Greek culture as in the demands of industrial technology. Our nostalgia for the Greek values of balance, clarity and purity of line – a nostalgia which Finlay warns us will last 'forever' – reaches its apogee in these superbly crafted aerodynamic objects, which have their origin as well as their function in the desire to master nature and to impose a certain civilisation on what we regard as barbarous. Finlay forces us to recognise that these artefacts are, in terms the West has long regarded as normative, indeed beautiful, compelling and even numinous.

Now to remark on the extraordinary coincidence of ideals of purity, order, and beauty with practices of power, violence and usurpation has long been a commonplace of postmodern literary theory. Truths often complacently rehearsed by the literati – as that the neo-classical order is constructed on a will-to-power (Foucault), that every strong text gains strength from dubious influences it would consciously like to disavow (Bloom), that each work of art represents a totalitarian suppression and co-option of alternates or of the work of the past in the name of a new link to absolute truth (Derrida) – are, however, remarkably disturbing when presented to our view pre-emptively, as it were, within extremely accomplished works of art. We are comfortable, even comforted when we read these truisms in critical prose, but even the literary theorist, so entranced, on the one hand, with the amoralities of non-referential systems of signs and so attached, on the other, to confident and fixed categories of political good and bad, bristles to find a Panzer in his wood, or a temple (taken seriously enough for Finlay to claim for it, provocatively if futilely so far, exemption from rates as a religious site) in his garden.

Finlay deploys the explosive shocks of this visual minefield he has planted to masterly effect. His emblems alone reveal, to our dismay, how often, in spite of our zeal for deconstruction, we turn a blind eye to the presence all around us of artefacts our society treats as taboo, unspeakable and beyond ordinary categories of ethical debate. While we are busy celebrating the complete evacuation of the sacred from our liberated consciousness, our militarised states are building all around us temples to pure art: power plants, launch pads, missiles, warships which, forbidden to the ordinary glance, nevertheless demand ceaseless human sacrifice in support of their sublime *technē*. Here are the ultimate blasphemies, idols peculiar to our time, which, unlike more 'primitive' ages, will not even recognise what it serves, or allow itself to discern beneath the camouflage the golden calf. Our refusal to tolerate the representation of these objects in art confirms their uncanny status and confirms as well the state power which has declared them, for the purposes of the 'average citizen', politically and practically invisible.

Finlay, however, and I want to end on this note, does not allow too easy a denunciation of these weapon-idols or of the political violence to which they point. Polemic, after all, may only be one way of denying or repressing the extreme power and fascination of the absolutist desire they express. Furthermore, in their uncanny, taboo status as objects of representation, the weapons and artefacts of war offer both a challenge to break this politically motivated concealment and an inescapable source not only of state but of aesthetic power as well. Here, indeed, as Yeats said of Easter 1916 in Ireland, 'a terrible beauty is born', and here is one source of that 'sacred terror' Henry James regarded as essential to all creative endeavour. Until we have confronted the depth of the ancient connection between *armis* and *litteris*, the pen and the sword, the power of art and the poetics of war, we cannot possibly make the ethical renunciations, heroic in a different sense, our current political situation requires of us. The dedication of the Garden Temple at Little Sparta 'To Apollo. His Music. His Missiles. His Muses' reminds us that only when we give the Gods of the thunderbolt, metaphorically speaking, their due, may we cherish even the possibility of avoiding the sacrifice of humanity in their service.

(1989)

Note

Roman numerals refer to Finlay and Costley, *Heroic Emblems* (Z Press, Calais, Vermont, 1977).

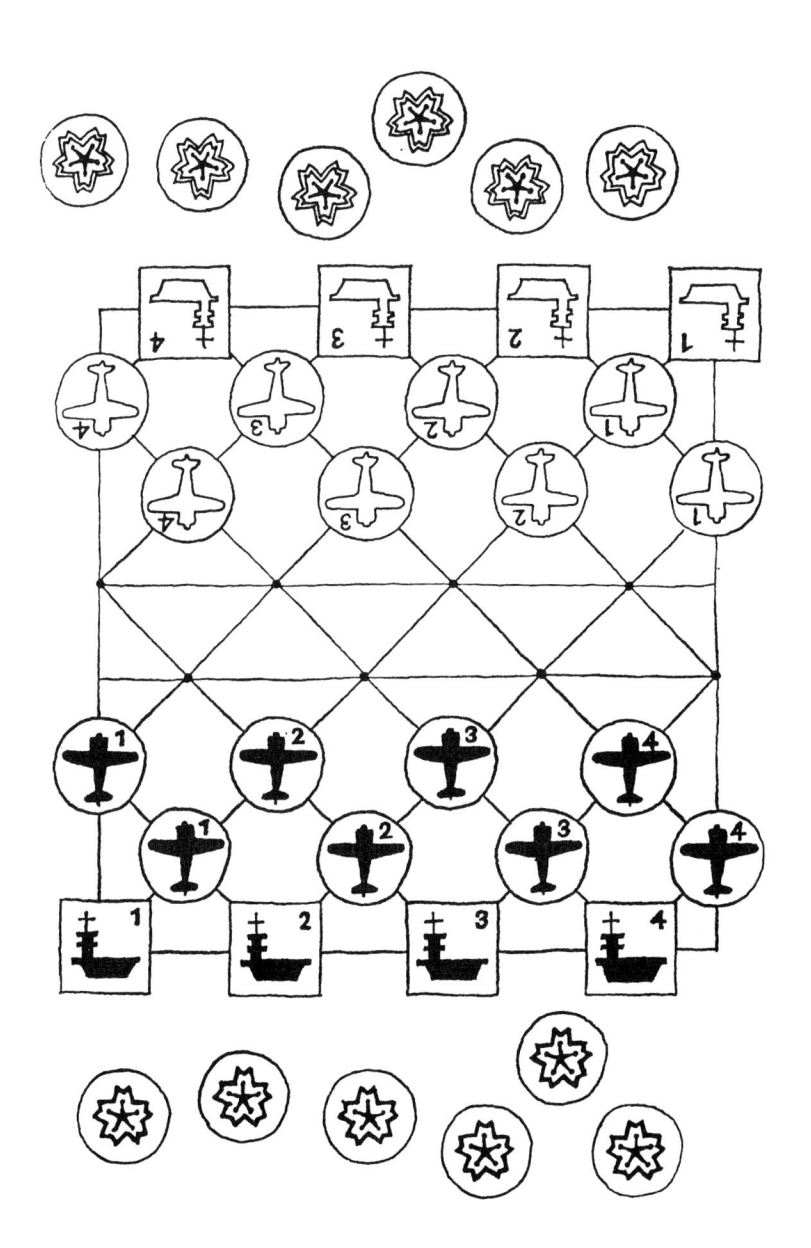

Pacific
Ian Hamilton Finlay, with Ron Costley, 1975

Poe and the Poetics of PACIFIC

MILES ORVELL

Over the last decade Ian Hamilton Finlay has made a series of assaults on the conventions of poetry: the materials, the conception, the status of the poem as object in the world – all these Finlay has forced us to re-examine. One is prepared for surprises in his work, but not, perhaps, for the advent of PACIFIC / TYPE A & B BOARD WARGAME FOR TWO PLAYERS. Looking at the board, or at the pieces (rectangular columns surmounted by aircraft carriers, round columns topped by planes) is not enough; one is expected – instructed – to 'play'. True, Finlay has previously designed a slate and marble chess set with austerely shaped pieces resembling submarine conning towers, but that was a contemporary invigoration of a traditional game: the usual chess artefacts had been transformed into submarine towers in a way not unlike Finlay's designs for aircraft-carrier bird-baths and fountains, or his many versions of the sundial. It was one thing to begin with a convention – chess, bird-bath, fountain, sundial – and superimpose thereon a militantly contemporary design: that was to erect irony upon artifice, that was the traditional mode (with certain differences) of the poet. It was quite another thing to invite someone to win or lose a game with another player. Finlay had lived for years in the Border country (England/Scotland; Art and Life), but what had this raiding game to do with the raid on the inarticulate (Eliot)? Poetry may be a superior kind of play, but can play be a superior kind of poetry? It is a question at least worth considering, especially since the game now appears in the context of a gallery exhibition of Finlay's works.

As a board game involving opposing sides, PACIFIC enters a tradition stretching back several thousands of years to the earliest amusements of China, India, Persia, and other ancient civilisations. Such games – predecessors of contemporary chess – were regarded as a kind of training for war, if not a sublimation of the barbaric impulse; they were also, in certain ways, ritual enactments of world order. As the American scholar Steward Culin observed in 1897 of a certain early form of Indian chess involving four sets of men, one can assume that the board, 'if not indeed all boards upon which games are played, stands for the world and its four quarters (or the year and its four seasons), and that the game itself was originally divinatory'. So many of Finlay's own works are rooted in the progress of the seasons and of the hours, and in the natural elements (see the emblem with central design of the aircraft carrier USS *Enterprise*, surrounded by the legend, 'A Celebration of Earth·Air·Fire·Water') that his gravitation to the ritual order of the board game seems wholly consistent. There may be another more purely local – or national – consistency in a Scottish poet's turning to the draughtboard, for we recall that during the nineteenth century Scottish players dominated world competition in draughts.

PACIFIC is neither chess nor draughts, though it is closer to the latter in the simplicity and economy of the rules governing moves. Unlike draughts, however, there are two kinds of pieces on the board: aircraft carriers (four to each side) and aeroplanes (two are 'attached' – by number – to each carrier). Only aeroplanes may attack opposing pieces and, by jumping them on a diagonal forward movement, remove them from action. If a carrier is jumped it is removed together with any planes that are attached to it. A plane reaching the opposing end of the board becomes a kamikaze, with freedom to move forwards and backwards (diagonally) across the board. What gives PACIFIC its peculiar quality as a game (and as a 'poem' – more of this later) is the rule governing aircraft and their carriers: for planes are limited in forward movement by the position of their base carriers. They can move forward only three positions beyond the carrier and may attack only from a point two moves beyond. In thus obliquely running, the planes have their limit, and when the plane far doth roam, to paraphrase Donne, the carrier hearkens after it.

Not in facsimiles of design nor in the other accidents of realism that entertain the commercial war-game enthusiast is PACIFIC tied to the real world; the pieces are designed with a simplicity that reinforces the purity of the rules governing their movements. Rather it is in the analogy of the limits imposed upon planes and carriers in *actual* warfare that PACIFIC connects with 'real life'.

As a dynamic intellectual process, PACIFIC turns not on the complexities of chess, with its elaborate orchestration of movements, but on the intensity and concentration of the chamber music strategist. The locus classicus for the aesthetic and conceptual differences between chess and draughts (and for the superiority of the latter) is the opening of Poe's *Murders in the Rue Morgue*, and since its applicability to the virtues of PACIFIC is so direct, I shall quote the extract at length.

> ... to calculate is not in itself to analyze. A chess-player, for example, does the one without effort at the other ... [The] higher powers of the reflective intellect are more decidedly and more usefully tasked by the unostentatious game of draughts than by all the elaborate frivolity of chess. In this latter, where the pieces have different and *bizarre* motions, with various and variable values, what is only complex is mistaken (a not unusual error) for what is profound. The *attention* is here called powerfully into play. If it flag for an instant, an oversight is committed, resulting in injury or defeat. The possible moves being not only manifold but involute, the chances of such oversights are multiplied; and in nine cases out of ten it is the more concentrative rather than the more acute player who conquers. In draughts, on the contrary, where the moves are *unique* and have but little variation, the probabilities of inadvertence are diminished, and the mere attention being left comparatively unemployed, what advantages are obtained by either party are obtained by superior *acumen*.

Poe's discussion (he goes on to celebrate the whist player) is part of an encomium to the analytic faculty, as opposed to the merely calculating, a distinction he likens to the one traditionally drawn between the imagination and the fancy.

> Between ingenuity and the analytic ability there exists a difference far greater, indeed, than that between the fancy and the imagination, but of a character very strictly analogous. It will be found, in fact, that the ingenious are always fanciful, and the *truly* imaginative never otherwise than analytic.

What Poe means by '*truly* imaginative' is a degree of acumen that, as he says earlier, borders on preternatural intuition. Poe's own poetry is so often accused of being mechanical and contrived in its effects (deliberately so, if we can believe *The Philosophy of Composition*) that we might dismiss this association of the analytic and imaginative faculties as ill-advised. But that would be a species of *ad hominem* argument, and we must rescue from Poe's observations the core of the matter – which is that concentrated analysis in a game like draughts – or PACIFIC – is akin to an imaginative trance: the mind tries out endless possibilities within a restricted field governed by rules, choices are made, effects are achieved, the world is at bay. (The purest example of this trance I have seen was in a mental patient who played draughts with me once, I being the 'recreational assistant' of the moment; during the game his normal swaying and humming became focused on the board, and in this trance of analytic lucidity – still swaying and humming, making abrupt, infallible moves – he was absolutely unbeatable.)

Anyone attempting a poetics of PACIFIC must start, then, with Poe, but the temptation to connect the game with certain characteristics of concrete poetry – given Finlay's own association with the movement – is irresistible. 'The new poem is simple and can be perceived visually as a whole as well as in its parts', the influential Eugen Gomringer observed in 1954. 'Its objective element of play is useful to modern man, whom the poet helps through his special gift for this kind of play-activity'. Many of Finlay's early works had evinced this quality of play, one of the most widely known – and it is relevant to a discussion of PACIFIC – being *Acrobats* (1964). In this poem the viewer regards a *representation* of a play area (the form suggests free-floating acrobats) that is itself a play area for the eye. *Acrobats* is a mirror-shape, in which the top half mirrors the lower half. Starting at either the top or the bottom line and moving towards the centre, each line repeats a single letter of the word 'acrobats' until you reach 's', which serves as the final letter for both top and bottom half. The eye can complete the word by starting from either top or bottom and moving diagonally down (or up) with many possible routes to travel. In its creation of a play-space with rules, in its grid-like arrangement of letters and diagonal movement, in its two opposing teams of words, *Acrobats* looks forward to PACIFIC.

Still another aspect of PACIFIC – what we might call its peculiar syntax – is related to certain other poems by Finlay, poems deriving from Gomringer. I referred earlier to the rule that planes in PACIFIC are limited in their movements by the position of their base carrier. It is the rule that most clearly distinguishes PACIFIC from draughts (and makes the former more complicated and more interesting than draughts, though still more concise than chess), for one must always plan the moves of the planes in conjunction with the moves of the carrier. One is constantly aware of the tension tying the two functions together, creating relationships that are constant in nature but variable in specific position. In the carrier/plane relationship we may be reminded of the analogous syntactical relationship that ties predicates to a nominative in a sentence, or, more simply, of the relationship between adjectives (planes) and nouns (carriers).[1] And I don't think it is stretching matters too far to see in the plane/carrier relationship an analogy to certain 'constellation' poems by Gomringer in which words are paired with one another, in varying sequences. One such poem begins 'cars and cars/cars and elevators/cars and men . . .'; another reads, 'you blue/you red/you yellow/you black/you white/you'. The latter poem (in German, 'du blau') Finlay uses as the basis for his own playful variation, 'Navy' – 'navy red/navy white/navy black/navy yellow/navy blue/navy' – which uses 'navy' itself as a hovering noun/adjective running like a nave with constellated colour-chapels throughout the columnar poem. How far can the associated words stray from the repeated base word? How far can the plane stray from the carrier?

If it is still difficult to imagine the leap from poetry to game, one further intermediate stage may be noted in the card, *Homage to Seurat* (1972). In this work, Seurat's painting of a marine basin filled with sailing-boats is abstracted into a line drawing that is only half-completed; the recipient of the card is thus invited not to win or lose, but to draw the lines connecting the numbered dots (43!), thereby completing the line-drawing. (This is pointillism with a difference!) By inviting the viewer's participation in the making-process, *Homage to Seurat* moves conceptually far beyond the invitation to the eye alone of *Acrobats*. PACIFIC, with its rules and full participation, lies ahead.

Having noted some ways that PACIFIC can in fact be likened to aspects of concrete poetry, one must hasten to assert the differences: *Acrobats* requires the viewer to make choices, but the arrangement of letters is *fixed*; Gomringer's (and Finlay's) constellations invite an abstract play of semantic forces, but the units are *verbal* and, again, the visual pattern is fixed. The Seurat card must be completed by the viewer, but the final product is predetermined. And in none of these instances is there a winner or loser. There is a beginning, a middle, and an end, but only the beginning and ending are at all predictable. PACIFIC is quite obviously not a poem; there is no 'text', merely a set of rules governing a social occasion. (We may be tempted to liken it to a set of rules like the sonnet, rather than to any *particular* sonnet, which is a poem – though of course no poem will ever result from PACIFIC).

Finally, a word about PACIFIC as a *war-game*, for the conception is merely a recent instance of Finlay's recurrent use of the vocabulary of armaments, which he has elsewhere adapted to prints, garden poems, fountains, and so forth. While each instance calls for its own examination, certain generalisations might be made regarding the tonal consistencies in these works. On the one hand, the simplified – even beautiful – designs suggest a respect for military machinery not unlike the serious respect rendered war by the traditional epic poet; on the other hand, the domestication of armaments within an ordered space implicitly mocks their power over our lives. But the playful reduction does not remove the charge of violence from the objects. Rather, it is the special order imposed on instruments of violent disorder that creates the tension and paradox in Finlay's armaments works. What gives PACIFIC its edge as a game is our not forgetting that behind the diagonal moves, the winning and losing amusement of a sunny afternoon, was a world of suicide pilots and forced crashes. Out in the Pacific – the blue ocean stretching like a field of play for aircraft carriers and planes – life was not very pacific. Poe, who quit the military academy at West Point to write poems about angels and tales of shipwreck, would have understood that tension and paradox.

(1977)

Note
1. I am indebted, for the latter observation, to a PACIFIC opponent, Professor Sharon O'Brien.

Nature Over Again After Poussin: these composed landscapes in the garden at Little Sparta refer to paintings by Claude Lorrain (top) and Albrecht Dürer. Ian Hamilton Finlay, with Nicholas Sloan, 1980.
Photos by Dave Paterson

Nature Over Again After Poussin: Some Discovered Landscapes

STEPHEN BANN

In his great essay, 'The School of Giorgione', Walter Pater reflects not so much upon an individual painter and the lesser 'school' who followed him, as on the very process by which an artist's achievement becomes an integral part of general culture. For him, the issue is not simply a matter of the threat posed to a 'great traditional reputation' by the incisive tools of modern scholarship; not merely a lament that 'what remains of the most vivid and stimulating of Venetian masters, a live flame, as it seemed, in those shadowy old times, has been reduced almost to a name by his most recent critics'. It is also a celebration of the way in which, running counter to the corrosion of criticism and time, a certain cultural value can be established which no longer strictly depends upon the tiny group of paintings which engendered it: not the value of Giorgione but, as Pater puts it, that of the *Giorgionesque*:

> ... for the aesthetic philosopher, over and above the real Giorgione and his authentic extant works, there remains the *Giorgionesque* also – an influence, a spirit or type in art, active in men so different as those to whom many of his supposed works are really assignable – a veritable school, which grew together out of all those fascinating works rightly or wrongly attributed to him; out of many copies from, or variations on, him, by unknown or uncertain workmen ... out of many traditions of

subject and treatment, which really descend from him to our own time, and by retracing which we fill out the original image; Giorgione thus becoming a sort of impersonation of Venice itself, its projected reflex or ideal . . .

It is not difficult to see that, in drawing attention to this process which is so much more subtle and more pervasive than the mere 'history of art' would lead us to believe, Pater is making a polemical assertion about the nature of culture. He is defending a concept of tradition which is both splendidly rich and radically under threat. For if the furtherance of culture, the preservation of tradition, is not simply a matter of guarding our treasures in the insulated conditions of the museum – if it is, on the contrary, a question of safeguarding and stimulating that 'weaving' process by which a cultural fabric is created in men's minds – then what are we to say when such a purpose is almost universally repudiated? The exceptional art historian will perhaps help us to diagnose the problem; just as Panofsky, in his essay on Poussin and the elegiac tradition, makes us aware of the almost infinite number of threads that went to compose the type of the 'elegy'. But only a contemporary artist, deeply imbued with the 'traditions of subject and treatment' of the past, can create the fusion of past and present which allows us to see the traditional as actual. He risks a great deal in this objective, it must however be said. For the deeply human and communal purpose of 'retracing' the 'original image' of our culture is too readily stigmatised as an individualistic act of exclusion.

And here, at the most general level, is the purpose – and the predicament – of this exhibition.[1] It exists to draw the visitor into the perspectives of a shared cultural inheritance. Its format is the individual enclosure, or 'corner', established by a series of photographed scenes. The visitor will stop in front of each one, his field of vision defined by the envelopment of the photographic image. As he observes, and meditates, his mind will play upon a series of associations engendered by the image: its relation, secured by the inscribed signature, to the work of a particular painter; its relation, through that painter, to a 'type' of landscape securely established within our culture; finally its relation, through the instrumentality of Ian Hamilton Finlay and his 'school' of craftsmen, to a certain polemical placing of landscape within the cultural debate of the present day. I refer, of course, to the 'ideal' visitor. What other visitor could I profitably refer to? But this introduction is above all concerned with the problem of that ideal visitor. Not only, does he exist, or not? But, how does the issue of his existence or non-existence affect the overall context in which the exhibition is inscribed?

With this broader question in mind, we can begin on the simplest level, though even here the deviousness of attribution and authorship obliges us to pause and think about the experience to which we are convoked. The photographs, by Finlay's longstanding photographic collaborator Dave Paterson, represent specific parts of the garden which Finlay has been developing, together with Sue Finlay, for more than a decade around their home, Stonypath, near Dunsyre in Lanarkshire. And yet, of course, these photographs do not simply represent the pre-existent garden. A judgement has been made about the *possibilities* of the garden, mediated through the instantaneous eye of the camera,[2] and the individual images have been produced from an equation between a particular detail or prospect, and the cultural 'type' of an Old Master as perpetuated in a certain kind of landscape. Sometimes this possibility of equation has required little additional help to bring it about. Thus the Altdorfer landscape is achieved miraculously through the clear light on young pines and vibrant undergrowth; Nicholas Sloan's inscription of the monogram of the artist is hardly necessary to locate this as the German Gothic vision of landscape. Equally, the curves of Corot's signature on a sun-blanched stone give us immediate access to a landscape which is post-romantic in its espousal of far distance, and blurred, intermediate fields. There is more artifice, necessarily, in the eighteenth-century Rococo landscape of Watteau, where flowers hang precariously beside the marbled and signed plaque, and there has been added a guitar to put us in mind of love-sick troubadours and a half-hidden sail to epitomise the delayed *Embarkation for Cythera*.

Besides this range of possibilities between the untouched and the artificial, Finlay and his collaborators have played upon a range of discriminations which are implicit in the very choice of artists. I wrote initially about Pater's notion of the Giorgionesque, which he exactly equates with 'such as in England we call "park scenery", with some elusive refinement felt about the rustic buildings, the choice grass, the grouped trees, the undulations deftly economised for graceful effect'. Such a description immediately sets us thinking about a corner of Stonypath that might be signed with Giorgione's name. But it also reminds us that Finlay is not making so substantial a claim for all his invited artists: culture, and the tradition of landscape, he seems to say, is made up of contributions which are not all so pervasive as the Giorgionesque. Indeed the inclusion of Gaspard Poussin in the company of his greater contempories, Nicolas Poussin and Claude, can only lead us to make a sharp discrimination between the qualities embodied in the one and the others. I borrow Finlay's own interpretation in suggesting that the distinctive feature of Gaspard Poussin is the very absence of the essential qualities which characterise the other two painters: 'It is the essence of Gaspard that he *lacks* an essence (as compared to the other Poussin or Claude)'. As a result of this clue, we might take the exhibition as offering us a wide range of modalities, some of which are less central than others to the creation of a landscape tradition, all of which offer subtly different prospects of engagement and enjoyment. In the 'Salvator Rosa', for example, the activity of the visitor might consist in enumerating the different elements that give the Neapolitan painter's work its gloomy, yet thrilling tone: dramatically lit shafts of wood, as if struck by lightning, scattered fragments of animal skulls, and even a hangman's noose. In 'Poussin' and 'Guercino', on the other hand, a more sustained and serious note is struck. In Poussin, it is the authentic elegiac tone, transfixed in stillness (as opposed to the 'Claude', where wind rustles the topmost leaves and simulates the effect of the artist's brush). In Guercino, it is a question of more indirect, iconographic references: to the first of all *Et In Arcadia Ego* pictures painted between 1621 and 1623, where a similar brick structure supports a death's head, and to Finlay's own *Footnotes to an Essay*, where Panofsky's original essay is used to support an intricate series of displacements from the theme of Death in Arcady.[3]

Implicitly, Finlay's strategy in this exhibition is to attack the vulgar disjunction of traditional culture and contemporary art. No more relevant example of this disjunction could be imagined than the comments of a contemporary commentator, Miles Hadfield, on Henry Hoare's garden at Stourhead. Hadfield proposes, with a semblance of relieving the reader of an unnecessary cultural burden: 'Disregarding the leafless trees, we see the lake and its banks as a superbly formed landscape, but Henry Hoare's incongruously mixed buildings (particularly as few of us now know the significance of their originals), delightful if absurd, seem perhaps to be a pioneering surrealist landscape'. It is no doubt fitting that Hadfield should combine a judgement that is tinged with a rather ludicrous sexual reductionism ('superbly formed landscape') with a reference to the 'half-baked, ignorant and journalese theory of surrealism' (Adrian Stokes's phrase). The experience of a great landscape garden is reduced to a banal reading of its outward contours, and a perverse reintegration of its neo-classical elements as if they were soft time-pieces or pipes that are not pipes. And indeed the most preposterous aspect of this type of exercise is the feigned concern for the limited capacities of the spectator, which could easily be read as a masquerading form of contempt. If 'few of us' now know the significance of the cultural references, then would it not be better to proceed with simple and methodical explanations? Is it really a benefit to the spectator that he should be offered the means of cultural euthanasia?

Such banality represents, no doubt, an easy target. But the issue is extended, and complicated, by a fascinating passage from Hans-Georg Gadamer's *Philosophical Hermeneutics*, which Finlay has quoted more than once in connection with this exhibition. In one sense, the passage confirms and strengthens the argument implied in Pater's definition of the Giorgionesque. But it also enables us to make a more searching examination of the cultural issue. Gadamer writes:

> The sharper reflection that Hegel brought to the question of the relation of natural and artistic beauty led him to the valid conclusion that natural beauty is a reflection of the beauty of art. When something natural is regarded and enjoyed as beautiful, it is not a timeless and wordless givenness of the 'purely aesthetic object' that has its exhibitive ground in the harmony of forms and colours and symmetry of design, as it might seem to a Pathagorizing (*sic*), mathematical mind. How nature pleases us belongs instead to the context that is stamped and determined by the artistic creativity of a particular time. The aesthetic history of a landscape – for

instance, the Alpine landscape – or the transitional phenomenon of garden art are irrefutable evidence of this. . . .

On the one hand, we could see this text as the programme of the whole exhibition. Finlay is inviting us to 'see' nature through 'art'. The individual photographs are in no sense substitute paintings, however precise and suggestive the references embodied in them. They serve to concretise the process whereby, in our wider experience of everyday life, we interpret the natural world through given modalities that refer to the history of our culture. Yet at the same time, Finlay would reject the assumption that derives, however unintentionally, from the statement that such a process is 'stamped and determined by the artistic creativity of a particular time'. Such an ideal notion of 'artistic creativity' comes close to implying a separate standpoint, clearly defined in the cultural topology, from which the interpretation of nature can be influenced. Yet the interest of studying landscape and the garden, in the context of general culture, lies precisely in the fact that such a standpoint cannot be achieved; that our perceptions of nature are determined by the widest possible network of interactions in the cultural field. Did Henry Hoare speak from the standpoint of 'artistic creativity'? Does Finlay himself, a poet assisted by stone-cutters, letterers and photographers (to name only a few of his collaborators), suggest anything other than a strategic emplacement, necessarily undetermined, within the mobile field of culture? In effect, Finlay uses the garden, and the landscape, not to irradiate that special aspect of our cultural life which is the perception of nature, but to illuminate, as in a microcosm, the tensions of contemporary culture as a whole. Stonypath has become, no less than Pope's garden at Twickenham, the emplacement of a political and cultural offensive which the poet directs toward the wider world.[4]

The point is clarified if we look at two further elements of the exhibition which are illustrated here, though they do not strictly belong to the sequence of photographs. The 'Fragonard' landscape introduces a musical score, based on the letters of the name 'Julie', which has been recorded by the lead-flautist of the Scottish Chamber Orchestra, after being set to music by the composer Wilma Patterson. Within the formality of the 'Fragonard', therefore, the introduction of the *Julie* theme forms both a musical interlude and a reference to the celebrated literary garden of Rousseau's *La Nouvelle Héloise* – a garden which the heroine, Julie, had herself created within the framework of a much larger, conventionally formal garden. Here we have the motif of the 'secret' or 'forbidden' garden, powerfully extended by Albert Speer's own drawing of his *First Stone Garden*[5] which he built during his period of imprisonment at Spandau prison, while ostensibly working on the conventional garden which the prison authorities had established as a way of occupying the 'leisure time' of their charges.[6] From Julie's 'secret' garden to Speer's forbidden garden – which could only be detected by lying in the middle of the lawn – the transition is a daring, but convincing one. The garden within a garden becomes not only an aesthetic microcosm which contrasts with the formal or conventional macrocosm of the enclosing area, but a model of cultural action as transgression. For Finlay himself, the garden at Stonypath has come to seem increasingly a secret or forbidden garden like these: set within the wider environment which accepts only the conventional notions of nature, culture and art, its integrity has been threatened by the cultural bureaucrats and local government officials who are as little able to glimpse its meaning and function as were bewigged French aristocrats or prison guards able to decipher the secrets of Julie and Speer. Essentially, Finlay is defending a conception of wholeness, or purity, against the fragmentation of contemporary culture. But another way of putting the issue would be to say that, for Finlay, the present-day garden is secular, made in the image of a secular society. Stonypath, the transgressive garden (transgressing the bar which separates tradition and the present) is also pre-eminently a *religious* garden.

I would hazard a guess that one day, and perhaps before long, the repression of religious discourse in discussion of contemporary culture may come to seem the most singular, and inexplicable, aspect of our current impoverishment. I write this partly because I have recently heard a very distinguished art historian talking about Caspar David Friedrich as if he were a kind of Kantian prefiguration of Greenbergian aesthetics; not concerned in the least with 'symbolism' but simply with the rendering of complex perceptual correlatives that are appropriate to our bi-focal vision. I also write because it seems appropriate to raise, in this particular context, the name of Cézanne, whose own concern to do 'Poussin over again after nature' is of course the unspoken prelude to this exhibition. What appears an arbitrary exclusion for Friedrich touches upon the bizarre when we recognise how little Cézanne's religious belief has been taken to imply for the development of his art. Like Zola, we moderns maintain particular pieties about modernism, the deepest of which is its foundation in the secular view. Yet when Cézanne talks of 'treating nature by the cylinder, the sphere, the cone', and theorises upon the laws of perspective, he also refers to 'the spectacle which the *Pater Omnipotens Aeterne Deus* sets out before our eyes'. When he confesses to Charles Camoin in 1903 that 'this is the most accurate letter that I have written to you', he continues with the one underlined word '*Credo*'. Cézanne's example stresses, with invincible force, the total implication of modern culture within the terms of religious discourse. And if it is the 'crisis' of that discourse which is in question, then such a crisis is not resolved by a vapid secularism. Ian Hamilton Finlay proposes to us, in this exhibition, a model of cultural wholeness which is far-reaching in its transgressive implications. But he presents us with no more important question than this one: whether Western culture has any meaning, or destiny, whatsoever, if it is divorced from the religious intuition of being.

(1980)

Notes

1. This exhibition featured photographs of the garden at Little Sparta by Dave Paterson. The landscapes were the work of Ian Hamilton Finlay and Sue Finlay, and the stone signatures were cut by Nicholas Sloan. The exhibition was held at the Collins Exhibition Hall at the University of Strathclyde, Glasgow, in 1980. The 'landscapes' refer to the following artists: Albrecht Altdorfer (1480–1538); Jean-Baptiste Camille Corot (1796–1875); Gaspard Dughet (known as Gaspard Poussin) (1615–1675); Albrecht Dürer (1471–1528); Jean Honoré Fragonard (1732–1806); Giovanni Francesco Guercino (1591–1666); Claude Lorrain (1600–1682); Nicolas Poussin (1594–1665); Salvator Rosa (1615–1673); Jacob Ruisdael (1628–1682); Antoine Watteau (1684–1721).

    The publications referred to are: Walter Pater, 'The School of Giorgione', in *The Renaissance*; Erwin Panofsky, 'Et in Arcadia Ego – Poussin and the Elegiac Tradition', in *Meaning in the Visual Arts*; Hans-Georg Gadamer, *Philosophical*

Hermeneutics; Maynard Mack, *The Garden and the City – Retirement and Politics in the Later Poetry of Pope*; Jean-Jacques Rousseau, *La Nouvelle Héloise*; Albert Speer, *Spandau – The Secret Diaries*; Paul Cézanne, *Correspondance*; Marcelin Pleynet, 'Cézanne sous l'oeil paternel', in *Documents Sur*, 4/5; William Shenstone, 'Unconnected Thoughts on Gardening', in *Essays on Men and Manners*.

2. Such a supposedly impersonal instrument as the camera might appear inappropriate for this task. But Finlay has pointed out that the critic Hugh Kenner refers to Pater's 'aesthetics of the glimpse'. Doubtless he has in mind a passage like the following, from the essay 'Joachim du Bellay': 'A sudden light transfigures a trivial thing, a weather-vane, a windmill, a winnowing flail, the dust in the barn door: a moment – and the thing has vanished, because it was pure effect; but it leaves a relish behind it, a longing that the accident may happen again'. Might the camera, then, perpetuate such an accident?

3. The attentive visitor to the exhibition will note, in the background and to the right of the brick structure, the bark of a tree which has been carved with the initials 'A' and 'M'. Angelica and Medoro, the lovers in Ariosto's *Orlando Furioso*, are depicted carving their names on a tree in one of Guercino's paintings.

4. I quote from the 'Epilogue' of Maynard Mack's *The Garden and the City*: 'To be a great satirist, a man must have, literally and figuratively, a place to stand. For Pope – so my argument runs – the garden and the grotto supplied this. They supplied a rallying point for his personal values and a focus for his conception of himself – as master of a poet's 'kingdom', a counter-order to a court and ministry that set no store by poets.... Through them his retreat at Twickenham became, not only in his own eyes but in those of a number of his contemporaries, a true country of the mind. In a world where the many lived as usual, as if they had a wisdom of their own, his house, grotto, and garden with all that they implied could be grasped, at any rate in the poetry, as Henry James's 'possible other case' – the case rich and edifying in the light of which the actuality of the other world seemed pretentious and vain.'

5. See also 'The Speer Garden', Stephen Bann's commentary on IHF's exhibition project and book (unpublished), and 'A Walled Garden' (with illustrations by Ian Gardner and a commentary by J.F. Hendry), in Yves Abrioux (ed.), *Ian Hamilton Finlay: A Visual Primer* (Reaktion Books, 1985).

6. The garden which Speer worked on was built with the most primitive means, using bombed bricks. In a letter to Finlay, dated 27 September 1977, he explained how, 'by lying on the middle of the lawn', he was able – he alone – to perceive a garden within a garden, portraying 'something of the fantastic world of architecture I lived in'.

Aphorisms on the Garden of an Aphorist

CHARLES JENCKS

Imagine a cross between Jonathan Swift and Monty Python with a dash of Solzhenitsyn thrown in: you wouldn't get Ian Hamilton Finlay, but you would get an aura close to his. Like Swift, Finlay has a polemical and bitter wit; like Monty Python his madcap antics are often performed for the media, and like Solzhenitsyn he is always trying to prove a moral point of a quasi-religious nature. All of which is to say that he is unlikely; so unlikely as to escape all categories of current professionalism.

Like one of his enigmatic stones, Finlay is often given a label – 'Scotland's Greatest Concrete Poet' – an inadequate description. Is he a poet-gardener, or a concrete epigrapher? Is he a landscape architect, an internationalist and pamphleteer, a bureaucrat-baiter, a boatsman, or the leader of the Saint-Just Vigilantes? This incomplete list of his activities makes him at once a Renaissance polymath and one of the great challenges to that non-hero of the twentieth century: One-Dimensional Man. Whatever else Finlay is, he is a very self-cultivated and courageous human being who is out to prove that the past, particularly of Western culture, can be updated and made into a provocation and indictment of the present. In him not only Swift *et al.* are combined; Pope, Shenstone and Poussin also sit together on the bench, and find contemporary culture guilty of specialisation and fragmentation.

Finlay and his wife Sue live in the Pentland Hills not far from

Edinburgh on an abandoned farm named Stonypath now renamed Little Sparta. As in Sparta, life on these hills is not easy although many visitors find the treeless vistas and wind-swept landscape very beautiful. It is also frightening and, like his work, sometimes sublime. Personally I find it, like death, rather boring when it extends indefinitely, and, although it has inspired Finlay's taste for sublime terror, I suspect that the creation of his garden was meant to be an antidote to infinite beauty. '*Le silence éternel de ces espaces infinis m'effrai*', complained an agoraphobic Pascal, and Finlay never leaves his oasis in space for the agora of the city: in effect he has been in self-imposed exile for almost twenty years, escaping from some of the acronymic bureaucracies that trouble him, such as the SAC (Scottish Arts Council) or SRC (Strathclyde Regional Council).

Building a symbolic garden as a private oasis away from the turmoils of public life is a venerable Chinese tradition (as well as a classical one) which prompted some of the great creations of this genre: 'The Garden of the Foolish or Unsuccessful Politician' (Suchow), 'The Garden of Solitary Confinement' (built by a famous historian in Luoyang), 'Angler's Rest' in Peking (as in the West, 'Gone Fishing' suggests opting out). These literary gardens, in which calligraphy and poetic inscription play such a key role, are so close to his own in spirit that they might have inspired Little Sparta, had Finlay not first responded to Western, eighteenth-century classical gardens, to Stowe and Stourhead, with their Temple of Ancient Virtue and Pantheon. His model is actually the idyllic Roman campagna, reconstituted in Scottish vernacular and cow-byres. And he is in many ways an eighteenth-century gentleman-poet who made a mistake only in being born in the age of the Welfare State (something for which he has yet to forgive it).

The layout of his garden is romantic and picturesque, following the layout of existing buildings and his changing fortunes and desires. There doesn't seem to be an overall plot which connects one temple or garden to another, although each sub-plot is carefully structured. The whole sequence is thus rather mysterious, like a Chinese garden, and full of surprising incidents. As each modest structure is decorated, labelled and transformed – usually into a classical allusion – it does however create a unifying idea and mood. This could be called 'The Subversive Classical', an oxymoronic clash between two traditions

Aphorisms on the Garden of an Aphorist

which Finlay admires: the eighteenth-century revolutionary moralism which inspired two of his heroes, Robespierre and Saint-Just, and the serene language of classicism which inspired many of his artistic exemplars, Poussin, Claude, J.L. David and even Albert Speer. Terror and serenity, morality and harmony, are usually considered incompatible pairs in our century and because Finlay combines them he is often misunderstood.

There has been a good book published on his work up to 1986 – *Ian Hamilton Finlay: A Visual Primer* by Yves Abrioux – which unravels some of the paradox.[1] Only by reading about and pondering on the significance of this work does its meaning become clear, and those who approach it only visually, or with the aesthetic mental sets of our time, are doomed to miss the point. Because the imagery and emblems seem relatively clear and straightforward, people are bound to think they have grasped their significance when all they have really seen is the glare of their own stereotypes. Finlay must enjoy creating this confusion because, like Pope and conceptual artists he often works with stereotypes. Thus the first clue to his work is understanding that everything is what it isn't. And the second is realising that one must be a detective versed in hermeneutics to tease out the hidden evidence. Only when one has passed through a string of interpretations, often contradictory and some supplied by Finlay himself, has one actually 'seen' the work. 'Eyes which do not see', Le Corbusier's challenging aphorism, could be rephrased as 'The Mind's Eye which does not stop to think'. Finlay's work demands a Borgesian process of reflections on reflections since he often interprets his own enigmas with enigmatic captions and explanations.

The now famous Garden Temple, scene of the break-in by the (un)law, is a case in point. At first glance one might think it is nothing but a 'decorated shed' in the Venturian tradition; the Scottish barn with classical orders realised in paint. It doesn't look very serious: the Ionic order is placed strangely above the Corinthian, the fluting is eroded in parts and the window proportion is, well, 1950s Welfare State. However, when one looks at the drawing by Nicholas Sloan and reads the explanatory caption, the depth of intention becomes more apparent. The blank, voided windows, often a sign of gravitas, and the dignified symmetry, are clearer here, and the book on Finlay reminds us that in ancient Greece the Muses often gave protection to the arts and sciences in garden buildings, or 'Musaea'. This philological reminder is a further clue to the dedication: 'TO APOLLO/HIS MUSIC/HIS MISSILES/HIS MUSES'. As one enters the temple door under 'HIS MISSILES', one is reminded of the name of the American rocket programme as well as of other acts of war carried out under the sign of the sun god. If governments can celebrate beautiful destructive power by invoking a Greek god of the arts, then so can Finlay.

This seems bizarre and shocking at first – as does his use of battleships and Nazi iconography – until one realises this is only the second level of interpretation and that there are still more clues to follow. Again we are mistaken if we regard them only aesthetically. A series of harmless-looking instruments are placed on pedestal-like altars, all with double meanings. There is a watering can with a tricolour; '*Arrosoir*' is the date the Robespierrists were guillotined, and as Finlay adds to the written caption near the watering can, Robespierre was described as 'regenerative' like an *arrosoir*. There is also an axe inscribed to Saint-Just ('HE SPOKE LIKE AN AXE'), two herm figures of Saint-Just, a beautiful wall of engraved stones carrying revolutionary slogans and, perhaps the most striking image of duality, a sculpture of paired columns set opposite a similar sculpture of the guillotine, the former marked 'VIRTUE', the latter 'TERROR'.

In effect, here, as elsewhere, Finlay is equating what our culture has polarised: the garden with warfare, terror with virtue, and the everyday with the beautiful. These equations seem so unlikely because in our century the military arts have been furthered and celebrated by megalomaniacs and philistines, whereas in the classical past the beauties and virtues of warriors were a cause for celebration by artists. Finlay reminds us of this awkward and surpressed truth and he is the first one since Marinetti to do so. Should we exile the poet because he presents unwelcome opinions? Clearly he is not supporting contemporary tyranny by portraying its beauty and ambiguity: witty slogans in a garden are only an incitement to meditation. The chapter in the book called 'The Destructive Element' discusses these problems at some length and comes to the conclusion, rightly to my mind, that Finlay's wit and sarcasm always give a double meaning to his images of war.

'The First Battle of Little Sparta' on 4 February 1983 was one of the zaniest engagements fought in the British Isles since William the Conqueror faked his rout from Hastings: at Little Sparta the only shots were fired by the Saint-Just Vigilantes, and they were black and white press shots handed out to the media soon after the event. These show our Arcadian heroes engaged in various military manoeuvres: spotting the enemy (the sheriff's officer in his car), then discussing battle tactics in the bunker, and finally surrendering with dark hands held high against the sky. The photographs bear comparison, in pose and gritty blackness, with some of the best shots of the Second World War. Indeed, like Jonathan Swift's bitter satire directed against the State, they give to ridiculous events an epic grandeur. That the SAC, SRC and other acronymics were drawn into and then memorialised in such a conflict is of importance in our age of the faceless bureaucrat, because it shows Finlay's genius at finding the heroic in the everyday, and the sublime in the banal. 'EVENTS ARE A DISCOURSE' is one of the slogan-emblems Finlay wishes to inscribe on Edinburgh's unfinished Parthenon, an epigram which is as appropriate to activist art as it is to eighteenth-century revolutionary classicism. This has not yet been cut into the stones on Calton Hill, but Saint-Just's phrase has been frozen into large stone blocks on the hillside at Little Sparta: 'THE PRESENT ORDER IS THE DISORDER OF THE FUTURE'.

This 'heroic emblem' is part of a genre that Finlay has reactivated from the past, especially from Renaissance Europe when epigrams were engraved in permanent materials. The danger of such aphorisms is that they sound like one-liners, advertisements; a danger Finlay overcomes by always making them ambiguous, turning them into at least two-liners with related meanings and combining them with clear, striking images. 'For [Finlay], the form of the emblem generates, in Gombrich's words, "a free-floating metaphor", formed from the conjunction of motto and image, setting it apart from more conventional methods of establishing meaning ... These "heroic emblems" are also intended to provoke meditation'.[2]

Your average aphorism always hits the nail on the head, whereas the Finlay aphorism always hits the hammer on the tail. 'SMALL IS QUITE BEAUTIFUL', a calculated miss-hit, is printed in sub-classical script on an ecological green card and elsewhere given extended exegesis by Finlay and his army of interpreters; these multiple texts *do* provoke meditation and *are* the meaning of the aphorism. Although it strikes quickly, as a snake-like epigram should, it bites into the mind and won't let go. Most aphorisms are more civilised and dissolve in the mind faster than disprin. However, instead of being the last word on the subject, Finlay's epigrams are intended to be the *continuous word* on the subject. 'THE WORDS WE HAVE SPOKEN WILL NEVER BE LOST ON EARTH' is carved in raised letters on ruined stone as if Saint-Just spoke in immortal chunks of imperishable limestone. Another phrase of his is inscribed on a votive column placed by the artificial Lochan Eck: 'THE WORLD HAS BEEN EMPTY SINCE THE ROMANS'. The Roman emphasis on the immortality of deeds, the permanence of heroic action and the memorialisation of the public realm are all invoked in these quotes of quotes. Finlay is determined to bring this pagan immortality back into an agnostic and confused age.

Part of his message is aimed against the mental and linguistic confusions of the Welfare State which mouths Christian pieties yet is even more secular than the atheist government of the French Revolution. The present state does not tax churches, charities or religious bodies, yet it does tax Finlay's shrine and, more importantly, will not discuss with him whether his Garden Temple is or is not a quasi-religious building. On a practical level this has led to the Little Spartan War, but on a philosophical level it has shown the contradiction of the reigning ideology. Holding a secular philosophy of liberal humanism, it nevertheless still supports a religion in which it does not profess a faith, and proclaims a democratic philosophy while actively supporting a law which favours the powerful. The Little Spartan War has revealed these contradictions again and again in case anyone has missed the point. For instance, after the raid on the Garden Temple and the confiscation of the art works within, their return was demanded by several owners including Finlay himself, but the only one returned belonged to an American who called in the US State Department to help him lodge his complaint. It takes this kind of hammer, evidently, to crack the bureaucratic sickle.

That Finlay should manoeuvre the SRC and its attendant legal arm into playing the role of the KGB to his Solzhenitsyn is a minor comic triumph. It recalls American acts of civil disobedience; Henry Thoreau, or more recently the eminent critic Edmund Wilson, who didn't pay

Aphorisms on the Garden of an Aphorist

income tax as a matter of principle. But however high-minded and just is Finlay's cause, it is also ludicrously funny and daft. The mock heroism of the battle, with model machine-guns stuck in haystacks as ersatz gun emplacements, reminds one of college pranks and of Monty Python. Finlay is not above using schoolboy jokes and farce in his epic war of wee David fighting the totalitarian Goliath.

The intent of the Finlay's art is not entirely polemical; it is also lyrical. One of the most beautiful and emotionally convincing parts of their garden is the Henry Vaughan Walk, a little pathway of brick cut into a dense forest-like area. Here one comes upon one short inscription after another, like stations of the cross or stills from a film, which have a narrative sequence. It is the appropriateness of the sayings to the melancholy forest and the build-up of the drama from one epigram to another that works so well here. This is the most moving part of the garden because image, setting and words are so well integrated. In some works, or parts of the garden, there is a certain let-down because the imagery, whether architectural or sculptural, has not been transformed to express or deny the words. Finlay sometimes seems content, like Moholy-Nagy or Sol LeWitt, to have an idea and then let others invent the particular visual vehicles. A certain dissociation and stereotype pervades this work, a mechanism that many committed to modern art will defend.

Whether Finlay will defend it or not is a moot point, because the mechanism is as much practical as ideological. Since he is no Michelangelo with a chisel or Michael Graves with a 4B pencil, he depends on others to draw or sculpt inventively at times and their invention is, alas, not always up to his conceptual and verbal wit. It is always fitting and well crafted, but sometimes flat and banal – a reason why some sculptors and architects dismiss the work before giving it a chance.

Its deeper meaning, however, overcomes these occasional drawbacks. And there are, of course, times when nothing is more suitable than a properly executed archetype: for instance Abbé Laugier's 'primitive hut' set as it should be by the water, but used by vicious Roman geese rather than noble savages. This tiny hut is an average neoclassical cliché, a mentally prefab Ledoux, but its columns, thatched infill and pediment are well proportioned, and its funny use and size give it a freshness which transcends stereotype. This is true of the garden as a whole, the creation of Ian and Sue Finlay which must rank as a major achievement. Put in context, it is a prime example of that moralistic postmodern classicism which has gained such strength in the last ten years: the work of Paul Georges, James Valerio, R.B. Kitaj, Hans Haacke, Leon Krier, Rita Wolff and other ethically inspired artists and architects. In a greater timeframe it asks to be compared to the great British classics – to Stourhead, Stowe and Hidcote – and the comparison is not always unfavourable to the Finlays' miniature version, which is certainly wittier than its precedents. In the end, Little Sparta is quite simply the greatest British garden created in the age of the Welfare State and a garden which raises questions about a public religion and morality. Oh woe to the SAC and SRC when they realise they have won the economic war against this martyr-poet only to have lost the Battle of Little Sparta, the battle for men's minds and hearts; for in the end they look small-minded and ridiculous and the Finlay's garden has become as immortal as it is possible to be. Surely there is a moral, and much stone-cutting, lying in this somewhere.

(1986)

Notes

1. *Ian Hamilton Finlay: A Visual Primer* by Yves Abrioux, with introductory notes and commentaries by Stephen Bann; (Reaktion Books, Edinburgh, 1985; second edition, 1992).
2. *Ibid.*, p. 97.

The Garden Temple at Little Sparta.
Photo by Antonia Reeve

On the Contemplative and Spiritual Use of the Temple at Little Sparta

MICHAEL CHARLESWORTH

At the centre of the garden at Little Sparta stands the Garden Temple: the Temple of Apollo. The sign of a Corinthian pilaster is carved into the stone of the old building, four times, and a golden inscription reads: TO APOLLO/HIS MUSIC/HIS MISSILES/HIS MUSES. The temple is best viewed across the garden pond, from where its inscribed signs shine out silver and gold against the grey Pentland sky.

It is with a shock, or with at least surprise, surely, that the visitor encounters the temple. While garden temples were once numerous in European and American gardens, they have, in general, long ceased to be made. Had Little Sparta's Temple of Apollo been created in, say, 1820, it could easily be assimilated as a nostalgic gesture of garden-making (nostalgic for a previous era of garden design, I mean). It was, after all, shortly before 1820 when the practice of building temples in gardens began to go into rapid decline. However, the century and a half – or more – that has intervened since then effectively forecloses such a simple explanation of Little Sparta's temple. Indeed, the circumstances of the Temple's making, after battle had been joined, as it were, in the war between Little Sparta and Strathclyde Region, also gesture strongly away from a purely garden-historiographical explanation. The question recurs, then, for the visitor: what does it mean to make a Temple of Apollo at the end of the twentieth century? Or rather, what does it mean to *find* one?

On one level, to find the temple is to find something to read. The inscription could be held to function as a short poem, with the invocation standing duty as its title.

TO APOLLO

HIS MUSIC. HIS MISSILES. HIS MUSES

The Temple's inscription seems to characterise Apollo by reference to certain modern attributes: music, missiles, muses. Music, Apollo's lyric poetry, we can assume, is a fitting attribute to invoke at the home of an important modern poet, but what about the missiles? The main images associated with the word in the 1980s and 1990s are surely intercontinental ballistic missiles, guided missiles, cruise missiles, nuclear missiles with their 'warheads' and their awesome destructive capacity. After this encounter with the uncompromisingly modern, and the astoundingly violent, Apollo's Muses can hardly be taken to designate only Thalia, Terpsichore and the rest of the ancient sisterhood; instead the word evokes, perhaps, the whole domain of the arts in modern Britain, arts now handmaidens of commerce, perhaps, Cinderellas of corporate sponsorship, but by the time we reach this conclusion, that disturbing 'missiles' has got firmly in the way. Are there now new muses that the years have added and I don't know about? The muse of sacred violence? The muse of surfeit? The muse of ballistic poetry? *Am I safe here?*

In rhetorical terms, after the invocation, 'TO APOLLO', the sequence is: metonymy (representation not of the thing itself but by a part or effect or attribute of the thing – HIS MUSIC); catachresis (the bringing together of two contradictory terms with an anomalous effect – HIS MISSILES); metonymy (HIS MUSES). Yet the restoration of the familiar trope is not so calming as it should be, and we can look again to the invocation to Apollo. In terms of structural linguistics, this should amount to metonymy (not the god himself but an attribute of him – his name). But what if in that invocation is couched the thing itself, recognised best by its unaccountably swollen attributes (an arrow, an Exocet; a discus, a Minuteman)?

Wittgenstein, the linguistic philosophers, even the great Lacanian unconscious itself, might seem to be awaiting the next stage of this meditation. Yet the poem is inscribed on an object, on a very solid and enduring building, which is, moreover, asserted to be, by its designation as temple, a sacred structure. Can the temple be a sacred, as well as a spiritual and contemplative, site?

Pliny the Elder tells us nearly all we need to know about the character of sacred status in a single sentence of his *Natural History*. A fig tree growing in the forum at Pompeii was considered sacred, he writes, because 'things struck by lightning were buried there'. From this ancient statement we can note several facts. For example, the sacred idea works by association: it was, of course, the *lightning* that was considered to be directly associated with the gods, and *that* therefore contains the sacred idea, which then creeps to the dead animals and to the tree in the forum. A second fact registers as an absence: sacredness is not confined to a site of worship, the building belonging to a functioning cult such as the Church of Scotland, for example. Or again, another fact: sacredness is allied to violence (here impersonal, unpredictable, ineffable, irresistible).

A moment's reflection will convince the reader that these facts can be redefined as *principles of the sacred*, true across the centuries and over many differing cultures. Taking our cue from 'HIS MISSILES', and focusing on the element of violence, for example, we can note that René Girard, in his engagingly titled book *Violence and the Sacred*, sees violence as 'the heart and secret soul of the sacred'. Taking this transhistorical view (though not a transcultural one: Little Sparta stands within the same cultural descent, just, as Pompeii, and the continuities between modern and classical culture are one of the themes of the garden) allows the facts provided by Pliny the Elder to be applied to Little Sparta and the Temple of Apollo. Certainly violence, albeit in symbolic form, has raged around the temple with greater and lesser intensity during its short life.

The question of the Temple of Apollo is, and yet so obviously is not simply, a question of definition. Such a question does not need to be decided on unhistorical grounds. There are certain persuasive parallels between Little Sparta and the eighteenth-century landscape garden made by the Marquis de Girardin at Ermenonville in France. Both gardens share a seriousness of purpose, a philosophical depth, and a resonant poetic feeling. At Ermenonville, as at Little Sparta, there was confrontation with other authority which claimed jurisdiction over the garden: the Charcoal Burner's Hut commemorates a court victory which successfully defended the poetic integrity of Ermenonville from the depredations of a member of the French royal family, the Prince de Condé.

Ermenonville was begun, in emulation of the English garden, in 1766. In the last months of the life of the philosopher Jean-Jacques Rousseau, Girardin harboured the great man, who botanised on the heath and enjoyed the company of Girardin's youngest son, Amable. On Rousseau's death at Ermenonville in 1778, Girardin interred his ashes in a neo-classical sarcophagus on the Island of Poplars in one of Ermenonville's artificial lakes (Rousseau was one of at least three people buried in the garden between 1778 and 1791).

Had Girardin sacralised his garden by burying there the freethinking deist? Other parts of Ermenonville indicate that Girardin was extremely suspicious of the sacred idea, and even wished to overturn or overthrow the grip of religion. While quarrying stone to build the garden's Hermitage, workmen dug up several skeletons, which were construed to be those of people massacred during religious wars of a previous time. An inscription was placed on the spot and became a garden feature:

> *Hic fuerunt inventa plurima*
> *Ossa occisorum, quando*
> *Fratres fratres, cives cives trucidabant.*
> *Tantum Religio potuit suadere molorum!*

(Here were discovered many bones of those massacred when brothers slaughtered brothers and citizens butchered citizens. How powerfully can religion incite to evil!)

The final line of the inscription is a quotation from the Roman author Lucretius that had been used by the English deist philosopher Matthew Tindal when he argued against organised religion because of its foundation, even in Christian times, in sacred violence. Reading Tindal's *Christianity as Old as the Creation* (1730) is often like reading Girardin two and a half centuries early.

The inscription over the old skeletons at Ermenonville tells us of Girardin's dislike of sacred violence. One can imagine his horror, therefore, when he learned that

> the celebrated opera dancer, Mlle. Theodore . . . [who] had an enthusiastic admiration of Rousseau . . . made a pilgrimage to his grave; and there, in the true spirit of enthusiastic homage, cutting off one of the long tresses of her fine hair, she hung it as an offering on his tomb.

Worse was to come. Helen Maria Williams continues, in her 1794 *Letters from France*, telling us that

> [two young Englishmen had swum to the island of Poplars, and] kneeling at the tomb of Rousseau, had burnt a book, published a short time after his death by Diderot, in which he had treated the memory of Rousseau with the most cruel indignity . . . Mons. Girardin was absent from home, when the sacrifice of Diderot's book was offered at the tomb.

In these strange gestures, so fitting on the eve of the French Revolution, we can recognise the inexorable logic of sacralisation. Rousseau's urn left Ermenonville, never to come back, and was exhibited in Paris beneath a small temple surrounded, like the tomb at Ermenonville, by a circle of Lombardy poplars. Hubert Robert, who had helped to design the original tomb, painted two beautiful watercolours of the Parisian catafalque.

Did the removal desacralise Ermenonville? Do the examples provided by Pliny and Ermenonville mean, by analogy, that Little Sparta is sacred? Is Finlay's assertion that the Temple of Apollo is a sacred building true? The answers to these questions are not obvious. What is clear, nevertheless, is that to answer 'no!' to them constitutes an act of violence.

The sacredness of Little Sparta could be defended by modern anthropological scholarship, but in the end such a recourse risks obscuring and misrepresenting the garden and what is at stake within it. Would not making such a defence be in some sense *missing the point* of the temple, which takes its strength from the nakedness of its stand, from its metaphor, from the charge of its *catachresis*? Taking off our anthropological armour, therefore, let us imagine a different case. Suppose that I make a garden and I declare it to be sacred. Another person, who has a garden of his own, says 'No, no! That's not sacred! Mine's sacred! Mine's the sacred one!' Then, because he has more violence at his disposal than I have, he invades my garden and damages it. I suffer, and his action is cruel. Surely we have the right to expect more than cruelty from our governments? How is sacredness to be judged? In quantity – a certain number of worshippers? Or in quality (true or false, pure or impure sacredness)? The questions are absurd. Our only response to the owner's or maker's declaration is acceptance, or cruelty (and cruelty brings hypocrisy in its train).

There are other sacred features at Little Sparta: the Temple of Philemon and Baucis, its miraculous transformation just beginning; the *lararium*, modelled after shrines to the household gods from Pompeii and Herculaneum, and containing its Apollo statuette. They form part of an extraordinary matrix of cultural and artistic allusion. On one level Finlay has collected a large number of references to cultural landmarks of the Western tradition, and has brought them back to Little Sparta, in transformations. A strong sense of delight comes to the visitor from perceiving this reconstruction on a few acres of the entire culture of the Western world, and the delight remains through the intellectual and philosophical challenges of encounters with individual works. For Ralph Austen, writing in the middle years of the seventeenth century, an orchard provided the opportunity for spiritual contemplation – an orchard being a lexicon of divine will – and the opportunity had not been fully exploited until the allegorical possibilities had been exhausted. In the twentieth century, Finlay's garden provides an opportunity for contemplation on the whole of Western cultural history, and the range of reference is so broad that full exploitation of the opportunities, expounded in the manner of Austen, would necessitate work on a encyclopaedic scale. What I had not been prepared for, in the case of the sacred features, was how *moving* they were. I have learned that Finlay's art eschews expressionism, and seeks to achieve an intervention in culture, and I suppose I had assumed the quality of being moving to be an expressionist quality (the direction of the brushstrokes around his bed in Van Gogh's famous painting, for example). Yet I was very moved by the encounter, and I am not very interested in working out why. Was it the humour, or the inventive appropriateness, or the sheer faithfulness of what I found? What matters is the fact, the opportunity I had, the power that the features have developed. For one visitor, at least, setting foot in Little Sparta brought the memory, despite the radically different weather conditions, of setting foot on the island of Delos, in the Cyclades of the Aegean Sea, where still (and by order of the Greek government) no visitor is allowed to sleep.

My feet are getting cold, standing here by the pond and gazing at the façade of the Temple. Perhaps the question of whether Little Sparta is sacred is irresolvable (perhaps: I do not believe so, but I introduce the possibility). Yet at least we need to abandon the polar opposites, the poles of opposition, sacred/secular. Sacred and scared are a simple typing error apart [so are worship and warship!], and 'cruel as' is an anagram of secular. Finlay himself has coined the term 'non-secular'. I hope that the Temple of Apollo, and Little Sparta as a whole, can survive for a long time as a real and concrete definition for that compound word.

(1994)

Elegiac Inscription by the Upper Pool, Little Sparta.
Ian Hamilton Finlay with John Andrew, 1975.

Photo by Dave Paterson.

Wood Notes Wild: A Tale of Claude

MURDO MACDONALD

Little Sparta is a temple in a wooded garden in the Pentland Hills overlooking Dunsyre, twenty-five miles south of Edinburgh. It is a place where groves of trees give shelter beside water, but even in summer it is a place where a light breeze can prickle the skin. Stevenson wrote of these same hills:

> Blows the wind today, and the sun and the rain are flying,
> Blows the wind on the moors today and now,
> Where about the graves of the martyrs the whaups are crying,
> My heart remembers how.

And for Ian Hamilton Finlay, as for Stevenson, the Pentlands are a place both natural and moral. They are a place where opposition – whether it be the beat of the curlew's wing against the wind or the fight of a band of Covenanters to defend a principle – has been a way of life.

Finlay's clearly stated cultural opposition is that of Dunsyre's Little Sparta to Edinburgh's Athens of the North, yet despite the Greek references both Edinburgh and Little Sparta look in the first instance not to Greece but to Rome. In particular they look to the Rome of the seventeenth century which attracted to itself the French painters Poussin (1594–1665) and Claude (1600–1682). Poussin's clarity of visual and intellectual purpose is a characteristic shared by Ian Hamilton Finlay. But where Poussin is clear, Claude is resonant, and this resonance – the plucking of a string of the psyche that allows the music of the spheres to be heard as if as an echo – is shared by Finlay also. Finlay has characterised this difference on a carved stone inscription in a glade by a pool in the garden at Little Sparta (*Elegiac Inscription*, 1975) '*See* Poussin, *Hear* Lorrain'. This epitomises the difference between the two artists: on the one hand each tree is almost chiselled in paint, but in the paintings of the other the air moves of its own accord because the artist allows it to and the wood notes wild can be heard. The tradition of Claude is thus the tradition of the real in the most poetic sense of that word. And where Claude is poetic, Poussin is controlled; yet both are working within a classical context. Finlay's virtue is to explore this counterpoint between poetry and control. In doing so he is a contemporary representative of the potent but little-explored artistic and intellectual tradition to which the work of Claude and his colleagues in Rome gave birth in Scotland.

This tradition is most keenly expressed in the eighteenth-century paintings of Jacob More and Alexander Nasmyth, the architecture of Robert Adam, and the nineteenth-century paintings of John Thomson of Duddingston and D.O. Hill. It runs much deeper than a mere visual influence. Claude is today routinely identified as a key step on the way to modern conceptions of landscape. This is no doubt true, and yet this interpretation misses his interests and intentions, for when Claude paints a figure on a small scale – perhaps Ascanius, aiming his arrow at the sacred stag of Silvia, or Psyche outside the castle of Eros, or Apollo and the Muses – it is not because he is uninterested in figures but because he is interested in landscape as a total narrative space; that is to say, spaces within which stories can take place, spaces within which figures must be of a scale which makes such narrative within the landscape plausible for the viewer. These are moral spaces, mythological spaces, poetic spaces; the Scottish artists who took Claude as their model understood this. They had a commitment to this Claudian narrative space, and were responsive to the need in each of us to explore the mythical and moral journey for ourselves, to encounter gods and mortals, nature and society in our own ways.

Thus, in order to understand the response of Scottish artists to Claude it is necessary to recognise this key aspect of his work as providing a model of narrative space. The beginning of this interest can be found in the workshop of the decorative painter James Norie

(1684–1757). His sons, James (1711–1736) and Robert (died 1766), painted a number of impressive works which show the influence of painters such as Claude's Roman colleague Gaspard Dughet (1613–1675) and indeed Claude himself, although the influences are somewhat difficult to disentangle since they came to the painters through the medium of engraving. A more immediate influence was the Italian-influenced English painter George Lambert, with whom both James and Robert studied in London. Perhaps as a result of Lambert's influence, Robert Norie took a key step in the 1740s when he began to integrate details of the real landscape of Scotland into his idealised compositions. This is a crucial moment in Scottish art, not because it led to realism, but because it led to a century-long exploration of the tension between the real and the ideal, between the actual and the imagined. This is mirrored by the concern of Scots mathematicians of the same period to preserve the status of geometry – the mathematical discipline in which the ideal and the real most clearly coexist – against the rise of the less philosophically rewarding technique of algebra.

Robert Norie's work cannot but have influenced that of Jacob More (1740–1793), who began painting as an apprentice in the Norie studios. More was also influenced by a landscape by the French artist Claude Vernet which hung in Dalkeith Palace at the time and acted as an important model for More's series of paintings of *The Falls of Clyde* (1771) which are among the outstanding European landscape paintings of the eighteenth-century. Although looking over their shoulder at Dughet and Vernet, these works seem to prefigure a confident drive to realism. However, they are best seen as part of the Scottish philosophical conversation between the real and ideal, since More turned his back on the possibilities of the real in favour of the possibilities of the ideal. At the end of the same year in which he had painted these pioneering works, he arrived in Rome, never to return to Scotland. As he worked in Rome, his work moved in style progressively towards the idealised landscapes of Claude. He became known as 'More of Rome', and was very successful, becoming one of the best-known artists of his day, and unusual among northern European artists in being asked to contribute a self-portrait to the Uffizi collection. Duncan Macmillan has pointed out that to modern eyes this period of More's work seems like little more than a pastiche of Claude, and, however much one may enjoy these works for what they are, it is easy to see why most of More's work so quickly drifted into obscurity after his death. But what is relevant here is the high level of More's commitment to Claude's example. It might be fairer to More to call his works homages to Claude rather than pastiches, for there is something very deliberate about More's fascination with Claude. There is an obsessive, respectful quality in the work, which in turn leads one to respect it. In short, More's love of Claude is very honest and it must have been precisely this honesty that his contemporaries in Rome saw in him, but it was also this obsession with Claude that constrained the development of his art. In a sense one may regret that More abandoned the approach to Scottish landscape shown in his *Falls of Clyde* series in favour of artifice derived from Claude, and yet in the light of his psychological and physical journey from Scotland to Rome it may be assumed that he knew where he was going. More the Claudian extremist is wholly continuous with More the Scottish landscape painter. His career can be seen as an exploration of this tension in the culture of Scotland between the actual and the imagined.

In the painting of More's younger contemporary Alexander Nasmyth (1758–1840), who visited him in Rome, one finds a kind of balance of the Claudian and the Scottish which owes a great deal to both phases of More's work and achieves a consistent synthesis which eluded More and perhaps did not interest him. Nasmyth went further in this synthesis: as an architect he designed Claudian temples in appropriate contexts, such as St Bernard's Well by the Water of Leith in Edinburgh. Nasmyth's paintings – like the buildings of Robert Adam (1728–1792) or the poetry of Robert Burns (1759–1796), each in their different ways exploring the interplay of actuality and imagination – must be seen as integral parts of the drama of ideas, philosophical, poetical, and visual, which is known as the Scottish Enlightenment. It is this drama which made Edinburgh the Athens of the North, and by extension, it is this drama which two hundred years later makes Little Sparta possible.

The Enlightenment is the intellectual and artistic drama out of which modern Scotland was born and Robert Burns has already been mentioned as integral to it. It is his Arcadian motto 'wood notes wild', a quote from Milton's *L'Allegro*, which gives this essay its title. Burns and Nasmyth were close friends, and it is to Nasmyth that we owe the famous image which has become the national icon of the poet. Burns's enduring role in the construction of modern Scottish identity is by no means unrelated to the fact that he, like Nasmyth, was an Enlightenment generalist: as well as being a brilliant popular communicator and pioneering folk-song scholar, in his poetry he could as easily write of ideas as of love or of politics. Thus his image can and does stand as a symbol of this key period of history.

To some extent and from a limited point of view, this begins to make sense of why Burns is such a durable cultural symbol in Scotland. Relevant also in the context of this essay is the image of Burns as the ploughman poet. This is often seen as a sentimentalisation of his rural background, and indeed it is. But it is also an image that encapsulates a belief in the working-class intellectual as a cultural force which leads from Burns through Hugh Miller and John Maclean to James Kelman. It is just as important to remember that this image of the rural poet was not created for Burns. It has a long history and relates as much to the classical conception of the rural as it does to eighteenth-century Scotland. It links Burns to the Roman poet Virgil. It is interesting to note in passing that both these poets came from peripheral, farming communities, both had to struggle, and both became celebrated in their respective capitals. Thus in Burns two key aspects of Scottish identity meet, namely classicism and working-class intellectualism, and this gives a further clue to his value as a cultural symbol. But what is also interesting for us here is that Virgil's poetry provided Claude with many of the subjects for his paintings. It is thus very fitting that Burns' portrait should have been painted by his late-Claudian friend, Nasmyth.

To conclude this tale of Scots Claudianism one can reflect on the extraordinary visual tribute to Burns made by David Octavius Hill (1802–1870), who, via Andrew Wilson, is in a direct line of teaching from Nasmyth. In 1841 over fifty of his images were presented in *The Land of Burns*, a major volume published by Chambers. Hill is one of the best-known figures of nineteenth-century Scotland, but his reputation today is based almost exclusively on the pioneering photographic work which he carried out in conjunction with Robert Adamson. As an artist he is most remembered for his record of the Disruption of the Church of Scotland in 1843. Much of the continued interest in that picture stems from the fact that, at the prompting of Sir David Brewster, Hill recognised the potential of the new art of photography for recording the features of the multitude of ministers who had seceded from the Kirk, before they were dispersed round the country, and thus began his interest in that medium. But while in international terms there is no doubt that Hill's significant contribution was to photography, we do not do him justice if we forget his other activities. He was an illustrator of considerable ability, particularly when it came to Burns; indeed one of the images from *The Land of Burns* is among the most intriguing works of art of mid-nineteenth-century Scotland. It appears on the title page of the book and is called *Lincluden: The Poet's Dream*. The figure of Burns is shown asleep among the ruins of Lincluden Abbey, his hand guided by faerie 'muses'. Surrounding him are characters from his poems: Bruce and Wallace on one hand, Tam o' Shanter on the other. For good measure (and among many other details) the archetypal tourist, Captain Grose, is there making sketches of architectural perspectives while Auld Nick plays the pipes in the middle distance. Essential to the composition are two contrasting but visually central features: in the far distance is a bright image of a classical monument to the poet himself while dominating the whole fantasy is a single figure outlined against the moon: a Celtic bard playing his harp. This latter figure is the Ossianic minstrel of liberty whom Burns conjours up in the verses of 'The Vision':

> He sang wi joy his former day
> He, weeping, wailed his latter times.

But the vision that Hill conjours up altogether exceeds the boundaries of that poem, becoming both a visual summary of the poet's achievement and, through its juxtaposition of classicism and celticism, a commentary on two of the cultural currents which have helped to shape so much Scottish thinking. Yet *The Poet's Dream* is far from typical of Hill. His other illustrations are landscapes or genre scenes, often of an expressive verve which links them to contemporary work by Turner (an example is the stormy *Turnberry Castle*) but also frequently drawing on, via Wilkie, a Netherlandish tradition, or, via Nasmyth, the classical landscape tradition of Claude, to which we can now return.

Like Nasmyth, Hill consciously applies insights from Claude to Scottish landscape, creating a set of memorable images of the places of which Burns wrote. What is interesting is that this classical approach, far from being an imposition on '*The Braes of Ballochmyle*' or '*Cassilis Castle*', tends to produce harmonious images which are appropriate to Burns' words while at the same time reminding the viewer that Burns' poetry is itself deeply informed by an awareness of the classical, and with that, among much else, an awareness of the tension between the real and the imaginary.

The fine thing about these engraved images is that, although by the time they were published both Burns and Nasmyth were dead, the inspiration of these friends, the poet and the painter, shows through. As such they transmit something about Burns and the classical ideas he took for granted, which has, for now, dropped out of sight. Similarly they remind one that the background to each of Nasmyth's portraits of the poet is a Scottish landscape certainly, but it is a classical landscape too. And finally they give reality to another aspect of that exceptional person, David Octavius Hill, who was both a pioneer of the new art of photography and the final representative of the mainstream Claudian tradition in Scottish landscape painting. In a number of later artists, not least William McTaggart, the influence of Claude's moral space can be felt, but the next explicit exploration of Claude is over a century later in the work of Ian Hamilton Finlay. For all that, the continuity is clear. And Claude, held in check for so long by the imperial antlers of the monarch of the glen, now shows himself again in Scotland.

(1994)

The Idiom of the Universe

THOMAS A. CLARK

> Ian Hamilton Finlay, *A Celebration of the Grove* (printed by the Parrett Press, 1984)
> Ian Hamilton Finlay, *Talismans and Signifiers* (Graeme Murray Gallery, 1984)
> Ian Hamilton Finlay, *Interpolations in Hegel* (Wild Hawthorn Press, 1984)

The bewildering variety of forms in which the work of Ian Hamilton Finlay has appeared has led reviewers into a small crisis of classification: is he 'the father of concrete poetry', a gardener, a sculptor or (the current solution) simply an 'artist', taking that word as a holdall for any odd or unpredictable behaviour? The problem seems an acute one in the case of a man who has a keen sense of where genres overlap and who insists on words, whether written or chiselled, meeting each other with a clean edge.

Certainly there was a stage in Finlay's development when there was some excuse for thinking of him as a writer who had abandoned words, or at least sentences and paragraphs. With recent publications and in particular the three books under review, this opinion is no longer tenable. Not only do the books reaffirm Finlay's status as a writer, they set out at some length the concerns and assumptions with which his more laconic works deal in an oblique or succinct fashion. They reveal Finlay as a writer concerned with problems of form, of change and intelligibility, of didacticism and dialectic, of light and shadow, oak and rock.

The seriousness of purpose that these publications display (not unspiced with levity, however) will not console those who persist in thinking of Finlay's work as whimsical and narrow in its range. The books take three forms: a proposal for several sculptures in an Italian olive grove; an investigation of the cube; reactions to the text of a great philosopher. As is usual in Finlay's work, the range of reference is bewilderingly and provocatively large; from pastoral sweetness to modern warfare; from landscape gardening to geometry; from Pythagoras to Wittgenstein, Vitruvius to Juan Gris, Virgil to Hugh MacDiarmid. The importance of culture is insisted upon at the same time as its various manifestations are put to the test.

A Celebration of the Grove is 'a proposal for the improvement of the olive grove at Celle'. Finlay was invited to create a work 'whose main raw material should be plants' but rather than alter the existing grove, he proposed the addition of four sculptures and a small temple in 'the spirit of the place'. In the plan of the grounds the grove is shown as a cultivated area between 'a prospect of olives' and the 'Forest of the Avant-Garde', an imposition of measure typical of Finlay's work. The temple and sculptures are to be placed in the grove according to Shenstone's principle, that 'objects should be less calculated to strike the immediate eye, than the judgement or well-formed imagination'. It is a standard far removed from those of the New Sculpture with which Finlay is sometimes linked.

The sculptures, a plough 'of the Roman sort', a plaque on an olive tree, a bronze basket of lemons, bear inscriptions of an elegiac character; 'The Day Is Old By Noon', 'Shadows Muse On Light', 'Silence After Chatter', and one which might almost serve as a motto of Finlay's Spartan intelligence, 'The Astringent Is Sweet'. The Italian setting has obviously inclined Finlay to a Claudian mood. One piece, a line of green porcelain bricks running in the earth between the trunks of the trees, might seem to have most in common with recent Land Art, yet it is intended as a literal representation of a quotation from Theocritus, 'a line of green among the trees', while its form and setting remind us of the eighteenth-century 'serpentine line' of beauty. The span of allusion in this one sculpture, from Theocritus to Carl Andre, is graceful and convincing, and its realisation might be as pleasing to the eye as to the 'judgement or well-formed imagination'.

The postscript of the book contains one of those 'dictionaries' which Finlay has issued in recent years, the form of which, consisting of a word and an imaginative definition, is perhaps a continuation (in reverse) of his early 'one-word poems'. The distance between the word and its definition is a sort of mild shock tactic which forces us to look more carefully at the word and our assumptions about it, surely one justification for the continuing relevance of metaphor in poetry. In this latest dictionary, words suggested by the setting of the grove are examined in terms of possibility and limitation: a volute is 'a form subsisting in the tree-bark'; peace is 'the simplicity of order'; the horizon is 'an explication'. The production of the book is very fine indeed, an edition of only twenty copies being printed at Parrett Press, with illustrations by Nicholas Sloan.

Talismans and Signifiers consists of photographs of small carved cubes, made in collaboration with Richard Grasby and Nicholas Sloan, side by side with quotations from various authors and with commentary by Finlay himself. The cubes, interspersed with an occasional rustic pebble, are inscribed with dots, words or patterns which may be seen as additions to, or subtractions from, the purity of the simple form. At any rate, it is owing to these markings that a play of meaning is able to accumulate around the little objects. Just as with the Celle sculptures, it is again the judgement rather than the eye which is being appealed to.

It is interesting to compare these works with the 'minimal' art of some American sculptors, Donald Judd, Sol LeWitt or Tony Smith. The last named produced a famous sculpture called *Die*, a six-foot steel cube intimidating in its proportions and material hardness. The purity of such a work consists in its 'dumbness', in its rigorous exclusion of meaning and the corresponding insistence upon naked being. By contrast, Finlay's cubes are small and manageable, the markings, even without the commentary, offer a purchase for the intelligence, and the fine craftsmanship of the carved stone places them immediately within a tradition of aesthetic discourse to which a whole cluster of ethical notions also adheres. We are in the realm of Proportion, Order, Harmony, the Good and the True. Seen in association with the texts, the works become specific, that is, they are changed from talismans to signifiers. The sheets of transparent paper which separate the photographs from the text are veils lifted from the talismanic aspect of the works.

The first cube is black with one corner roughly broken away. It is accompanied by a quotation from Proclus: 'Now we observe that physical beauty exists only when form prevails over matter'. Later Vitruvius and Plato are evoked to describe the cube as that which 'stands firm and steady' and is 'the most retentive of shape', and the human implications of these formal concerns are set out by Plotinus: 'In the universe as a whole there must necessarily be such a degree of solidity, that is to say, of resistance, as will ensure that the earth, set in the centre, be a sure footing and support to the living beings moving over it, and communicate something of its own density to them'. As evidence against these, there are quotations from Sallustius, who reminds us that the golden apple of the world is formed of opposites and is 'thrown by Discord', and Heraclitus, who teaches the difficult lesson that 'it rests by changing'.

The drama of this conflict, between solidity and change, between form and chaos, is accepted by Finlay and is responsible for the antagonistic and elegiac attitudes his work often assumes. It is painful and difficult work when set beside that of many contemporary artists who simply aspire to a state of rude and unthinking being.

If the title *Interpolations in Hegel* is impertinent, it is with a refreshing sort of impertinence. Who reads Hegel nowadays? Is Hegel himself not something of a joke, the last absurd edifice that reason managed to raise in complete retirement from praxis? The wit of Finlay's title is directed at these assumptions rather than at Hegel, whose text he may counterpoint or disagree with but which he never treats either as a joke or as a sacred relic. The implication in this book as in the others is that culture is no more something we can package into a body of scholarly knowledge than it is something we can afford to ignore.

Hegel is generally regarded as the last great systematic philosopher, but Finlay makes no attempt to come to terms with the philosophy as a system. Rather, he engages Hegel in a kind of Socratic dialogue, answering him or interrupting him with an aphoristic acumen quite equal to Hegel's own. The aphorism is usually a didactic form, but by placing his own sentences beside those of Hegel, Finlay breaks open the closed form of the aphorism, making it more dialectical. We do not receive the words of either man as encapsulated wisdom, but are forced by their juxtaposition to think beyond them and confront the problem directly for ourselves.

There are usually other characters lurking behind the scenes in this confrontation, who give their opinions in the notes at the end of the book. For instance, the first Hegel quotation reads: 'As regards the individual, each, whatever happens, is a son of his time'. Finlay's comment on this is: '*A man's associates are his fate*'. If we turn to the notes we find that this aphorism is a contradiction of Heraclitus: 'A man's character is his fate'. It is not that Finlay is having the last word, or asking us to choose between the different quotations. Indeed he would probably maintain that all the views are in some sense true. The value of the exercise is perhaps more apparent when we remember that a certain school of political thought, deriving from Hegel, has already made a different choice on this matter and turned its choice into a dogma.

The formal concerns of *Talismans and Signifiers* are again prominent, this time less remote from their social and moral implications. To Hegel's sentence, 'It is from conforming to finite categories in thought and action that all deception originates', Finlay replies '*The social earth is flat; it is only for the spirit that the world is round*'. Another reference to Heraclitus states that '*inconstant man cannot step into the same river twice*'. And elsewhere, echoing Wittgenstein, '*That whereof we cannot speak, we must construct*'. But the importance of a concern for otherness and the integrity of forms is most convincingly set out, first by Hegel, 'The tendency of all man's endeavours is to understand the world, to appropriate and subdue it to himself: and to this end the positive reality of the world must be as it were crushed and pounded, in other words, idealized', and then by Finlay, '*Facts, rather than property, are the first common property in the rational State*'.

The 'interpolations' form which Finlay uses in this book may be a development or variation of the 'unconnected sentences' which, after the eighteenth-century practice of Shenstone or Diderot, he has been using recently. One of the interpolations in the Hegel book says '*Consecutive sentences are the beginning of the secular*'. The presence of Heraclitus (whom Finlay calls the philosopher of form rather than of flux) in much of this work is, therefore, not an accident. Finlay is here returning the sentence to its Pre-Socratic adventure, using it as a poetic probe rather than as a logical machine. The lack of connection is essential if he wishes to leave the world intact rather than 'appropriate and subdue it'. The multiple viewpoints which the unconnected sentences allow might be compared with those of a cubist painter, a point which Finlay wittily makes with regard to a Hegelian discussion of 'limits': *'The guitar is the limit of the pipe and the fruit-dish, the music-sheet is the limit of the pack of cards'*. It is a spiritual or moral practice rather than a purely aesthetic one, because in freeing the mind from a single perspective both object and viewer are returned to their own integrity and possibility.

Ian Hamilton Finlay once described the concrete poem as 'a model of order . . . set in a space full of doubt'. He still investigates and constructs such models of order and obviously sees them as a necessary and humanising activity. Yet it becomes ever more evident that no order is more than a locality within Finlay's almost cosmic sense of doubt. A man's associates may be his fate but we are also told that *'Destiny is not necessity: Destiny is the universe's idiom'*. The attempt to confront the provisional nature of all systems of order has given Finlay's recent work a new toughness and incisiveness. It is almost as if he had embarked upon a *via negativa*, discarding successive forms as unworthy of his rigorous demands of order. The gaps between the sentences are a condition of their non-secular aspiration.

(1985)

Finlay in the 70s and 80s

EDWIN MORGAN

What immediately impresses anyone considering the productions of Ian Hamilton Finlay and the Wild Hawthorn Press over the last two decades is an astonishing fertility of ideas, linked intimately to a fertility of forms and genres, with publications of books and booklets, cards flat and folding, poem-prints and posters of varying size and shape, and proposals for architectural/sculptural/horticultural installations in many parts of the world. His printed works – I am not concerned here with his three-dimensional works or with the garden at Stonypath, Little Sparta – have a characteristically and pleasingly clean-cut, crafted appearance, are often made in close collaboration with a chosen artist, and range from the almost completely pictorial to the almost completely verbal, an interplay of word and image being carried forward, through various metamorphoses, from the early days of concrete poetry right into his latest publications. Readers and spectators hot for certainties will not find it easy to plump for 'visual poet' or 'conceptual artist' or any other restricting definition of him, though his own description of Robert Louis Stevenson as 'man of letters' (R.L.S.) seems also germane to the author of 'Dzaezl' (1979), where permutations of the letters in the world 'dazzle' present the idea of camouflage by their layout on the page. Using one of his favourite words, 'net', one could say that his work casts a net over a number of categories, and if I still want to claim him as a poet *of some kind*, and his work as *poésie* (in Cocteau's sense) *of some kind*, this is partly as a reaction to the art historians who appear to me to have been a shade proprietorial in their interpretations, and to have neglected the broad human context within which any poet or artist must be judged. No one would deny that a good deal of his work asks for art/historical knowledge to be brought to bear, and we are all in debt to those who have supplied such knowledge, but there is more to be said. A human being of the late twentieth century stands facing a Finlay poster. Let us say it is a long red banner with the message 'Reverence is the Dada of the 1980s as irreverence was the Dada of 1918'. What are his or her thoughts? That the whirligig of time brings in such natural reverses in any case? That yes, perhaps so, but is this necessarily a good thing? That if Leningrad is to be re-named St Petersburg out of a new-found reverence towards the past, why should Volgograd not be re-re-named Stalingrad out of reverence towards the fearful Finlayesque 'sublime' of its battle during the last war, i.e. is reverence such a simple concept after all? Or – slicing through the doubts – right, and what could be a more pithy aperçu?

The compression, the one-offness, the insight, the sudden perception, and often too the wit, the apparent paradox, the surprise, the shock, the provocation, of an aperçu are hallmarks equally visual and verbal in Finlay's work, and link his fondness for a large number (hundreds) of individual cards and prints with his belief in individual sentences as against connected discourse. Hence such titles as *Detached Sentences on Gardening*, *Detached Sentences on Public Space*, *Camouflage Sentences*, *Selected Dispatches of Louis Antoine Saint-Just*: collections of aphorisms inviting or indeed demanding reader response. Hence also the fact that, among the many separate aphorisms in *Table-Talk of Ian Hamilton Finlay* (Barbarian Press, Vancouver, Canada, 1985), we are told: 'Consecutive sentences are the beginning of the secular'. If Pre-Socratic gnomic sayings are numinous in a way that most post-Enlightenment connected philosophical and scientific discourse is not, then we must refresh ourselves at these antique springs (though in a contemporary manner), rediscover the fact that soul is the wit of brevity, and find cast down what for the majority of readers will be a new set of co-ordinates, still however to be co-ordinated by us reading the runes, into a world-view. Grappling with the *Table-Talk* will be strenuous ('Vengeance is an act of good faith' – which goes beyond Bacon's 'Revenge is a kind of wild justice'), poetic ('Land and sea are the warp and woof of the world'), perfectionist ('The artist has this disadvantage: he has no equivalent of the word "etc." '), single-minded ('A satirical age scarcely deserves its warships'), and above all active ('That of which we cannot speak, we must construct' – the Achilles' heel of Wittgensteinian rigour). With aphorisms goes quite naturally an interest in dictionaries and definitions, imaginary dictionaries with new definitions, definitions that provoke and force new thinking through the defamiliarisation of exploiting totally but consistently overturned expectations. Examples are at their sharpest in *A New Arcadian Dictionary*:

> *Arcadian*, adj. leafy, dangerous; n. a native of Arcadia, variously a shepherd, a commando, a nymph, a satyr, a Waffen-SS man; according to Lord Byron, a blackguard.
> *Lyre*, n. a double-barrelled quick-firing gun.
> *Neoclassicism*, n. a rearmament programme for Architecture and the Arts.
> *Schutzenpanzer*, n. one of the Awesome forms assumed by Pan.

These Arcadian definitions, many of which also appear as images on cards and prints, open up some of the wider themes which became central in Finlay's work, the relation of the world of nature to the worlds of art, politics, war, and revolution. A natural progression could be traced from the early sundial mottoes (like the beautiful EVENING WILL COME/ THEY WILL SEW THE BLUE SAIL) to the emblemised word-plus-image of *Heroic Emblems* (Z Press, Calais, VT, 1977), the recycled pictures of *Et In Arcadia Ego*, and the word-plus-image-plus-motto-plus-relief of *A Wartime Garden* (Graeme Murray, Edinburgh, 1990). Renaissance emblem books and heraldic coats-of-arms could range from the simplest illustration to the most recondite and riddling relationship between image and words. In his series of *Heroic Emblems* Finlay revives both the clarity and the mystery of this centuries-old tradition, but in a context which (as the title suggests) seeks to remind us that classical links between pastoral and epic are not to be ruled out because we are living in modernist (or postmodernist) times. As Virgil moved from his *Eclogues* to the *Aeneid*, so Spenser moved from his *Shepheardes Calender* to *The Faerie Queene* (where battles purportedly spiritual are fleshed out by violently realistic images of the war between the English and the Irish which Spenser had experienced at first hand), and so also Milton graduated from the pastoral world of *Arcades* and *Lycidas* to the cannons of the War in Heaven in *Paradise Lost*. It is worth recalling too that the Scottish poet William Drummond, a delicate adept at pastoral evocation, had an avocation devising and patenting fearful weapons of war (Hawthornden as the Wild Hawthorn Press of the seventeenth century). There is therefore ample precedent for the fact that *Heroic Emblems* shows a tank in a glade, a camouflaged battleship in a grove, or the Battle of Midway in a garden of beehives. Perhaps the most striking of these heroic emblems is one where a double motto runs round the oval frame of the image: a one-line poem by Emmanuel Lochac, 'Éternelle action du Paros immobile' (eternal action of motionless Paros [marble]) is recycled by Finlay as 'Éternelle action des Paras immobiles' (eternal action of motionless paratroops), with the suggestion that the latent energies of the static marble sculpture have an equivalence in the latent actions of a scatter of paratroopers fixed in the sky at the moment of ejection; both the art and the war are 'unnatural' but are the frame of the 'natural' image of a rose-bush climbing up through an umbrella-shaped pergola, the scatter of roses and leaves descending like paratroopers but the entire pergola presenting its own image, like close shot after long shot, of a parachute descending, so that the natural rose-bush, as in so much pastoral, is, in the older, pre-pejorative sense, artifice. The repeated emphasis on *action* in the two quotations, whether one envisages a 'frieze' of real parachutists or a real frieze of 'parachutists', suggests that both pastoral epic and epic pastoral are possible categories. Or, as one of the apophthegms in *Table-Talk* asserts, 'Up at five and fold hammocks is the rule in Arcady'.

But nothing hearty will placate the dark gods. The death which might lie in wait for the paratrooper as he descends, or which he might inflict on those he descends among, will always keep the true Arcadian alert and vigilant, and sometimes make him melancholy and downcast. These thoughts permeate Finlay's *Et In Arcadia Ego* variations on pictures by Guercino, Poussin, Cipriani, and Kolbe. The powerful old tag, correctly translated as 'I too [i.e. Death] am (or was) in Arcadia', sometimes misrendered in nostalgic-sentimental mode as 'I too had a time of happiness', or in a less romantic extension as 'I know; I've been there too', is given a new life, mainly in its original meaning though with some qualifications, in Finlay's metamorphoses. In an early Poussin version of the theme, two shepherds and a shepherdess in a pastoral landscape examine the Latin lettering on a tomb which has a skull on top of it as a *memento mori*; they are tracing with their fingers and spelling out that 'ET IN ARCADIA EGO' which can only be ominous but retains an element of the enigmatic. In Finlay's reworking, the scene is exactly the same, but the inscription on the tomb has to be deciphered by the troubled pastoralists, now time-travellers, from the German: 'Wenn alle Brüder schweigen' (When all the brothers are silent), the Waffen-SS anthem based on an earlier patriotic song; the shepherds might well be terrified if they knew anything about these death-dealers, but all they know is that the death-dealers have in turn been dealt death, have gone to dust as shepherds do.

Poussin's second assault on the theme, a few years later, removes both skull and inscription and shows the pastoralists examining a large old blank tomb which fails to explain itself in any way other than by reminding them that the awe of tombs is the presence of the past. Finlay's re-creation of the picture has swept away all the human figures but reproduced the half-open, half-bosky landscape, and replaced the ancient tomb with – again one thinks of science fiction – a more modern functional-looking tomb in process of pupating into a tank; the absence of both human figures and inscription leaves this object, which is more monument than machine, in a status of unfocused, unfinished menace – and yet the menace may be undermined by a reverse thought that possibly a tomb is struggling to emerge from a tank, not a tank from a tomb. No such doubts attend his treatment of Cipriani's picture of the motto, which has no less than nine pastoral figures clustered in a startled group about an elaborate urned and plaqued tomb with death's-head and Italian inscription, 'Ancora in Arcadia Morte' (even in Arcadia there is death). Finlay does away with the figures, keeps the landscape but adds some trees and bushes to it, and replaces the tomb with a tank, tracked and viable this time, its turret garnished with the SS flash and its side painted with the same Italian motto as in Cipriani; a glade devoted to death and destruction but still beautiful, still un-ravaged, its foliage half concealing a hideous power held in reserve. As if to take the story further forward, and regain a more elegiac human ambience, Finlay takes a German Romantic artist, Kolbe, who shows two lovers in a lush forest pausing at a scarcely visible tomb, and transforms nothing except the tomb, which becomes an overgrown, decaying, abandoned tank; the lovers languidly and without panic gaze at the stencilled letters on the tank, 'Auch ich war in Arkadien' (I too was in Arcadia), to them a message once of war but now of love: they too, as well as Death, will be able to say that they have been in Arcadia. In the midst of life we are in death. In the midst of death we are in love.

In the very fine reliefs, strongly carved in Portland stone by John Andrew, of *A Wartime Garden* (1990), Finlay returns from the pastoral countryside to the garden and reminds us that (as in one of his *Unconnected Sentences on Gardening*) 'Certain gardens are described as retreats when they are really attacks'. Here, a fountain is a battleship symmetrically firing its guns; a grove is a tank camouflaged with greenery; a precipice is an aircraft carrier; a lawn is the sea seen from deck, with an aircraft-bird flying off into the distance. These and similar ideas and transformations go far back into his earlier work, revealing his sense of nature as an arena of very powerful forces which will not be tamed by 'picnic areas' at one end of the scale or 'land art' at the other. The mythologising of nature by Greek and Latin writers has appealed to Finlay because it was a way of acknowledging the impact of these forces, largely mysterious as they still were, in terms of character and story that invited continual meditation and discussion. Since the Renaissance, it has been felt at various times that classical myth was 'worked out'. Dr Johnson thought Milton was flogging a dead horse in *Lycidas*. Keats feared it might be too late to use classical mythology, and left his 'Hyperion' unfinished. Yet these myths have proved surprisingly resistant to relegation, as much poetry in our own century, from Pound to Olson, has shown. Finlay's use of the Apollo and Daphne story is of particular interest. It is a myth that invites richness of interpretation; the god of poetry and music pursues a virgin who rejects him and runs from him, and as he is about to catch her she is saved by being turned into a laurel tree – the god vainly embraces bark and leaves. So on one level a love has been lost, but Apollo by his art can sing of his love and his quest and can therefore be crowned by the laurel wreath his very loss has provided; and further, since Daphne has 'become nature', his laureation, the laureation of the poet who is also the sun-god, can express a mystical wedding, half-tragic though it is, of sun and earth. In his print version of Apollo and Daphne *After Bernini* (1977), Finlay emphasises the extreme wildness of the 'nature' which his Apollo is about to catch, as his Daphne is already partly swallowed by the camouflage greenery of an SS uniform. The best comment on this is his card of 1987:

> 'Nature is the Devil in a fancy waistcoat.'
> *Samuel Taylor Coleridge*
>
> Translation for our time:
> 'Nature is a storm trooper in a camouflage smock.'
> *Ian Hamilton Finlay*

Finlay never loses his sense of the immediate and simple charm of nature which is so evident in his early works, as witness cards like *Rowan* and *Willow* from 1987, or the booklet *A Country Lane* (1988) which sets out with affectionate commentary his designs for a 'lane with four stiles' (of course in four styles!) at the Glasgow Garden Festival. And his *Table-Talk* of 1985 delightfully claims that 'Nature has, as it were, an extraordinary facility in rendering far-off trees'. But increasingly we find him militarising and politicising nature. Another saying in the *Table-Talk* warns: 'In Revolution, politics become Nature'. The 'wildness' of the Bernini variation referred to above is reinforced in his 1978 booklet *SF*, a sequence of script symbols with a note explaining how in 'the progression (or descent) from the civilised script [of the eighteenth-century] – in which 'f's were customarily substituted for 's's [this is not strictly true: the so-called 'f' was not printed with the full crossbar of a real 'f' and was in fact a 'long s' which had been in use for centuries] – to the runic rendering or double lightning stroke of the SS uniform and banners, we therefore follow the gradation between "Culture" and "Nature" '. The forces concealed in that aspect of nature represent terror, violent upheaval, a dreadful test which once begun has to be dealt with, a 'turning over of the earth' rather different from the innocent kinetic *Autumn Poem* of 1966. This theme haunts much of his later work. Three stark prints of 1990 – *Two Scythes, Scythe/Lightning*

Flash, and *Sickle/Lightning Flash* – instead of turning swords to ploughshares or pruning-hooks turn scythe and sickle, images of harvest and fecundity, into the SS lightning flash, reminding us that death is the grim reaper but also that politics and revolution are a part of nature. The German connection is strong, and obviously problematic. Although the SS flash is half a century old, and appears playfully with make-believe menace in heavy metal circles, it has by no means lost its force, as was instanced in March this year when Lithuanian demonstrators in Vilnius held up banners saying USSR but with the two central letters transformed into the SS flash: no motto was needed to make the point about violent suppression of rights. On the other hand one must sympathise with the message on Finlay's 1987 card:

> Myriam Salomon* owns the Second World War and you are not allowed to mention it.
>
> * *Assistant editor, Art Press, Paris*

It has always been one of Finlay's aims to provoke thought and discussion where thought and discussion seem to him to be inhibited by contemporary timidity or liberal consensus. Rather as Christopher Logue in his translations has tried to remind us that what Homer wrote about in the *Iliad* really *was war*, Finlay defends his neo-classicism ('Neoclassicism needs YOU' is his card variant of a famous First World War recruiting poster) as a removal of comforting delusions, an inevitably hedgehog realism that will spike out all round and give useful offence.

During the 1980s, the theme of the French Revolution emerges more and more strongly. At the time of his fight with Strathclyde Region over the rating of the Garden Temple at Stonypath, the formation of the support group of 'Saint-Just Vigilantes' was a first blast of the trumpet in foregrounding Saint-Just (1767–1794) as an exemplary Revolutionary figure, and in the context of the approaching bicentenary of 1989 Finlay produced a mass of highly original material which was celebratory at the classically severe, often ferocious, end of the spectrum, pro-Jacobin and anti-Girondin, making much use of the revolutionaries' own cultural markers – the new calendar, the Phrygian cap – and of the overriding, self-determining image of the guillotine.

> The French Revolution
> Scorned circumlocution.
> 'It depends what you mean'
> Meant Madame Guillotine.
> (From 'Clerihews for Liberals', 1987)

Saint-Just, guillotined at 26, is *A Young Blade* in Finlay's card of that title, which shows his head-and-shoulders portrait, cut concavely at the bottom to suggest a descending blade. The sharp, decisive, dangerous imagery is continued in another card with a long black axe inscribed in white HE SPOKE LIKE AN AXE – BARÈRE ON SAINT-JUST. In the end the axe spoke like Saint-Just, equally incisively. There are so many links backward and forward in Finlay's work that it is impossible not to relate Saint-Just to the *Apollo and Daphne* print already mentioned in the German connection; a decade later, in 1987, the old legend and the Bernini image resurfaced, with a different Apollo and Daphne print, *After Bernini*, and a complementary poster, *And even as she fled ...(2)*. By slightly altering the words of the story in Ovid's *Metamorphoses*, Book I, Finlay gives it a new meaning:

> AND EVEN AS SHE FLED
> THE REPUBLIC CHARMED HIM
> THE WIND BLEW HER GARMENTS
> AND HER HAIR STREAMED LOOSE
> SO FLEW THE YOUNG REVOLUTIONARY
> AND THE SHY REPUBLIC
> HE ON THE WINGS OF LOVE
> AND SHE ON THOSE OF FEAR[1]

In the print, Daphne is beginning to turn into a tree, but is clearly girdled with the tricolour of the young French Republic, and Finlay's note asks us 'to see Daphne as the Virtuous Republic and the over-ardent suitor Apollo as the young Saint-Just. The Republic flies, the Revolutionary pursues her. It is the all-too-brief period of the pursuit of a perhaps impossible Ideal'. The theme of Love in pursuit of Virtue, couched in political terms, is the theme of every revolution, and the Terror implicit in the extremity of the chase is suggested in the print by the Gorgon-like transformation of her hair and hands, already arboreal and twisting in anguish. She is Nature, and Terror, but she is also Revolution, and Virtue; her flourishing, once the trauma is over and has become a part of history, will produce bay leaves for the brow of Saint-Just – for some, though not for all, historians!

The Apollo and Daphne story has a rural setting, and no matter how urban revolutions tend to be (and the French one was no exception), Finlay remains true to his feeling (natural to one whose life has been lived very largely against a Scottish rural background) that even cities are set in a world of nature, in ground, in earth, there is no escape from it. His French Revolution cards and booklets, posters and installations, frequently make their political points in terms of plants and flowers, domestic and garden objects, baskets that would have appealed to Theocritus or Rousseau. A little time-bomb of a booklet, *4 Baskets* (1990), with drawings by Kathleen Lindsley, saunters through its homely pastoral with a 'Domestic' basket of loaves and wine, a 'Pastoral' basket of grain and nets, a 'Parnassian' basket of bay leaves, and (one can go no higher) a 'Sublime' basket containing two guillotined heads resting on straw. 'Whatever is in any sort terrible, or is conversant with terrible objects, or operates in a manner analogous to terror', said Burke, 'is a source of the *sublime*'. Something similar occurs in *Thermidor* (1989), a booklet with a sequence of drawings by Laurie Clark, illustrating the plants (and one animal) of the re-named first 'week' of Thermidor (Month of Heat) in the Republican Calendar; this time, nothing outwardly gruesome supervenes, but the final day, Arrosoir (Watering-Can), shows the watering-can with a ribbon tied round its spout to mark the fact that the guillotining of Robespierre and his group took place at that time. A note by Finlay reminds us that the Republican Calendar was inspired by Rousseau. We are in one of the *rêveries* of that *promeneur solitaire*. *Naturam expellas furca, tamen usque recurret*. If pitchforked nature returns, does this mean that man's hopes of art, as distinct from his victories over oppression, or accident, or opposition, are small-scale, short-term, provisional almost? Life is not a walk across a field, as the Russian proverb says. Nature is Pompeii, Lisbon, Krakatoa. So what can we set up? In an early letter (to the French poet Pierre Garnier, 17 September 1963, published in *Image* [1964]), Finlay argued against any art that had a '*glittering* perfection', as if it could cut itself off from man's earthly home. 'New thought', he said, 'does not make a new man; in any photograph of an aircrash one can see how terribly far man stretches – from angel to animal'. An unpretentious victory, however, could still be strong, a 'tangible image of goodness and sanity' which at that time he was able to find in concrete poetry. What a well-made concrete poem offered was 'a model, of order, even if set in a space which is full of doubt'. His farewell (so far) to the French Revolution comes in a card of 1991 which shows a scaffold with a guillotine set up in readiness, and the motto is a self-quotation: 'A model of order even if set in a space filled with doubt'. If that is something of an in-joke for those with long memories, it still says something relevant and important. Wars and revolutions, heads rolling not metaphorically as they do nowadays but really and truly, mythologised or unmythologised events of terror, do indeed take place in a space filled with doubt, as even the most devoted historians would agree. Eugen Weber, Professor of Modern European History at the University of California, recently described Saint-Just as 'bloody-minded, suspicious, intolerant of criticism, pretentious, vain, and power-hungry' (can this be Finlay's 'young blade'?), but also had to admit his 'great sense of greatness, of history, and of his role in history' (can this be Finlay's Apollo outwitted by a naked Daphne?). The model of order is not really the guillotine, but the guillotined pages of a folding card or a flimsy booklet, produced with care and diligent collaboration to give the reader a shock not of recognition but of cognition, which is much harder and much more valuable.

(1991)

Note

1. The sources are as follows: Ovid, *Metamorphoses*, Book I, Fable XII; Ipotesi, *Saint-Just & l'Antiquité*; Pater, *Apollo in Picardy*; Wittkower, *Bernini*; Mignet *Histoire de la Révolution Française*.

'*A dream is always the sentiment of a truth that exists no more.*' – Saint-Just
Ian Hamilton Finlay, with Kerstin Curwin, 1993.

'Saint-Just the Stern'

Saint-Just resembled Pater's 'Hyperborean Apollo' – 'a certain seductive summer in winter', even as a youth 'a titanic revolt in his heart'. Through contemporary portraits invariably show him with dark hair, he is almost always described – even by his enemies – as having long, golden or fair hair, reminiscent of the god. In addition, his characteristic emblems echo those of his Olympian counterpart, not the *bow* and the *lyre* but the *blade* and the *flute*. In his *Memoirs* a fellow-member of the Committee of Public Safety, Bertrand Barère, wrote: 'What distinguishes Saint-Just is his audacity. It was he who saw that the secret of the Revolution lay in the word *dare*.' Ian Hamilton Finlay First published in '*Poursuites Revolutionnaires*', Exhibition catalogue, Fondation Cartier, Jouy-en-Josas 1987.

Terror is the Piety of the Revolution

ALEXANDER STODDART

Of the five massive inscriptions in the Garden Temple at Little Sparta, *Terror is the Piety of the Revolution* stands alone. It is a profoundly Neo-classical work, yet it breaches the usual perimeter of this idiom in several places. At root the problem lies with its difficulty in reconciling form with concept; simply, where form (shape, letter, sound) normally exists to clarify meaning, in this case it tends to confuse. But the way in which the resounding *tone* of the work conceals its rationale is, in itself, contributive to a further conceptualisation – that of demarcating the very edges of its territory. The work must be viewed as a bold herm standing at the frontier of formalism.

The Neo-classical tendency is persecuted largely because it adheres to Doctrine. But it is also *feared* because it is well known to be quite capable of contravening the letter of that Doctrine in the cause of saving the whole. Hence, while the ordered phalanx is the appropriate military manifestation of the neo-classical impulse, the tactic of guerilla action (its antithesis) will be recognised, when necessary, to *effect* the ordered phalanx. *Terror is the Piety of the Revolution* will be persecuted, also feared. Neo-classicism recognises it and will march upon its precedence. But neither Red nor White shall fully trust it; each can anticipate it issuing from the lips of the other. Thus it rings *Red* when shouted in the Convention, and all scatter as though a quiverful had been loosed upon them . . . yet a White light shines when its riddle does not hammer home after a few seconds' contemplation. And again – it appears to legislate like the falling blade . . . yet the motion jams at the penultimate moment and presently a jury assembles around the scaffold. Now the printer's workshop echoes to the chant – now it accompanies a 'tut' overheard at a diplomatic function. In short, Finlay has devised a perfect sample of *Revolutionary Talk* – a wildfire rumour, a Tactic.

Thus while the *meaning* of the words 'Terror is the Piety of the Revolution' might remain undefined, the *purpose* of the *effect* of the aphorism becomes clearer. Simply, it clears a no-man's-land between the Neo-classicist and Modernist factions. The latter instinctively recoils, the former advances through it, its action a discourse on danger, exalting, through repetition – Virtue.

(1986)

151

Idylls
Ian Hamilton Finlay, with Michael Harvey, 1987

Pastorals

THOMAS A. CLARK

The Pastoral flourishes in a late time. Whether we go back to Theocritus and Bion or to Virgil and Ovid, the genre conjures a simplicity already lost or on the verge of loss. In the first Eclogue of Virgil, for instance, we find mention of civil war, evictions, the countryside in chaos or, on the other hand, privilege through the favour of a patron. In short, in the midst of the pastoral landscape, we find politics. Meliboeus, ruined, driving his goats into exile, meets Tityrus 'at ease under the awning of a beech'. They discuss the state of the world and Meliboeus is invited to partake, for one last evening, of the country's hospitality.

Of course this is not an overtly political poetry. The unrest is there to throw into relief the trappings of pastoral stasis. It is the shade, the bees among the willow blossom, the pleasures of song, the smoke from the rooftops, that are insisted upon. If we are, like Meliboeus, exiled from simplicity, the poem serves to remind us that it is nevertheless our home. Politics and complexity constitute a fall and, while we necessarily engage in them, the image of our early innocence may serve to orientate us in our fallen state.

The Pastoral is generally criticised for being nostalgic, and certainly the backward glance and a sense of ease and comfort are inseparable from it. But such critics too literally interpret the imagery presented. We are not being asked to regress to a pastoral economy. The sheep, the flute, the country love affairs, are emblems of a directness of relations, a more felicitous association between person and person, between humans and animals, between society and the natural world. We are being asked to consider value. The images remind us of essential ingredients in a civilised life; productive labour leavened by dance and song, gracious social relations, closeness to nature. They teach us that tenderness and joy are not additions to but vital constituents of a fully human condition. The work of Ian Hamilton Finlay is, in one aspect at least, militantly political. There are revolutionary slogans, guillotines and axes, tanks and aircraft carriers. In another, perhaps less evident, aspect, as in the books *Interpolations in Hegel* (1984) and *Unnatural Pebbles* (Graeme Murray, Edinburgh, 1981), or the recent exhibition at ARC in Paris (*Poursuites Révolutionnaires*) it is speculative and philosophical. But by no means the least resourceful part of this artist's wide-ranging work has made continuing use of the Pastoral. Many early works exploit the fact that, for example, fishing-boats with such names as *Amaryllis, Shepherd Lad* and *Zephyr* are registered in Buckie, Kirkcaldy and Inverness. No larger permission was needed for legitimising pastoral motifs in what was a self-consciously modern art.

The first work we meet in the present exhibition[1] reminds us, like the background to the first Eclogue, that the world is violent. The four Pre-Socratic elements[2] are not static but, as the presence of the Exocet missile indicates, liable to erupt and destroy whatever civilised grace we manage. More disturbingly, our own control over the power of the elements is far in excess of our social cohesion. With this cautionary work in the entrance, we can view the interior of the gallery as a clearing, a glade in which fauns and dryads dance, all the more lovely and miraculous for the darkness and violence that surround it.

In the glade of the exhibition, and in the space available here, it is impossible for me to notice all the ramifications of the conceits and idylls that Ian Hamilton Finlay's imagination and the craft of his collaborators have summoned before us. But I will mention a few, as discreetly as I can, in the spirit of one who points to a bird among the branches while aware that there are furtive presences poised at the edge of his gaze. If some of these conceits are abstruse, others are camouflaged, and with this artist's work it is necessary not only to look and to think but also to wait and allow a nuance or metaphor to come into the mind unbidden, as a deer might come into a clearing. A certain patience and reverence is required, for, as the inscription on the brick and stone altar says, quoting Mallarmé, 'Every holy thing wishing to remain holy surrounds itself with mystery'.

There is also the problem that the shyness and modesty of such 'holy things' is part of their being. They fly away or evaporate at any coarse delineation or too direct approach. So we find Daphne, pursued by Apollo, on the point of metamorphosis, her form partially camouflaged by the grain of the wood she has become. Further on, the nymph has already stepped into the rusticated column and capital, leaving in her haste a little pair of golden sandals. These and many other of the pieces included are necessarily oblique, addressing their subject with great care and tact. They are traces of traces. In enduring wood and stone, they attempt to pay homage to the evanescent, to a music scored 'for flute and roses'. Nevertheless, such checks and subtleties guard over values which the artist would attest and maintain. Their first requirement might be the moral injunction, from Epicurus, 'LIVE UNKNOWN'.

In the seven slate *Idylls*[3] we have a form linking the pastoral theme to Ian Hamilton Finlay's early 'concrete' poems. By the difference of a letter or two, a play is established which, to quote the Oxford English Dictionary's definition of 'idyllic', is 'full of natural simple charm or picturesqueness'. The first two (identical) words create a context or habitat which the third word enlivens with incident. A barque (which an earlier Finlay poem allows us to associate with the baroque) sails among tree trunks; a faun sports with two young fallow deer; a song tries itself upon the air. But this poem (if we again consult the *OED*) yields further variations: obsolete meanings of the word 'aire' include the nest of a hawk or falcon, and 'an altar'.

Modesty and secrecy again occur in the slate inscribed 'vale/vale/veil'. The English word 'vale' is already poetic, a heightening of the more usual 'valley'. The word is sweet, slightly archaic. The veil might be mist, haze or dusk, and the conceit of the poem is of the personified vale retiring, preserving its sweetness from scrutiny or intrusion. We have here a gentler illustration of the Epicurean commendment already mentioned, a less patrician example of Mallarmé's holy things. The poem impresses by being entirely realised. We are not summoned to piety but shown an instance of it. The veil may of course be lifted, to reveal the promised ripeness of the vale, but its presence is sufficient guarantee against vulgarity and display.

Virgil is, of course, an acknowledged presence in this exhibition and many of the works have what Erwin Panofsky, referring to Virgil, called 'that vespertinal mixture of sadness and tranquillity'. But there is also an element, reminiscent of Ovid, of more robust celebration. There is vigour, invention, humour. However learned the allusions and references may be, the imaginative movement in all the works presented here is simple, a recognition or delight entirely consonant with the pastoral genre to which they belong. This constitutes perhaps no more than a glade within the larger work of Ian Hamilton Finlay, but its importance should not be overlooked. Adumbrated here are some of the values, part of the fabric of civilised life, which more combative works seek to defend. Placed next to the Virgil tree-column is one dedicated to Rousseau, whose Social Contract might be seen as a modern version of Pastoral. It is a fiction to which we look back in order to remind ourselves of what our first freedom was, what we were without the chains of perspicacity and guile.

(1987)

Notes

1. *Pastorales*, Galerie Claire Burrus, Paris, 19 September to 9 November 1987.
2. *Presocratic Inscription*, a stone relief inscribed 'EARTH WATER AIR FIRE EXOCET'. Ian Hamilton Finlay with Ralph Beyer, 1987.
3. *Seven Idylls*: the texts are as follows: 'AIR/AIR/AIRE'; 'FRUIT/FRUIT/FLUTE'; 'VALE/VALE/VEIL'; 'FLUTE/FLUTE/FLUTE'; 'FAWN/FAWN/FAUN'; 'EAVES/EAVES/EVES'; 'BARK/BARK/BARQUE'.

Eye, Judgement and Imagination: Words and Images from the French Revolution in the Work of Ian Hamilton Finlay

YVES ABRIOUX

> Objects should be less calculated to strike the immediate eye, than the judgement or well-formed imagination.
> William Shenstone

> My art does not consist in words, my art is all action.
> Jacques Louis David

It is common knowledge that the French Revolution has long fascinated poets and artists. Early evidence of this fascination in Britain is provided by Wordsworth's great autobiographical poem, *The Prelude*, composed at the beginning of the nineteenth century, which tells of the poet's journey on foot through France and over the Alps just as the great Revolution was dawning. It is true that the outbreak of the Terror, justifying in the eyes of most people the anti-revolutionary wars fought by the monarchies of Europe, reunited the hearts of George III's subjects. Burke's defence of legitimacy won the day, and the young Wordsworth's troubled fascination remained secret, the *Prelude* only being published after the death of its author. It remains that the Revolution did not only forcibly strike the romantic imagination. It has even been taken to explain the genesis of the romantic movement as such. At the end of the nineteenth century, for example, that most subtle of English critics, Walter Pater, described romanticism as an essentially French phenomenon, and as the result of the 'storm' which the Revolution had constituted. 'In 1815', he writes, 'the storm had come and gone, but had left, in the spirit of "young France", the *ennui* of an immense disillusion', leading to a yearning for 'the spectacle of beauty and strength', which the works of the romantics set out to assuage. It is interesting to note that Pater in no way takes up the revisionist view, derived from Burke, adopted by the English romantics. For Pater, 'the love of energy and beauty, of distinction in passion, tended naturally to become a little *bizarre*'. Beauty and catastrophe went together: '*Are we in the Inferno* – we are tempted to ask, wondering at something malign in so much beauty'. Pater also cites as the epitome of romanticism Victor Hugo's description of the French National Convention in the year of the Terror, in which the assembly is compared to the sublime spectacle of a mountain peak. Hugo's Himalayas thus echo Wordsworth's Alps.

It will be necessary to return to the question of the sublime. Let us begin, however, by observing that Ian Hamilton Finlay's treatment of the French Revolution is as far removed as it could be from romanticism. Quite the contrary, Finlay openly espouses the neoclassical idiom favoured by the Revolution itself. It is known that the Revolution was marked by a great number of obviously pedagogical and commemorative works: prints, almanacs, ceramics, songs, monuments, festivals, etc. Finlay in no way denies this heritage. He once took up the text of an appeal by Saint-Just, calling on the ladies of Strasbourg to give up German fashions 'because their hearts are French', to make posters for the walls of a gallery, without so much as changing a word (Victoria Miro, London, 1985). More remarkably still, some ten years ago Finlay declared that he was probably the only living poet or artist who would have been happy to help organise the Festival of the Supreme Being in the re-baptised Second Year of the Revolutionary calendar (statement for the Tate Gallery catalogue, 1978). It was of course the painter David who organised the festival. Finlay has systematically adapted David's homages to Marat, Bara or Lepelletier. The grandiose *Chant For a Regional Occasion*, intended for two thousand voices, which he sketched out in 1983, was probably also inspired by David's example.

One cannot, however, limit Finlay's work to the type of pedagogical programme carried out by the Revolution. Nor does it simply commemorate its heroes. If, for example, Finlay has designed a fountain for the grounds of the Palace of Versailles for the bicentenary of the Revolution, he bypasses the Revolutionary iconoclasm which wreaked considerable ravages here and there, as the monarchy collapsed and the nobility fled into exile. The fountain of course takes up symbols of the Revolution: the water sprays red, white and blue; the motto 'Liberty, Equality, Fraternity' is carved into its base. However, the context for which the fountain has been proposed must not be forgotten. For Versailles, Finlay has planned a finely calculated deviation from the court's waterworks.

Finlay's work characteristically operates by means of comparable deviations. However, deviation in this case is in no way synonymous with perversion. What is involved, rather, is a process of complexification aimed at enriching the cultural fabric with which any cultural project must work. What Finlay strives after is both to question what makes up our culture, and to prolong and develop its aesthetic, philosophical or ethical energies. Let us return, then to the question of the sublime. For Edmund Burke, sublimity is terror – but terror observed from a distance, so that there is no immediate threat, just an imposing spectacle. All therefore depends on the point of view. This doubtless explains why the sublime passages in Burke's *Reflections* on the French Revolution – and there are indeed such passages – refer, not to the Revolutionary protagonists of terror, but to characters at a safe historical distance (Cromwell among others). For, as Tocqueville was quick to observe, if Burke and de Maistre regarded the Revolution as a monster, this is because they were too close to the events themselves, and too directly involved with them to be able to see their real shape.

Finlay, however, attacks the question of point of view head on. This explains why the installation he created for the Kassel Documenta of 1987 is called *View to the Temple*. Four life-sized guillotines, bearing on their blades short statements referring to the sublime, frame – like so many classical arches – a small neo-classical temple on an island at the far end of a park. This work can be analysed in terms of the principles set out by the poet and gardener William Shenstone, quoted at the head of this essay. In a major exhibition of contemporary art, it is obvious that Finlay's guillotines will immediately strike the visitor's eye, for nothing has been done to make their sharp reality aesthetically pleasing. However, things cannot remain there. The work is set out in such a way as to ensure that an act of reading – bringing in the judgement – will take over from the immediate visual effect, nevertheless without ever glossing over its contours. By way of the quotations on the blades, certainly, but also by means of the plastic 'rhyme' (guillotines – arches) and the effect of the perspective itself, which mimes the historical relationship between the sublime and the classical, observers are called upon to meditate on the problematics of the sublime. This should help to form their imagination, which they can immediately test by turning to the other works exhibited at Documenta and taking stock of them.

It is easy enough to check that Finlay's imagination is itself well formed. For *View to the Temple* condenses a series of historical and cultural facts. So it is, for example, that a few years ago the French poet Michel Deguy described the sublime as a crisis accentuating what is at stake in the present moment of any poetic act aware of the distance separating it from the sacred origins of art; a definition recently echoed by the art historian Daniel Arasse in a book on the guillotine. Arasse writes that the blade of the horrific machine 'gives shape to the moment' as a crisis or paroxysm in the movement of time. Nothing links the poet and the historian's statements, if not *View to the Temple* itself, which is why it can be said that if the installation constitutes a visual or concrete poem, it is 'all action'. Any visitor to Finlay's exhibition (Poursuites Révolutionnaires) will also encounter the inscriptions on the four guillotine blades from Kassel. However, here they are inscribed on pieces of slate and they frame a passage quoted from Albert Mathiez, historian of the French Revolution, and itself inscribed on a blackboard resting on an easel. The quotation refers to Robespierre as the severe schoolmaster of democracy. The question of the sublime thus applies here more directly to politics than to aesthetics.

How can a disposition such as this best be described? I propose here to make use of a term employed by Walter Pater, who gave the collection of essays from which I quoted earlier the title *Appreciations*. An appreciation is not simply a celebration, and it implies something different from sublime delectation. It must weigh up the forces involved. By playing on the eye, the judgement and the imagination in action, Finlay confronts different elements of our culture: the sublime and the beautiful, aesthetics and history in *View to the Temple*, but also, as we shall see, the traditional or the classical and the modern, nature and culture, etc. In what follows, I shall not attempt to impose any one exclusive reading on works which can in any case always be approached from different angles, but simply to give some indications of Finlay's poetic and iconographical procedures, and also to set out some aspects of the intertextual fabric with which he works. However, it is impossible to give a purely formalistic description of Finlay's work. He is an artist who works less with pure forms than with the forms of our understanding. The pleasure which one derives from his texts or objects necessarily involves both formal appreciation and an act of interpretation. It will thus be necessary to interrupt the discursive and iconographical analysis at some points, in order to deal more directly with the principles and ideas Finlay has developed.

It would be useful at the outset to get rid of two possible misunderstandings. The way Finlay privileges both the French Revolution and the Third Reich can cause problems, inasmuch as neither of these historical phenomena is situated at a distance sufficient to guard against over-hasty polemics. This is in any case partly what draws Finlay to them, for his intent is never merely archaeological. Two approaches have been followed in attempting to ward off the discomfort which the artist provokes in the beholder. Finlay has been accused of an indecent fascination with military matters, and even of producing fascist art. This is, however, an attempt to salve one's own conscience by (deliberately?) ignoring the formal work involved in creating the pieces incriminated, and is an obvious misreading. Other critics have sought to share their clear conscience with Finlay, by attributing to him an ironical intent. This second approach is scarcely more acceptable than the first. Finlay never seeks to assume the position of silent superiority that characterises the ironist. His work is involved with forces which haunt us too closely to allow ironic distance to come into play. If there is irony, then this can only be in the root sense of the term. *Eironeia* means 'questioning'. As the rhetorician Bernard Dupriez reminds us, the reader is thus expected to ask himself what any ironic statement can really signify. This is what irony strictly speaking amounts to. And it is the test – frequently a radical trial – one must go through whenever the eye, judgement and imagination confront the work of Ian Hamilton Finlay.

This being said, it is possible to make things easier for oneself – in the first place, by being aware of the high degree of formal and poetical sophistication which has always characterised Finlay's work. It should be recalled that if Finlay's earliest works (dating back to the late 1950s) are fairly traditional in technique, they nevertheless allowed the problem of the continuity of the tradition to rise to the surface. The syntactical disruption of his concrete poems of the 60s, and the moments of tension and stasis this implies, represent a highly original and pertinent response to the modernistic tradition of the new, and to the ritualised breaks engineered by successive avant-gardes. It is important to note that concrete poetry (for Finlay, in any case) was a late modernist phenomenon which of necessity referred back to the heroic moments of early modernism. It engaged in a play on similarities and difference, proximity and distance, which the artist was to prolong and increasingly to underline in the neo-classical idiom he adopted in the early 1970s. Finlay's work characteristically involves creation by formal variations involving iconographical or linguistic terms; over a quarter of a century, it perpetually plays on similarity and difference, on proximity and distance. It is now possible to pay closer attention to his formal procedures. Some of these operate on the iconic dimension, others involve linguistic values.

The addition, subtraction, permutation and repetition of linguistic elements (to begin with, of letters and words in particular) are common features of concrete poetry. The elements on which such operations are carried out need not be *in praesentia*, but can be *in absentia*, if quotations or clichés are involved, so that their shadow can be sensed behind the created work. A text such as *Clay the Life, Plaster the Death, Marble the Revolution* (1987) thus draws attention to itself, not only by means of its formal repetitions – a common enough poetic tool – but also by what it does not say: what it will not say, or corrects. In this piece, the meaning (a statement on sculpture or monuments) as well as the form (a huge piece of marble) both evoke the aesthetics of neo-classicism. The first two statements are commonly attributed to Canova. However, in such a context, the word 'Revolution' sticks out. As a matter of fact, the sculptor's declaration has traditionally been completed by 'Marble the Resurrection'. As for Finlay's correction, it is inspired by an appeal made by Saint-Just: 'Bronze Liberty'. Marking the way the Revolution laid hold of neo-classicism, Finlay's work shows its fighting spirit, even if the assurance communicated by its monumental proportions seems to deny, or even repress, any polemical intentions. Unlike so many other modern poets or artists, Finlay is not obsessed with the idea of making a clean sweep of the past. Nor, however, does he fall into that other trap awaiting modernists: the patchwork of citations. This is what gives his work its essentially polemicological texture. It gets its strength by imitating predecessors, by repeating them with deviations. Yet it imposes its own presence. I have sought to explain this process elsewhere in terms of a play between the visible, on the one hand, and the figurative or the readable on the other. Once again, the eye, the judgement and – given the work's iconic and poetic development – the imagination are all involved.

The other monumental inscription in this exhibition is a translation of a work shown for the first time in 1983 and subsequently installed in Finlay's garden at Little Sparta. A Dutch translation can also be seen in Holland. The pieces of stone composing *The Present Order is the Disorder of the Future – Saint-Just* are all very heavy. This makes the work a challenge. Whoever aspires to intervene in, let us say, our cultural order, must expect to accomplish a heroic act, worthy of a Hercules. Just try to move the stones around. In spite of its epic stature, *The Present Order* recalls the games played in concrete poetry. An earlier version, printed on a card (1983) invited its readers to cut up the text and place the words in order. As for the miniature version shown at the Chapelle Sainte-Marie, Nevers, and the Galerie Eric Fabre, Paris, in 1985, it can sit on a table and allows the reader to carry out the permutations which the very texture of the work encourages. Between them, these two versions clarify the link between Finlay's monumental piece and the formal context which gave birth to it. The relationship between *The Present Order* and concrete poetry, which it imitates and repeats, is polemicological. It is concrete poetry, but with a heroic difference. And it is just this heroism which gives the measure of Finlay's ambition.

The formal context Finlay imposes on his texts should never be forgotten. Finlay presents a quotation from Saint-Just without any obvious formal apparatus, except for the fact that the stone on which it is inscribed is broken. However, it is just this fragmentary appearance – the peculiar mixture of fragility and durability which is characteristic of architectural remains – that acts on the text. Saint-Just had loudly proclaimed that the declarations of the Revolution had eternity before them: *The words we have spoken will never be lost on earth* (1985). In a context recalling classical architectural ruins, the words lose their original bravura and acquire a pathos which incorporates both their triumphant force and their death. Finlay is here applying the 'ruins' test devised by architects keen to imagine what a projected building would one day look like, in order to ensure that the plan and the materials would produce a handsome ruin. If Albert Speer, for instance, spoke of the 'law of ruins', Finlay's polemological energies takes up the principle in order to return to the question of neo-classicism's awareness of its own mortality, even if this appears to contradict the splendour of its projects.

I shall stay with Saint-Just long enough to evoke one of the monuments at Little Sparta. A small column beside the lochan bears the inscription *The world has been empty since the Romans – Saint-Just* (1983). The words are from a speech in which Saint-Just galvanised the National Convention against factions. In this work, the renewing context is provided by the monument and the lochan, and indeed by the aesthetic presiding over the whole of the upper part of the Finlays' garden. This is the classical inspiration of a Claude, whose work very largely inspired the 'natural' style of eighteenth-century English landscape gardens. For the ideological value ascribed to nature by English landscape gardeners reacting against French gardens owes as much to the classical ideal as it does to a plain return to nature. In his garden, Finlay takes pleasure in underlining the intertextual quality of landscape aesthetics. The monument with the Saint-Just citation recalls Claude's architectural elements, but the barrenness of the site is more evocative of the pathos of a Corot (Corot being a painter even further removed from classical origins). He also injects into the garden a political dimension, which the English landscape garden can absorb without the slightest difficulty, as its origins also go back to struggles involving Whigs and Tories. The move towards the French Revolution, which marks much of the garden at Little Sparta, of course makes the link between cultural and political spheres more complex. In many ways, as we shall see in a little while, the Finlays' garden constitutes a meditation on the ideological value imposed on nature. Indeed, it re-writes the whole question.

While one must insist on the discursive complexity obtained by the formalism underlying even the most forceful of Finlay's works, this should not be allowed to blunt the impact obtained by a straight interpretation. In 1983, when Finlay put up small posters next to *The Present Order is the Disorder of the Future*, exhibited at the Hayward Gallery, London, the purpose was to underline the work's immediate message – both political and ethical. The authorities of Strathclyde Region, where Finlay's home and garden are situated, fully understood this. Strathclyde was explicitly named in the posters, in the context of the long struggle in which it was involved with Finlay, and the authorities tried to have them removed. Finlay's posters of quotations from Saint-Just, or his own sentences on revolution, also printed on posters for a group exhibition in Paris in 1984, constitute political and moralistic maxims, the ethical dimension springing straight from aesthetic considerations. For all that, Finlay does not purely and simply return to a moralistic tradition in art. The statements by Saint-Just repeated and reworked for *The Ivory Flute*[1] owe their peculiar force to the historical echoes which Finlay has underlined. And the three stones dated 1794, the year the Robespierrists fell, are deliberately enigmatic. The ethical commitment they express can only be read through their historical and cultural fabric. This is indeed what makes them so enigmatic.

Brevity Ran to Wit[2] could be taken as an elegy for Saint-Just, whose laconic style has been recognised as an essential instrument of his system of thought, and of its development into action. After Thermidor, Saint-Just's sharpness must thus be considered to have degenerated into mere wit (the process of degeneration being underlined by the way Finlay's turn of phrase echoes expressions like 'to run to fat' or 'to run to seed'). *Brigands/Bacchantes*, lifted from a speech by a Girondin attacking the National Convention, takes the form of a programme for a poet or painter, who is being instructed to compose a work mingling the sublime and the bucolic, the wild reaches of nature and groves set in pleasant countryside. *A Beheading of Bouquets* reminds us that Robespierre, holding pride of place at the Festival of the Supreme Being, carried a bouquet. The bouquet beheaded here with the casual cruelty of a stroller swinging his walking stick to right and left, however, also represents the Robespierrists, who were executed just weeks after the festival. Thermidor is re-written here in a light but brutal idiom, worthy of a host of cruel pastorals. In each of these inscriptions, History and the history of artistic styles and genres meet in an enigmatic fashion. The enigma goes hand in hand with the unfinished aspect of the stone fragments. Readability becomes the issue here, and its questioning involves an assessment of the status of artistic discourse in our society. Finally, when Finlay refers to the popular art of the Revolution in the samplers and furnishings of a room intended for a young Jacobin, the sentences and themes which the works illustrate do not slip over into repetitive moralising, but continue to develop his work on our cultural sensibility.

Finlay's use of the idiom of the French Revolution involves a gesture similar to the one which led him to convert the gallery in his garden into a neo-classical temple. (While being dedicated to Apollo, this temple is strongly marked by the Revolution and its protagonists.) In both cases, the distance separating us from the model Finlay invokes is immediately perceptible. The young Jacobin's bedroom and the temple at Little Sparta are environmental works. As such, they remind one of works produced by the neo-avant-garde of the last twenty-five years. However, they awaken quite different associations, and thus cause one to ponder over contemporary procedures.

This type of procedure can at times take on surprising proportions, as in the installation showing the heads of four personalities associated with the world of the arts as if they had been guillotined. This acts as a reminder of a time when the stakes were quite obviously higher; it is evidence of a will to make an argument even more dramatic, and is justified in Finlay's eyes not on the basis of simple disagreements, but on the grounds that the personalities he has incriminated have all failed to stick by the most elementary standards of fairness. There is perhaps no other way to emphasise the importance of what is at stake. The National Trust and the publishers Jonathan Cape are, elsewhere and for similar reasons, assimilated to the assassins of Lepelletier, a martyr of the Revolution, whom David commemorated. Whenever Finlay's adversaries refuse to enter a fair discussion, he calls upon the Saint-Just Vigilantes to bombard them with cards and tracts. Discourse takes on the appearance of a military campaign and the conflict can, by way of sundry spectacular interventions, be transformed into a happening – but of a significant order – for the media to seize upon. It is significant that the first appearance of the Saint-Just Vigilantes, acting as guerillas for Finlay, occurred in one of the artist's own works,[3] and not in concrete reality. Action and its principles emerge from the work, and continue to bear the mark of its aesthetic and ethical considerations. It is worth returning for a second to the four guillotined heads. A few years ago, in a discussion of the way modern sculpture had become an autonomous sphere, Rosalind Krauss put particular stress on the part played by the bases of sculptures. If sculpture no longer produces works that can be characterised as monuments, if it no longer knits in with social life, this state of affairs can be discerned in the disappearance of the bases which linked works to public space. Krauss links the fragmentation of the human body in sculpture to this disappearance of bases. The heads Finlay places in baskets are in this sense sculptures without bases, even if he reintroduces the base by way of a theatrical staging intended to recall the platforms of guillotines. Thus is the issue of the base re-formulated in fully historical terms – as it indeed is throughout the exhibition at the Fondation Cartier. For if Finlay has insisted that as many works as possible should be shown on bases resembling packing-cases, this is to produce an effect of a modest rusticity worthy of Rousseau, and so with the aim of questioning anew the social relations of art, just as he has done in setting up his temple. Even when the words Finlay uses are playful, it is serious games that they play.

Finlay's way with words has long involved a similar procedure of challenging, or indeed modifying, discursive forms through re-contextualisation – as when a citation culled from Saint-Just ('I know only what is just'), is used as a sundial motto, thus conjoining philosophical and ethical connotations in a way that brings out their similarity.

The sundial, which Finlay has often made use of, lends itself particularly well to questioning what constitutes a model, or what it is to be exemplary. Situated between nature and culture, it involves mimesis and reflection, recalling, for instance, the Platonic shadow which repeats but weakens the luminous idea. This is taken up in the motto to a sundial in the Royal Botanic Garden, Edinburgh,[4] which states *Umbra Solis Non Aeris* – the shadow of the sun, not of the bronze, or gnomon. The astute articulation of a natural force and a network, which stems from man's capacity for measuring and calculating, in fact goes beyond what is debilitating in Plato's concept of mimesis. For the result is an instrument for capturing and transforming – for setting to work – the source upon which it depends. In this way, the sundial constitutes a working model of Finlay's own poetic procedures.

Finlay's work on models, which also provides a model for his own poetics, is pursued in the series of tree/column bases which appeal more directly to the aesthetics and philosophy of the French Revolution. As in the pantheon of anagrammatical busts, Finlay here mingles ancient and modern, political, philosophical and aesthetic. In the Sacred Grove created for the Rijksmuseum Kröller-Müller in the Netherlands (1982), Robespierre stands next to Lycurgus, Rousseau, Michelet and Corot; while at Little Sparta one also finds tree column bases dedicated to Saint-Just, Caspar David Friedrich, and others. The linking of stone and vegetation, which transforms the trees into living pillars, evokes the origins of culture. For instance, the way in which the trees affirm their vertical quality recalls what Heidegger says of the eruption of *phusis* achieved by the intervention of *techne*. One feels as if one were in at the very origins of mimesis. However, the transhistorical quality of Finlay's sacred groves cannot be put down to an obsession with origins. The reverence implied by the inscribed stones (which, for Finlay, kneel in adoration of the trees) can just as appropriately be taken to define an intertextual logic. One comes to understand that granting a predecessor the status of classic does not, in Finlay's eyes, mean transforming his work into a rigid or deadly body of doctrine. Nor does it involve fantasies of a spontaneous natural presence. It is a question of entering into a peculiar form of mimesis, which is not *imitatio* or repetition, but which takes into account, not only death (for the columns are works of commemoration, as were the colossi of ancient Greece), but also the departure implied by difference (for the space left between the tree and it base contributes fundamentally to the passage from nature to culture enacted here).

The figuration by the tree/column bases of what is an essential component of our cultural relations owes a lot to the French Revolution's dual reference to nature and antiquity. In the sacred grove at the Kröller-Müller, it is placed under the aegis of Saint-Just, whose name is quoted in the subtitle *Corot – Saint-Just*. Finlay in fact goes further than the young revolutionary's theoretical and institutional writings, obviously inspired by Rousseau, in which he never manages to conceptualise the loss of narcissistic plenitude which constitutes the loss of the state of nature. He also radicalises the neo-classical reference to antiquity which shaped Saint-Just's rhetoric and imagination, with the result that the young revolutionary becomes the centre point of a meditation on the exemplary.

All of Finlay's work on revolution and nature complexifies the notion of a model in this way. It is thus totally opposed to any ideology of the merely natural. One of the artist's favourite means of linking culture, revolution and nature involves pastiching dictionary definitions. Finlay thus provides definitions of 'temple', 'capital', 'wild flower', etc., which resemble dictionary definitions in appearance only. 'Revolution' is defined in the following manner:

> REVOLUTION n. a scheme for the improving of a country; a scheme for realising the capabilities of a country. A return. A restoration. A renewal. (*Revolution*, n., 1986)

The words 'scheme', 'improving', 'capabilities', although not incomprehensible here, retain a degree of opacity. This is due to the fact that they belong to the vocabulary of the aesthetics of eighteenth-century English landscape gardening. The echo is partly justified by the political dimension the creators of landscape gardens gave to their work. However, Finlay's work implies more than simply reconstructing a state of mind typical of the eighteenth century so as to shed a perhaps surprising light on the origins of the French Revolution (remember, however, the figure of Rousseau in the gardens of the Marquis de Girardin at Ermenonville). His oblique passage by way of an anachronistic terminology also serves, thanks to the way 'improving' or 'capabilities' resist a contemporary reader's understanding, to complexify his approach to the banal, yet rhetorically effective imagery that assimilates revolution to a natural process. This cliché, which acts like irrefutable evidence of the inevitability of revolution, and which thus constitutes a modern myth, is also wittily questioned by the seed packets[5] which complete *Revolution, n.*

These seed packets lead us to the iconic aspect of Finlay's aesthetics. The objects which have constantly cropped up in his work over the last twenty years or more also establish contexts for fathoming such and such a word, phrase or ideology. (It should perhaps be recalled that Finlay was making little wooden toys even before he encountered concrete poetry, and that – as he himself has observed – that facilitated this stage of his work.) Finlay has thus had inscribed on to the handle of a sickle a declaration of Saint-Just's expressing a bucolic reverie which some will find surprising: *A cottage, a field, a plough* (1985). And the handle of an axe bears the text of a declaration by Barère, which expresses the horror Saint-Just inspired in him: *He spoke like an axe* (1987). Like the packets in *Revolution, n.*, these tools recall in a concrete manner the pastoral dimension of the Revolution's ideal – an ideology doubtless derived from Rousseauistic musings – which can be sensed even in Saint-Just's *Institutions Républicaines*. Finlay has described this posthumous text – written by a man whose draft constitution formed the basis of the Republican constitution actually adopted in 1793 – as a visionary political pastoral, Spartan in its severity, which could have been illustrated by Claude.

Instruments such as a sickle or an axe emphasise the domestic and pastoral aspects of the Revolution. Finlay does not however oppose such imagery to the Terror conducted during the rule of the Robespierrists. If there are watering-cans dedicated both to Saint-Just and Robespierre, on which are inscribed their names and dates of birth and death, this is to be explained by the fact that they were both guillotined in Thermidor (month of heat) on a day called Arrosoir (watering-can) in the Revolutionary calendar. It is this chance date which draws attention to the parallel between political conflict and a natural process (the struggle between fire and water). As for the axe inscribed with Barère's words, it should be observed that if it is not an executioner's axe, but a domestic or rustic one, this acts against any illusions we might have regarding the sweetness of the natural life; while the scythe has, of course, a long iconographical history as a *memento mori*, taken up both by the two inscribed scythes that hang in the temple at Little Sparta, and by the Saint-Just sickle. What is concrete or visual does not in such cases simply represent a pedagogical tool illustrating abstract ideas. It imposes itself by its very presence, and owes its force to the manner in which it provides a new angle on the ways we imagine or rationalise our situation.

The 'visual rhyme', which is another essential aspect of Finlay's iconographical concerns, derives from Juan Gris' synthetic cubism. By establishing correspondences between forms more often than not drawn from quite different spheres, Finlay is able to pursue his strategy of confronting cultural values. In the 1960s, he made extensive use of images of fishing-boats (and later of warships). Formal criteria, certainly, but also historical details or names of ships come into play in the context of a poetics based on the generalisation of analogy, which has played a prominent part in the production of the cards, prints and other publications which constitute a major part of Finlay's production. *The Little Drummer Boy* (1971) uses a visual rhyme to bring together two kinds of popular imagery whose sentimental impact is guaranteed: the sea, since the work is a print of a sailing ship seen side on; and military iconography, because its title – printed as a caption – invites the observer to decode the image as a little drummer boy with his drumsticks proudly raised. Twelve years later, Finlay returned to the drummer boy/sailing ship for his first *Hommage à David* (1983), doubtless encouraged by the fact that the original work was red, white and blue. This chance use of emblematical colours contributed to *The Little Drummer Boy*'s adoption as a Revolutionary icon. The process was completed by way of an incident from the war against the counter-revolutionaries from Vendée. A brave little drummer boy named Bara found himself surrounded by Chouans who ordered him to shout 'Long live the king'. Because he responded 'Long live the Revolution!', he died at their hands. The drummer boy from the 1971 print thus becomes this very Bara, whose death David painted, Finlay's card pursuing his efforts to destabilise the dichotomy one too easily establishes between innocence and force.

Finlay pursued the Bara theme in a second *Hommage à David* (1983), which is a little cardboard drum to be cut out and stuck together. If the fragile quality of the work recalls the tricolour rosette which one can just see clutched in the hands of Bara's mortal remains in the painting by David, the smallness of the drum underlines the distance separating us from the heroism celebrated by the painter, rather than the pathos of sacrificed youth. Every age has its own image of childhood. In Finlay's projected *Temple of Bara* (1985), the play on scale is prolonged by means of a spectacular reversal. The temple is a 'postmodern' bandstand (the quotation marks are Finlay's own) crowned by a very large cockade. This deliberately eccentric gesture suggests that Finlay is seeking to give his monument the status of a folly. However, the bravura of his response to David's discretion is an answer to the mania for flat, timorous citation which characterises so many of the postmodern buildings that have gone up over the past few years. Finlay's eye, playing on scale and point of view, may indeed slip over into mannerism here. Nevertheless, spectacular as the distortions the artist obtains may be, they are minutely calculated so as to take into account the historical dimension, and thus the work is placed clearly within the tradition.

The *Temple of Bara* does not evoke the little drummer boy only by way of its projected use (one immediately thinks of military bands but Finlay, conscious as ever of the differences between historical periods, imagines it taken over by 'strolling musicians' giving impromptu performances, as at a street corner). Column drums (a traditional architectural feature) are incorporated into the temple, the columns thus producing a pun which Finlay underlines by giving these architectural drums the appearance of a drummer boy's side drum. This is once again a visual rhyme, and leads us to the central motif of the homage to Bara at the Fondation Cartier . Finlay sets out here to give equal weight to each of the components of the drum 'rhyme'. There is thus a monument to Bara, which is a severely truncated column bearing the boy martyr's name. The two bronze drumsticks laid on top of this column underline the analogy with a drum (*Monument to Joseph Bara*, 1986). But there is also a column of toy drums (1987), in which one senses the artist's desire to correct the formal play by means of which a number of contemporary artists recycle debris and other sundry objects. Elsewhere, Finlay adds a further twist to the analogy by using neo-classical pillars which are fluted in order to evoke the military flutes and drums.

Finlay's brief *Thoughts* published in the catalogue to his recent ARC (Paris) exhibition insist on the militant dimension of neo-classicism.[6] However, they also suggest that neo-classicism forms an ambivalent supplement to the classical; all the more so in view of the fact that virtue, which in Finlay's eyes replaces beauty as an ideal for neo-classicism, is expected of a movement that must 'withhold' itself as it 'emulates' classicism. These *Thoughts*, which demonstrate once more the awareness of a belatedness with respect to origins that constitutes modernism, mull over problems similar to those posed by the four guillotines in the Kassel installation. The most incisive verbal formulation is inscribed not only on one of the Kassel guillotine blades, but also on a stone plaque hanging in the temple at Little Sparta. The proposition *Terror is the Piety of the Revolution*, as harsh a statement as one may find, should not be read simply as a slogan. The reader will already be sufficiently aware of the way Finlay deliberately renders any statement difficult and enigmatic, and thus prepared to grant this sentence the attention it deserves. As Alexander Stoddart has rightly remarked in his convincing commentary, what characterises the neo-classical artist is not the fact of unquestioningly adhering to the proposition Finlay has formulated. It is the will to face up to the risk it communicates. A guillotine face to face with a fragment of a classical colonnade constitutes a visual echo of the sentence, using a visual rhyme to revive the debate on terror and virtue, classicism and Revolutionary neo-classicism.

The fine *Marat Assassiné* installation (1986)[7] also uses a visual rhyme to confront once more the political and the aesthetic. Finlay reverses David's famous dedicatory inscription in order to underline what history owes to the painter. As to the three avatars of the wooden block forming the centrepiece of the painting Finlay cites, the first simply recalls the original in an almost literal fashion, the second looks like a plain wooden packing-case, and the third evokes a tombstone. The work thus alludes both to a typically modernistic medium and to the kind of monument to which David was himself discreetly evoking. The visual rhyme has here an iconographical component upon which one is invited to ponder. By pastiching minimalism (as he also did in the series of five cubes shown in *Inter Artes et Naturam* at ARC in Paris in 1987), Finlay strives to correct the formal reductionism of late modernism. As has already been shown with reference to numerous works, Finlay gives precedence to the inscription of his work within the tradition, so as to question its cultural dimension, and not to a search for the *a priori* constituents of art.

The success of the operation of course depends on the force with which any given work imposes the deviations which it brings about. It is essential that the eye should be caught, if the judgement and imagination are to be put to work. It is not however in every case necessary to have recourse to the kind of maximalist impact that a guillotine (for instance) will be sure to provoke. The means can just as easily be discreet, as in the case of the goddess wearing round her neck a red silk thread, like those worn by the relatives of people beheaded on the guillotine (*Aphrodite of the Terror*, 1987). The thread is enough to show that the goddess is in mourning: logic would have it, for the gods. And who might have killed them, if not the Enlightenment, which sought to replace religious sentiment with the profane goddess of reason? The gods are thus in Finlay's eyes victims of the counterterror. The work also reminds us that violence was endemic on Mount Olympus. It is after all not by accident that Anatole France entitled his novel on the year of the Terror *The Gods are Thirsty*. Finlay's minimalistic intervention produces effects that are in no way dogmatic.

Finlay systematically equates Apollo, symbolising the classicism of ancient Greece, with the revolutionary Saint-Just. *Apollo in Strathclyde*, a card published in 1986, states that at Little Sparta the god is identified with Saint-Just, but immediately insists that this Apollo is hyperborean, like the reincarnation imagined by Walter Pater in one of his 'imaginary portraits', *Apollo in Picardy*. The northerly climes inhabited by this latest avatar of the god are in evidence in the photograph of a field of Scottish turnips, which is accompanied by a caption underlining the distance between this lost corner of Europe and the cradle of our civilisation: 'The wine-dark sea, the turnip-marbled field'. The formal coherence of this Homeric line of verse and the paradoxical effect of the evocation of marble further complexify our perception of the distance evoked. All of Finlay's work on the composite character represented by Apollo/Saint-Just partakes of a similar instability, acutely questioning the continuity of our culture. Finlay makes use of a significant intermediary to further the parallel between Apollo and Saint-Just. This is a sculpture of Apollo pursuing Daphne by Bernini. Bernini's Apollo, armed by Finlay, appears in various small statues at Little Sparta, the weapons being a modern translation of the god's bow. Bernini's Apollo and Daphne are of course those we read of in Ovid, where the nymph hotly pursued by the god is transformed into a laurel. The theme of the work thus already involves metamorphosis, and Finlay provoked further metamorphoses, not only by means of historical mutations (a 1977 print preceding the works evoking Saint-Just refers to camouflage and the Second World War), but also through internal variations, as in the series of three cut-outs shown at the Fondation Cartier (*Poursuites Révolutionnaires*) and the Galerie Claire Burrus, Paris (*Pastorales*).

The metamorphoses of Apollo and Daphne (who give the Fondation Cartier exhibition its title) can be taken as emblematising Finlay's procedure as a whole. Should the repeated use of such a motif be taken as allegorical? It will perhaps be useful to end by considering this question, since Finlay's neo-classical aesthetics and the balance he strives to achieve between the concrete and the conceptual make it unavoidable. The variations on Bernini are accompanied by an allegorical re-writing of Ovid's tale. If, therefore, there is indeed allegory, one should, when dealing with Finlay, follow the contemporary theoreticians for whom the revaluation of allegory depends on a willingness to welcome its artificial quality. This was the grounds for its condemnation by romantic philosophers, who preferred the supposedly natural symbol. However, artificiality provokes a frequently enigmatic gap between literal and figurative meanings, thus accentuating the question of the link between the eye and the judgement or the imagination. It forces one to question what constitutes a reading, and also the legitimacy of a cultural continuity which has recourse to such apparent tricks to assert itself. The allegorical flavour of so much of Finlay's work can therefore not be taken as a rudimentary substitute for clear thinking. It constitutes a question addressed to our culture and – to the extent that the reader/observer is able to assimilate the work in a meaningful manner – an instrument for safeguarding and developing what has to be called our 'cultural competence': the formal and encyclopaedic apparatus which allows us to understand the works of our culture. At a time when the death of ideologies and of the historical logic they imply has been loudly proclaimed, allegory is never in Finlay's work merely a matter of illustration. It constitutes a procedure that is both rigorous and open, and which seeks to preserve a continuity which it considers to be threatened, not on the level of material or ideational substance, but by means of the relations which it continues to provoke. Such is the 'revolutionary pursuit' in which Ian Hamilton Finlay is engaged, and which the French Revolution – through its words, its images, its energies . . . and its example – has helped him to formulate in all its complexity.

(1987, 1994, translated and abridged by the author)

Notes

1. *The Ivory Flute: Selected Despatches of Louis Antoine Saint-Just*, edited by Ian Hamilton Finlay, *Poursuites Révolutionnaires* exhibition catalogue; reprinted in *Edinburgh Review*, no. 89, Spring 1993.
2. From *3 Inscriptions*, Ian Hamilton Finlay with Richard Grasby (1987).
3. *The Third Reich Revisited* (1979).
4. The sundial is no longer on display in the Botanic Garden.
5. Each seed packet bears the name of one of the members of the Committee of Public Safety.
6. A selection of Finlay's detached sentences on neo-classicism appeared in the exhibition catalogue *Inter Artes et Naturam*, ARC, Musée de la Ville de Paris, 1987.
7. A note by Finlay describes this installation:

Marat Assassiné: J.L. David's *Death of Marat*, 'the first modern masterpiece', is completed by the artist's dedication – added to the box which stands by the bath – 'À MARAT, DAVID'. Reversing this, 'À DAVID, MARAT', inscribed in increasingly classicised versions, presents Marat's martyrdom as a gift to David, and to the Revolution.

'For our sake Marat suffered. He trusted humanity and it stabbed him'. (Michael Levey)

'A model of order...'
Ian Hamilton Finlay, with Gary Hincks.
Card, 1991.

A View to the Temple,
installed at Documenta 8, Kassel, 1987. With Gary Hincks, Keith Brookwell, Nicholas Sloan, Sue Finlay, Andreas Gram and Markus Grüchtel.
Photo by Monika Nicolic

Models of Order

STEPHEN SCOBIE

> The French Revolution
> Scorned circumlocution.
> 'It depends what you mean'
> Meant Madame Guillotine.
>
> Ian Hamilton Finlay,
> From 'Clerihews for Liberals' (1987)

1989 was the 200th anniversary of the French Revolution. For visitors to Paris that year, the iconography of the celebration afforded an interesting study. Images of the Bastille were everywhere, the tricolour abounded, and postcards offered endless risqué variations on the theme of 'sans-culottes'. Conspicuously absent, however, was any evidence of what is, arguably, the Revolution's most potent visual symbol: the guillotine.

The guillotine is the dark shadow of the Revolution. It's fine to proclaim Liberty, Equality, and Fraternity, but no one in Paris in 1989 wanted to celebrate the Terror. In what is now the orthodox historical interpretation, the French Revolution is exemplary among revolutions in showing how the fervour of high ideals degenerates into factional blood-lust: how, in the famous words of the Girondin Pierre Vergniaud, 'it must be feared that the Revolution, like Saturn, successively devouring its children, will engender, finally, only despotism' (quoted in Schama, 1989, p. 714). The guillotine is the emblem of this degeneration, the visual image of the Terror. As an image, it still has the power to terrify, to disturb, to disrupt the complacency of any 'politically correct' celebration.

What are we to make, then, of the emblem *A Model of Order*, presented in 1991 by the Scottish poet Ian Hamilton Finlay? The image, drawn by Gary Hincks, is based upon an engraving now in the Musée Carnavalet, and reproduced in Daniel Arasse's book *The Guillotine and the Terror*. In the original, the caption at the foot reads:

LA VÉRITABLE GUILLOTINE ORDINAIRE
HALEBON SOUTIEN POUR LA LIBERTÉ!

Finlay's text – 'A model of order even if set in a space filled with doubt' – is somewhat more ambiguous, not least because it is a quotation. But before I discuss the relevance of the source for that quotation, I would like to consider the words as they stand. That the French Revolution was 'a space filled with doubt' is obvious enough; but in what sense, then, was the guillotine 'a model of order'?

Certainly, it was as 'a model of order' that the machine was first proposed to the National Assembly, in 1789, by Dr Joseph-Ignace Guillotin.[1] It was part of a typical Enlightenment proposal for the rational reform of the criminal laws; the guillotine would be the most efficient, humane, and egalitarian method of execution. It did away with the wide variety of different methods – most of them long-drawn-out exercises in torture, or else liable to hideous botching by incompetent executioners – which were applied, on a random and unequal basis, in *ancien régime* France. Henceforth, no one would be broken on the wheel or hung, drawn, and quartered; beheading, once the 'privilege' of the nobility, would now be the common lot of lord and peasant. Engravings presented by Dr Guillotin[2] show the executions taking place in private, rural settings; they suggest, as Simon Schama says, 'dignified serenity rather than macabre retribution' (1989, p. 621). By the time the guillotine was finally adopted, in 1792, it had also become very important for the state to reclaim the legal control of violence.[3] The guillotine replaced not only more barbaric methods of official execution but also mob lynchings, the kind of indiscriminate massacre that took place in the Paris prisons in September 1792.

In every sense, then, the guillotine was 'a model of order'. It stood for the values of rationality, humanity, and control which formed the Revolution's ideology. Most of the Revolutionary politicians, including Robespierre and Saint-Just, had gone through a school system which included intensive study of the oratory of the Roman Republic. The stern Roman ideals of civic duty, memorably presented in David's painting of Brutus and his dead sons, were at the centre of the Revolution's idea of Virtue. Virtue is no longer a very fashionable idea among politicians, and it is customary to scoff at the protestations of Robespierre and Saint-Just, to see their 'virtue' stained by the blood spilled by Dr Guillotin's humanitarian device. But they themselves saw no contradiction here. In a folder of cards entitled *4 Blades* (1986), Ian Hamilton Finlay presents four linked quotations, each one printed on a drawing of a guillotine blade:

> Frighten me, if you will, but let the terror which you inspire in me be tempered by some grand moral idea.

> The form of each thing is distinguished by its function or purpose; some are intended to arouse laughter, others terror, and these are their forms.

> The government of the Revolution is the despotism of liberty against tyranny. Terror is an emanation of virtue.

> Terror is the piety of the Revolution.

The first quotation is from Denis Diderot; the second from Nicolas Poussin; the third from Maximilien Robespierre; the fourth is by Finlay himself. To read the interaction of these quotations with each other, and with the simple visual form in which they are presented, is a complex matter – and is, indeed, an exemplary exercise in the 'reading' of Finlay's poetry. Diderot's reputation is that of a moderate, reasonable man, the epitome of the Enlightenment; Robespierre is usually dismissed as a totalitarian fanatic. Yet both insist on the moral function and value of terror. Poussin's description of form as determined by function relates not only to the aesthetics of painting but also to the single-minded efficiency of the blade on which it is inscribed; and his evocation of terror as one of the purposes of art echoes back to Aristotle and the classical doctrine of catharsis. Finlay's dictum hinges on the very equivocal reaction which a late-twentieth-century secular audience is liable to have to the word 'piety'. None of this is to argue that Finlay is, in any simple-minded way, endorsing terror (The Terror; terror-ism); it is to suggest that the issues are nowhere near as simple as the conventional historiography of the French Revolution has come to imply.

4 Blades is balanced, in Finlay's work, by a lethally simple booklet entitled *4 Baskets* (1990). Each page features a drawing of a wicker basket by Kathleen Lindsley; the drawings are detailed, realistic, and charming. Each drawing has as a title a single word, an adjective drawn from the cultural repertoire of the Enlightenment. The first basket is entitled 'Domestic', and it contains three French loaves and a bottle of wine; the second is entitled 'Pastoral', and it contains a net and an abundant sheaf of corn; the third is entitled 'Parnassian', and it contains a wreath of laurel leaves; the fourth is entitled 'Sublime', and it contains two severed heads.

The alliance of Terror and the Sublime was a central aspect of Enlightenment aesthetics,[4] first proclaimed (ironically, since he was a bitter opponent of the French Revolution) by Edmund Burke:

> Whatever is fitted in any sort to excite the ideas of pain, and danger, that is to say, whatever is in any sort terrible, or is conversant about terrible objects, or operates in a manner analogous to terror, is a source of the *sublime*. . . .
>
> I know of nothing sublime which is not some modification of power. . . . That power derives all its sublimity from the terror with which it is generally accompanied. . . .
>
> Indeed terror is in all cases whatsoever, either more openly or latently the ruling principle of the sublime.
>
> (Burke, 1958, pp. 39, 64–5, 58)

Finlay follows through on this association on numerous occasions: for instance, in the print *Two Landscapes of the Sublime* (1989), which juxtaposes the guillotine with the most traditional 'natural' instance of the Romantic Sublime, the waterfall. The same point is also made in a folding card entitled *SUBLIME* (1992) which takes a sentence from 'FH' (Friedrich Hölderlin) and adds to it a sentence by 'IHF':

> Where the eagles circle in
> darkness, the sons of the
> Alps cross from precipice
> to precipice, fearlessly,
> on the flimsiest rope
> bridges.
>
> In the Place de la Révolution
> the man-made mountain
> torrent clatters
> and clatters.

(The 'man-made mountain' is also an allusion to the fact that the Jacobin faction in the Constituent Assembly was popularly known as 'The Mountain'.)

For Finlay, then, the association of Terror and the Sublime is brought firmly into the political arena (in ways of which Burke would have utterly disapproved). A modest folding card from 1989 bears the title *A Proposal for the Celebration of the Bicentenary of the French Revolution*; inside, in large red letters, one reads simply: 'A REVOLUTION'. In 1984, he designed a medal (struck in bronze by Nicholas Sloan; reproduced in Abrioux, 1985, p. 223), one side of which shows two classical columns flanked by the word 'Virtue', while the other side shows the two vertical columns of the guillotine, flanked by the word 'Terror'. Virtue and Terror become, quite literally, the two sides of the same coin. In Finlay's work, this conjoined evocation of Virtue, Terror, and the Sublime *within a political setting* is not simply an exercise in eighteenth-century antiquarianism, but a direct challenge to the political values of contemporary liberal, secular society.

One of the best commentaries on this challenge comes from Finlay himself, in a letter quoted by Yves Abrioux. Finlay is describing a 1984 emblem, which juxtaposes a line from Herman Hesse's 'Ode to

Hölderlin', 'For the temples of the Greeks our homesickness lasts for ever', with a drawing of a German battleship:

> As you will appreciate, there is a comparison being made, between the small and perfect (aesthetically perfect) warship, and the Greek temple (Greek temples are usually small, too – of frigate-size, one might say, as opposed to Roman temple-cruisers or even battleships –); the ungiven, implicit text is Goethe's 'Kennst du das Land, wo die Zitronen blühn . . .' – Do you know the country where the lemon trees flower –: which I am taking as an invocation of the South-land of classical culture – German 'homesickness' for which has always had an ambiguity, allegorised by the ambiguities of German classical architecture (whose longings, notoriously, were not confined to flowering lemon trees, or rather, which notoriously did not present itself as an actualisation of a merely verdant ideal). (The period of German idealist philosophy is also the period of the birth of German nationalism.) What the warship and the temple share, is an absolute (neither is a secular construction). This is why they can be interchanged, or is why the 'aesthetic' parallel is not merely whimsical. Democracies are not at ease with their weaponry, or with their art, since both involve (take their stand on) other values – those of the 'South-land'. Perhaps democracy should be homesick for its own unbuilt temples – alternatives to weaponry, a truly democratic pluralist art – or perhaps such alternatives, and such art, are just not possible. Classicism was at home with power; the modern democracies (whose secularism has produced extraordinary power) are not. The warship is an unrecognised, necessary temple. From the citizen armies of the post-Revolution period, there is a return to mercenary armies (the soldier as outsider). Pacifism, which should be the real 'creed' of democracy, is obviously no more than a form of the utilitarian (the convenient, the easy) (i.e. as presently understood and 'lived'). The homesickness for classical culture was an impetus towards wholeness, and since this clearly included the gods, and power (for gods without power are a contradiction), it had an ambiguous aspect; it was in our terms *dangerous*.
>
> (quoted in Abrioux, 1985, pp. 155–6).

This passage opens up many important topics in Finlay's work, not all of which I can explore here.[5] For the moment, I would just like to stress that extraordinarily suggestive phrase, 'Democracies are not at ease with their weaponry, or with their art'. It offers some explanation for the tremendous uneasiness which greets Finlay's presentation of the guillotine – or, equally, his mounting of an Oerlikon anti-aircraft gun as a sculpture entitled *Lyre* (1977); or his substitution of a German Panzer tank for the gravestone in Nicolas Poussin's *Et in Arcadia Ego* (1977); or, indeed, almost any of his major works in the last twenty years. By its reinsertion of the Sublime (as Virtue, as Terror) into a society which finds such an equation *unacceptable*, it underlines (at the very least) the *distance* which separates our society from one that could, authentically, long for the Classical past. Stephen Bann writes of Finlay's

> inclination [towards] those moments of classicist sensibility, in which the new Classicism moulds itself – but in a minor key, as it were – on the major of the past. His Classicism is intimately linked to a sense of estrangement from the Classical, and, for that reason, it has its most clear affinities with the art of those epochs when estrangement from the past was the dominant tone.
> (Bann, 1972, p. 11)

There is, in fact, a *double* distancing here. The Jacobin idealists longed for a Roman past from which *they* felt separated; Finlay, as it were, longs for that longing. 'The world has been empty since the Romans', wrote Saint-Just elegiacally. For Finlay, one might say, the world has been empty since Saint-Just; but his words remain, inscribed in stone at the base of a classical column set in the wildest, loneliest section of Little Sparta.[6]

In 1986, Stephen Bann again commented on this sense of distance and distancing, while writing about Finlay's use of the figure described by Walter Pater as 'the Hyperborean Apollo'.[7]

> Pater, like Heine and Nietzsche, recounts the myth of the Greek God who is displaced from his original setting and visits the far-off northern regions: 'the hyperborean Apollo, sojourning,

in the revolutions [sic] of time, in the sluggish north for a season, yet Apollo still, prompting art, music, poetry, and the philosophy which interprets man's life, making a sort of intercalary day amid the natural darkness; not meridian day, of course, but a soft derivative daylight, good enough for us'. It is to this deity that the Garden Temple at Little Sparta is dedicated. Inevitably he is a displaced deity, whose present situation can and must be treated on occasions with irony. Thus 'Apollo in Strathclyde' appears on one of Finlay's cards . . . with the Homeric 'wine-dark sea' reinterpreted as Dunsyre's 'turnip-marbled field'. But irony is not the same as pastiche. Irony can comprehend both the pathos of estrangement and the insistence of an actual, historical situation. 'In Little Sparta the Hyperborean Apollo is identified with Saint-Just'.

(Bann, 1986, p. 42)

The signs of this irony in Finlay's work are those of wit, and often of reduction of scale. (As Finlay proclaims, in a massive stone inscription, 'Small Is Quite Beautiful'.) Questions of scale are always at the centre of Finlay's poetry, and of his gardening: he has often insisted that the art of garden design lies in the manipulation of perspectives. Thus, while the images of the modern Sublime are sometimes presented in their full force, they are equally subject to all sorts of ironic modulation of scale. Take, for example, the aircraft carrier. In several of his *Heroic Emblems* (Z Press, Calais, VT, 1977), Finlay associates the aircraft carrier with the four elements (water as the element they sail on; earth as the landing strip they offer to their planes; air as the element of those planes; fire as their destructive power); these elements in turn are related to Pre-Socratic philosophy. In one stunning juxtaposition, he identifies the Battle of Midway in the Pacific War with Dante's 'midway . . . in a dark wood' in the first line of the *Inferno* (see *Heroic Emblems* 31, 43; Abrioux, 1985, p. 101). Yet at the same time, the garden at Little Sparta includes stone representations of aircraft carriers which are also designed to be bird-tables or bird-baths, with little birds instead of warplanes, landing and taking off. The effect, as always with Finlay, is a complex ironic interplay between different modes: the high Sublime of the aircraft carrier as the embodiment of elemental nature, and the mock-heroic reduction of the bird-bath.[8] This interplay is further commented on by Miles Orvell (1977), in relation to PACIFIC (1975) a board game which Finlay developed, based on the Pacific war:

> On the one hand, the simplified – even beautiful – designs suggest a respect for military machinery not unlike the serious respect rendered war by the traditional epic poet; on the other hand, the domestication of armaments within an ordered space implicitly mocks their power over our lives. But the playful reduction does not remove the charge of violence from the objects. Rather, it is the special order imposed on instruments of violent disorder that creates the tension and paradox in Finlay's armaments works. What gives PACIFIC its edge as a game is our not forgetting that behind the diagonal moves, the winning and losing amusement of a sunny afternoon, was a world of suicide pilots and forced crashes. Out in the Pacific – the blue ocean stretching like a field of play for aircraft carriers and planes – life was not very pacific.

Finlay's irony, then, is always in some sense complicitous with its subject. The irony marks the irreducible historical distance from a society in which Virtue could be proclaimed without embarrassment as the goal of civic life; or, further, the irony marks the distance which is *always* present, the sense in which the Jacobins longed for the Romans, and the Romans in turn longed for Arcadia, and Arcadia itself was not free of the presence of death. It is an irony which for many critics is also marked by that problematic prefix 'post-' much of Finlay's work could be accounted for in terms of the theories of irony and parody which Linda Hutcheon advances as characteristic of postmodernism. For Finlay, however, the ironic prefix is more often 'neo-'. Consider another pamphlet of four images, to set alongside *4 Blades* and *4 Baskets*. This one is called *Four Monostichs* (1991). Each page is folded over, so that at first the reader sees only the title, and has to open up the fold to read the text:

> *Classical Biography*
> No man is a hero to his valley.

Classical Warfare
  The capital fell to an enemy column.

Neoclassical Thaumaturgy
  The gods fly faster than sound.

Neoclassical Statuary
  The gods and heroes retain their arms.

The difficulty of 'reading' a poem such as this stems from the fact that Finlay places so much trust in his reader's ability to respond to nuances of tone and context. Each one of Finlay's works is itself small-scale (he prefers individual booklets or postcards or prints to conventional 'collections' of poems), yet they do also relate to each other and build up intricate patterns of cross-reference. (The joke on 'arms', for instance, recalls several instances in which Finlay has reproduced classical statues and supplied them not only with complete limbs but also with machine-guns or hand-grenades.) No discursive statement is made: Finlay never says anything as crude as 'I approve/disapprove of aircraft carriers and/or guillotines'. Rather, he presents images in a context (both of his own works and of cultural history) in which the reader has to negotiate between several opposing views, and many layers of ironic distance.

If this is difficult enough to do with works consisting entirely of words, it becomes even more difficult when the works juxtapose words with visual images. The visual image is, for our society, always stronger and more potentially disturbing – it is also more difficult to 'read', since we no longer have a cultural training in iconography, or the habit of responding in complex ways to non-discursive statements.[9] It is for this reason that Finlay is so interested in the tradition of the emblem, in which Renaissance books often provided pages of commentary for each visual image. The commentary was, in effect, *part of* the emblem – or, I would say, they were each other's supplements. In Finlay, the process of supplementarity is continuously at work. Arguments about whether he is a poet or a visual artist are, in this sense, beside the point. His visual art has always demanded the supplement of words, even if these words have largely been implied and unspoken.

And his poetry reached its crisis point when it felt the inadequacy of a merely verbal syntax. In one sense, Finlay's work is utterly individual; no other contemporary artist compares with him. But in another sense, in its compelling demonstration of the supplementary relation between word and image, I would argue that Finlay is the most representative artist of our time.

'A model of order even if set in a space filled with doubt'. Within the ironical mode in which Finlay situates both his admiration for the Jacobin revolution and his distance from it, it is now perhaps possible to see the extent to which the guillotine is indeed a 'model of order'. But the irony of Finlay's card stretches farther when one also situates the quoted text within *its* original context. It comes from a letter which Finlay wrote to the French poet Pierre Garnier on September 17, 1963; this letter has been widely reproduced[10] as one of the founding manifestos of concrete poetry.

> One of the Cubists – I forget who[11] – said that it was after all difficult for THEM to make cubism because they did not have, as we have, the example of cubism to help them ... For myself I cannot derive from the poems I have written any 'method' which can be applied to the writing of the next poem; it comes back, after each poem, to a level of 'being', to an almost physical intuition of the form ... to which I try, with huge uncertainty, to be 'true'. Just so, 'concrete' began for me with the extraordinary (since wholly unexpected) sense that the syntax I had been using, *the movement* of language in me, at a physical level, was no longer there – so it had to be replaced with something else, with a syntax and movement that would be true of the new feeling (which existed in only the vaguest way, since I had, then, no form for it ...). So that I see the theory as a very essential (because we are people, and people think, or should think, or should TRY to think) part of our life and art; and yet I also feel that it is a construction, very haphazard, uncertain, and by no means as yet to be taken as definitive. And indeed, when people come together, for whatever purpose, the good is often a by-product ... it comes as the unexpected thing. For myself, on the question of

'naming', I call my poems 'fauve' or 'suprematist', this to indicate their relation to 'reality' ... (and you see, one of the difficulties of theory for me is that I find myself using a word like 'reality' while knowing that if I was asked, 'What do you mean by reality?', I would simply answer, 'I don't know ...').[12] I approve of Malevich's statement, 'Man distinguished himself as a thinking being and removed himself from the perfection of God's creation. Having left the non-thinking state, he strives by means of his perfected objects, to be again embodied in the perfection of absolute, non-thinking life. ....'. That is, this seems to me, to describe, approximately, my own need to make poems ... though I don't know what is meant by 'God'. And it also raises the question that, though the objects might 'make it', possibly, into a state of perfection, the poet and painter will not. I think any pilot-plan should distinguish, in its optimism, between what man can construct and what he actually *is*. I mean, new thought does not make a new man; in any photograph of an aircrash one can see how terribly far man stretches – from angel to animal; and one does not want a *glittering* perfection which forgets that the world is, after all, also to be made by man into his *home*. I should say – however hard I would find it to justify this in theory – that 'concrete' by its very limitations offers a tangible image of goodness and sanity; it is very far from the now-fashionable poetry of anguish and self ... It is a model, of order, even if set in a space which is full of doubt ...[13] I would like, if I could, to bring into this, somewhere the unfashionable notion of 'Beauty', which I find compelling and immediate, however theoretically inadequate. I mean this in the simplest way – that if I was asked, 'Why do you like concrete poetry'? I could truthfully answer 'Because it is beautiful'.

(taken from Solt, 1968, p. 84).

The 'model of order', then, is concrete poetry itself, and it intervenes in the doubtful space of contemporary culture, countering the 'now-fashionable poetry of anguish and self'. As a model of order, it was based, for Finlay as early as 1963, on an idea of classicism which was to evolve through the years to that state of neo-classical irony in which its image would be the guillotine blade. Commenting on the 1991 card, and setting it correctly within the context of the 1963 letter, Edwin Morgan writes: 'The model of order is not really the guillotine, but the guillotined pages of a folding card or a flimsy booklet, produced with care and diligent collaboration to give the reader a shock not of recognition but of cognition, which is much harder and much more valuable'. I agree that the double sense of 'guillotine' is present, and that the 1963 context suggests that the model of order does reside in the aesthetic sense of 'care and diligent collaboration' which has always characterised Finlay's work. But I think that Morgan is too defensive when he claims that the model is 'not really the guillotine': there is, again, the liberal uneasiness with weaponry, a certain shying away (like Dr Guillotin himself) from the shadow of the Terror. Finlay's card is more of a challenge than that: it insists that there is a continuity in his work, and that those aspects of it which make his readers uncomfortable ('Terror is the piety of the Revolution') cannot be neatly separated from its more easily accepted and likeable motifs.[14]

At the same time, the letter to Garnier (and, by extension, the card which re-inscribes the letter) recognises the danger of 'a *glittering* perfection which forgets that the world is, after all, also to be made by man into his *home*'. Another of Finlay's folding cards (1989) proclaims the very classical slogan 'Order Is Repetition', and adds, as a subtext, 'as in Rat-a-Tat'. The multi-levelled irony of Finlay's evocation of Jacobin or Nazi models never fails to recognise their destructive potentiality, or that 'piety' is all too often reinforced by machine-guns. The catastrophic Sublime is not, after all, exactly the same thing as the 'theoretically inadequate' Beautiful.

The letter to Garnier indicates also the extent to which Finlay's aesthetic was formed by the artistic movements of the early twentieth century; its reference points are cubism, fauvism, and suprematism. The recourse to painting arose, the letter explains, at the point where verbal language in itself seemed inadequate: 'with the extraordinary (since wholly unexpected) sense that the syntax I had been using, *the movement* of language in me, at a physical level, was no longer there'. Painting – or, more generally, 'visual language' – provided (for Finlay, and for many other poets at the time) a way out of this impasse: not by discarding words, but by supplementing them. The 'movement' of language became a visual movement, because poetry is already implicated in images, and painting is already a linguistic structure. Thus, cubism was a particularly apt model for Finlay, since it is exemplary among modern movements for its self-consciously semiotic character.

The distinguishing point of concrete poetry has always been its relation to syntax. In ordinary language, and thus in conventional poetry, it is syntax which provides the connectives, which ties one word to the next and advances the reader in a linear manner through the poem. Poetry has often utilised other schemes of connection (rhyme and metre; metaphor and image-pattern) which run counter or across the linear progression of syntax; poetry, in other words, has always aspired towards a spatial form which will inhibit its progression in time. But only concrete poetry has succeeded in establishing convincing alternatives to syntax. It is at this point also that the possible analogy between concrete poetry and cubism becomes most suggestive, in terms of an analogy between linear syntax in poetry and linear perspective in painting.[15] Those movements in modern painting which abandoned representation altogether also, by definition, abandoned perspective; other movements, like impressionism and fauvism, came to uneasy compromises, in which elements of traditional perspective survive, as it were, squashed up to the surface. Only cubism succeeded in establishing a means of organising representational pictorial space which was a fully coherent alternative to perspective. In the same way, concrete poetry reorganised poetic space in non-syntactic ways without abandoning referential language.

Even those concrete poems which retain a syntactical element usually subordinate that element to the visual design of the poem. That is, the way in which one reads a concrete poem, the connections one makes between its different components, and the conclusions one draws from these connections, are all determined visually, not by a discursive movement of linear syntax. Take as an example (and it relates directly to the Garnier letter) Finlay's 'Homage to Malevich'.

This poem retains, obviously, a high degree of semantic content, in the meanings and associations attached to the words 'black', 'block', 'lack', and 'lock'. But the relationships between these meanings are suggested not by syntactic means but by visual ones: the fact that the words form a black block which is locked together; or that 'lock' and 'lack' are formed by the lack of the b, which runs down the right hand edge, lacking its completion; or that the insistence on black in this square (and in Malevich's) suggests the lack of white, or the locked-in binary of black and white; etc. The reference to Malevich, and to his famous suprematist painting of the black square, places this verbal construct within a pictorial context. As with the later emblems, the visual image calls for the supplement of commentary. And as so often in Finlay's work, it is Stephen Bann who provides it:

> Here it is a question of the equivocal status of the edge, the bordering limit which both separates language formally from the surrounding 'blank' space and also (as it were) bisects the semantic units 'black' and 'block', leaving an oscillation of the resolved and the unresolved in the terms 'lack' and 'lock'. Finlay expresses a tension which will prove crucial to his further development as an artist: that of form and non-form, language and non-language, being set not merely in opposition, but *in a dialectical relationship*. If Malevich, in his 'Square' series, achieves dialectical expression of the painter's problem of figure and ground, Finlay carefully avoids the implication that such a problem can simply be transposed into poetic terms. For language is in itself presence and absence, in terms of Saussure's distinction it comprises both *signifier* and *signified*. In 'Homage to Malevich', the space 'of doubt' is not simply the white page, but the dimension of meaning whose incompatible signs (lack/lock) are in contrast with the certainty of typographic structure.
>
> (Bann, 1977, p. 11)

So the 'Homage to Malevich' too is a 'model of order': not only in its typographic fixity, and not only in its evocation of the formal ideals of suprematism, but also in its adherence to the generic conventions of the *hommage*. In a 'homage', one artist brings his or her own sensibility to bear upon another's; the result is a statement about each artist individually, and also about the way they relate to each other in the continuity of culture. The homage is paid, indeed, not just to the artist named but to that very continuity; the homage asserts the continued vitality of the past, at the same time as it marks a certain distance from it. Just as Finlay's tributes to Robespierre and Saint-Just contain an elegiac element, an implicit statement of loss, so too the 'Homage to Malevich' locks into the present the lack of Malevich's presence.

In Finlay's homages, that distance is often marked by an ironic wit, what Bann called 'a minor key': a diminution of scale which is friendly and playful, but not without a certain edge to it. The *Homage to Pop Art* (1973), for instance, re-states Cézanne's 'the cylinder, the sphere, the cone' in terms of ice-cream; the *Homage to Seurat* (1972) transforms the artist's pointillism into a dot-to-dot painting kit. Other homages are less obviously playful, but not less complex. The *Homage to Vuillard* (1971) consists of the single word SINGER, printed in warm shades of yellow and brown which recall the intimacy of Vuillard's interiors. The literal meaning of the word (Vuillard as the 'singer', or celebrator, of domestic life) is both reinforced and slyly commented on by the association of 'Singer' as the leading trade name of sewing machines. Most generally of all, the print *Homage to Modern Art* (1972), realised by Jim Nicholson, shows a sailing-boat, in deep, subdued browns and blues, with a vividly printed insignia on its sail: a yellow triangle inside a blue triangle inside a yellow triangle. The bright colours of the insignia set up an immediate figure-and-ground problem which goes straight to the heart of modern art's problematic of surface and depth: the yellow and blue stand out 'in front of' their ostensible support (the sail), and are ostentatiously 'flat', whereas a 'realistic' image would require them to reflect the uneven surface of the sail. The yellow and blue triangles are, in the words of Maurice Denis (1890), 'a flat surface covered in colours arranged in a certain order'. In the established heraldry of naval flags, no specific meaning attaches to this design: it is pure pattern; it is, as it were, an abstract painting within a representational form. Yet, as ground, the image of the boat retains its referential and associative force. This *Homage to Modern Art* registers, in a controlled and witty way, the major debates and uncertainties of the modernist period; it is a model of order, even if set in a space filled with doubt.

For the concerns of this essay, the most relevant of such Finlay homages is of course the one to Kahnweiler (1972). Finlay's reduction of 'Life and Work' to 'Knife and Fork' is in tune with this whole mode

Models of Order

of affectionate distancing; but it also has further resonances, which may be seen by juxtaposing Finlay's homage to Kahnweiler with Gertrude Stein's homage to Juan Gris:

> Therein Juan Gris is not anything but more than anything. He made that thing. He made the thing. He made a thing to be measured.
>
> Later having done it he could be sorry it was not why they liked it. And so he made it very well loving and he made it with plainly playing. And he liked a knife and all but reasonably.
>
> (Stein, 1927, pp. 160–2).

So here is Juan Gris (1887–1927); and here is his knife ('reasonably': Gertrude Stein, in tribute to her friend); and here are his knife and his fork (and a glass, and a bottle: in, say, one of those gorgeous blue-grey proto-cubist still life paintings from 1911–12), and here are also his life and work, recorded faithfully by Daniel-Henry Kahnweiler (*Juan Gris. Sa Vie, Son Oeuvre, Ses Ecrits*, Gallimard, Paris, 1946; *Juan Gris: His Life and Work*, translated by Douglas Cooper, 1947; revised edition, 1969); and here is Ian Hamilton Finlay (Stonypath, 1974), paying tribute to Kahnweiler paying tribute to Gris (and of Finlay himself could it not well be said, here as everywhere, that he has 'made a thing to be measured', and that he 'made it very well loving and he made it with plainly playing'?); and here, finally, is Ian Hamilton Finlay, in a letter of 25 August 1970 to Stephen Scobie:

> I'm delighted you liked the Kahnweiler book (as I knew you would, which is a compliment to you). As a matter of fact, I can't honestly say when I read it, because you know I read a lot of books on Cubism when I was about fourteen[16], and the whole thing is surrounded by a romantic glow (the way I daresay poetry is, for some people) and sits as squarely in my heart, as fishingboats do. I do know that I *re*-read the Kahnweiler book carefully when we were in Easter Ross, about four years ago . . . I agree with you, Kahnweiler's book is crying out for a concluding chapter on concrete poetry – one could almost write it *for him*, and that, by the way, would be a thing you could do: write the

unfinished chapter on concrete poetry, by Kahnweiler – what a splendid idea. I grow more enthusiastic about that, every second.

Finlay's attraction to Kahnweiler, and to Gris, can best be explained in relation to that phrase of Stein's: Gris 'made a thing to be measured'. More than that of any of the other major cubist painters, Gris' work is distinguished by its *clarity*, its cleanness of conception and line. Kahnweiler defines Gris as a classical artist, as opposed to the more romantic Picasso (and also, surprisingly, Braque) (see Kahnweiler, 1969, p. 132). For Finlay, this classical sense of clarity (the fine cutting edge, one might say, of the guillotine) is fundamental: one of his highest compliments is to call something 'uncluttered'. But Stein further perceives (what all too many of Gris' critics have failed to perceive) that Gris' clarity is not cold and unemotional: 'he made it very well loving and he made it plainly playing'. Kahnweiler says of Gris' painting, and of cubism generally, that they 'made us "see" and love so many simple, unassuming objects which hitherto escaped our eyes' (1969, p. 168). This love for 'simple, unassuming objects' is clearly visible throughout Finlay's work, and the element of play is also plainly displayed.

Many of these themes are recapitulated in a later 'homage', the *Analytical Cubist Portrait* of *Daniel-Henry Snowman* (from The Mailed Pinkie, Verlaggalerie Leaman, Germany, 1982). The 'snowman' is perhaps a joke on the reputed 'coldness' of Gris' work; if so, it re-situates that coldness within the friendly warmth of a children's game. The highly recognisable pipe [17] is a parodic allusion to the recognisable details which Picasso, especially, would include in his cubist portraits (such as the precise little moustache in his *Portrait of Daniel Henry Kahnweiler*, 1910, or indeed the pipe in *Man with a Pipe*, 1911), and which Kahnweiler would insist on as 'clues' to the legibility of cubist paintings. The pipe also appears in a booklet of Finlay's entitled *Picturesque* (1991), which reads:

> 'It is hardly necessary to remark how the view from the house would be enlivened by the smoke of a cottage –'

– or a Picasso portrait by the inclusion of a recognisable pipe.

Analytical Cubist Portrait
Daniel-Henry Snowman

Ian Hamilton Finlay, with Gary Hincks, 1982

The quotation which makes up the first half of this poem is taken from Humphry Repton (1752–1818), one of the great figures in the history of English gardening. The various associations and ramifications of this pamphlet will provide an opening into the richness and complexity of Finlay's own 'picturesque' garden at Little Sparta.

The booklet *Picturesque* is itself an expansion of an idea which occurs in one of Finlay's *Unconnected Sentences on Gardening*: 'In cubist portraits the pipe has the homely air of a cottage chimney' (*Nature Over Again After Poussin*, Exhibition catalogue, Collins Exhibition Hall, University of Strathclyde, Glasgow, 1980, pp. 21–2). Finlay has issued several series of 'unconnected' or 'detached' sentences on gardening,[18] the model being William Shenstone's 1764 essay 'Unconnected Thoughts on Gardening'. Among Finlay's more memorable sentences, I would pick out the following:

> Superior gardens are composed of Glooms and Solitudes and not of plants and trees.

Gardens are always for *next* year.

Garden centres must become the Jacobin Clubs of the new Revolution.

British Weather is often warmer at *weeding* level.

Certain gardens are described as retreats when they are really attacks.

Shenstone's garden at The Leasowes in Warwickshire, created between 1745 and 1763, is one of the few precedents for Finlay's garden at Little Sparta. *The Oxford Companion to Gardens* (p. 331) describes The Leasowes thus:

> The visitor followed a prescribed route which presented scenes of grandeur, beauty, and variety. Latin inscriptions and dedications invoked classical associations, and urns were dedicated to the memory of friends to provide a desirable tinge of melancholy. There were also modest garden buildings, a grotto, bridges, numerous cascades and waterfalls, and the picturesque ruins of the priory.

'Picturesque' – when the term was first introduced, in the eighteenth century, it had the specific meaning of 'making landscapes in the manner of pictures, in particular the drawings of Claude Lorrain and Gaspard Poussin, the brother-in-law of Nicolas Poussin' (*Oxford Companion*, p. 431). Progressively, the term degenerated, until today it means little more than a superficial kind of prettiness: the exact opposite, really, of the Sublime. But in the 1790s, the picturesque was championed in England in a series of essays and books by William Gilpin, Payne Knight, and Uvedale Price. The odd coincidence of dates should not pass unnoticed: Gilpin's essays were published in 1792, the year in which Dr Guillotin's machine was first put to public use in Paris; and Knight and Price both published their major books in 1794, the year in which Robespierre and Saint-Just were executed, in the month of Thermidor, on the day designated in the new Revolutionary calendar as Arrosoir, the Watering-Can.[19] In their advocacy of the picturesque, Knight and Price were particularly critical of the landscape designs of Humphry Repton, who replied to their attacks in his *Sketches and Hints on Landscape Gardening* (1795).

For Finlay to quote Repton in a pamphlet entitled *Picturesque* is not, then, without irony. 'While mouldering abbeys and the antiquated cottage with its chimney smothered in ivy may be eminently appealing to the painter', Repton wrote, 'in whatever relates to man, propriety and convenience are not less objects of good taste than picturesque effects' (quoted in *Oxford Companion*, p. 431). The difference, that is, is between a cottage chimney 'smothered in ivy' and a working one which 'enlivens' the scene with its smoke. Repton saw his interventions in landscape as 'improvements'. His goal was not simply the creation of an interesting visual effect, but the setting of the garden within a cultural context, 'whatever relates to man'. In 1967, on the first occasion that I met him, Ian Hamilton Finlay remarked to me: 'In an age when man has learned to control vast areas of his environment which were formerly left to chance and Nature, we simply cannot *afford* decadent art'.

Little Sparta contains many examples of the 'picturesque' in the original sense. Corners of the garden are carefully arranged to reproduce the effects of certain painters, and then their 'signatures' are inserted in the landscape. Blocks of masonry are 'signed' by Claude; the monogram initials of Albrecht Dürer are hung from a tree. Beside a pond, a stone inscription reads *See* POUSSIN *Hear* LORRAIN. Stephen Bann comments: 'it is the ambiguity of the landscape, which may be read as Poussin's visual clarity and stillness, or may vibrate to Claude's perceptibly more atmospheric touch, that engages our absorbed attention' (Bann, 1981, p. 136).

What is involved here is an extremely subtle instance of what I have described, throughout this book, as the supplementarity of word and image. This piece presupposes, in the first instance, that the 'reader' will be familiar with the paintings of Poussin and Lorrain, and will be able to make the kind of association that Bann suggests, to Poussin's 'visual clarity' or Lorrain's 'atmospheric touch'. Like so many of Finlay's works, it situates itself within a continuity of culture, and not the least important of its assertions is the idea that a Scottish poet in the late twentieth century can make a meaningful response to French painters of the seventeenth. Finlay's words are themselves a commentary on (or a supplement to) the original paintings; they bring to the paintings a whole discourse on synaesthesia (how does one 'hear' a painting?) and the primacy of visual values in classical art. (At the same time, Finlay's words obviously need to be supplemented by the paintings; the poetic text is in itself incomplete.) Both the paintings and the poetic text are in turn supplemented by the landscape in which they are set: an actual pond, a daily interaction of water and light on a Scottish hillside. In one sense, the pond is 'reality'; it is neither 'signifier' nor 'signified' (in Saussure's terms), but is the *referent* which stands behind those signs. Step into this poem and you'll get your feet wet. But at the same time, *the pond itself is also a sign*. It is a 'picturesque' landscape, 'improved' by Finlay. The stone inscription supplements the landscape, and so transforms it into a controlled image: a *framed* image. Then a further layer of supplementarity is added by the *photograph*, which selects a particular angle on this image, excluding the farther horizon. The photograph frames the image: but the literal frame of the camera only doubles the frame which is already implied by the placing of the stone.

The gesture of 'signing' a landscape might be seen as an ultimate form of 'linguistic imperialism'. Is it not arrogant of Finlay thus to appropriate a natural spectacle, and claim it in the name of the signature? The signature itself is doubled: the stone may say 'Poussin' or 'Lorrain', but both of those signatures are in turn 'signed by' the name of Ian Hamilton Finlay. All art, one might say, is appropriation; since no work exists in a vacuum, what one signs is never 'original', but only a part of the intertext. To a greater degree than either poetry or painting, gardening is always an art of supplementarity: the gardener never really controls nature, but must always co-operate with it (supplement it).[20] What Finlay insists upon is that gardening is also a discourse, that the very idea of 'a garden' is something already situated within language. Thus the garden at Little Sparta, isolated among the Pentland hills, is nevertheless a social statement, as central to its culture as any publishing house in London or art gallery in Paris.

On the hillside above the farm buildings of Little Sparta, a small wooden sundial faces west. On it is carved an inscription (I take the layout of the words not from the sundial, but from its earlier publication as a print):

Models of Order

            EVEN
            -ING
            WILL
            COME

            THEY
            WILL
            SEW
            THE
            BLUE
            SAIL

Considered as a brief lyric poem, the text is very beautiful. Rhythmically, the one-word-per-line arrangement gives it an 'uneven' movement which eventually 'evens' out, just as visually, on the page, the break of 'evening' into 'even / -ing' is an evening out of the line-length. Literally, the sewing of sails is something that might be done in an evening, after a day's work; but the association of evening with the end of day suggests also the end of a life, the sewing of a shroud; and is there not a hint of something sinister in that unspecified 'they'? Metaphorically, the 'blue sail' links the elements: it is the blue of both sky and sea, and the action of the sail unites air (wind) and water (boat). The sewing of the blue sail brings land and sea together, as the evening fall of darkness renders them indistinguishable from each other.

A lovely poem; but even a text as full as this one seeks the supplement of visual form. It was first published as a long, vertical print, the words in delicate white lettering against a rich blue background. As a sundial, however, the visual form is an even richer supplement. It is, of course, a working sundial; like Repton's cottage chimney, it 'smokes'. The curved line which marks the hours 'rhymes' (in the manner of Juan Gris) the shape of a sail. From Little Sparta, it faces west, towards a sea which it cannot see; but in the metaphorical interplay of elements, the sea is always a part of Finlay's inland garden. Facing west, it works as a sundial only in the even-ing hours, only when they sew the blue sail. Facing west, it also bears the full force of the Scottish weather – and, as the years have gone by, this sundial has weathered too. Moss grows on the wood; already the carved lettering is worn and evened down.

Marking the passage of time on a yearly as well as hourly basis, the sundial too is a living thing which approaches its ending. For it too the even-ing will come; they will sew the blue sail.

Notes

See also Stephen Scobie, 'Rhymes and Reasons: Kahnweiler, Gris, Finlay, Stein', in *Collaborations* (exhibition catalogue, Kettle's Yard, Cambridge, 1977).

1. Guillotin did not 'invent' the guillotine. Machines of similar design had long been used in Europe; Arasse's book contains several illustrations, including a device called 'The Maiden', used in Scotland in the sixteenth century. Guillotin improved the efficiency of the design; his proposal for its use was a rather minor part of a sweeping, and very progressive, reform of criminal laws relating to punishment. For all his reasonable outlook, however, Guillotin came to share something of the terror which the machine evoked, and he bitterly resented the fact that his name had been attached to it. Arasse quotes a wonderfully ironic statement from the funeral oration delivered for Dr Guillotin when he died in 1814: 'How true it is that it is difficult to benefit mankind without some unpleasantness resulting for oneself'.
2. See Arasse, 1989 (unpaginated), and Schama, 1989, p. 620.
3. On this point, see Schama, 1989, especially p. 623: 'At each successive phase of the Revolution, those in authority attempted to recover a monopoly on punitive violence for the state, only to find themselves outmanoeuvred by opposing politicians who endorsed and even organized popular violence for their own ends... The core problem of revolutionary government, then, turned on the efforts to manage popular violence on behalf of, rather than against, the state'.
4. Discussing this topic in his book *Ian Hamilton Finlay: A Visual Primer*, Yves Abrioux cites a passage from Harold Bloom: 'in the European Enlightenment, this literary idea [the Sublime] was strangely transformed into a vision of the terror that could be perceived both in nature and in art, a terror uneasily allied with pleasurable sensations of augmented power' (*Agon*, p. 101). The quotation comes from an essay by Bloom entitled 'Freud and the Sublime: A Catastrophe Theory of Creativity', in which he further argues that 'The greatest shock of *Beyond the Pleasure Principle* is that it ascribes the origin of all human drives to a catastrophe theory of creation (to which I would add: "of creativity")' (*Agon*, p. 104). Bloom does not mention that Friedrich Schlegel described the French Revolution as 'the happy catastrophe' – but Finlay uses this quote as the basis for a short poem (*The Happy Catastrophe*, booklet, 1992):

THE HAPPY CATASTROPHE

Be-

falls.

5. For example, the references to 'temples' allude to Finlay's continuing battle with Strathclyde Regional Council over his classification of one of the buildings on his property as a garden temple: a dispute which is especially instructive about the embarrassment of a secular government in trying to deal with an absolute (or with the Sublime). Further, I have confined this section to a discussion of selected Finlay works on French Revolutionary themes; I have not attempted here to extend the discussion into the even more highly charged and problematic area of Finlay's confrontation with the iconography and architecture of the Third Reich.
6. The farmhouse and land which Finlay occupies at Dunsyre, some twenty-five miles south-west of Edinburgh, used to be called, simply, Stonypath. Finlay's renaming of it as 'Little Sparta' carries a complex ironic charge. As 'Sparta', it stands in an adversarial relationship to 'the Athens of the North' (Edinburgh); at the same time, as 'Little Sparta', it accepts its own reduction in scale, and offers a friendly, almost cosy familiarity. 'How many times', asks Stephen Bann, 'do his titles and his works employ the word "little"?' (Bann, 1972, p. 13). Sparta, however, remains Sparta, and is quite prepared to fight its battles. Historically, 'Little Sparta' was the name given to the Parisian district of the Cordeliers, one of the strongholds of the Jacobins, by Camille Desmoulins (see Schama, 1989, p. 499). Desmoulins, in employing the diminutive, was already someone to whom one might apply Francis Edeline's charming coinage, *'très finléenne'*!
7. Apollo, it should be remembered, carried weapons as well as lyres: he is another figure with whom secular democracies are ill at ease. The Garden Temple at Little Sparta, which so disconcerts the bureaucrats of Strathclyde Region, is dedicated 'To Apollo·His Music·His Missiles·His Muses'. Various Finlay works have reinterpreted the myth of Apollo and Daphne: she metamorphoses, not into foliage but into foliage-based army camouflage; or, in a rewording of Ovid:

AND EVEN AS SHE FLED
THE REPUBLIC CHARMED HIM
THE WIND BLEW HER GARMENTS
AND HER HAIR STREAMED LOOSE
SO FLEW THE YOUNG REVOLUTIONARY
AND THE SHY REPUBLIC
HE ON THE WINGS OF LOVE

AND SHE ON THOSE OF FEAR
(*And Even as She Fled 2*, 1987)

(Again, the equation of Apollo with that "young blade," Saint-Just.)

8. See also the print (Abrioux, 1985, p. 13) in which rows of warplanes on a carrier deck are depicted, with their wings neatly folded, under the title *Lullaby* (1975).
9. To some extent, Finlay courts mis-reading by his use of provocative visual symbols, such as the guillotine, and, even more, Nazi emblems such as the lightning-flash double S of the SS insignia. Some of his critics have argued that the very presence of these emblems visually overpowers any context in which they might be placed, and that any work containing the SS is *ipso facto* Nazi. This is a terribly simplistic argument, and it has lead to vicious and unfounded personal attacks on Finlay. But it is the unjustifiable overstatement of the difficulty which Finlay himself identifies in the very form of his works.
10. It appeared first in the British magazine *Image*. Its most influential reprint was in Mary Ellen Solt's anthology *Concrete Poetry: A World View*.
11. Almost certainly Picasso. I have found two possible sources for what Finlay recalls. In *Picasso* (1938), Gertrude Stein wrote: 'Picasso said once that he who created a thing is forced to make it ugly. In the effort to create the intensity and the struggle to create this intensity, the result always produces a certain ugliness, those who follow can make of this thing a beautiful thing because they know what they are doing, the thing having already been invented, but the inventor because he does not know what he is going to invent the thing he makes must have its ugliness' (Burns, 1970, pp. 14–17). More directly, there is a 1960 interview, included in Dore Ashton's *Picasso on Art: A Selection of Views*, in which Picasso himself states: 'Moreover, to know that we were doing cubism we should have had to be acquainted with it! Actually, nobody knew what it was. And if we had known, everybody would have known. Even Einstein did not know it either! The condition of discovery is outside ourselves; but the terrifying thing is that despite all this, we can only find what we know' (Ashton, 1972, pp. 62–3).
12. This is a good example of what Derrida means by the necessity of putting certain terms 'under erasure'.
13. This is how the phrase appears in the letter as reprinted by Solt. I have no idea why the guillotine card alters the punctuation, and changes 'full of' to 'filled with'.
14. When I first became interested in Finlay's work, in the late 1960s, his major motif was the Scottish fishing-boat; and much of my early writing on him extols the homely charms and

warm friendliness with which he presented this theme (and to this day, I cannot walk through Pittenweem harbour without seeing, all round me, a certain kind of beauty which Finlay taught me to see). When the shipping in his work changed from fishing-boats to aircraft carriers, I was greatly disconcerted, and it took me many years to come to terms with the gods and heroes who retain their arms.
15. Inter-artistic analogy is always difficult, since 'analogy' itself is such a tricky and shifting concept. See, for instance, Wendy Steiner's whole discussion of four-term and three-term analogy in *The Colors of Rhetoric*, pp. 1–19. The propositions in this paragraph are put forward more as suggestive points for consideration than as any kind of rigorous theory of analogy.
16. Finlay was born in 1925. Kahnweiler's book was first published in English in 1947.
17. A secondary allusion may be to Magritte's *Ceci n'est pas un pipe*, which has become a *locus classicus* for the separation between sign and reality. Much later, in 1992, Finlay also gave a challenging re-statement to Magritte's painting, where the title is attached to an image of a sub-machine-gun, in which the holes along the gun barrel do very much have the appearance of the stop-holes on a (musical) 'pipe'.
18. Edwin Morgan connects Finlay's 'fondness for a large number (hundreds) of individual cards and prints with his belief in individual sentences as against connected discourse'. Morgan quotes one of Finlay's aphorisms – 'Consecutive sentences are the beginning of the secular' – and comments: 'If Pre-Socratic gnomic sayings are numinous in a way that most post-Enlightenment connected philosophical and scientific discourse is not, then we must refresh ourselves at these antique springs (though in a contemporary manner), [and] rediscover the fact that soul is the wit of brevity' (Morgan, 1991).
19. Finlay has exhibited several installations on the theme of the days of Thermidor, in which a small black ribbon is tied to the spout of the watering-can.
20. Is there any finer illustration of what Derrida means by 'supplement' than the compost heap?

References

Abrioux, Yves. *Ian Hamilton Finlay: A Visual Primer*. Edinburgh: Reaktion Books, 1985.

Arasse, Daniel. *The Guillotine and the Terror*. Trans. Christopher Miller. Penguin, 1989.

Ashton, Dore, ed. *Picasso on Art: A Selection of Views*. New York: Viking, 1972.

Bann, Stephen. *Ian Hamilton Finlay: An Illustrated Essay*. Edinburgh: Scottish National Gallery of Modern Art, 1972.

Bann, Stephen. 'Ian Hamilton Finlay: An Imaginary Portrait'. In

Ian Hamilton Finlay, exhibition catalogue. London: Serpentine Gallery, 1977, pp. 7–36; reprinted herein.
Bann, Stephen. 'A Description of Stonypath'. *Journal of Garden History*, vol. 1, no. 2, 1981.
Bann, Stephen. 'Apollo in Strathclyde'. *Cencrastus: Scottish & International Literature Arts & Affairs*, 22, Winter 1986, pp. 39–42.
Bloom, Harold. *Agon: Towards a Theory of Revisionism*. Oxford University Press, 1982.
Burke, Edmund. *A Philosophical Enquiry into the Origin of our Ideas of the Sublime and Beautiful*. Ed. J.T. Boulton. New York: Columbia UP, 1958.
Burns, Edward, ed. *Gertrude Stein on Picasso*. New York: Liveright, 1970.
Ian Hamilton Finlay: Collaborations. Cambridge: Kettle's Yard Gallery, 1977.
Jellicoe, Geoffrey and Susan, Patrick Goode, and Michael Lancaster, eds. *The Oxford Companion to Gardens*. Oxford: Oxford UP, 1986.
Kahnweiler, Daniel-Henry. *Juan Gris: His Life and Work*. Trans. Douglas Cooper. Revised ed. New York: Abrams, 1969.
Morgan, Edwin. 'Finlay in the 70s and 80s'. In Murray, 1991, pp. 37–46; reprinted herein.
Murray, Graeme, ed. *Ian Hamilton Finlay and The Wild Hawthorn Press 1958–1991*. Edinburgh: Graeme Murray Gallery, 1991.
Orvell, Miles. 'Poe and the Poetics of Pacific'. In *Ian Hamilton Finlay: Collaborations*, pp. 17–22; reprinted herein.
Rubin, William. *Picasso and Braque: Pioneering Cubism*. New York: The Museum of Modern Art, 1989.
Schama, Simon. *Citizens: A Chronicle of the French Revolution*. New York: Knopf, 1989.
Solt, Mary Ellen, ed. *Concrete Poetry: A World View*. Bloomington: Indiana UP, 1968.
Stein, Gertrude. 'The Life of Juan Gris The Life and Death of Juan Gris'. *transition* 4 (July 1927), pp. 160–2.
Steiner, Wendy. *The Colors of Rhetoric: Problems in the Relation between Modern Literature and Painting*. Chicago: University of Chicago Press, 1982.

Ehrentempel Model, 1993.
Photo by Simone Gänsheimer

Wild Flowers
Wild Flowers of the Ehrentempel: The DeNazification of Neo-classicism

PATRICK EYRES

This exhibition, *Wild Flowers*,[1] represents a climactic moment in Ian Hamilton Finlay's continuing programme of deNazifying neo-classicism. Neo-classicism was the style employed for the public buildings of the Third Reich. In the wake of the Second World War this architecture became tainted with the holocaust, and neo-classicism in general was stigmatised. Finlay's deNazification programme is motivated by the necessity to prevent 'a thousand years of architecture being thrown away due to a régime lasting thirteen years'.[2] This programme can be traced back over a decade to *The Third Reich Revisited*, an exhibition at the Tartar Gallery during the 1982 Edinburgh Festival. *The Third Reich Revisited* was subsequently enlarged for an exhibition organised by Southampton Art Gallery which toured Britain throughout 1984–86.[3]

Wild Flowers is climactic because it presents proposals specific to sites in Munich. One is for the Haus Der Kunst. The other two are for the reconstruction of the Ehrentempel. While the former addresses the stigmatisation of neo-classicism in general, the latter engage with the ruins of a neo-classical site which once enshrined Nazi ideology. Moreover these two proposals entertain the possibility of the physical as well as the hypothetical deNazification which characterises *The Third Reich Revisited*. The significance of the Ehrentempels to Finlay's deNazification agenda was manifested by their inclusion in *The Third Reich Revisited*:

> Hitler's first architect, Paul Ludwig Troost, designed the Ehrentempel (twin-Temples of Honour) as a memorial to the martyrs of the NSDAP 1923 *putsch*. Troost's widow wrote, 'No damp vault encloses the coffins of the fallen. Surrounded by pillars they rest under the open sky of the homeland . . .' At the end of the War, the Americans decided to blow up these examples of heroic classicism . . . a high principled but barbaric vandalism . . . (This was the time of the DeNazification Tribunals).[4]

Wild Flowers, at the Lenbachhaus in Munich, comprises three rooms each containing sculptures and prints. The arrangement of the rooms implies a sequential progression. In Room One neo-classicism is explored as problematic. The work in Room Two articulates Nature as a political emblem. Room Three contains the proposals for the Ehrentempel. Appropriately, the exhibition not only coincides with the 70th anniversary of the Munich Putsch, but the Ehrentempel plinths are also visible from the gallery.

It was the sixteen Nazi casualties of the abortive putsch who were enshrined by the subsequent erection of the Ehrentempel. The anniversary will necessarily raise the historical spectre of Nazism and evoke the contemporary virulence of neo-Nazism. The systematic terror inflicted by neo-Nazis on ethnic minority communities is more apparent in Germany than, for example, in Britain and France. But the murder of Turkish families through firebombing is symptomatic of a resurgent European menace. It would be dangerous to identify these forces exclusively in terms of Germany. They are not solely 1990s versions of the Nazi Kristallnacht – when similar tactics were unleashed against the Jewish population of German cities. Thus it is fitting that Finlay's deNazification acknowledges the horror of the Third Reich's geopolitical and racial programme and implies its spectral reincarnation through European neo-Nazism. Thus it is also fitting that the warning of Finlay's deNazification is that the *continued* presence of Nazism should not *continue* to be confused with neo-classicism. The artist regards neo-classical architecture as a metaphor of European culture. His warning is that, as the perceptions of an audience are culturally determined, neo-classicism will remain stigmatised unless distinctions are made between ideology and cultural form.

Meaning in Finlay's work is communicated, as in the European emblem tradition, through the associations generated by the coupling of text and image. *The Third Reich Revisited* exemplifies this process. Each of the fourteen works comprises a drawing, a title and a commentary. Each one engages with a site of neo-classicism which is either specific or imaginary. Half of these works 'Revisit' the Third Reich, while the other seven evoke the Europeanness of neo-classicism through Scottish examples in Edinburgh.

The Third Reich Revisited also exemplifies the manner in which Finlay provokes cultural debate through the purposeful use of irony. Thus the commentary to one work, 'Sundials at the Zeppelinfeld', acknowledges 'German geopolitical ambitions, Germany Over All', while another, '*Little Fields* at Nuremburg', suspends 'questions of blood and soil and Reich expansionism'. It is the entrenched and emotive post-war taboo that Finlay confronts when, in the commentary to 'St Andrew's House, Edinburgh', he draws attention 'to the fact that neo-classicism was not, as is generally thought, a specifically German phenomenon of the inter-war years. Rather, it was – as much as the Corbusier and Gropius esperanto – an international style'. Indeed, it was deployed by totalitarian states and pluralist democracies alike. Moreover, within the particular context of Germany, it is ironic to note that the nursery of architectural modernism provided the cradle for Nazi architecture. Indeed, the tripartite organisation of architecture favoured by the Third Reich was established before the First World War by the innovative modernism of the Deutsche Werkbund. The Werkbund had advocated neo-classicism for public buildings, a vernacular arts and crafts style for mass housing, and the utilitarian or modernist for industry (later extended by the Third Reich to fortification). This was apparent at the Werkbund's influential exhibition in Cologne during 1914, and particularly through the work of Peter Behrens' studio which employed Le Corbusier, Gropius and Mies van der Rohe. It is equally ironic that the progress of post-war modernism has been stimulated by Third Reich fortifications. Indeed, the military architecture of the Atlantic and West Walls, the U-Boat pens and the urban flak-towers contributed to the evolution of that austere brand of modernist architecture, known as Brutalism, which flourished during the 1960s and 1970s.[5] Strangely enough, the utilitarian modernism of the concentration camps has not lead to a moral interdiction on that type of architecture. It is precisely the ironies generated by the interrelation of architecture and politics that form the vehicle for Finlay's deNazifying programme.

Room One: Neo-Classicism as Problematic

The works herein dramatise the popular perception of neo-classicism as dangerous. Simultaneously, they question this view: 'Camouflage represents cultural fantasy, not the view of Ian Hamilton Finlay'.[6] Two sculptures, twin sets of three columns, articulate the artist's perception. One set is camouflaged in the 'panzer' tank manner, while the related print, *Three Columns*, images the three variously camouflaged columns combined with a citation from 'An Architecture of Desire' by Leon Krier:

> Architects consider the erection of a single classical column to be morally more questionable than the building of a nuclear reactor, and the construction of a splendid colonnade alarms the profession more profoundly than a line of panzers leaving the Krupp factories.

This citation is the key to the exhibition's discourse and particularly to Room One. The other set of three columns has added 'kill rings' like those painted on gun barrels to record kills (the destruction of an enemy vehicle). These are placed where the 'necking grooves' would occur on a Doric column. Similarly, a related print demonstrates the progression from the classical column to the 'panzer' gun barrel: *Column to Gun (A–D), Necking Grooves to 'Kill' Rings (1–4)* 1993.

The Krier citation is reiterated in the very large print, almost five feet long, which is the *Proposal for the Haus Der Kunst, Munich*. To emphasise that architects make more fuss over one classical colonnade than over all the tanks that roll off the assembly line at Krupps, the proposal adds armbands to each column of the rear, uninterrupted, façade of the building. These armbands alternately bear the

German and English words, in red and black, 'Verboten' and 'Forbidden'.

However, the most dramatic visualisation of 'dangerous' neo-classicism is the *Man with Panzerschreck*. This sculpture is a bronze cast from an original Greek statue entitled *Man with Javelin*. By substituting the modern Panzerschreck for this antique weapon,[7] Finlay elegantly reiterates the point made in 'Apollo in George Street' from *The Third Reich Revisited*. The commentary to this work, a statue of Apollo (after Bernini) which is armed with a modern sub-machine-gun, explains that 'Apollo's emblems are the bow-and-arrow, and lyre; the gun is only the former, approximately updated (though unlikely to be approved of by present fashion)'. The union of classical figure and modern weaponry confronts the 'present fashion', which recoils in horror when culture and politics are overtly coupled.

Room Two: Nature as Political Emblem

The works in this room introduce another consistent aspect of the artist's neo-classicism. This is the integration of politics and culture through Nature. In Room Two it is the wild flower that manifests Nature as a political emblem; 'The wild flower is ideological, like a badge'.[8] The politicisation of Nature is elucidated through the example of the French Revolution. Revolutionary ideology was articulated through Nature as interpreted by the philosopher, Jean-Jacques Rousseau:

> The Republican Calendar, composed by Fabre d'Eglantine, was intended to allegorise the French Revolution as a new beginning in history. The twelve months, poetically renamed, were each divided into three weeks of ten days. Just as the author had earlier changed his name from Philippe François Nazaire Fabre, to Fabre d'Eglantine, so he named the Republic's days after fruits, flowers, and vegetables, together with animals and agricultural implements. This was in keeping with a Revolution which, under the influence of the writings of Rousseau, explicitly venerated Nature.[9]

These sentiments are emphasised by a wooden stand bearing inscribed flowerpots whose wild flowers re-create the card and print, *Les Femmes de la Révolution – after Anselm Kiefer* (1992).

> Representing Nature, the opposite to all that is artificial, the wild flower is a 'text' which can be moralising, or ideological, or indeed subversive. We need only to think of the role of Nature (and of wild flowers) in the French Revolution and the writings of Rousseau, which preceded it.[10]

While the proposals in Rooms One and Three specifically refer to architectural sites in Munich, this room creates such associations through allusion. As a direct consequence of the outbreak of the French revolution, Karl Theodore of Bavaria had, in 1789, commissioned the design and construction of the English Garden in Munich. This decision, to provide a green space for the recreation of his subjects, was motivated by the desire to defuse any potential unrest stimulated by events in France. In so doing, Karl Theodore was employing the very same form of landscape gardening that had influenced Rousseau's vision of Nature as a symbolic model for the human condition. The English landscape garden of the eighteenth century had been designed to be as natural as Nature itself. Wild flowers were at liberty.

Finlay uses the wild flower to link the Nature politics of the 1790s in Paris with those of the 1990s in Munich. Through the phrase, 'Das Wort aus Stein – The Word out of Stone', Hitler defined the role of architecture as the monumental realisation of ideology. The phrase is painted on the wall of Room Two and reiterated on a stone vase based on the columns of the Ehrentempels. The vase contains wild flowers, and it is wild flowers that have become the words 'uttered' by the stone plinths of the ruined Ehrentempel.

With dramatic irony Nature, generally ravished by the polluting encroachments of human 'progress', had organically colonised the plinths. The wild flowers, self-seeded, had created a pastoral *rus in urbe* out of the Nazi ruins, a 'countryside within the city' to which Green activism could enthusiastically respond. Since the Americans blew up the porticoes and removed the sixteen bronze coffins, the Ehrentempel plinths have become so overgrown that the city authorities have listed the bushes and trees and a great variety of wild flowers for the benefit of the public. In 1990 the authorities launched a competition to redesign the area and it was the intense political debate surrounding the various proposals that brought the Ehrentempel into focus as Green emblems. Indeed, the Green Party argued to preserve each overgrown plinth as an urban nature reserve. However, at the time no proposal was accepted and so Finlay regards the competition as implicitly open.

Room Three: The Proposals for the Ehrentempel

This room is the climax both of the exhibition and of Finlay's decade-long programme of deNazifying neo-classicism. The focus is upon the two sculptures which are models of the reconstructed Ehrentempel. Each sculpture, accompanied by a drawing and commentary, constitutes the proposal for a particular Ehrentempel site. The commentaries for each proposal are as follows:

Two Proposals for the Munich Ehrentempel Sites

1. *Legend*: Modest bronze plaques replace the grandiose coffins of the original Nazi martyrs. They are inscribed with the names of the 'fallen' – the wild flowers which sowed themselves on the Ehrentempel plinths after the columns and roofs were punitively destroyed by the American occupying force in 1947. The flowers – and trees – are removed to allow the 'DeNazified' restoration which acknowledges the intense public debate which took place over the future of the Ehrentempel sites.

2. *Legend*: In place of the descending terraces which once led to the eight bronze coffins, there is now a pool dramatically edged with polished black marble. Through the open roof, the clouds reflect themselves in the still water, while on the frieze is inscribed a phrase from the Roman philosopher Varro, AETERNA TEMPLA CAELI, 'The eternal temples of the sky'. (For the Romans, any area of the sky marked off for the purpose of divination was a 'temple'.) That the clouds *suggest* the eternal and *are* conspicuously ephemeral confirms the passive, elegiac aspect of the reconstructed building.

The combination of sculpture, drawings and commentaries in this room is reminiscent of the focal work in the original *Third Reich Revisited* exhibition, 'Actaeon and the National Gallery of Scotland'. Indeed, the present drawings are in the same idiom and by the same architect, Ian Appleton.

Another *Third Reich Revisited* work, 'National Monument, Calton Hill, Edinburgh', provides the key to the methodology of the deNazification programme. Finlay has 'added lettering to the frieze of the . . . embarrassingly . . . unfinished classical monument'. The inscription, which reads 'Events are a Discourse', is as much the text for this exhibition as the Krier citation. It foregrounds Finlay's acknowledgement, in the current proposals, of 'the intense public debate which took place over the future of the Ehrentempel sites'; and it confirms that changing political events transform the meaning of a site and generate the drama and irony which are the tactics of Finlay's strategy. Now, through changing political events, the Ehrentempels are as ideologically entangled as Nature's exuberant overgrowth. This former Nazi shrine, destroyed by post-war 'deNazification', has become a verdant sanctuary celebrated by the Green Party.

The seed of the current proposal lies in the deNazifying imperative of *The Third Reich Revisited*. Over a decade ago Finlay had specified the Ehrentempel as a site wherein

> the interior frieze, framing the 'open sky', was used for a deNazifying inscription . . . [thus] retaining the *architecture* while altering the *sense* . . . It preserves the transcendental aspect of the original architecture while managing to avoid both the old militarist/heroic and the new democratic/secular.

Thus the deNazification, which began in 1947 through destruction and defamation, is completed through rehabilitation; and the Ehrentempels are reclaimed for the classical tradition – from which, as his models, Troost had plucked the small pair of open-roofed temples at the entrance to the Ornithon, proposed by Pirro Ligorio in 1559.

This imperative is enhanced by the current proposal through the possibilities offered by the greening of the plinths. Indeed, by neoclassicising the pool that had already formed in the sunken area of one of the plinths, Finlay activates the citation from Varro, which is accessibly inscribed alternately in Latin and German. While the reflections of the clouds evoke the polar opposites of eternity and the ephemeral, they also invoke a further irony: that, just as the clouds are ephemeral, so too was the Third Reich in the span of human history. Simultaneously, the reconstructed neo-classicism asserts Finlay's determination to prevent 'a thousand years of architecture being thrown away due to a régime lasting thirteen years'.

(1993)

Notes

1. This essay was written to contextualise the exhibition at the Lenbachhaus in Munich, 9 September, 1993–9 January, 1994.
2. Ian Hamilton Finlay, conversation with the author, 17 September 1993.
3. The exhibition was titled *Liberty, Terror & Virtue: The Little Spartan War and The Third Reich Revisited*. It was co-organised by the New Arcadian Press, which published *New Arcadian Journal* no. 15 as a contextual companion. *NAJ* 15 is the only publication to reproduce all fourteen works of *The Third Reich Revisited*.
4. Ian Hamilton Finlay, 'Ehrentempel, Munich', *The Third Reich Revisited* (illustrations, Ian Appleton), *New Arcadian Journal*, no. 15, New Arcadian Press, Leeds, 1984. All references in this essay to *The Third Reich Revisited* are drawn from this source.
5. Cf. Ian Hamilton Finlay, 'The Atlantic Wall (William Gilpin Annotated)', (illustrations, Ian Gardner), *New Arcadian Journal*, no. 14.
6. Ian Hamilton Finlay, conversation with the author.
7. Panzerschreck: a German World War Two version of the hand-held anti-tank 'bazooka' type weapon.
8. Ian Hamilton Finlay, *A Book of Wildflowers*, Wild Hawthorn Press Christmas, 1994.
9. Ian Hamilton Finlay, *Fructidor (Month of Fruit)*, folding card, with Kathleen Lindsley, Wild Hawthorn Press.
10. Ian Hamilton Finlay, *Wildflower, n.*, folding card, with Gary Hincks, Wild Hawthorn Press.

Features in the Park: Ian Hamilton Finlay's Garden at Luton

LUCIUS BURKHARDT

What a strange kind of art it is that needs explanation – hasn't art to be beautiful and nothing else? Indeed, for Ian Hamilton Finlay's work some explanation *is* required, but such explanation is not like the answer to a riddle. You don't say 'Aha' because the problem is answered – we think of explanations that will increase the beauty of the work.

We begin our walk by entering a landscape garden. Such a garden is a representation of a landscape. So here we meet our first difficulty: a work of art in which representation and the represented coincide. This very English style of gardening began in the eighteenth century, and indeed you can imagine that there were people who had never before seen such a garden and said 'you have worked so much and spent such a lot of money, and now it looks like landscape anyhow. A meadow, surrounded irregularly by bigger and smaller trees, with some sheep grazing – you can see that anywhere'! These early visitors to English gardens were helped by the owners introducing signs which served as interpretation. A small round temple, a stone tower or grove signalled 'You are not just anywhere, you are in England, but you are also in Rome. You are entering a representation of the Roman Campagna'. The artist Ian Hamilton Finlay began as a poet: his work begins in language. His representations, even in gardens, start with the word. By using words, Finlay has brought about a revival of the art of gardening. Gardening everywhere is losing its significance: larger and larger tulips are bred and more of them are planted, so every border of tulips seems to be small because there are larger ones on television or in gardening catalogues. But even the largest bed of tulips does not satisfy, because it has no meaning. Finlay's contribution to gardening is to postulate a garden which has a message, which has something to communicate. Landscape, nature, tree and tulip don't tell us anything unless we succeed in making them speak.

Thus, at the entrance in Stockwood Park, we find a plaque for us to read: it is an Appeal to the Muses. In the Roman age every poem began with an Appeal to the Muses. Through this Appeal the garden is transformed into a poem. Into what kind of poem? A Pastoral poem. The Pastoral poems of antiquity were the first descriptions of landscape. They always begin with a shepherd saying to another shepherd 'I know a beautiful place...', then he will describe it and say '...so let us go there and sing and play the flute'. And through these Pastoral poems written by citizens for citizens, the citizens began to recognise the countryside around his city and to identify it as beautiful landscape.

'I sing for the Muses and myself'. Who is it who talks to us in the first person? We don't see any antique shepherds: the species seems extinct. Is it the tree carrying the plaque which speaks? The wind that sings in its branches? Or perhaps it is the garden itself which wants to tell us that it has found a language – a language in which it can discourse on landscape?

A group of stones lies in the foreground. 'Foreground' is a word we generally use only in the context of landscape painting. Indeed, the stones occupy the place where a landscape painter of old would have placed his flock of sheep and his shepherd playing the flute. Neither sheep nor stones tell us anything, except for one stone which has an inscription in the idiom of a dictionary, explaining the word 'flock'. A flock, we are told, is defined by the fact that its number is fixed and it constitutes a unity. This presupposes a shepherd. It is for us to imagine him, playing his flute – so the picture is completed. But why this strange decision to use the idiom of a dictionary? It is because we, as latecomers, cannot see the landscape otherwise than in an alienated and reflected language: we are no longer a part of it, in no way shepherds.

Two pedestals of the kind used to bear classical columns 'bear' two birch trees. The trunks of the birches become columns, and we remember that in the past architecture used columns and beams to echo timber constructions. The classical Roman architect Vitruvius thought that the first builders of temples supported their beams on living trees.

Through the addition of an inscription, the birches become monuments. Let us read who is honoured. 'Betula pendula' is inscribed on the first base, and on the second the same thing in modern language: 'Silver Birch'. So the birch becomes its own monument twice over, by the name used in natural science, since Linnaeus, and the name used in modern English. These are two ways in which alienated man can approach Nature: by way of science, or by way of the old knowledge of the countryman.

We come now to a curved wall with inscriptions. In some way it reminds us of the wall of the Temple of British Heroes in the garden at Stowe. The meaning of the wall at Stowe is that England has its own antiquity, and that there are others who can stand alongside Brutus, Livius, Augustus, and Pericles in Hades. But here at Luton, Finlay has worked with an antique subject. First we read the title 'The Errata of Ovid', and then there follows a supposed list of errors: 'for Daphne read Laurel', and so on, and then a strange corrigendum, 'for Narcissus read Narcissus'. Ovid's stories are well known: when Apollo tried to touch the chaste nymph Daphne, she transformed herself into a laurel. Ovid leads us into a special landscape, the landscape of deception. It is the realm of Bacchus, god of wine, and of his followers, absorbed by counterfeit. In vain Narcissus is looking for his friend Echo. He cannot find her. Then, in a pool, he perceives a beautiful boy, falls in love with him and plunges into his mirror-image – an error, a misprint. On the linguistic scale, a printer's error.

At the other end of the garden, near its edge, we find a capital partly covered in earth. Such fragments of antique buildings are to be found in the Roman Forum, or on the sites of imperial villas as at Tivoli or Baiae. The painter Claude Lorrain ennobled his landscapes with such signs, as if to say 'The Romans were here'.

Were the Romans at Luton? Was there a villa at Stockwood? Here Finlay uses a literary figure from antique rhetoric, *pars pro toto*: you mention a part and mean the whole. The antique capital is privileged beside the ruins of today: it is a part from which you can develop the whole building. Take a volute of a capital, and a learned architect knows the order to which it belongs and what, in consequence, the other parts of the building were like, which bases were beneath the columns, what the intervals were between the columns, what kind of beams sat on the entablature of the capitals and how the architrave was decorated.

Finally, at the far end of the garden, we meet a herm, a garden monument dedicated to Aphrodite, the goddess of love. The inscription on the herm consist of three anagrams, three lines which each use the same letters to form different words. Here Finlay is practising his old art, the art of concrete poetry, a poetry which reflects on the fact that words are made from letters and that significance can arise without a normal sentence structure. We are reluctant to offer an easy access to the discoveries of the 'Hard Poet'.

(1991)

Note

See also 'Ian Hamilton Finlay's Expressive Garden', *Anthos*, no. 4, 1984.

Flock, with Nicholas Sloan, 1988
Photo by Stephanie Record.

Aphrodite Herm, with Nicholas Sloan, 1991
Photo by Stephanie Record.

A Luton Arcadia: Ian Hamilton Finlay's Contribution to the English Neo-Classical Tradition

STEPHEN BANN

One of the most interesting, yet elusive themes, to emerge in this symposium[1] has been the issue of subjectivity in garden design. Edward Harwood raised it in a fascinating way in his paper on 'Personal identity and the eighteenth-century English landscape garden'. In broad terms, he traced a process whereby the assertion of selfhood in the early-eighteenth-century garden was made more and more difficult as the century drew on: Capability Brown finally swamped the garden of the self by replacing personal with generic treatment. Yet this challenging formulation opened up further questions of method and interpretation. In what sense was it possible to think of the creator of a garden as exercising a full, untarnished subjectivity? In what sense could there be 'gardens of desire'? Such an issue could not be determined on historical grounds alone. It was also necessary, no doubt, to have some working hypothesis about the subject, in linguistic or psychoanalytic terms, before the more substantive questions could be answered.

One might characterise very briefly the implications of such hypotheses by looking at two influential models of the subject, one drawn from linguistics and one from psychoanalysis. The French linguistician, Emile Benveniste, has had a pervasive effect on interpretation in the human sciences with his distinction between *énonciation* and the *énoncé* (sometimes translated as 'the act of uttering' and 'the utterance').

The difference is that, in the first case, the speaking subject assumes responsibility for the act of speaking, while in the second case the subject is absent. Is a garden *énonciation* or *énoncé*? Is it, so to speak, a discourse enunciated by a subject, or is it a statement from which the signs of utterance are eliminated? Do certain gardens fall into one category, and others into the second, and can this distinction be correlated with historical changes?[2]

Such a formulation might seem to be merely a rephrasing of Edward Harwood's proposition. But the question of 'desire' inevitably brings in the psychoanalytic dimension. The psychoanalytic subject, from Freud to Lacan, is a split subject: that is to say, the cleavage between the conscious and the unconscious mind engenders a dialectic of desire and lack. In these terms (to define the issue very summarily) there is no desire without lack: desire is indeed produced by lack, and to talk of it being fulfilled is a contradiction. The 'garden of desire' would therefore have to be thought of not, perhaps, as the fulfilment of the self's intentions in pleasurable experience, but the realisation, in the very intensity of the sensory stimuli, of the self's own radical lack of consistency. Roland Barthes' well-known distinction between *plaisir* and *jouissance* is designed to express this dichotomy, and we might well want to ask if, parallel to Barthes' listing of the texts that fall into these alternative categories, there might be gardens of *plaisir*, and gardens of *jouissance*?[3]

These preliminary remarks are, in fact, directly relevant to my own subject, the Stockwood Park garden of Ian Hamilton Finlay. But before turning directly to that, I would like to pick up a further theme which is also germane to my topic. Michael Charlesworth has spoken not indeed directly about the self, but about 'The Sacred Idea', which takes for granted a very special and culturally mediated investment of the self. His interest was in showing how, in the same period as that covered by Edward Harwood, religious convictions 'emerge in the motivate garden design'. Here we have an issue which, in its very form, inevitably brings up the question of selfhood, but at the same time requires it to be set within the specific types of social and political practice existing at the time. Indeed the raising of the issue of sacredness in the garden is valuable, in my opinion, precisely because it requires us to discriminate clearly between quite different functions of the sacred, which were evident in the eighteenth century and have arguably never lost their pertinence.

Without claiming to get very far in discriminating these different functions, I can at least make a start by suggesting that there are at least three, which I shall call functional, ideological and subjective. Of the functional use of the sacred, there is little to say except that sacredness is obviously one of the most direct ways of signifying the dimension of infinity as a structural requirement within the design of the garden. Another way, as Bernard Lassus has shown, is the referencing within the garden of features relating to travel, voyages and the exotic. In the Temple built to commemorate the voyages of Captain Cook, erected at the Château de Méréville, we have a concatenation of the themes of sacredness and the voyage, which is moreover *functionally* justified as it exists at the extreme boundary of the park, over a stretch of water which thus becomes invested with the character of an outer limit.[4]

Of the ideological use of the sacred, which is of course not incompatible with its functional use, there is perhaps little to say, since its message has been diffused so widely in the current state of landscape and garden history. If we take ideology as meaning the construction of a set of imaginary relations which mask political and social reality, then we can see that, in the eighteenth century particularly, the idea of the sacred often contributed to this process. In Michael Charlesworth's paper, the constitution of Rievaulx Abbey as a place redolent of medieval superstition, viewed from the terrace as if from the superior stance of the enlightened eighteenth century, is an excellent example, as is Christopher Sykes's classicising of the church at Sledmere. But it would be a great mistake to suppose that the ideological, and the functional, aspects exhaust the use of sacredness in the garden design of the period. Michael Charlesworth also mentions the antiquarian William Stukeley, and his reverent if eccentric treatment of objects which had an intense personal significance: he writes about Pope, who was certainly saturated in ideology but equally concerned with the concrete realisation of features connected to his family and his religion. To treat these examples seriously is not to commit the mistake of reifying the notion of 'sacredness' and substituting 'airy nothingness' for the hard data of political and social life. It is to commit oneself to a more scrupulous

A Luton Arcadia

investigation of the stakes of subjectivity. The question is not, then, 'did Pope really believe in God?' or even 'what difference would it make to our reading of his garden if we accepted that Pope believed in God'? It should be turned round, perhaps, in the following way: should we read such and such a garden as the enunciation of a 'believing subject', given that a 'believing subject', like a 'desiring subject', is inevitably caught up in a dialectic of plenitude and lack, fulfilment and unfulfilment? Such an enterprise may appear to be a needless complication in the prosaic agenda of garden history. Equally, it might be seen as a way of revitalising our awareness of why the garden continues to matter, as part of a lively cultural debate, in the present day.

Coming right at the end of the period allotted to the 'English Arcadia' in this symposium (and indeed technically just outside it), the Stockwood Park garden by Ian Hamilton Finlay is at the same time a retrospective meditation on the neo-classical tradition and a revaluation of it. Finlay's work as a poet and gardener is known particularly as a result of his remarkable transformation of the upland landscape around the small farm where he has lived since 1966: Stonypath (or, as it was re-named in the 1970s, Little Sparta) remains his definitive creation, since it reflects the cumulative effect of landscape modifications and the siting of permanent works over a quarter of a century. Yet at the same time as he has continually added to Little Sparta, Finlay has engaged in distinct projects for quite different sites. These are, by their very nature, conceived as complete in their own terms. They therefore enable us to trace a certain logic in the development of his guiding ideas. The Stockwood Park garden was certainly made possible by the fact that only in the last few years were professional gardeners sufficiently aware of Finlay's reputation to envisage so complete a landscape project in collaboration with him. But it was also made possible by the development and clarification of his concepts. It forms, in every respect, a mature statement of belief.

I shall therefore concern myself here with the pre-history and the achievement of Stockwood Park. But it is important to begin by underlining a fundamental point about Finlay's approach, and one which sets him apart from other contemporary garden designers. Finlay was, in the early 1960s, an avant-garde poet of international importance, with multifarious links to fellow members of the concrete poetry movement, which he developed through his Wild Hawthorn Press. By the end of the decade, however, he had become disenchanted with this spectrum of activity. A significant pointer to his change of heart is the poem entitled 'Arcady', published shortly after his arrival at the farm of Stonypath, in which he invited his readers to see the letters of the alphabet not reductively (as in many of the latter-day expressions of concrete poetry) but as a classical landscape.[5] From the last years of the 1960s dates the initial cross-fertilisation between his work as a poet and his incipient activity as a gardener. The small book *Stonechats*, published in 1967, comprises a collection of brief, sometimes 'one-word' poems which were destined for a place as inscriptions in new features of Stonypath such as the 'Sunken Garden'.[6]

Just as Finlay's concern with the landscaping of Stonypath was itself implicitly a critique of the sterility of the concrete poetry movement, so his further development and 'neo-classical rearmament' of the garden in the 1970s was itself intended as a critique of the state of international modernist art. It was not that he abandoned the practice of contemporary poet and artist, in order to become a gardener. Quite the opposite, being a gardener as well as a poet and artist gave him a basis from which to work polemically against the contemporary art world: the garden did not completely displace the gallery, but it remained a kind of alibi – a concrete place in relation to which the more ephemeral manifestations would implicitly be judged. Louis Marin has well understood this crucial aspect of the garden by placing his study of 'Le Jardin de Julie' in a sequence of essays on Utopia, comprised in his *Lectures traversières* (1992). For him, the logic of the garden is precisely analogous to the logic of the text, and thus of the imagination: 'displacement of the space of nature into a privileged place where its infinite diversity, its inexhaustible profusion, its production are condensed and summed up in a product, a representation, which is a substitute and a replacement'.[7] Rousseau, walking in the 'Jardin de Julie', halts and meditates precisely at those places where a stone inscription, emerging from this microcosm of the natural world, puts him in mind of an alternative history and culture to the one which he is experiencing: 'if this inscription be of some ancient nation which exists no longer, it extends our soul into the regions of infinity and gives

A Luton Arcadia

it the sentiment of its own immortality, by showing it that a thought has survived the very ruin of an empire'.[8]

I want to suggest that the Stockwood Park garden, coming as it does twenty-five years after the first work at Stonypath, is Finlay's most conclusive statement to date of the 'logic' which Marin traces here: of a deep interconnection between nature, in its condensed and representational form, and the text as a relay between past and present, signalling the possibility of Utopia in the very act of imagination which it imposes on the visitor. But in order to define its special quality, I need first of all to spend some time describing two earlier landscape projects which indicate his growing confidence in handling the antique theme. That these could best be characterised as interpolations, or indeed interventions, within the discourse of the contemporary sculpture park is not their least important feature.

The *Sacred Grove*, for the Rijksmuseum Kröller-Müller (Dutch National Sculpture Collection) at Otterlo, was completed in 1982. A site had originally been selected for a project by Finlay in the vicinity of the museum, within easy distance of the many conventionally sited pieces of modern sculpture. What was eventually selected, however, was a very different type of space, which allowed him to design a total and compelling environment. Over recent years, the patronage of the museum had extended to offering artists like Claes Oldenburg and Jean Dubuffet the possibility of designing large-scale works for a broad belt of cleared woodland which formed a circuit at some distance from the museum. Here the most dramatic use was made of the terrain, with works deliberately accentuating their own artificiality (as with Oldenburg's *Trowel*, from 1971, or Dubuffet's *Jardin d'Email*, from 1972–73). Finlay chose to situate his project at the very centre of this belt, in an area previously inaccessible to the public and hemmed in by rhododendron bushes. A pathway of laid stones was created to offer a serpentine entry, and the inner space was simply cleared of bushes, leaving a fine group of mature trees. The *Sacred Grove* was to be, on one level, simply the enhancement of these existing trees, which had their lower branches cropped so that they formed slender 'columns': all that was added to them was a sequence of stone 'column-bases'.

Yves Abrioux has written perceptively about these 'tree columns' as instances of the contemporary practice of collage.[9] So they are, indeed, and the carefully designed and individual stone bases must inevitably appear in visual terms as cultural grafts on to a natural scene. But obviously Finlay is not creating the same effect of sharp disjunction as his colleagues on the other side of the bushes. The *Sacred Grove* is the enhancement of nature through an act of cultural implantation: one-word inscriptions complete the process by dedicating the individual tree-columns to Lycurgus, Rousseau, Robespierre, Michelet and Corot. It is interesting to consider the syntagmatic chain formed by that particular set of names, especially as it both borrows from and revises similar, well-known gestures of homage at Stowe and Ermenonville. Finlay's theme is not 'British Worthies' or 'Philosophers of Nature', but figures connected with the French Revolution. Yet the fact that Lycurgus, its mythic Spartan law-giver, and Rousseau, its philosophical enabler, are juxtaposed with Robespierre, its historical actor, and Michelet, its historical commentator, indicates the multiplicity of discourses within which the event needs to be set. There is, moreover, Corot, to remind us that the intensity of a neo-classical style is itself a significant postscript to the historical phenomenon.

At Otterlo, Finlay's *Sacred Grove* is an interpolation in the modern sculpture park, and an intervention in its bland, eclectic discourse. At the Villa Celle, near Pistoia, where Finlay's project was completed in 1984, the strategy was one of lateral displacement, out of the 'Forest of the Avant-Garde' and into the Olive Grove, which was to be 'celebrated' and 'improved' at the same time. In the original proposal, *A Celebration of the Grove*, his brief was given as creating a work whose 'main raw material should be plants' and whose site was to be 'some agricultural land next to the park'.[10] Rather than uproot the existing olive trees, he determined to supplement them with a trio of bronze objects, all testifying to the Georgic or Virgilian tradition of country life. Once again, it is striking how Finlay's easy adaptation to the existing condition of the landscape contrasts with, and forms an implicit criticism of, the avant-garde sculpture which adjoins it. The work in the park, or 'Forest of the Avant-Garde', for the most part vaunts its modernist or high-tech affiliations, though an exception must be made for the dramatic Baroque water feature of Anne and Patrick Poirier, and perhaps for the concrete line threading the woods in the manner of Kent's watercourses, which is the work of Danni Karavan. Finlay alludes neither to modernism, nor to the grand tradition of garden design. His oval bronze tree-plaque, with a text interchanging the properties of 'The Silver Flute' and 'The Rough Bark', is a no more constraining adjunct than the Otterlo column-base. His bronze plough, 'of the Roman sort', tells us that 'The Day Is Old By Noon', as if to remind us that the agricultural round is timed differently from the schedule of private views and gallery visits. Finally, a 'Basket of Lemons', again in bronze, evokes the motif of refreshment – 'Silence After Chatter', 'The Astringent Is Sweet' – which underlines the effect of this Georgic interlude arising in the sequence of overemphatic and clamorous sculptural works.

I have stressed the fact that these two major projects by Finlay indicate a counterdiscourse within the discourses of contemporary art: in particular, they intervene within the institution of the sculpture park, a contemporary and necessarily hybrid form of garden whose aesthetic has perhaps been taken for granted for too long. In a sense, Finlay's strategy is precisely to recall to the attentive visitor that these spaces are, or should be, gardens: gardens, that is to say, in the full historical and cultural sense of the term, and therefore of necessity incorporating philosophical and political themes. But it will be clear that, in this context, his gesture is bound to be a partial one. He can create an island or a Utopia, within its own limits. He cannot, however, change the character of the institution itself. The Celle Olive Grove is a timely reminder of this fact, since in its present state of realisation it represents only a part of the original scheme. Finlay also designed a 'Small Circular Temple', which was to be used for viewing the Virgilian Grove, and a 'Line of Bricks, of green porcelain' which were to run in the earth between the trunks of the olive trees. Without these elements, the visual syntax was bound to remain inadequate, and the relation to the other parts of the park insufficiently defined.

My point is that, in the course of these two projects, Finlay began to conceive of the possibility of a more integral expression. This was to be neither the strategic intervention of the sculpture park, nor the gradual accretion which continued to take place in the context of Little Sparta itself. It is possible, I believe, to see the kind of change involved if we compare two further projects from the second half of the 1980s. His *Proposal for a Monument to Jean-Jacques Rousseau* (1986) takes the form of a presentation of 'before' and 'after', in the style of Humphry Repton, but it is essentially a dynamic reinterpretation of an existing garden. Gary Hincks' fine drawing demonstrates the function of the 'Urn' in framing a section of the landscape, and therefore celebrating Rousseau's role in giving new ethical and political content to the idea of Nature. Like the stone column-base, the Urn, in its negativity, complements and transforms the existing vegetation. In a later project also involving Gary Hincks, *A Proposal for the Forest of Dean* (1988, completed 1989), the allusion to a drawing by William Kent is not simply a historical point of reference but a model for a complete landscape feature. Finlay uses a sequence of tree-plaques simply to emphasise and specify the mood attaching to the landscape. It should not, however, be forgotten that his use of the word 'silence', in its linguistic variants, harks back to a classic short poem of the heyday of the international concrete poetry movement, by the German poet Eugen Gomringer.

I would conclude that the Stockwood Park Garden, completed in 1991, came at just the right moment in Finlay's development as a poet, artist and garden designer. Here, for the first time, the idea of 'Arcady' nurtured from the first days of his arrival at Stonypath could be carried out in a context which was still, inevitably, critical in relation to the modes of contemporary art and garden design, but nevertheless a certain way removed from the exigencies of immediate polemic. It is important right at the outset to mention the crucial role of Robert Burgoyne, the Master Gardener who initiated and carried through the whole scheme, with a restraint in the use of bedding plants which implies a truly heroic renunciation in the case of an English public park! Stockwood offered Finlay not a virgin site, which would have been immensely costly and time-consuming to develop, but the best of both worlds: a large fragment of a mature garden, with several fine trees and a vestigial ha-ha, which could be replanned as a complete entity. On one side, the fine brick wall of the original kitchen garden kept at bay a picturesque medley of rockeries and souvenirs of the largely destroyed big house, whilst on the other, the adjacent golf course gave a pleasing extension to the wider views, without offering too much disturbance or distraction.

The further context of the Stockwood Park garden is worth

A Luton Arcadia

mentioning, since this forms a kind of frame to the achievement. Luton is a town which, in the post-war years, has largely destroyed its historic centre, and is perhaps most associated in the popular mind with the possession of a busy airport (whose arrivals and departures are easily visible from Stockwood Park). The park in which the Finlay garden is situated performs a medley of functions for the urban community: exhibition of pictures and *objets d'art* in the outbuildings of the previous house, provision of swings and roundabouts for intrepid children, and demonstration of local crafts and products for the casual visitor. At the same time, it is placed almost adjacent to the M1, Britain's motorway *par excellence*, and therefore accessible from London in one direction, and from the Los Angeles of the Midland Counties, Milton Keynes, in another. Motorway drivers are already well aware of the attractions of Woburn Abbey, a classic English garden with supplementary wild beasts which extends for many acres on the other side of the motorway. Some of them may indeed be aware that Woburn has recently lost its prime work of neo-classical art, the *Three Graces* of Canova, which was removed from the Temple specially constructed for it by a former Duke of Bedford and sent to an American destination, an action justified by the official argument that, since it was physically capable of being detached from its setting, it formed no integral part of the Temple and could be alienated.

I am not simply free-associating about the environs of Stockwood Park. It seems to me that all of the elements mentioned here bear on an issue which integrally concerns Finlay's garden, and conditions its meaning. What is the force of classical reference, or indeed any form of historical and cultural reference, today? What is the relationship between the demands of mass housing and mass transport, on the one hand, and the need for recreation, in the most etymologically precise sense of the term? Who could or should take responsibility for conserving, or protecting, what is now generally described as our heritage? What role does the individual artist have, or hope to have? It is clear that many visual artists have begun to comment critically on the gap between the conditions of everyday life and the ideality of the image offered to us by classical art. Victor Burgin, in his series of photo-panels on the city of Grenoble, juxtaposes the Claude in the local museum with the raw and graceless expression of nature in the setting of the modern suburb.[11] Bernard Lassus, working not only as a trained artist but also as a veteran of imaginative architectural schemes, actually displaces the Roman façade of the Temple at Nimes (made redundant by a Norman Foster building) on to a motorway site where he is creating a formal garden, and a Belvedere based on the *Tour Magne* which at the same time offers a prospect of the adjacent city. His solution is not simply the critical exposure of the gap, but the creative development of a series of productive interchanges: the *aire d'autoroute* becomes a microcosm of the adjacent site.

Stockwood Park relates to both of these possibilities, while remaining entirely specific and original in its solution. To confront the designs, again by Gary Hincks, with the actual state of the garden, in this early phase of its development, is to be struck by the disparity between the classical, Claudian vision and the contemporary, still unweathered sculptural work. Finlay will have shepherds and their flocks, temples and mountains, in his Claudian designs, though no shepherd has been seen in Luton for quite some time, no mountain exists in the Midlands, and the Temple of the Graces has (as mentioned earlier) been profaned. Of course, it does not matter. The disjunction serves precisely to raise the stakes of the classical reference, and to make the inscription a vehicle for the imagination – 'showing it that a thought has survived the very ruin of an empire'. When Finlay appends to one of the oldest and most distinctive trees a stone plaque bearing the text, 'I sing for the Muses and myself', he sets himself within a chain of references: to the Emperor Julian who favoured the phrase, and yet also to the previous poet whose precedence Julian acknowledged. The interminable chain of gestures of homage to the preceding poet is both a symbol of the endurance of the classical tradition, and an indication that the self is bifurcated by its acceptance of latecoming: the 'Muses' are the constant guarantee of the persistence of genres.

All this is, at present, a promissory note, in the sense that the discreet and delightful planting schemes have still to mature. But, of course, it is destined to remain a promissory note, in a more definitive sense. The opening of Stockwood Park was greeted in a variety of different ways. Certainly there was intelligent response and indeed acclaim on the national scale, while on the local scale a wholly misinformed debate about the cost of the scheme, revolving around Finlay's most minimal feature, created an unproductive furore. The substitution of blocks of stone for the Claudian sheep – in a work which resembled Finlay's well-acclimatised sculptures at Eindhoven and San Diego – excited incomprehension and hostility. At the same time, it is obvious that such a distribution of informally sited large elements, in the space extending beyond the excavated ha-ha, peoples the prospect in a convenient and satisfying way. Finlay has in a sense acknowledged that this is not an easy garden to appreciate, but one which challenges its visitors to the indispensable act of imaginative empathy. Language, in its transformations which include the apparently random form of the anagram, betrays the critical stance of the poet, as when the anagram of Aphrodite, inscribed on a woodland Herm, yields, as its first scrambled message, 'I HARD POET'. How much lies buried beneath the surface, not only in terms of the archaeology of a land once part of the Roman Empire, but also in the layering of mental strata which testifies to the possession, even now, of a common culture? That is Finlay's question, at Stockwood Park, and indeed his challenge. The landscape is, for him, a 'landscape with a buried capital', in that we can only perceive its cultural dimension (be it William Shenstone, or Quatremère de Quincy) through seizing hold of the fragment. In its dual movement of apprehension and abnegation, the self can none the less accede to the point of saying 'Et In Arcadia Ego'.

I need to make some final remarks which will draw together the general considerations of subjectivity with which I began, and the more particular evocation of Finlay's work up to and including the Stockwood Park garden. In a sense, my whole argument has been a matter of positing the conditions for the self-assertion of the 'I' in the contemporary garden: 'I HARD POET'; 'I SING FOR THE MUSES AND MYSELF'. Only the poet-gardener, the 'believing subject', is qualified to do this, I am inclined to suggest, and only he can provide the place which the garden visitor can then occupy, in turn. But is this indeed the appropriation of Arcadia? Is this the position suggested in the complex and contradictory historical fortunes of that famous phrase, 'Et In Arcadia Ego'?

Louis Marin, whose remarks on the 'Jardin de Julie' have already been quoted, has an important point to make about Poussin's painting of the *Arcadian Shepherds* (Louvre version) where the phrase so memorably occurs:

> The obliteration of the name and the verb in the inscription points out the operation enacted by the representational narrative process and represents it as the concealment of the 'enunciative' structure itself, thanks to which the past, death, loss, can come back here and now by our reading – but come back as representation, set upon its stage, the object of a serene contemplation exorcising all irony.[12]

In this reading, the lacunary nature of the inscription – who precisely is 'Ego'? – serves precisely to conceal the *énonciation*, that is to mask the instrumentality of the subject: we therefore see 'Arcadia' as representation, the representation of absence which is the condition of Poussin's painting itself. Yet here there is a crucial difference between the painting and the garden. The garden may indeed be a representation, in Marin's terms 'a substitute and a replacement' for the 'infinite diversity' and 'inexhaustible profusion' of nature itself. But it is also, potentially, a Utopia, projecting the visitor into a concrete experience which is not limited by the borders of the picture frame or predetermined by the imperfect enunciation of the inscribed message. 'I HARD POET' may be an anagram, and thus a masking of the subject through the free play of the signifier. But 'I SING FOR THE MUSES AND MYSELF' is the differential placing of the poet in the sequence of a tradition, and thus the sufficient assertion of subjectivity in the concrete discourse of the garden as representation.

All this will make little impact on the commentators who describe the garden developed at West Green House by Lord McAlpine as 'the best post-war garden in Britain'.[13] It will cut no ice with those who regard Quinlan Terry's designs for follies at West Green as 'a welcome reminder that art is not dead – and Arcadian visions can still be realised'.[14] But it is precisely in the need to distinguish Little Sparta and Stockwood Park from West Green House that we find ourselves requiring new definitions of subjectivity and selfhood, which will help us to distinguish between ideology and the sacred, and between true and false Arcadia.

(1992)

Notes

See also Stephen Bann, 'A Description of Stonypath', *Journal of Garden History*, vol. 1, no. 2, April–June, 1981.

1. Symposium 'Rediscovering the British Garden', organised by the American Institute of Architects, Washington, DC, May 1992.
2. For a example of the application of Benveniste's concepts to a specific discourse, see Roland Barthes, 'The Discourse of History', in Elinor Shaffer (Ed.) *Comparative Criticism*, 3 (1981), pp. 3–20.
3. See Roland Barthes, *Le plaisir du texte* (Le Seuil, Paris, 1973).
4. For a discussion of this feature, see Stephen Bann, 'From Captain Cook to Neil Armstrong: Colonial exploration and the structure of landscape', in Simon Pugh (Ed.) *Reading Landscape – Country, City, Capital* (Manchester University Press, 1990), pp. 214–30.
5. For an early discussion of this poem and its significance in Finlay's development, see Stephen Bann, 'Ian Hamilton Finlay's *Ocean Stripe 5*', *Scottish International*, March/April 1967, p. 47. Although post-dated in some bibliographies, the poem was already circulating in December 1966.
6. See Stephen Bann, 'A description of Stonypath', *Journal of Garden History*, vol. 1, no. 2, 1981, pp. 114ff.
7. Louis Marin, *Lectures traversières* (Albin Michel, Paris, 1992), pp. 70–1 (my translation).
8. *Ibid.*, p. 71 (my translation).
9. Yves Abrioux, 'Dissociation: On the Poetics of Ian Hamilton Finlay's Tree/Columns', *Word and Image*, IV, 1988, pp. 338–44.
10. Ian Hamilton Finlay, *A Celebration of the Grove* (printed by the Parrett Press, 1984), unpaginated.
11. See Victor Burgin, *Between* (Blackwell, Oxford, 1986), pp. 100–7.
12. Louis Marin, 'Towards a Theory of Reading in the Visual Arts', in Norman Bryson (Ed.) *Calligram* (Cambridge University Press, 1988), p. 86.
13. Gervase Jackson-Stops, *An English Arcadia 1600–1990* (American Institute of Architects Press, 1991), p. 154. The remark is unattributed.
14. *Ibid.*, p. 22.

Ian Hamilton Finlay

TOM LUBBOCK

It is difficult to read Ian Hamilton Finlay's work in a way that sounds quite straight. Writing, for instance, about the role of the French Revolution, Jean de Loisy says: 'For Finlay, the French Revolution is not a theme which he illustrates, as one might ordinarily say of an artist and his subject. It is a hyperbolic, interiorised metaphor for the artist's moral attitude in the world'. A large claim seems to be in the offing here. The Revolution is not merely subject-matter, it represents some sort of design upon the world. But before we arrive at the world, this is qualified by a large proviso. The Revolution is not, on the other hand, more than a metaphor, a hyperbolic, interiorised metaphor, for a moral attitude – those words apparently stressing that the Revolution is not something that Finlay believes in, in a straightforward way, not directly his *cause*. In fact, thus stated, the idea of the Revolution could hardly be set at a further remove from danger or commitment. It becomes – what? – only a way of lending drama to a difference of opinion?

I dwell on these remarks because I think they conform to a common tendency in commentary on Finlay's work – a tendency, that is, to assert its moral and ideological credentials, while being hesitant to spell out what those credentials are, or to address the question of whether there's anything you might or might not agree with. Yet I also believe that this turn of thought is likely to inflect, in some form, any response to Finlay's art. If I suggest that speaking of 'metaphor' here is to avoid a decision, then it does nevertheless register a tension which may be hard to resolve. To put this in one rough and general way: the work often seems to make claims about and upon the world and our life in it. But then, on reflection, these world-involving claims, and the conflicts they imply, seem to be dealt with or worked through within the work itself; and perhaps to be not capable of any other expression than that which the work gives them. To put it another way: it is hard to give an account of Finlay's work that does not either seem too 'arty' or appear to deny the fact that it is art.

The questionable word 'art' is at the heart of the question. Can or must the work be viewed as art? Is its material presented to us as a contained experience for our contemplation? Is it untranslatable into any forms other than its own? Or is it something more than, other than, an art of this pure, fine sort? A religious art, an ideological art, a programmatic or propagandist art? My case is that, when considering Finlay's work, these questions will continually arise in one way or another, and that they cannot be given a stable answer. Nor are they only questions for the viewer/reader; they are questions which the work itself encounters and negotiates. Here are various instances and aspects.

The Temple

To take this embattled example: do we see the Garden Temple as, somehow, a working 'neo-classical' temple, a place of worship? Or is it a work which propagates the possibility of such a temple, and does this by presenting us with an example of one? Or is it a work of art which meditates on the idea of a temple, which takes this idea as its subject – albeit, again, in concrete form? Whatever view you take, the dispute itself is a real one – even though it may also have representative value as an instance of something larger, an incident in a wider cultural conflict. It turns on the official acceptance and recognition of a certain idea of a temple, or at least on making this idea the subject of public debate. Perhaps the final result will be only a proof that there is indeed no public place for this idea, as things stand. But you can't say the challenge has not been made openly, and on the letter of a point of law.

The Revolution

A theme? A cause? A metaphor for a moral attitude? Granted, nothing in Finlay's work simply urges a re-run of the French Revolution. But neither is that Revolution and the idea of a revolution generally treated as a merely historical phenomenon, something 'in the past'. The object of invoking the Revolution, you might say, is in part to emphasise how remote its values are from our own (which is to be lamented; it is not just a matter of a historical 'contrast'). But then, would it involve another revolution if this state of affairs were to change or be changed? And can we deny that Finlay's work does imply some such change, however obscure or remote that possibility may be? Or is it, itself, only a work of lamentation? At the very least, to invoke the idea of a revolution at all is to give a particular force and focus to a moral attitude. Moral attitudes, after all, we have plenty of. This must suggest one with a comprehensive scope and a stance of radical opposition.

A 'Cause'

Finlay and commentators working with him have on occasion set his work in opposition to the modern world – a world whose values are characterised (adversely) as 'secular', 'liberal', 'pluralistic', 'materialistic' and 'utilitarian'. Counter to this, some re-spiritualisation, some idea of a whole culture and a right relation to nature is suggested, in accord with what is called a 'Western tradition'; and some history of loss is implied. Similar-sounding calls come from many quarters. But Finlay's seems to be distinct, in not being alignable with any prevalent marxian or conservative tradition (nor with 'ecology') and especially in eliding almost entirely christianity (it is neither affirmed nor contested; it is scarcely referred to). What is lost, roughly speaking, are the values and vision of the classical world, and their various reiterations and revisions in history. These are, in some way, to be reaffirmed and perhaps re-realised; and a temporal scheme of 'original truth – loss – restoration' suggests itself.

But this is to put roughly what it is very difficult to put more definitely. If we find intimations of ideology in Finlay's work, this only leaves us with a range of questions. Do they amount to a position or a cause? Is it a matter of critique only, a collision of value systems which envisages no further issue? Or are there designs upon the world? Could this position or cause be stated as apart from its expression in the work – and be believed in, acted upon by others? Should we take the work itself as an exposition, a promulgation of it?

A 'World-View'

Writing about Finlay's printed work, Edwin Morgan refers to 'what for the majority of readers will be a new set of co-ordinates, still, however, to be co-ordinated, by us reading the rules, into a world-view', and probably the majority of readers/viewers would assent to that perception with regard to Finlay's work as a whole. We encounter such dominant themes as classical antiquity, the French Revolution and German Romanticism, and many variations on motifs of warfare, architecture, nature cultivated and nature wild. Finlay's central topics are to an extent unfamiliar ones and certainly unfamiliar in combination; their scope is wide-ranging; and there is a web of interconnections between individual works. All these factors, supported by some sort of *auteur* theory perhaps, encourage us to seek a unifying account. As Morgan says, we must then read the runes, piece it together.

But it is another thing to suppose that an attempt at co-ordination will be rewarded, that there is anything that could be called a world-view involved in forming the work. At least, the question is open. It could be that Finlay's work constitutes a series of individual points rather than a coherent whole, and that the sense of coherence is an effect, an illusion, of art, achieved at the level of imagery only (or it could be that it really does cohere, and this is then figured in art). Again, it could be that such coherence as it does have is really a psychological matter, something peculiar to the artist's personality, which we might try to diagnose but hardly to give sense to (or again, the coherence of this world-view might be publicly definable).

A 'Vision'

All these are problems. But there would be a way to set them aside, to make them not matter – and it is surely a temptation, though it should be resisted. This would be to consider Finlay's work as 'a vision'. We would see Finlay as constructing a 'little world' of his imagination, a private 'mythology', something which, on its own terms, may appear complete or persuasive and within its limits and which we might, in imagination, enter or entertain for a while – but which does not claim us. What gives it value for us, ultimately, is that it means something to the artist, and this might not be so far from saying that what we have here is a personal 'case', a matter of 'obsessions' to be appreciated for their strangeness and single-mindedness – or dismissed as a fantasy, a dream-world. At any rate, this would be a way of taking the work 'artistically' (in a rather debased sense of the word). Thus, it is no business of the work of art to 'make sense'; nor need we be concerned about whether its ideas are definable or coherent, or whether they have any purchase or designs upon us and our world. No, it is a world of its own.

Of course, we could allow all these points, and indeed read the work as plainly ideological, and still deflect this with some suspension of disbelief or a positive revelling in disbelief – as with Soviet art; or we might put aside the question of our own assent by bracketing off Finlay's ideas as themselves an artistic 'creation' or 'spectacle'. The aesthetic *cordon sanitaire* is almost infinitely elastic, and it is a barrier which Finlay's work must often encounter. But this is to stray from my line of argument, which concerns those responses which his work prompts; and it does not prompt this form of response, even though it can hardly prevent it.

Discourse

I say that it is an error, though a tempting one, to treat Finlay's work as an enclosed, personal vision. But any enquiry into it from the other point of view is going to be difficult. We have inklings of a position, a cause, a world-view, etc. We have no clear or complete picture. But if we then look around elsewhere, we find that the ideas that are in play, the points made, the perceptions offered, do not – so far as one can tell – find a place in any established current debate, public or academic or 'cultural'. They are not in the discourse. Finlay has from time to time intervened in such debates – but from a point of view which appears to be outside them. Then again, though Finlay's work takes as its bearings many historical landmarks, the selection, reading and synthesis of these 'sources' appears to be his own. There is no established and self-conscious tradition of thought and belief of which his work is an expression. I think any view of his work must conclude that Finlay is, if a thinker at all, then an original one; and that his position is a singular and isolated one. He is also an artist. So the difficulty can be put like this: if we seek a world-view, etc., informing the work, it is only to be discovered, pieced together, from the work itself. There are no other firm, external bearings to assist us. This is why there is the temptation to treat the world-view itself as either an intransitive artistic construct, or as a personal case. The world view is, it happens, contained in this one particular expression of it. The ideological, the artistic and the personal in Finlay's work may in theory be distinguishable – but they are, as things stand, congruent.

Moreover, Finlay does not operate as an original and singular ideologue might. He does not expound his thinking in a systematic way. He works rather as an artist *to* a body of ideas, as if assuming that the topics and terms of his work were already a going concern, and by adopting this procedure the work, as it were, projects from itself a (putative) discourse-community among whom these things *are* already the subject of an on-going conversation. I do not mean a following, a movement attached to the work, but something more like a movement to which the work itself was attached. Nor do I merely mean that the work is sometimes hard to understand; more, that its difficulties feel like those an 'outsider' would experience. (For example, in the equation of Saint-Just and Apollo: do you take this as a 'standard' typology, or a startling conceit?) But I think this sense that the work is in discourse with something outside itself contributes to our sense of its conviction. It, at least, has the effect of subduing the suspicion of personal 'visionariness', though I agree that it could also be further evidence for Finlay's being completely 'in a world of his own'. Either way, we are left with these paradoxical responses. Finlay seems to us an original thinker – yet he works as if his ideas were in circulation. His position seems to us singular and isolated – yet his work supposes and implies a discourse-community with whom it is in conversation.

Now, if the work really were part of an established discourse, past or present, wide or narrow, then its situation would be very different. It would be under less pressure to declare by itself its world-view, clear and entire. That would be available elsewhere as it is, for example, for a christian art – and we could judge then how far Finlay's own expression of it was a partial, variant or personal version. There would be less question also whether the work *itself* spoke for its cause. That cause would have other spokesmen, other manifestations, where the issue of our assent or otherwise might arise. And with all that, we would be able to take the work more artistically (in a quite respectable sense) – neither as exposition nor as propaganda, but as some form of meditation.

Meditation, Propaganda

But then, why shouldn't we do this anyway? It could be objected that the whole account so far given makes Finlay's work too programmatic. Remember that Finlay is an artist; it is no business of the artist to be an ideologue, and nor does he work as one. Jean de Loisy's denial notwithstanding, why shouldn't we take the relation of the work to its material as a relation of art to subject-matter: a meditation, a discussion, a dramatisation, a presentation, a treatment of some sort? To be sure, you can approach the work in terms of themes and imagery, concerns and references, and this approach will afford an almost complete critical description of it. You might indeed take Finlay's project to be purely scholarly – a study of various historical and cultural topics, albeit a particularly vivid and inventive one. Or you might allow (you could hardly not) that there are definite tendencies in forming this study, but still maintain that its *handling* of these is essentially contemplative. The work raises questions, entertains ideas, stages conflicts, but holds them so to speak in suspension. It does not step over the bounds of art. It does not, in doing this, promulgate. It does not itself challenge our belief.

But for reasons given before, this reading cannot be steadily maintained. However much it goes against the grain of the work's own ways, there is for us a pressure to ideologise it – simply because there are no other expressions of its thought available onto which this pressure can be displaced. So, to the extent that there are intimations of a worldview, we must take the work as expounding this; to the extent that there are intimations of a cause, we must receive the work, however obliquely, as propaganda for it. It may, on the other hand, make more sense, go more with the grain of the work, to presume a supposed discourse-community. No need to expound or to propagandise to 'them' – but the work reads well as an artistic reflection upon, embodiment of, an inspiration to the ideas and beliefs of this imagined community. And then, we may see this procedure as itself a wise tactic upon ourselves – persuasion through the assumption of assent. At all events, the admonition to remember that Finlay is an artist only goes so far. His work may confine itself to the business of art. But it may still have within it impulses which go beyond what art alone can accomplish. Likewise, criticism may observe the proprieties of interpretation – and yet acknowledge that its object raises questions beyond this strict scope.

'Aestheticism'

What complicates further an attempt to talk about a world-view and its possible designs on our world in Finlay's work, is that some of its basic terms seem to constitute a specifically artistic language, whose grip on the world is uncertain. 'Artistic' in this sense: the world and our life in it is seen very largely through artistic genres and modes, the pastoral, the heroic, the elegiac, the idyll, the sublime. And we may wonder, are these categories a figurative language, a way of putting things for the purposes of art, which could be expressed in other terms? In that case, how do they translate out? (Into what politics? what ethics?) Perhaps we must see Finlay's work as operating with a closed system of symbols, internally articulate, but with no external purchase, really only 'about art'. Or on the other hand, there may be no question of translating out, because these categories are to be taken as literal models of our life in the world, or models at least of how it might be – life in effect translated into art. In that case, you might say that Finlay seems to take artistic 'conventions' much too literally, or that he is wilfully aestheticising – these visions never were and never could be true. Overall, the issue would be whether Finlay was offering an artistic treatment or version of the world (to be converted by us, into other terms) or whether he saw the world as essentially a work of art (or to be remade according to art's orders).

It may not be possible to resolve this question, but it can be clarified. Finlay is often accused of 'aestheticism', meaning that his art softens the hard edges of the world, or that it absorbs it, without due resistance, into a symbolic system. But this is to miss the point, or what I take to be Finlay's point at least. His 'aestheticism', his employment of an apparently artistic language in the depiction of the world, is not a matter of a knowing or deluded play of fictions – not exactly. Rather, his work specifically opposes the idea that the forms of art are merely 'fictions', arbitrarily constructed and imposed. The pastoral, the heroic, the idyll etc: these are proposed as idealisations. They are held up specifically as ideals, as the needful terms in which the world and human life is to be made meaningful; in that sense to be believed in. These are the terms in which Finlay's art speaks of the world, the language in which his reflections take place – but it is offered neither as a solely 'artistic' language, nor as the language of one man's 'personal mythology'. It claims a purchase on the world, as an idealisation of it. Furthermore, it is exemplary: it proposes itself as a public language – according to those terms, these ideals, we too should live. So it is a vision both put into practice in Finlay's work, and envisaged as the condition of the world generally.

At this point, of course, the same questions about translation and truth may recur. How should these terms, this vision have a bearing on our lives? What kind of credit or authority, even as ideals, can they be given? I don't know what answers there could be. But what can be said in a general way about Finlay's position is that our age has a widespread paranoia of meanings – finding them everywhere, and finding them always false or oppressive. Finlay, by contrast, seems to envisage a world which is filled with declared meanings – though very different ones from those now prevailing – and sees their maintenance, rather than their dismantling, as the necessary and difficult project. And from this point of view, art itself is given a special place in the world, as the bearer of these meanings (again, an art of a very different sort from that whose natural home is the modern art gallery). But one should observe that in a world – such as our own – where neither these ideals nor this role for art is acknowledged, the artist (Finlay) may be obliged to adopt a more tactical and more complex *modus operandi*. I'll return to this.

'Idealism'

Another proviso is necessary. Any sense of a cause, of another world envisaged and to be realised, is itself compounded in Finlay's work with opposing tones. Every positive, idealistic motion is beset by a conscious sense of loss, defeat, struggle. The classical world is looked back to, but long gone; its distance is recognised, even while its values are revived. The Revolution is defeated, consumed by its own idealistic energies; this defeat is to be mourned and memorialised, made as important as its aspirations. Every human good is opposed by forces of destruction – a Heraclitan motif, emphatically marked. So though the work may hold up ideals, it does not hold out much hope. And you might say that this returns it to the condition of art, simply for reasons of 'content': it offers no cause that could be actively subscribed to – it offers only a meditation on themes of greatness and catastrophe, the good life and its end.

But maybe the sense of a cause is not quite lost. True, if we picture still an ideal world from Finlay's work, certainly it is not of any familiar kind. It is neither the joyful collaborative effort of some progressive thought, nor the contented order-in-variety of conservatism. It is a world full of mournful reflections, struggle against the odds, piety towards 'the gods' in both tutelary and menacing roles. But at least that valuation, those meanings (albeit tragic ones) are present in it. At least the realisation of that sense of the world could be its cause. Or what was the stance of critique and opposition to the 'secular' or the 'liberal' concerned with in the first place?

Yet perhaps the temporal scheme which that stance seemed to imply (of original truth – loss – restoration) was misleading. Perhaps that scheme should be seen only as an analogy for – a way we can't help viewing – a permanent situation, where the supposed ideal is always lost, always to be borne in mind, always out of reach; where the revolution is held only as a perpetual possibility, perpetually beyond accomplishment. The vision comes down to an attitude; the cause, to maintaining it. But surely now we will say that this vision is essentially an artistic one, insofar as it has itself the structure of a work of art, a dynamic stasis, a balance of forces held in tension. Or might we say again that Finlay is only giving an artistic version (him being an artist) of something which, given a more worldly expression, might still lay claim to our more active commitment?

Realisation, Self-Reflection

Let me, for the last time, put this another way in terms of the role of works of art themselves. Finlay's world-view gives a particular place to art: it has a central place in the world as the bearer of meanings and ideals. He envisages a public, a religious function for art, and thus a world in which it would perform this function. So what the artist does is, in a sense, a form of 'direct action'. He can create work which performs this role; or at least offers to perform it, and the work becomes not a picture of the world it envisages, but an instance of it (an anticipatory instance). The vision may to an extent be realised, by being enacted in this way.

We can see Finlay doing this. Just as his work in general seems to project from itself an imagined discourse-community, so sometimes it also projects a world of belief. Not only the Temple and the Sacred Grove, but many individual works employ a mode of prophecy, by implying a world in which they would have a recognised place – standing, so to speak, as the sacred objects and places to a belief that is yet to be realised. And we, as viewers, may then imaginatively enter into the believing role this offers to us. (The Garden itself is too rich and complex a manifestation of Finlay's vision to make this point clearly. It is both an image and a microcosm of a world which declares its meanings at every corner; it is also an act of observance, a working model of pious cultivation.)

On the other hand, this realisation through art can never be a complete one. The artist cannot do it all; cannot just designate such functions to a work. It will never be a matter simply of filling up the world with the right sort of art. The world must comply – and the world as it is, is not such that art can perform the function aspired to. The actual situation of Finlay's art, like anyone else's, is as a marginal intervention. Now some artist might embrace the role of dissident, or of marginal nudger; this is the role that Finlay's work does perform, but not one that it fully accepts. Another artist, meanwhile, might naively try to perform this ideal function, regardless of how the world otherwise went creating indeed a dream-world of private belief. But a self-conscious art in this situation, both aspiring to this ideal function and aware that it is not now available (not anymore, being lost, or not yet, but in some possible future) is drawn into self-reflection. It must consider its position, as between the art that it is, and the art it aspires to be. It must picture itself.

This takes two forms. In one, the work stands also propaganda – propaganda by example – it consciously stakes a claim for a world in which it would have this role (The Temple is propaganda for Temples.) In another, it turns to reflection upon this lack and becomes a meditation upon the loss and out-of-reachness of the place it desires. (The Temple is a monument to Temples.) In the face of this predicament, it must tell of as well as instantiate its designs; it must dwell upon its present state as well as dwelling hopefully in a possible future, registering that future's present remoteness, and take on an aspect of longing. Finlay's I think, is such a self-conscious art. It assumes a position in the world which it in fact lacks – and then, in response to this adverse circumstance, it makes that sense of lack and distance both its cause (something to be urged against) and its theme (something to be meditated on).

We may be tempted into thinking that Finlay's designs upon the world are in fact fully realised in this art. For what matter does it leave over? What further realisation does it hold out? All its active impulses seem to be absorbed into its own reflections. Even any residual sense of a 'cause', being so far from accomplishment, may itself finally become only a further theme for contemplation. The work, and the responses it asks of us, would revert to a mode of stilled longing (perpetual lamentation, perpetual anticipation). But the question remains: is this only a response to circumstance, a work for the time being? Is this mode of unfulfillable longing the very heart of Finlay's vision – which would again make the vision itself art-like? Or is it rather an artistic handling, an artistic recognition of the world as it is – but which might conceivably, remotely change, and then the art would finally come into its own?

Note

See also Tom Lubbock, 'The Once and Future Revolution', *Independent on Sunday*, 9 February 1992.

Appendix A
Poor. Old. Tired. Horse.:
Contributors, 1961–67

NUMBER ONE
Contributors: Pete Brown, Ian Hamilton Finlay, Anselm Hollo, Tatsuji Miyoshi, Lorine Niedecker, Alan Riddell, Gael Turnbull, and Fyodor Tyutchev (translated by Edwin Morgan).

NUMBER TWO
Contributors: Tuomas Anhava, Dave Ball, George Mackay Brown, Cid Corman, Attila József, Shimpei Kusano, Lesley Lendrum, Vladimir Mayakovsky, Jerome Rothenberg, and Gerry A. Zdanwicz.

NUMBER THREE
Contributors: Guillaume Apollinaire, R. Crombie Saunders, Larry Eigner, Lawrence Ferlinghetti, Robert Garioch, Libby Houston, Giacomo Leopardi, Edwin Morgan, César Lopez Nunez, Veng, and Jonathan Williams.

NUMBER FOUR
Contributors: Helen B. Cruickshank, Spike Hawkins, J.F. Hendry, Bernard Kops, Suzan Livingstone, Tom McGrath, Alexander McNeish, Heinrich von Morungen, Lorine Niedecker and Georg Trakl.

NUMBER FIVE
Contributors: Hans Arp, Pete Brown, Tao Ch'ien, e.e. cummings, Theodore Enslin, Robert Garioch, Pekka Lounela, William McGonagall, Alexander McNeish, Marvin Malone, Pablo Neruda,

Appendix A 247

Vasko Popa, Alan Riddell, Armand Schwerner, and Andrei Voznesensky.

NUMBER SIX
Contributors: Augusto de Campos, Larry Eigner, Günter Grass, Spike Hawkins, J.F. Hendry, Attila József, Bernard Kops, Marcelo Moura, Michael Shayer, Mary Ellen Solt, Pedro Xisto and Louis Zukofsky.

NUMBER SEVEN
Contributors: Paul Blackburn, Paul Celan, Robert Creeley, Piero Heliczer, Richard Huelsenbeck, Hamish McLaren, Alexander McNeish, Bud Neill, Crombie Saunders, Kurt Schwitters, Robert Simmons, Mario Trufelli and Andrei Voznesensky.

NUMBER EIGHT
Contributors: Ian Hamilton Finlay, Spike Hawkins, A. Khlebnikov, Velemir Khlebnikov, El Lissitsky, Vladimir Mayakovsky, Yury Pantratov, Mary Ellen Solt, Peter Stitt, Alexander Tvardovskii, Andrei Voznesensky and Jonathan Williams.

NUMBER NINE
Contributors: Paul Fort, John Gray, Libby Houston, Ronald Johnson, Paulo Marcos de Andrade, Lorine Niedecker, and Rocco Scotellaro, with decorations by Peter Stitt.

NUMBER TEN
A '*concrete number*' with contributions from Augusto de Campos, Ian Hamilton Finlay, Robert Frame, Eugen Gomringer, Anselm Hollo, Dom Sylvester Houédard, Robert Lax and Edwin Morgan.

NUMBER ELEVEN
Contributors: Guillaume Apollinaire, J.F. Hendry, Horace, Renzo Laurano, Ann McGarrell, Christian Morgenstern, John Picking, Michael Shayer, Kurt Sigel and Robert Simmons.

NUMBER TWELVE
Contributors: Lewis Carroll, Ian Hamilton Finlay, J.F. Hendry, Dom Sylvester Houédard, Ernst Jandl, Edwin Morgan, Mary Ellen Solt, and Paul de Vree. Optical designs from paintings by Jeffrey Steele.

NUMBER THIRTEEN
Contributors: Guillaume Apollinaire, Ian Hamilton Finlay, Ronald Johnson, Marvin Malone, Lorine Niedecker, Nicole Rabetaud, Jerome Rothenberg and Mary Ellen Solt. Drawings by John Furnival.

NUMBER FOURTEEN
'– *Visual* – *Semiotic* – *Concrete* –' Contributors: Pierre Albert-Birot, Ian Hamilton Finlay, John Furnival, Heinz Gappmayr, Mary Ellen Solt and Pedro Xisto.

NUMBER FIFTEEN
Contributors: R.L. Cook, Theodore Enslin, Ian Hamilton Finlay, Libby Houston, George Mackay Brown, Hamish McLaren, Edwin Morgan and Eli Siegel. Drawings by Margot Sandeman.

NUMBER SIXTEEN
'*STICKS STONES/NAMES BONES*' Contributors: Pierre Albert-Birot, anonymous copywriter, Barry Cole, Ian Hamilton Finlay, Spike Hawkins, Hermann Hesse, Ernst Jandl, Francis Ponge, Eli Siegel, Tristan Tzara, Enrique Uribe, Jonathan Williams and Edward Wright.

NUMBER SEVENTEEN
Contributors: poems Robert Lax, drawings Emil Antonucci.

NUMBER EIGHTEEN
Contributors: Drawings and layout by Bridget Riley, England. Writings and script by Ad Reinhardt, USA.

NUMBER NINETEEN

    io and the
    ox-eye
    daisy

Contributors: Ronald Johnson, design John Furnival.

NUMBER TWENTY

    the tug
    the barge . . .

Appendix A   249

Contributors: Ian Hamilton Finlay, drawings by Peter Lyle.

NUMBER TWENTY-ONE

>   ilha
>   brilha
>   tranqüïla

Contributors: Edgard Braga, Augusto de Campos and Nigel Sutton.

NUMBER TWENTY-TWO
Contributors: Charles Biederman: *An Art Credo*, Typographer: Philip Steadman

NUMBER TWENTY-THREE
teapoth 23
Contributors: Pierre Albert-Birot, Theodore Enslin, Ian Hamilton Finlay, Ronald Johnson, George Mackay Brown, Edwin Morgan, Eli Siegel, Gael Turnbull and Max Weber. Designed by John Furnival.

NUMBER TWENTY-FOUR
Concrete Poetry at the Brighton ('67) Festival, a record in photographs by Graham Keen. Contributors: Stephen Bann, Claus Bremer, Kenelm Cox, Ian Hamilton Finlay, John Furnival, Eugen Gomringer, Hansjörg Mayer and Edwin Morgan. Designed by Alistair Cant.

NUMBER TWENTY-FIVE
'ONE WORD POEMS'
Contributors: Alkman, Oswald de Andrade, Stephen Bann, Kenelm Cox, Hugh Creighton Hill, Ian Hamilton Finlay, Astrid Gillis, Giles Gordon, Ernst Jandl, Edward Lucie-Smith, George Mackay Brown, Stuart Mills, Alan Riddell, Jerome Rothenberg, Aram Saroyan, Martin Seymour-Smith, Dick Sheeler, Eli Siegel, Gael Turnbull, Jonathan Williams, Jerome Rothenberg, Pedro Xisto and Douglas Young. Design and Calligraphy by Jim Nicholson.

Appendix B
Ian Hamilton Finlay: Serpentine Gallery Exhibition 1977: List of Works

(Commentaries by Stephen Bann)

I Neo-classical Room

We are to imagine a neo-classical interior, perhaps a small temple opening upon a garden as at Stourhead or Stowe. The emblems, inscriptions and other objects assembled here testify to the reinvocation of classical themes. But this is on a scale of intimacy which suggests the generic title of 'chamber sculpture'. The classic from the modern period, Max Bill, is paid the delightful homage of a 'Marble paper boat' reminiscent of his work, while the mythical Homeric hero receives the tribute of a contemporary *graffito*. As Stephen Bann writes of the emblems – images and texts conjoined – which form the major part of this section, Finlay 'mobilises the gap between the modern period and that of the Renaissance, just as the emblematists themselves signified the gap between their own period and the Graeco-Roman world through the choice of classical tags and quotations. He sets before us a cultural tissue in which these various levels – the Classical, the Renaissance and the Modern – are indissolubly united'.

'Even Gods Have Dwelt In Woods'. 1976
Stone. With John Andrew
Lent by the Scottish Arts Council

Ulysses Was Here. 1977
Bronze fibreglass. With Leicester Thomas

Small Is Quite Beautiful. 1976
Stone. With Richard Grasby
Lent by the Scottish Arts Council

'Big E' (at Midway). Set of 3: plain 'E', bronze 'E', and gold 'E'. 1976/7
Stone. With John Andrew
Plain 'E' lent by the Scottish Arts Council

Amphorae (aircraft carrier torsos). 1976
Stone. With Keith Bailey

'Woodland Is Pleasing To The Muses'. 1977
Slate. With Richard Grasby

'A Niun' Altra'. 1977
Slate. With Richard Grasby

Marble Paper Boats (set of 3). 1976
With Christopher Hall

'Of famous *Arcady* ye are'. 1977
Slate. With Michael Harvey

'Et In Arcadia Ego' – After Nicolas Poussin. 1975
Stone. With John Andrew
Lent by the Scottish National Gallery of Modern Art

'Et In Arcadia Ego' – After Giovanni Francesco Guercino. 1977
Stone. With John Andrew

'Cominus Et Eminus'. 1977
Stone. With John Andrew

'Éternelle action des Paras immobiles'. 1977
Marble. With John Andrew

Lyre (Mk. 2). 1977
Stone. With John Andrew

'Semper Festina Lente'. 1977
Stone. With John Andrew

Apollo and Daphne (after Bernini). 1977
Granite, marble. With Richard Grasby

'Italy Cast a Shadow'. (Elegiac World Cup Inscription). 1977
Stone. With Richard Grasby

Angels, Bandits, Saints. 1975
Slate. With Keith Bailey

In Memoriam 'The Roberts'. 1977
Marble. With Keith Bailey

NOTE: 'Even Gods Have Dwelt In Woods', 'Woodland Is Pleasing To The Muses', 'A Niun' Altra', 'Cominus Et Eminus', 'Éternelle action des Paras immobiles', 'Semper Festina Lente', and 'Angels, Bandits, Saints' are based on the emblems printed in *Heroic Emblems*, Ian Hamilton Finlay and Ron Costley, Z Press, USA

II Neon Room

The neon poem is the successor to the 'fauve' poems of Finlay's first collection of concrete poems, *Rapel* (1963). Its intense luminosity, replacing the original strategy of coloured printing inks, allows an immediacy to the effects of metaphor which excludes any but the simplest of texts. The impression is at one and the same time voluptuous and ascetic, like Walter Pater's prose in its striving to convey the immediacy of pure sensation. Finlay takes this Paterian ideal back to its Platonic antecedents, proposing the poem as 'plain sensation refined till it becomes an aspect of The Good'.

Sea Pink
Wave Ave
Lily-Cobbled
Wave Sheaf
Strawberry Camouflage

1977. With Ron Costley and Merson Signs

III Midway Room

The Battle of Midway was fought between the fleets of the United States and Japan in June 1942. The Japanese strategists had long been preparing for a 'decisive fleet action' in the Pacific, and the Commander in Chief of the Japanese fleet rightly calculated that a threat to Midway Island – the westernmost outpost of the Hawaiian island chain – would compel the Americans to engage their comparatively weaker forces. In effect the battle was finally decided in America's favour, and marked the turning point both of the War in the Pacific, and, arguably, of the entire World War.

In another emblem, Finlay equates the entry into the 'dark wood' of the battle with the famous opening lines of Dante's *Divine Comedy*. Here he uses the cover of a Renaissance pastoral to enact the conflict of 4 June 1942, when the four ships of Admiral Nagumo's Carrier Striking Force were destroyed by dive-bombers from their American counterparts, Enterprise and Hornet (Yorktown being the major American casualty). The dramatic success of this action depended on the fact that the American planes were able to engage the Japanese fleet at its most vulnerable – whilst each of the carriers bore a full deck load of armed and fuelled aircraft. The effect of American bombing was therefore to ignite petrol tanks, bombs and torpedoes, causing unquenchable conflagration. The analogy of the Renaissance garden, familiar from the original emblem books, shows us the carriers as antique hives and the American attack planes as swarming bees; the conflagration must be imagined as one of overspilling honey. Rose trees in tubs fill out the pastoral conception, while signifying at the same time the Ocean, in whose lush distances the opposing carriers were concealed from one another.

Battle of Midway, June 1942, Tableau
The Tableau was constructed with the assistance of James Stodart and James Boyd. The 2 silkscreen prints, 'Battle of Midway' and 'Midway Inscription' were realised with Ron Costley, 1977. The photographs of the Battle were lent by the Japanese and American Embassies. A version of 'Battle of Midway' was realised as a tile, with Laurie Clark, 1975.

IV Embroideries

Douglas Hall writes of Finlay's collaboration with Jud Fine, on which this series of embroideries is based: 'It is not merely that he has found a collaborator to express, still within the strict limits of a visual poem, an "epic" quality, a "fierceness" that he longed for. It is also that for the first time a degree of personal expressionism through artistic gesture or handwriting has become an element in the work, to be reckoned with alongside the verbal, conceptual element, and over above the charm and perfection that his other collaborators had always imprinted on his work. If I am right in seeing this as a bridge that has been crossed, the possibilities that it opens up are limitless and exciting'.

8 embroideries, with Pamela Campion. 1977

Poire/Loire
Paper Boat/Hat
Sail/Pear
Sea/Sky/Line
Art/Decal
Hard-Edged
Ark/Arc
Patch

These embroideries are based on drawings done with Jud Fine, 1975/6.

    V Outdoor Room (with screened-off area for slides)
Although the effect of Finlay's garden at Stonypath cannot be successfully recreated, Dave Paterson's slide sequence gives a memorable impression of it. and And in the great variety of objects assembled in this room, the 'pastoral' element in his work is consistently stressed. The customary garden furniture of benches, sundials and tubs is pressed into poetic use – even watering-cans, flowerpots and paving stones are qualified to become poetic. 'Wild stones' removed from the sea-shore and inscribed with texts remind us of Finlay's constant reference to the Ocean, whilst the bronzed fibreglass tortoises as Panzer Leaders push the metaphor from tank warfare into unexpected territory.

'Panzer Leader'. 1977
Bronze fibreglass. With Richard Grasby

A Small Interruption In The Light (Locus Brevis In Luce Intermissus). 1977
Slate. With Michael Harvey

3 inscribed stones (set). 1977
Stones from the seashore. With Keith Bailey

Daisies. 1977
Bronze fibreglass. With John Andrew

Tree-Shells. 1972/77. Tub, label, tree

Homage to K(ettle's) Y(ard). 1977
Large English pebble. With Keith Bailey

'Even Gods Have Dwelt In Woods' (plant trough). 1977
Stone. With John Andrew

2 Watering-Cans. 1977
With Peter Grant

'Snow Bark' (bench). 1977
Stone. With Maxwell Allan

Boat Names/Numbers:
D19 (HMS Glamorgan, Guided Missile Destroyer)
Coastal Boy (Fishing boat: A534)
Fern (Fishing boat: BF205)
1977. Painted wood. With Peter Grant

Selection of tiles published by Ian Hamilton Finlay's Wild Hawthorn Press, 1975/7

Butter poem. 1977
Wood, butter. With John R. Thorpe

H)our Lady (folding sundial). 1977
Wood. With John R. Thorpe.
This sundial is based on the page from *Airs Waters Graces*, Ian Hamilton Finlay and Ron Costley, 1975

The Sea's Waves (folding poem). 1977
Wood. With John R. Thorpe.

This is based on the Wild Hawthorn Press card, Ian Hamilton Finlay and Stuart Barrie, 1973

Improvisation No. I, photograph. 1976
With Carl Heideken

Ceramic collaborations, Ian Hamilton Finlay and David Ballantyne, 1976–7
Collaborations, Ian Hamilton Finlay and Denis Barns (Livingston Town Artist), 1977

Named after Warplanes
Ian Hamilton Finlay and Dave Paterson. Set of 6 photographs, with texts based on Japanese WW2 warplane categories. 1977

Max Planck Institute Garden Poems. 1977
Ian Hamilton Finlay with Ron Costley
Set of photographs of the poems in the garden of the Max Planck Institute, near Stuttgart, West Germany. Architect: J. Brenner & Partner, Stuttgart. Project Manager: H. Buchwald.
The poems were commissioned by the Max Planck Society, Munich. Photographs by P. Walser, Stuttgart.

Stonypath
35 mm slides of Ian and Sue Finlay's garden, taken by Dave Paterson. 1976

VI Information Area/Print Room

This is a small selection of the enormous number of printed works which Finlay has published through the Wild Hawthorn Press. It is supplemented by other works on a modest scale, bronze Pierrots and anagrammatical busts concealing the names of ancient and modern worthies – aspects of his most recent work juxtaposed with new versions of older poems like 'Wave Rock', which now appears in a folding version.

3 Pierrots. 1977
Steel, pewter, copper, on wood. With Andrew Coomber.
Based on Ian Hamilton Finlay's miniature balsa glider, 'Meadow Ranger'.

Wave Rock (folding poem). 1977
Incised and painted on wood. With John R. Thorpe.
This is based on the calligraphic version of Wave/Rock realised with George L. Thomson for the new edition of his book, 'Better Handwriting'.
See also Wave Rock, glass, 1966

Lemons, Netted. 1977
Painted wood. With Peter Grant

3 Anagrammatical Busts. (Apollinaire, Epicurus, Juan Gris.) 1977
Ceramic. With Roger Bunn

Ulysses Was Here (small version). 1977
Bronze fibreglass
Edition of 15

Selection of Ian Hamilton Finlay postcards, published by the Wild Hawthorn Press

Selection of recent Ian Hamilton Finlay prints, published by the Wild Hawthorn Press

'*Trophies of War*' (stone reliefs from the collection of the Scottish Arts Council). Ian Hamilton Finlay, with John Andrew, Richard Grasby, and unidentified Saint-Just Vigilante letter-carvers, 1975/85.

The original title of this Relief was '*Small is Quite Beautiful*' (1975). It is one of the two Reliefs that in Finlay's words 'were removed from the S.A.C. Charlotte Square HQ in the famous 'commando raid' carried out by an international volunteer squad of Saint-Just Vigilantes. Some of the names were added to the reliefs in an earlier episode (involving snow and sledges and other elements of melodrama!); other names are those of the 'war guilty' (of i.e., The Little Spartan War) – added at the rate of two letters each day while the S.A.C refused to uphold its own legal Charter by giving advice to Strathclyde Region (on Little Sparta's Garden Temple).'

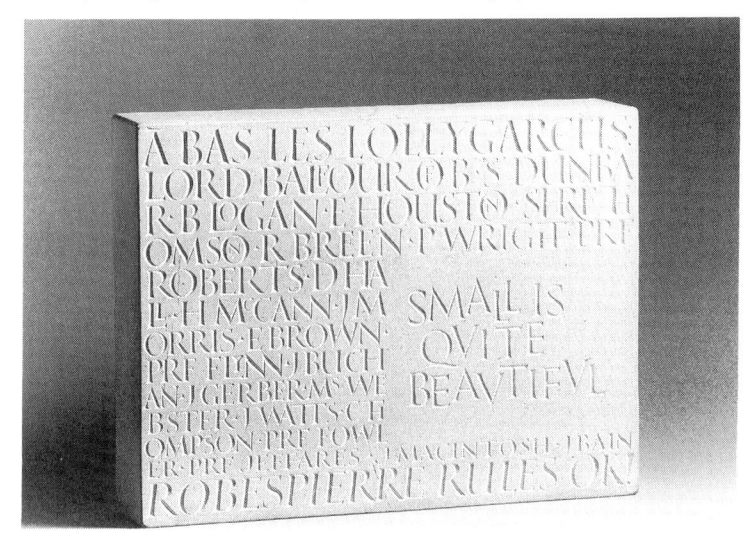

Appendix C
Spartan Defence: Ian Hamilton Finlay in conversation with Peter Hill

PH: Before we speak about the problems you have had to face over the past year or so it might be worth speaking about the philosophy behind your garden temple at Little Sparta. As one of the most beautiful collaborations between man and nature that I have ever seen, I wonder how it all began?

IHF: Every question can be answered on different levels, or, that is, has a number of different answers. As a building, the garden temple began as a cow-byre which we converted into a gallery and then, over a period, into a garden temple, or as we at first described it a 'Canova-type temple' – referring to the temple built by the Italian neo-classicist. This was not to equate our garden temple with Canova's temple but to explain it by means of a precedent: a building which housed works of art but which did not present itself specifically as an 'art gallery'. But in another way one could say that our garden temple began because we had a garden, and we have a garden because we were given a semi-derelict cottage surrounded by an area of hillside (wild moorland). This moorland represented a possibility, and produced our response. (I say 'our' to include Sue Finlay who has been, from the beginning, my collaborator on the garden.)

PH: For well over a year you have been engaged in battle with the Hamilton Rates Authorities. How did this begin, and is there an end in sight?

IHF: Our battle is not with the Hamilton Rates Authorities but with Strathclyde Region, of which the Hamilton authority is a minor detachment, taking its orders from above. The dispute began when the Region withdrew the discretionary rates relief on our building, initially justifying this on the grounds that we had no Scottish Arts Council grant, and were unknown: 'No one here has heard of you'. Subsequently, the dispute became a War, a term I use to acknowledge the 'limitless' aspect of what has been happening, the absence of law (legality) as a fixed point in the Region's thinking, the use of force, the refusal of discussion by the Region's bureaucrats. As you know, the Saint-Just Vigilantes have removed two stone reliefs of mine from the Scottish Arts Council's public collection, and the names of the guilty (in the Little Spartan War) are being added to these, as well as an inscription. This inscription reads 'EVENTS ARE A DISCOURSE'. Now, in a civilised society such a 'discourse' when it has gone on for a long time, and contains disorderly and violent aspects, (in this case, the use of the Sheriff's Officer and the Police, the Saint-Just Vigilante 'commando type' counterattack on the SAC's Charlotte Square HQ, the confrontation between the Region and the US State Department and therefore – implicitly – the US Sixth Fleet, etc.) would naturally, by a general agreement or desire, become a verbal discourse. But discussion is excluded (as I have said) by the Region's bureaucrats. And events are a discourse for a few people only; generally speaking, they remain emblematic, obscure – emblems *without* their accompanying commentaries, which should be supplied by the culture, the press, and the critics. As you know, there has been a total absence of comment from the Scottish art critics. One has to say that there is a deliberate refusal to look at the content of the conflict and to bring that into consciousness (on all sides) to resolve the dispute. The War is simply the mode of utterance of a barbaric society which *won't speak to itself.*

PH: Over the past year you have invoked the help of the Saint-Just Vigilantes. Who are they, and how have they helped you?

IHF: The Saint-Just Vigilantes began as an entirely imaginary organisation, invoked in the prose commentary on one of my pieces in the exhibition – in collaboration with Ian Appleton – 'The Third Reich Revisited'. The complete version of this exhibition will be shown at the

Appendix C 261

Southampton Civic Art Gallery during 1984. (The original showing was at the Tartar Gallery, Edinburgh, in 1982). In one of the sequences, the 'scenario' assumes an Iranian-type revolution, leading to a process known as 'Desecularisation'; the Scottish Arts Council HQ, and Charlotte Square itself, are thrown (as it were) to the corrective forces of Imperialist Ecology – in short, they are taken over by pine trees and foxgloves; but the verbal commentary explains that the original sacking of the SAC was accomplished by the 'Ayatollah Aesthetes' and the 'Saint-Just Vigilantes' (two groups, it is clear, with a decent dislike of democratic-pluralist state-aided art). Subsequently, it was decided – who knows exactly how – that the Saint-Just Vigilantes should have an actual existence. Appropriately, their first appearance was in a demonstration which took place outside the SAC HQ in the autumn of 1982. Now, Saint-Just has been called 'a thinker of actions' and action is in fact the basis of the S-J Vs: they have discovered themselves (their identity) in action; their leaders have emerged in the course of action: there is no list of members, and there is no list of rules saying what an S-J V is. Yet, the S-J Vs are undoubtedly an organisation in so far as it is the role of an organisation to have aims and to have the capacity to carry them out in a deliberate way. As you know, the works stolen from our garden temple by the Region are now in the vault of some unnamed bank; amusingly, several people (including one newspaper features editor) have seriously asked me why the S-J Vs don't identify the bank and carry out a raid to recover the works. Such is the *mythological identity* of the S-J Vs.

PH: Could you describe the First Battle of Little Sparta and your subsequent encounters with Sandy Walker, the Sheriff's Officer?

IHF: It is impossible to describe The First Battle of Little Sparta as history has not yet decided what actually took place. The Monument (bronze and brick) will be erected in the Spring of this year, at what was 'Checkpoint Sandy' – Little Sparta's Southern Frontier for that day. *Poetry Nation Review*'s extensive photodocumentary on the Battle begins with a quotation from Gratien's Introduction to Saint-Just's *Oeuvres choisies*: 'Giving oneself up to this sculpture presupposes a fundamental lack of respect towards what is considered to constitute reality'. This could define the Battle as a kind of 'heroic' extension of the Gilbert and George mode. Alternatively, one knows the 'sculpture' to which Saint-Just 'gave himself up'. To adapt Marianne Moore's famous definition of poetry, this was not 'an imaginary garden with real toads' but a real garden, and not with imaginary but real Police. In his *Despatches From The Little Spartan War* (a chronicle of the War composed in episodes), Patrick Eyres says of '4th February 1983', 'Choreographed with military precision, art confronted political reality and, in triumph, captured the imagination of the public... Icy, bleak dawn reveals defence in depth astride the single approach... "Checkpoint Sandy", named in honour of the Sheriff's Officer Alexander 'Sandy' Walker, stands before the bridge. YOU ARE NOW ENTERING LITTLE SPARTA warns the red and white counterweight barrier reminiscent of the Berlin Wall. The Checkpoint is covered by a camouflaged Mk. IV Panzer hull down to enfilade. Minefields stretch as far as the eye can see. Two flags rustle in the morning air. The Red Cross locates the Casualty Clearing Station and offers safety to neutrals. . . .' One could describe the Battle as allegorical – that is, as a dramatic allegory of the fact that ideas were in conflict; but one cannot describe as merely allegorical an event in which the presence of the *actual* was more obvious than the presence of the *idea*.

PH: How do you feel the Scottish Arts Council has emerged from the whole situation, and following on from that do you have any strong feelings about the support you have had, and have not had, from various quarters?

IHF: The Scottish Arts Council is a public body with a legal charter, and this charter unambiguously sets it out as an object of the Council that it should (I quote) 'develop and improve the knowledge, understanding and practice of the Arts . . .' and 'advise and co-operate with Departments of our Government, local authorities and other bodies on any matters concerned whether directly or indirectly . . .' with the Arts. In so far as the War may be considered as a rates dispute, it hinges on the nature of the disputed building. As is well known, the SAC has consistently refused to advise the Region as to whether it considers the building to be a garden temple, or not. Therefore, the SAC has not acted in terms of its own legal charter. In this, it obviously has the support of its various committees, Literature Committee, Art Committee,

Appendix C 263

and so on. Clearly, officials and committee members who cannot accept the legal basis of the organisation, should not be part of the organisation. Moreover, apart from the question of the building (temple or not), there are the serious questions concealed in the rating dispute. These cannot be separated from the 'knowledge, understanding and practice of the Arts'; yet the SAC has persistently set them aside, and those on its committees who have been approached by members of the public, in correspondence, have refused to discuss them. As for the question of support 'from various quarters', I do have strong feelings, not about the having or not having support, but about the deliberate refusal of the culture – by which I mean the art critics, the art editors, the gallery directors, the artists (etc.) – to try to look seriously at the *implicit* and *general* (not particular, not financial) questions involved. Scottish art editors and art critics have carefully distanced themselves from the press reporting of the War. The culture has behaved as if its existence is something entirely separate from what *actually goes on.* This is how the Greeks understood barbarians – people who are *unable* to discuss.

PH: One of your short stories, *The Money*, describes the problems faced by an artist attempting to claim social security benefit. To what extent do you feel the state should support the artist, especially the young artist who these days is forced to live on £25 per week, at best, who probably leaves college, or whatever, full of energy and enthusiasm and who very quickly becomes disillusioned with the established art world and with the society which perpetuates its position?

IHF: The story is not about the problems of an artist on social security but about the contrast between a naïve aspiration towards objectivity and a social temporising. The question of the extent to which the state should support the artist, cannot be seriously considered apart from the questions of the *nature* of Art and the nature of the state. For example, I have just said 'state' with a small 's' when it is perfectly possible to have State with a capital 'S'; and though the Arts Council Charter uses 'Art' with a capital 'A', it should really – where the Arts Council is concerned – be used with a small 'a', the Arts, or arts, being regarded by the Arts Council as somewhere between a tourist attraction and a social service of a less essential sort. If anyone doubts this, let him (or her) consider the typical statement quoted in the *Scotsman*: 'We want to see Scottish Opera providing a reasonable service of opera within Scotland within the funds available'. This is Mr H. McCann, Deputy Director of the Scottish Arts Council; the incredible thing is not that he said this, but that it is quoted without comment by the newspaper's Art Editor and it will be read as a reasonable statement on an aspect of the arts. 'We want to see the Scottish Gas Board providing a reasonable service of gas within Scotland within the funds available'. The fact is, that it is the 'pluralist democracies' – the states with a small 's' – which have reduced the art critic, art editor (etc.), to functionaries of the state. And the so-called 'avant-garde' is simply democratic state art. What I am saying is, that your question cannot be answered (just now) because it conceals too many other questions; and these are the questions which there is a general agreement – general as regards the Arts Council, the artists, the press, the culture as a whole – to *suppress*. Inadequately, one can say that there is a total and as yet unacknowledged contradiction between the idea of pluralist democracy and the state-aided art. And that this contradiction reveals itself in the characteristic feeling of an absence of *necessity* in exhibitions today.

PH: What are the major influences behind your work and how, once these bureaucratic interruptions are over, do you see your work progressing?

IHF: The 'bureaucratic interruptions' are part of my work, in the sense that they arise from the nature of my work, and are not resolved because the culture is unable to move from the incoherent or emblematic statement of the event (as such), to the conscious statement, in terms of thought – here, of between art and law. I am interested, therefore, in changing the culture. Till one actually does this, one is merely challenging it. I am extremely concerned with the details of Art – that things should be properly and professionally done: at the same time, I am personally impatient of the categories of 'artist', 'poet', 'sculptor', 'gardener', and so on: these are useful and essential categories but I see that gardening, for instance, easily passes into politics – and this is factually confirmed by the history of gardening, as witness Stowe, or Girardin's Ermenonville (where Rousseau died); it is in this perspective that I regard my *Five Columns for The Kröller-Müller*, which is

Appendix C

subtitled *A Fifth Column for The Kröller-Müller* or *Corot-Saint-Just*.

PH: Your work unites language and image, or language and matter, in a very precise way. Do you see the two as indivisible?

IHF: My relation with language is extremely difficult. I have never understood the 'easy' relation with language of other (present-day) Scottish writers. Language is an aspect of being, and as there is no single *kind* of being (qualitatively speaking) so there is no single 'being of language'. I understand language (in my work, as opposed to correspondence, casual conversation, and so on) as an effort to find a mode of language which is true to a relevant mode of being. In fact (practically speaking), it always turns out that the temporary resolution of the language difficulty occurs through a temporary intuition of a suitable form. The influence on my work is the Western Tradition (unacknowledged, as one knows, by Strathclyde Region, which is in essence one of the most barbarous and backward states in the USSR). I am particularly interested in the Pre-Socratic Greeks. And for some time I have felt inspired by the neo-classical triumvirate of Robespierre, Saint-Just and J.L. David. These three created that astonishing idealist pastoral, the French Revolution (whose Virgil was Rousseau). Presumably my work will 'progress' towards my being in prison, unless the necessity of a revolution (a return to Western Traditions) is understood first.

PH: An article written by Patrick Eyres entitled 'The Third Reich Revisited' published in *Cencrastus* focuses on an exhibition of your work held at the Tartar Gallery, Edinburgh. What were the influences behind this body of work?

IHF: 'The Third Reich Revisited' was The Little Spartan War in an earlier form. It was – is – an attempt to raise (in a necessarily roundabout way) the questions which our culture does not want to put in idea-form. The exhibition consists of drawings and commentaries. Most of the drawings are of buildings, some imaginary, some real (or some which were real in Hitler's time). Likewise, the commentaries include invented and actual history, used in such a way that one can't be sure what is 'true' and what is not. For example, one drawing shows a set of my sundials on the outer wall of Speer's Zeppelinfeld (scene of the Nazi rallies). The sundials are invention (it is necessary to say this because one or two people actually thought I had created sundials for the Zeppelinfeld), while the commentary contains a quotation from Speer, concerning the sundials – not (as you might think) another invention, but Speer's comment to me on the drawings (on which I had asked his opinion). This mixture of the real and invented is important because it gives a kind of *pressing* quality to the projects; they are not mere mythology (far less whimsies); and they are therefore related to events – things which happened, or might happen: and after a time the exhibition seemed to extend itself, as it were, into The Little Spartan War. In the case of the War, the position is reversed; instead of drawings and commentaries which might have been events, one has events which might turn out to be Art (except that the Police and Sheriff's Officers are not a normal 'art content'); the similarity lies in the fact that both the exhibition and the War are a kind of *circumlocution of incoherence*, a pun or play on unidentified ideas – which is just how Robert Cockcroft sees his long poem ('Gritstone Upon Granite') on The First Battle of Little Sparta: '. . . Where the four champions (led by Metaphor) / Rode out, I sat in spirit and pun / In the Red Cross Minor Traveller...' (The Minor Traveller was the ambulance which attended the Battle.) The War had produced a quantity of art; what it has not yet produced (in Britain as opposed to Europe) is serious, didactic *thought* on its *causes* – the chief of which is, that where the Arts once overlapped with Religion, they now overlap with tourism and entertainment, and there is no form or mode for the non-secular in our society.

(1984)

Copyright Acknowledgements

EDWIN MORGAN, 'To Ian Hamilton Finlay' from Collected Poems. © Edwin Morgan 1966, 1990. Reprinted by permission of Carcanet Press, Manchester.

Early Finlay, from *Cencrastus*, No. 22, 1986. © Edwin Morgan 1986, 1991. (This was reprinted in *Crossing the Border*, Carcanet Press, Manchester, 1990.)

Poor. Old. Tired. Horse. from *Lines Review*, No. 26, 1968. © Edwin Morgan 1968.

Finlay in the 70s and 80s, from *Evening Will Come They Will Sew The Blue Sail*, Graeme Murray, Edinburgh, 1991. © Edwin Morgan 1991.

SUE INNES, from the *Scotsman* magazine Vol 9, No. 3, 1988. © Sue Innes 1988.

STEPHEN BANN, Concrete Poetry, from *Architectural Review*, Vol. 139, No. 830, 1966. © Stephen Bann 1966.

Ian Hamilton Finlay – An Imaginary Portrait, from *Ian Hamilton Finlay*, exhibition catalogue, Serpentine Gallery, London, 1977. © Stephen Bann 1977. The exhibition was presented by the Arts Council of Great Britain.

Nature Over Again After Poussin: Some Discovered Landscapes from *Nature Over Again After Poussin*, exhibition catalogue, Collins Exhibition Hall, University of Strathclyde, Glasgow 1980. © Stephen Bann 1980.

A Luton Arcadia: Ian Hamilton Finlay's contribution to the English Neo-classical tradition, from *Journal of Garden History*, Vol. 13, Nos 1 & 2, 1993. © Stephen Bann 1992.

(From a talk given at the symposium, 'Rediscovering the British Garden' organised by the American Institute of Architects, Washington, DC, 1992.)

SIMON CUTTS, The Aesthetic of Ian Hamilton Finlay, from *Form*, No. 10, 1969. © Simon Cutts 1969.

KATHLEEN RAINE, 'Stonypath' from *Collaborations*, exhibition catalogue, Kettle's Yard, Cambridge, 1977. © Kathleen Raine 1977.

R.C. KENEDY, Ian Hamilton Finlay from *Art International*, Vol. XVII/3, 1973. © Robert Kenedy 1973.

IAN STEPHEN, Versed in Vessels, from *Chapman*, 78/79, 1994. © Ian Stephen 1994.

CLEO MCNELLY KEARNS, *Armis et Litteris*: Ian Hamilton Finlay's Heroic Emblems, from *Verse*, Vol. 6, No.1. 1989. © Cleo McNelly Kearns 1989.

MILES ORVELL, Poe and the Poetics of Pacific, from Collaborations, exhibition catalogue, Kettle's Yard, Cambridge 1977. © Miles Orvell 1977.

CHARLES JENCKS, Aphorisms on the Garden of a Aphorist from *Art & Design* magazine, Vol 2, 1986. Revised by the author. © Charles Jencks 1986.

MICHAEL CHARLESWORTH, On the Contemplative and Spiritual Use of the Temple at Little Sparta, from *Chapman*, 79/79, 1994. © Michael Charlesworth 1994.

MURDO MACDONALD, Wood Notes Wild: A Tale of Claude. © Murdo MacDonald 1994.

THOMAS A. CLARK, The Idiom of the Universe, from *P N Review* 47, Vol 12, No.3, 1985. © Thomas A. Clark 1985.

Pastorals, from *Pastorales*, exhibition catalogue, Galerie Claire Burrus, Paris, 1987. Revised by the author. © Thomas A. Clark 1987, 1994.

ALEXANDER STODDART, Terror is the Piety of Revolution, first published by the Wild Hawthorn Press, Little Sparta, 1986. © Alexander Stoddart, 1986, 1987.

Copyright Acknowledgements 269

YVES ABRIOUX, Eye, Judgment and Imagination from *Poursuites Révolutionnaires*, exhibition catalogue, Fondation Cartier, Jouy-en-Josas, 1987. © Yves Abrioux, 1987, 1994. (This is an English translation abridged by the author.)

STEPHEN SCOBIE, Models of Order. © Stephen Scobie 1994.

PATRICK EYRES, Wild Flowers from *Wildwachsende Blumen*, exhibition catalogue, Städtische Galerie im Lenbachhaus, Munich, 1993. © Patrick Eyres 1993.

LUCIUS BURKHARDT, Features in the Park: Ian Hamilton Finlay's Garden at Luton, from *A Guide to the Ian Hamilton Finlay Garden at Stockwood Park*. Published by Luton Borough Council. © Lucius Burkhardt and Luton Borough Council Museum Service, 1991.

TOM LUBBOCK, Ian Hamilton Finlay, © Tom Lubbock 1994.

Appendices

Poor. Old. Tired. Horse.

Nos 1–25 Issues and Contributors 1961–7

From *Ian Hamilton Finlay & The Wild Hawthorn Press, a Catalogue Raisonné, 1958–90*, Graeme Murray, Edinburgh, 1990.

Ian Hamilton Finlay, Serpentine Gallery 1977.
List of Works

From the catalogue of the exhibition organised by the Arts Council of Great Britain 1977. © Stephen Bann 1977.

Spartan Defence
Ian Hamilton Finlay in conversation with Peter Hill.

From *Studio International*. Vol 196, No. 1004, 1984. © Peter Hill 1984.

Notes on the Contributors

Duncan MacMillan is the author of the prize-winning *Scottish Art 1460–1990*. He is currently curator of the Talbot Rice Museum at the University of Edinburgh.

Edwin Morgan's *Collected Poems* were published by Carcanet Press, Manchester, 1990. His most recent books are a translation of *Cyrano de Bergerac* into Scots and *Sweeping out the Dark*.

Sue Innes is a journalist, writer and illustrator from the north-east of Scotland. She lives and works in Edinburgh, contributing a weekly column to *Scotland on Sunday* and looking after her two daughters.

Stephen Bann has taught at the University of Kent since 1967, and is at present Professor and Director of the Centre for Modern Cultural Studies. His recent books have included *Utopias and the Millennium* (co-edited, with Kishan Kumar, 1993) and a translation of Julia Kristeva's *Proust and the Sense of Time* (Faber, 1993).

Simon Cutts is a poet, publisher, curator and critic. In the 1960s he edited Tarasque Press with Stuart Mills. Two collections of his poetry, *Pianostool Footnotes* and *Seepages*, have been published by The Jargon Society. He is currently active as publisher of Coracle Press and editor of the Little Critic series, based in the Norfolk village of Docking.

Kathleen Raine is a well known poet and art critic.

R.C. Kenedy worked at the Victoria and Albert Museum. He was a poet and art critic.

Notes on the Contributors

Ian Stephen is a poet and storyteller. He works as a coastguard on the Isle of Lewis, in the Outer Hebrides. His latest collection of poetry, accompanied by his own photographs, *Providence II*, appeared from the Windfall Press, Isle of Lewis in 1994. He has also edited an anthology of poetry from Lewis and Harris, *Siud an t-Eilean/ There Goes The Island* (Acair, Stornoway, 1993).

Cleo McNelly Kearns writes on literature, religion and theology. She is the author of *T.S. Eliot and Indic Traditions: A Study in Poetry and Belief* (CUP, 1987) and of articles on a number of postmodern critics and theories. She is associate Professor of Humanities at the New Jersey Institute of Technology, where she teaches courses in world religion, comparative literature and English composition.

Miles Orvell is Professor of English and American Studies at Temple University in Philadelphia. He is the author of *Flannery O'Connor: An Introduction* and *The Real Thing: Imitation and Authenticity in American Culture, 1880–1940* (co-winner in 1990 of the American Studies Association's Franklin Prize).

Charles Jencks is a writer and designer. He has just finished a book on contemporary architecture and culture, *The Cosmos: Complexity and Architecture, A New Language of Design*.

Michael Charlesworth edited *The English Garden: Literary Sources and Documents* (3 vols, 1993) and contributed a chapter, 'The Ruined Abbey: Picturesque and Gothic Values' to *The Politics of the Picturesque* (1994). His essays on garden history, photography and nineteenth-century painting have appeared in *Word and Image, Journal of Garden History, New Arcadians' Journal, Garden History* and *Landscape Journal*. He is Assistant Professor of Art History at the University of Texas at Austin.

Murdo MacDonald lectures at the University of Edinburgh and has written previously on Ian Hamilton Finlay in the *Scotsman* newspaper and in the magazine, *Variant*. He is a former editor of *Edinburgh Review*.

Thomas A. Clark was born in Greenock and now lives in Gloucestershire where he co-runs the Cairn Gallery, a venue for contemporary art. His latest collection of poetry, *Tormentil and Bleached Bones*, was published by Polygon in 1993.

Alexander Stoddart is a Neo-classical sculptor. His latest commission is a statue of David Hume for the City of Edinburgh.

Yves Abrioux is the author of *Ian Hamilton Finlay: A Visual Primer* and of numerous articles on contemporary art, literary theory and landscape. He is a regular contributor to the periodical *Untitled* and has just edited an issue of the magazine, *T.I.F.* (université de Paris VIII) on chaos theory and literature.

Stephen Scobie was born in Scotland in 1943 and has lived in Canada since 1967. He teaches at the University of Victoria, BC. He is the author of numerous books of poetry and criticism, including works on bpNichol, Leonard Cohen, Jacques Derrida and Bob Dylan.

Patrick Eyres is a Senior Lecturer in Art and Design at the Bradford and Ilkey Community College. He is also the editor-publisher of the *New Arcadians' Journal*.

Lucius Burkhardt was born in Davos in 1925 and had held a professorship in the field of town planning/landscape planning at the Polytechnic of Kassel since 1973. He is the author of *Die Kinder fressen ihre Revolution – Planen, Bauen, Wohnen, Grunen (The Children are Devouring Their Revolution – Planning, Building, Living, Landscaping)*, DuMont Verlag, 1985.

Tom Lubbock is a freelance art-critic, radio critic for *The Observer*, currently writing for *The Independent* and a variety of contemporary art journals and magazines.

Alec Finlay is editor and publisher of Morning Star publications. His childhood years were spent at Stonypath where his parents Sue Finlay and Ian Hamilton Finlay created the garden now known as Little Sparta. He has lectured on Ian Hamilton Finlay's poetry and art in Britain, America and Europe.

Index

Works by Ian Hamilton Finlay will be found indexed under 'Finlay'; collaborators and exhibitions will also be found listed there for convenience of reference.

Abrioux, Yves 14
Adam, Robert 125, 127
Adorno, Theodor 68
Albers 7

Bann, Stephen xvi, xvii, 8, 78, 90–1, 82, 183–4, 192, 197, 249, 250
Bara, François-Joseph 170
Barère, Bertrand de 145, 148, 169
Barr, Ian 165
Bernini, Gianlorenzo 2, 143, 174
Between Poetry and Painting (ICA, London, 1965; including IHF) 30, 32, 61
Biederman, Charles 20, 248
Bill, Max 28, 35, 250
Braque, Georges 194
Burke, Edmund 156, 158, 180
Burns, Robert 127–8, 129, 130

Campos, Augusto de 65, 247, 249
Canova, Antonio 229, 259
Cézanne, Paul 104–5, 192
Cipriani, Giovanni Battista 140, 141
Clark, Thomas A. xvi
Claude, *see under* Gelée
collaborators with IHF, *see under* Finlay
Collaborations (exhibition at Kettle's Yard, Cambridge) 67, 79, 200
Conan, Michael 8
Corot, Jean Baptiste Camille 163, 167, 168
Creeley, Robert xiv, 21, 247; and title of *P.O.T.H.*, 21

David, Jacques Louis 156, 166, 170–1, 172, 179
de Campos, Augusto *see* Campos
Diderot, Denis 179
Dughet, Gaspard, *called* Poussin 196
Dürer, Albrecht 197

Epicurus 154
exhibitions/installations by IHF, *see under* Finlay
Eyres, Patrick 262

Finlay, Alec 11
Finlay, Ian Hamilton
collaborators with:
  Allen, Maxwell 31, 255
  Andrew, John 123, 142, 250, 251, 258
  Appleton, Ian 213, 260
  Bann, Stephen 78, 80–1, 82
  Brookwell, Keith 176
  Burgoyne, Robert 228
  Clark, Laurie 51, 146, 253
  Costley, Ron 54, 80–1, 89, 252, 253, 254, 255
  Curwin, Kerstin 148
  Fine, Jud 68–9, 253–4
  Finlay, Sue xxiii, 8, 10, 100, 256, 259
  Furnival, John 30, 248, 249
  Gardner, Ian 106, 214
  Gram, Andreas 176
  Gnüchtel, Markus 176
  Grasby, Richard 133, 251, 252, 254, 258
  Harvey, Michael 49, 151, 251, 255
  Hincks, Gary 50, 52, 176, 178, 228, 230
  Kujundzic, Zeljko 16
  Lindsley, Kathleen 146, 180, 214
  Nicholson, Jim 192
  Paterson, Dave 45, 69, 95, 97, 100, 254, 256
  Paterson, Wilma 103
  Picking, John 16
  Sandeman, Margot 51, 248
  Sheeler, Dick 29, 66–7
  Simig, Pia xxiii
  Sloan, Nicholas 97, 100, 109, 133, 176, 181, 219
  Thorpe, John R. 38, 255, 256, 257

exhibitions/installations by (see also: *works*)
- at Celle, Italy; see *A Celebration of the Grove* under *works*)
- at Kassel, see *A View to the Temple* under *works*
- at Luton (Stockwood Park) 216ff., 223 ff.
- at Versailles, fountain, 158; see also *Jardin Révolutionnaire* under *works*)
- in Edinburgh: Graeme Murray Gallery, 71, 133–4; Tartar Gallery, 206, 260, 261; in West Princes Street Gardens, 10
- in Glasgow (Collins Exhibition Hall, 1980) 99ff.; see also *Nature Over Again After Poussin*, under *works*
- in Jouy-en-Josas (Fondation Cartier) 10, 13, 166, 174
- in London (Serpentine Gallery) xix, xx, 55, 79
- in Paris: ARC, 10, 172–3; Galerie Claire Burrus, 10, 174
- in Southampton (Art Gallery) 206, 260–1
- in Stuttgart (Max Planck Institute) 44, 70, 256
- *Collaborations* (Kettle's Yard, Cambridge, 1977) 67, 79, 200
- *Homage to Watteau* (Graeme Murray Gallery, Edinburgh, 1976) 71
- *Ian Hamilton Finlay* (Serpentine Gallery, London, 1977) xix, xx, 55, 79
- *Inter Artes et Naturam* (ARC, Paris, 1987) 10, 172–3
- *Liberty, Terror & Virtue: The Little Spartan War and The Third Reich Revisited* (Southampton Art Gallery, 1984) 206, 260–1
- *Midway* (Bibliothèque Nationale, Paris, 1987) 10
- *Nature Over Again After Poussin* (Collins Exhibition Hall, Glasgow, 1980) 99ff.; see also under *works*
- *Pastorales* (Galerie Claire Burrus, Paris, 1987) 10, 174
- *Poursuites Révolutionnaires* (Fondation Cartier, Jouy-en-Josas, France, 1987) 10, 13, 166, 174
- *Talismans and Signifiers* (Graeme Murray Gallery, Edinburgh, 1984) 133–4
- *The Third Reich Revisited* (Tartar Gallery, Edinburgh, 1982) 206, 260–1
- *A View to the Temple* (Kassel Documenta 8, 1987) see under *works*
- *A Wartime Garden* (Tate Gallery, London, and Graeme Murray Gallery, Edinburgh) 106, 139
- *Wildwachsende Blumen* ('Wild Flowers of the Ehrentempel'; at the Lenbachhaus, Munich, 1993–4) xix, xx, 205, 206ff.

themes in the work of:
- the concrete-poetical xvi, 19, 21ff., 28ff., 32ff., 57–9, 60ff., 69, 161, 187–8, 190–1, 224, 252
- the French-Revolutionary xv–vi, 9, 144–7, 149–50, 156ff., 178ff., 210–1, 234, 235–6, 242, 265
- the garden/landscape xv, xxiii–iv, 41, 104, 108, 113–4, 163–4, 184, 195–6, 197–8, 215ff., 220ff., 244, 254
- the maritime 2, 18, 23, 34, 42–3, 46ff., 73–4, 170, 202, 254
- the military 2–3, 12, 19, 42–3, 51–2, 57, 78–9, 83ff., 90, 95, 110–1, 117, 140–1, 143–4, 153, 170, 174, 182–3, 185–6, 189, 202, 206ff., 252–5
- the neo-classical 9, 87, 109, 116–7, 124ff., 139, 142, 172, 183, 206ff., 230, 235, 236, 250, 259
- the pastoral 2, 4, 12, 139, 141, 152ff., 169, 216ff., 241, 253

works by:
- 'A bas les lollygarchs' 258
- *Acrobats* 29, 93–4
- *After Bernini* (Apollo and Daphne) 143, 174
- *After Magritte* 263
- *Ajar* 29–30, 66
- 'Altdorfer' (*Nature Over Again After Poussin*) 100
- *Analytical Cubist Portrait* 194, 195
- *And even as she fled . . . (2)* (Apollo and Daphne) 145, 201
- Aphrodite herm (Stockwood Park) 218, 219
- *Aphrodite of the Terror* 173
- *Apollo and Daphne* 174; see also: *After Bernini*, *And even as she fled*
- *Apollo in Strathclyde* 173
- 'Arcady' 224
- 'ark/arc' 66
- *Apollo Saint-Just* (in *lararium*) 121
- *Arrosoir* 110, 146, 169
- *The Atlantic Wall (William Gilpin Annotated)* 106
- *Autumn Poem* 23, 143
- *Battle of Little Sparta, Monument to* 261
- *Battle of Midway* 2, 54, 252–3; see also: *Through a dark wood . . .*
- 'Betula pendula' (Stockwood Park) 217
- *Big 'E' at Midway* 78–9, 251

Index

A Beheading of Bouquets 165
Blue Lemon 49
The Boy and the Guess 17
Brevity Ran to Wit 164
Brigands/Bacchantes 165
Bring Back the Birch 42
Canal Stripe Series 3 66
Canal Stripe Series 4 22
'Catch' 18
A Celebration of the Grove (Proposal for Celle) 132–3, 226–7
Chant for a Regional Occasion 157–8
Le Circus 62
'Claude' (*Nature Over Again After Poussin*) 97, 197
CLAUDI stone (*Nature Over Again After Poussin*) 97, 197
Clay the life . . . 161–2
Cloud Board 31, 35
Concertina 16, 19, 66
'Corot' (*Nature Over Again After Poussin*) 100
Corot-Saint-Just, see *Five Columns . . .*
A Cottage, a Field, a Plough . . . 169
The Dancers Inherit the Party 16, 32, 48
Detached Sentence 210, 214; see also *More Detached Sentences. . . . Unconnected Sentences . . .*
A dream is always . . . (Saint-Just the Stern) 148
'Dürer' (*Nature Over Again After Poussin*) 97
Dzaezl 137
Ehrentempel model 205
Elegaic Inscription (See POUSSIN/Hear LORRAIN) 75, 123, 125, 197
The Errata of Ovid (version on the Ovid wall, Luton) 217
Et In Arcadia Ego 80, 101, 139, 140–2, 183, 251
'Eternelle action . . .' (*Heroic Emblem*) 140, 251
Evening will come . . . (westward-facing sundial) 38, 53, 139, 198–9
Events are a discourse . . . 213, 260
Les Femmes de la Révolution 211
First Battle of Little Sparta, Monument to 261
A Fifth Column for the Kröller-Müller, see *Five Columns . . .*
Five Columns for the Kröller-Müller 167, 168, 225–6, 264–5
'Flock' (Stockwood Park) 216, 219
Footnotes to an essay see *Et In Arcadia Ego*
4 Baskets 180

4 Blades 179–80
'Four Heads' 13, 165
Four Monostichs 185–6
4 Sails 64
'Fragonard' (*Nature Over Again After Poussin*) 103
from 'Clerihews for liberals' 145, 177
Fructidor (Month of Fruit) 210, 214
Garden Temple, see Temple to Apollo
'The Gift' 18
Glasgow Beasts 16, 18
The Great Piece of Turf 75
'Guercino' (*Nature Over Again After Poussin*) 101
The Happy Catastrophe 200–1
A Harbour of Roses 50
'He spoke like an axe . . .' 145, 169
'He was the first schoolmaster of democracy . . .' 159
The Henry Vaughan Walk 113
Heroic Emblems 78, 80, 81, 82ff., 139, 140, 184
'hic jacet . . .' (Pond inscription) 70
Homage to Kahnweiler 192–3
'Homage to Malevich' 25, 60–1, 63–4, 71, 190–2
Homage to Modern Art 192
Homage to Pop Art 192
Homage to Seurat 94–5, 192
Homage to Vuillard 192
Hommage à David (1) 170
Hommage à David (2) 171
'I was published by Jonathan Cape . . .' 166
'I Sing for the Muses and myself' (Stockwood Park) 216
Idylls 151, 154
Interpolations In Hegel 134–6
The Ivory Flute 164
Un Jardin Révolutionnaire 10, 15
Julie's Garden 104
KY 35
letter of 1963 to Pierre Garnier 58, 146–7, 187–8, 189
'Liberty, Equality, Fraternity' (Versailles fountain) 158
The Little Drummer Boy 170
Little Fields 30
Lugger 45
Lyre 57, 183, 251
Man with Panzerschreck v, 210
Marat Assassiné 172
'Marble Paper Boats' 250, 251
'A model of order . . .' 147, 176, 178, 187, 189
The Money 263

Monument to Joseph Bara 171
Monument to the First Battle of Little Sparta 261
More Detached Sentences on Gardening... xiv
'Nature is the devil...' 143
Nature Over Again After Poussin 71, 97, 100, 101, 103, 197; see also under exhibitions
'Navy' 94
NETS weathercock 34
A New Arcadian Dictionary 139
Nuclear Sail 11, 70
Ocean Stripe Series 3 22, 49
Ocean Stripe Series 5 49, 73–4
The Old Stonypath Hoy 52, 57
'Order is repetition' 189
Ovid wall (Stockwood Park) 217
PACIFIC 89, 90ff., 189
part-capital (Stockwood Park) 217–8
Peterhead Fragments 51
Picturesque 194–5
'Poem on My Poem on Her and the Horse' 18
'Pond inscription' (hic jacet...) 70
Pond Stone 24, 31
Poor. Old. Tired. Horse. (shortened to *P.O.T.H.*) 16, 19–22, 26–7
Prescocratic inscription 155
The present order... 10, 111, 162
Proclamation ('Les Citoyennes de Strasbourg...') 157
Proposal for a Monument to Jean-Jacques Rousseau 227–8
A Proposal for the Bicentenary of the French Revolution 181
A Proposal for the Forest of Dean 228
Proposal for the Haus der Kunst, Munich 209–10
Rapel 19, 63, 75–6; see also 'Homage to Malevich'
A Remembrance of R.L.S. 10, 137
'Reverence is the Dada of the 1980s...' xiv, 138
Revolution, n. 168–9
'Rosa' (*Nature Over Again After Poussin*) 71
'Scene' 19
Scythe/Lightning Flash 143–4
The Sea-Bed 16
'The Sea-Bed' 17
Sea-Poppy 1 49
Sea-Poppy 2 49
'See POUSSIN/Hear LORRAIN' (Elegaic Inscription) 75, 123, 125, 197

Seven Bollards 51
7.01 xvii, 139
SF 143
Sickle 170
Sickle/Lightning Flash 144
Silhouettes 51
'Small is quite beautiful' 111, 184, 251, 258
Standing poems 66
Starlit Waters 10, 74
Stonechats 24, 35, 224
'Straw' 17
Sublime 181
Table Talk of Ian Hamilton Finlay 138–9, 140, 143
Talismans and Signifiers 133–4
Tea-leaves and Fishes 21
Telegrams from my Windmill 21
Temple of Bara 171
Temple of Philemon and Baucis 121
Temple to Apollo (Garden Temple) xvi, xvii, xviii, 11, 85, 87, 88, 109–10, 115, 116ff., 149–50, 165, 201, 235, 259
Terror and Virtue 181
Terror is the Piety of the Revolution 149–50, 172
Thermidor 146
The Third Reich Revisited 206, 207, 208, 210, 265–6 (see also under exhibitions)
Three Columns 209
Tree-column base 155, 167
Trophies of War 258
'Through a dark wood...' (*Heroic Emblem*) 54
Two Landscapes of the Sublime 180–1
'Two Proposals for the Munich Ehrentempel Sites' 212
Two Scythes 143, 170
Umbra Solis Non Aeris 167
Unconnected Sentences on Gardening xxi, 142, 195–6
'U.S.S. Enterprise' (*Heroic Emblem*) 78, 81
A View to the Temple 10, 158–9, 160, 176
A Wartime Garden 106, 139
Water Weathercock 34
'wave/avè' 53
Wave Rock 35, 62–3, 256, 257
'Watteau' (*Nature Over Again After Poussin*) 100
Westward-facing Sundial (Evening will come...) 38, 53, 139, 198–9
Wildflower. n. 211, 214
'The words we have spoken...' 112
'The world has been empty...' 112, 163, 183

Index

Finlay, Sue xxiii, 8, 10, 11, 69, 100, 107, 256, 259

Gadamer, Hans-Georg 102–3
Gänsheimer, Simone 205
Garnier, Pierre, Pierre Garnier (letter of IHF to, 1963) 58, 146–7, 187–8, 189
Gelée, Claude, *called* 'Claude' or 'le Lorrain' xix, 1–2, 75, 76, 97, 101, 124ff., 130, 163, 197
Gilonis, Harry xiii
Giorgione (Giorgio da' Castelfranco) 98, 99, 100–1
Girardin, René Louis, Marquis de (Ermenonville garden) 70, 118, 119, 120, 168, 226, 264
Gombrich, Ernst 66
Gomringer, Eugen 28, 58–9, 64–5, 93–4, 228, 247, 249
Gris, Juan 170, 193, 194
Guercino (Giovanni Francesco Barbieri, *called*) 101, 140
Guillotin, Dr Joseph-Ignace 178, 196, 200

Hall, Douglas 253–4
Headley, Gwyn 165
Hegel, G. W. F. 134–6
Heidegger, Martin xviii, 59–60, 167
Henderson, Hamish xiv
Heraclitus xviii, 134, 135
Hill, David Octavius 125, 128–30
Hölderlin, Friedrich xix, 181–2
Horace 247

Ian Hamilton Finlay (exhibition at the Serpentine Gallery, London) xix, xx, 55, 79
installations/exhibitions by IHF, *see under* Finlay
International Exhibition of Concrete and Kinetic Poetry (Cambridge, 1964; including IHF) 61

Jandl, Ernst 23, 247, 248, 249
Januszczak, Waldemar 165
Judd, Donald 133
Julian 'the Apostate' 230

Kahnweiler, Daniel-Henry 192, 193–4
Kenedy, Robert 69–70
Kolbe, Georg Wilhelm 140, 142
Krauss, Rosalind 166

Lassus, Bernard 8, 222, 230
Lax, Robert xxiii, 247, 248
Lepeletier, Louis-Michel 166

LeWitt, Sol 133
Lochac, Emmanuel 140
Loisy, Jean de 12, 234
'Lorrain, le', *see under* Gelée
Lucretius 109
Luton (Stockwood Park) 216ff., 223 ff.

MacDiarmid, Hugh xiv, 20
McGuffie, Jessie xxiii, 8, 53
Macmillan, Duncan 126
Malevich, Kazimir 3
Marat, Jean Paul 172
Marin, Louis 224–5, 231–2
Mathiez, Albert 159
Millet, Catherine 165
Milton, John xxiv, 4, 127, 140
More, Jacob 125, 126–7
Morgan, Edwin xvii, 20, 46, 189, 237, 246, 247, 248, 249

Nasmyth, Alexander 125, 127, 128
Nature Over Again After Poussin (exhibition at Collins Exhibition Hall, Glasgow) 99ff.; see also under *works* b
Niedecker, Lorine xxiii, 246, 247, 248
Nikolic, Monika 176
'Noigandres' group 58
Norie, James (father) 125–6
Norie, James (son) 126
Norie, Robert 126

Orvell, Miles 185
Ovid xix, 2, 145, 152, 155, 174, 217

Panofsky, Erwin 155
Pastorales (exhibition at Galerie Claire Burrus, Paris) 10, 174
Pater, Walter 55, 56–7, 98–9, 157, 183, 252
Paterson, Dave 31, 38, 123
Picasso, Pablo 194, 202
Pleynet, Marcelin 71–2
Plutarch 78–9
Pliny the Elder 118
Poe, Edgar Allan 92–3
Poursuites Révolutionnaires (exhibition at the Fondation Cartier, Jouy-en-Josas) 10, 13, 166, 174
Poussin, Nicolas xvi, xix, 75, 76, 80, 101, 124, 141, 179, 196, 197, 231–2
Proclus 134

Record, Stephanie 219
Reeve, Antonia v, 115
Reinhardt, Ad 20, 248
Repton, Humphry 195, 197

Rilke, Rainer Maria xiii
Robespierre, Maximilien-François-Isidore xix, 159, 165, 167, 169, 179
Rousseau, Jean-Jacques xviii, 104, 119, 120, 146, 155, 166, 167, 224–5

Saint-Just, Louis-Antoine-Léon xv, xix, 4, 144, 145, 147, 148, 163, 164, 166, 167, 168, 169, 173–4, 179
Saint-Just Vigilantes xix, 144, 166, 258, 260–1
Sallustius 134
Schwitters, Kurt 23
Scobie, Stephen 21
Shenstone, William (The Leasowes garden) 70, 132, 156, 159, 195, 196; see also 'Detached Sentences' under Finlay, *works*
Simig, Pia xxiii
Smith, Tony 133
Speer, Albert 104
Stein, Gertrude 193
Stevenson, Robert Louis 10, 124, 137

Stockwood Park (Luton) 216ff., 223 ff.

themes in the work of IHF, *see under* Finlay
Theocritus 132, 152
Thomson, John 125
Turnbull, Gael xxiii, 246, 249
Twentieth Century Studies 54

Varro 212, 214
Vasarely, Victor xxiii
Virgil xix, 2, 128, 152, 155
Vitruvius 134

Wildwachsende Blumen (exhibition at the Lenbachhaus, Munich) xix, xx, 205, 206ff.
Wittgenstein, Ludwig xvii, 135, 139
Wordsworth, William 156
works by IHF, *see under* Finlay

Zukofsky, Louis xxiii, 247